whispering shadows

The Navarre Chronicles Book Two

whispering shadows

Whispering Shadows

Copyright © 2021 by Lilac Daggers Press LLC

All rights reserved. Printed in the United States of America. No part of this book may be used or reproduced in any manner whatsoever without written permission except in the case of brief quotations embodied in critical articles or reviews.
This book is a work of fiction. Names, characters, businesses, organizations, places, events and incidents either are the product of the author's imagination or are used fictitiously. Any resemblance to actual persons, living or dead, events, or locales is entirely coincidental.

Trigger Warning : contains scenes with general violence and torture elements (including children), mild language, and some nudity.

For information contact :
Lilac Daggers Press LLC
9429 Monticello Drive
Twinsburg, OH 44087
www.worldofsydneyhawthorn.com

Cover design by CelinGraphics
Map design by Lizard Ink Maps
ISBN: 978-1-7349004-4-6

First Edition: June 2021

10 9 8 7 6 5 4 3 2 1

To Gram, Rita Greenbaum, for not only believing in me from the very beginning, but for showing me again and again what true strength is.

preface

The crystal castle's council room was silent. It had been that way for hours, since they gave up on the useless discussion.

King Reul Elirona released a sigh from his seat at the head of the red oak table. He pinched the bridge of his nose, long silvery-white hair dancing about his muscular frame in the breeze passing through the open balcony archways. Only Larina dared approach him, squeezing his arm gently as the council members dispersed. Her turquoise eyes met his, sad and tired. Reul gave his sister a brisk nod before pushing up from the table, straightening his gold-embellished collar, then wiping a hand over his face.

Gods save them all. Aeron was rising.

Centuries of peace succumbed to darkness and there was nothing he or his court could do about it; Aeron had seen to that one hundred years ago when his henchmen slaughtered Reul's children and murdered any Demi-God offspring who might be able to stand with them.

Fae, Witch, Dwarf, and Mortal.

It had been three hundred years since the Second Demon Wars, since the four royal bloodlines came together to protect the realm from the Demon King in command of the Shadowplains and its army of darkness. The Demon Wars left Navarre in ruin; the Redhorn

Mountains and the Eswye Channel alike ran red with blood. But as the years passed, history became myth, and the Demon King's strength still rose in the shadows.

The mortal Waeshorn Kings had long forgotten Aeron's terrors. The Dwarfs of house Ashguard, despite his prying, hadn't emerged from the Redhorn Mountains since the wars ended. As for the covens of Rekiv, no one was certain of the she-demons who reigned in the north, or dared reach out to inquire their allegiance. Even Larina's legion, stationed in the southern town of Ebondenn, didn't dare send scouts to press the witches they came across for answers.

The Fae alone maintained the seal, the ever-present war raging along Dorwynn's borders only proving Aeron's growing power. But Reul's reign was halfway over. With his children slaughtered, Kira barren, and none of his kin with heirs who could serve as his successor, they were running out of options.

Soon, the realm would writhe in chaos.

The castle's white marble halls were empty save for the core members of his cadre stationed at each looming archway, ivy vines creeping up the smooth stone at their backs. Reul nodded to each as he passed, keeping his expression blank, his movements graceful and cat-like. White ash trees lined the open walls, blooming phosphorescent flowers gleaming like lanterns in the setting sun.

Queen Kira stood at the balcony towering above the small garden courtyard visible from their private chambers. Thin braids pulled silvery hair away from her face on either side, revealing delicately elongated ears. A sprig of jasmine accented the silver pins securing the tiny braids.

She turned to him, eyes narrowed but kind. "You were longer than you promised."

Reul closed the door, walking to her. He savored her embrace, her aura calming the fear and despair heating his blood. "Apologies, my love."

She splayed delicate fingers on his broad chest, grey eyes shimmering with moonlight. "The council meeting didn't go well."

"Larina demands more soldiers in the Ebondenn camp on the

border. First and foremost, she wants to make sure Raenya is protected. Gaelin says the seas are swarming with unknown monsters, and Ralovaris refuses to let me go anywhere." He bit his lip. "Goddess damn them all to The Twelve, I'm a king, not a child."

"But you are also their brother. They only want to protect you."

"I don't need protecting."

"What did you tell Larina?" Kira's voice was gentle as she dropped the subject.

"What am I supposed to tell her, Kira?" The words came out harsher than he wanted.

"She's your sister, and commander of your most secure army outpost."

He swore, gnawing at his bottom lip again. "The vote remains uneven. Half the council wants to storm Badraol to search for the Dwarves, others want to march on Rekiv to confront Queen Rowena. Some want to demand King Nathaniel open his eyes to the truths his ancestors have forgotten. With no sign of his daughter…"

Kira tucked a loose strand of silver hair behind his ear; another comforting touch. "If the Waeshorn Princess was in Aeron's hands, he would have struck already. I truly believe that."

Reul sighed. "She's the only one left who can possibly save us all. And even with her safety ensured, who's to say she could defeat him without the other royal children beside her?" He ran a hand through his hair. "Gods above, they were supposed to be there for her."

Kira waited a moment before speaking. "No word from Fallon?"

Reul shut his eyes, pinching the bridge of his nose.

"Have you tried speaking to him?"

"After six centuries, I have to trust Fallon knows what actions to take should chaos fall upon us. I trust him to do what's right." He pushed away, bracing himself against the pale, carved balcony. The amethysts embedded within the stone shone in the sunset.

"My love, Fallon was…*is* your chief advisor and most trusted friend."

"I haven't heard from him since…I know he still blames himself." Reul rubbed his eyes. "Conan has seen him, he promised me he's alright."

A pause, a sigh. Reul turned back to her.

"I must trust him. If Aeron discovered any communications, the fighting could spread not only along the Dorwynn border but throughout Navarre. I cannot in good conscience force war on King Nathaniel if he wants no part in it. We will find another way."

Kira was an ever-present calm at his side. "You cannot fight this war alone. Aeron is too powerful, even against the entire might of Dorwynn. Please, do not ask me to watch you fail." She touched his arm. "Send word to Fallon."

A sharp knock cut off Reul's response. The door creaked open. "Apologies for the late intrusion, Your Majesties…"

Kira took the letter the page offered, waving a dismissive hand. The boy bowed and left as she handed it to Reul, who read it several times before looking up.

"What is it?" Kira asked.

Reul's lips twitched into a smile. "Fallon found Princess Joseline."

one

Dax was dead, and it was her fault.

This abandonment was her fault. Her punishment. A cruel, sick joke for those she couldn't save. Now, the one person she'd dared open the confines of her heart to after she'd barred it for so long was gone.

Dead.

It didn't feel real.

Her heart threatened to explode from the pain. The cold, damp, darkness of the spiraling staircase only made the agony more surreal, more unbearable. Shadows swarmed around every turn, her footsteps echoing at each corner.

He'd been so kind to her. Kind despite eighteen years of hatred. Hatred he didn't deserve.

Her breath came in choked sobs, rasping and uneven. A numb sorrow enveloped her, the torment of raw with unspoken emotions. Her cheeks stung, her hands shook, and she could barely move. Each time she slid to the ground, she forced herself to stand, blood-stained hands scrubbing at tear-stained flesh.

I killed him. He's dead because of me.

Another choked sob.

Then another.

She stumbled, her fingers reaching for something, anything to break her fall into the descending darkness. But Evalyn tumbled downward, the torch sputtering, vanishing into whispering shadows. She rolled, rough stone clawing at pale skin and bit her lip, breaking flesh as her skull cracked against stone, at last slowing her tumble.

Her knees burned, a hot, sticky stream of blood trickling down her chin. She touched the tender spot where her lip split and hissed, pulling back her fingers.

Shaking, she drew her knees into her chest, the sobs ripping from her lungs. This time, she could not rise.

She hated herself. She hated the truth of what she'd done to the man she might have loved. Her head fell into her hands. Blood, sweat, and tears ran down her neck and onto her tunic.

His tunic.

She couldn't do this. She couldn't force the look of agony in his eyes from her mind, his blood flowering his stomach as she whimpered and turned away. She couldn't watch him die, not as she'd watched her mother. But now she couldn't stop the fear and loneliness from swallowing her whole. Not alone, not again.

Not without him.

"Gods," she whimpered. "Why, why did it have to be him?"

The salty breeze echoed in response, whisking around her from the stairs.

"Why?" she all but screamed into the darkness, not caring who might hear as she choked back another sob and bit her knuckle, relishing the rewarding sting.

Stand up.

The voice resonated through her mind, shaking away the foggy numbness.

Stand up, it repeated.

She obeyed, the movements not quite her own—one step, then another. She pushed steadily down the stairs, one hand brushing, guiding along the stone. It took all her strength to keep her bruised knee from buckling beneath her weight, but she gritted her teeth. The breathing became easier somehow, the will to move less demanding and more necessity. Bits of light flashed in the distance, the stairs evening out to solid ground.

Evalyn blinked. How long had she been walking? She focused on the flickers growing nearer, until at last it opened against an uneven cliff face.

Freedom.

The exhilaration was so strong, for a moment she forgot the fear and sorrow.

You can climb the ledges if you're careful, though I'm afraid there's no real path. Stay to the left, and it'll lead you to the port. The memory of his voice brought the pain rushing back, crashing into her as violent as the waves.

Pebbles tumbled down the steep cliffside and into the churning waters, vanishing into the foaming depths. Keeping her back to the mountains, she edged along, careful not to misstep. Her memory flared, overcome with images of a younger child with unbound silver hair running barefoot through the trees, a house burning behind her.

It had been her sixth birthday, the day the nightmares became reality.

Shining stars danced amidst a navy and lilac sky, weaving between scattered clouds. The Dorwynn sky was always magnificent in spring. Her mother, Zaria, even let her help cook the evening meal on those days, the delectable smells of hazelnut soup and freshly-baked rolls still on her tongue as she sucked on a sugar-coated honey drop. It took three rounds of brushing to free the gooey sweetness from her teeth. Then, per Evalyn's request, Zaria told the story of the first royal Dorwynn twins. She loved the magic of the shapeshifter Fae and their ability to change forms into two wolves—one resembling the light, the other darkness. The wolves were the sigil of the royal Elirona house, loyal, strong, and fearless protectors of the Fae people with the Goddess Noria's faithful Faeries at their sides.

Eva adored the mysterious tales full of magic. They made her think of her own twin brother, who had gone missing two years before—wondering what magic they might have been capable of together.

Once the story ended, Zaria kissed her goodnight. Not long after, the first shadow creature appeared, its form looming against her wall from the moonlight streaming through her open window. The smell hit her, thick and smoky.

Her mother, fast as lightning, grabbed Evalyn from bed and ushered her silently outside. The night was quiet, peaceful, and full of illusions. Zaria knelt before Evalyn, tears sparkling in her eyes as she squeezed her small hands fiercely. "No matter what happens, you remember what I'm about to tell you, Eva, do you understand?"

Evalyn nodded, eyes wide, flickering to the moving shadows within the house, pulse hammering in her chest.

With a smile, Zaria wiped at a loose strand of silver hair dancing across Eva's face and tucked it behind her ear. "I love you, forever, my sweet little flower. You shine, and keep shining for all the world to see. Don't be afraid, and your light will always shine as bright as the stars and pure as the Gods."

A hiss sounded from the trees, and Zaria's head snapped toward the noise. But the woods were empty. Zaria released a sigh, pulling Eva close. She wished the hug could last forever. "Now run, Eva. Run and don't look back." Her mother kissed her forehead, then urged her down the back steps. Eva was almost inside the trees when she heard Zaria scream.

That scream shattered her.

Eva glanced over her shoulder for only a moment, and she couldn't conceal her gasp. She clutched her sides with shaking hands, fighting the nausea spreading through her body.

Blood dripped down the wooden stairs from her mother's broken body. A creature gripped her silvery hair in one hand, a sharp nail tracing down her chest, ripping flesh. Tears streaked down her face, leaving a trail through the blood on her cheeks.

The dark, soulless eyes of the shadowy nightmare met Eva's the same moment her mothers did.

Run. A whisper, a final plea on cracked, bleeding lips.

Evalyn ran.

The monster's shadow tendrils reached for her, always a step behind. She ran until she no longer could, until she hit the Eswye Channel. She tried to swim it, pushing through churning waves, desperate to outrun the murderous darkness. The night enclosed around her, but she refused to let the panic seize her frantic thoughts, her gaze fixating on a ship further down the channel.

Help, her mind begged. She reached with shaking hands for the ship that couldn't see her in the dark. The deep green flag waved mockingly in the distance, the sea dragon amidst the sails taunting her. *Please, help me. Save me.*

Her small legs beat against the current, but the current was stronger, fighting her strength until at last she succumbed, her body twirling into the chill water filling her lungs.

The effort to breathe was unbearable as she fought to swim toward the surface. The water engulfed her, almost blinding. The energy slowly ebbed away as the movements became more difficult. She shook, her legs beating against the vicious current struggling to pull her back, to suck her down into her frigid blackness. One more second, and she would be free. If she could just break through the darkness...

Strong arms pulled her up, out of the viscous, swirling waters, and held her close despite her frantic thrashing, then set her down on the deck of an enormous ship. She glared at her indigo-eyed rescuer.

"Calm down, little one, you're alright." He smiled that crooked smile, extending a ring-covered hand. Eva, despite the racing panic, had scowled at him.

A sob lodged in her throat at the memory, threatening to erupt just as she rounded the curving mountain ledge onto wider ground, but the voices on the docks stopped it.

Eva froze. Fear coursed through her, but she forced her breath to calm and the shaking to settle, gripping Dax's cloak more firmly around her chest. The dawn light peeked over the mountains, spreading blood-red hues and metallic puffs of ash along the crumbling rocks, shimmering crimson on the water. The large ship in the harbor took her breath away, the other smaller vessels unnoticed in its shadow.

You'll know her when you see her, he'd said.

The *Seraphina*. She was impossible to miss. Forest-green sails whipped in the breeze, the sea dragon at her bow painted a golden sheen, tail winding around the side of the ship. The dark brown wood had faded with time, but she was still gorgeous. Cautiously, Eva moved across the rocky earth to crouch behind several barrels stacked along the dock near the boarding plank. The smell of salt engulfed her senses as the wind blew toward her.

"I told you this was a bad idea." A woman's voice.

Evalyn dropped closer to the ground, gripping the fabric of her breeches. She closed her eyes, praying to the Gods they couldn't hear her thundering heart.

"Bet yer arse it was, but I'm not stupid enough t' argue with him." A second, gruffer voice. "Ya know how he gets about defiance when he's made his mind up."

Evalyn peered out between two barrels, Dax's thick cloak preventing her long silver hair from whipping about her face.

"Well, now he's dead." The softer voice came again.

Only then did she hear the gongs echoing against the mountains. *So, they found his body, then.* Evalyn fought the urge to bite her swollen lip, covering her mouth with shaking hands.

"What's the holdup?"

She wanted to run as far from that Shadow Beast's hissing voice as possible.

"Nothin'. We were discussin' the death of *our* leader." There was bitterness when the pirate spoke.

The Shadow Beast came into view, and Eva ducked behind the barrel once more. "That isn't my fault."

"No?" The woman challenged. "He wasn't dead until you lot started raising demands."

"Is that a threat, *mortal*?"

At the sound of a strangled gasp, Evalyn dared to peer out from behind the barrels. The Shadow Beast had lifted the taller pirate off the ground by the throat. The stockier one drew a cutlass, holding it up to the monster towering over him.

"Drop her," he growled, his lips tightening into a firm line.

The Shadow Beast snarled but released his companion.

"Now," he said, helping her to her feet and sheathing his blade, "if you'll excuse us, we're goin' inside fer a moment."

"How dare you command me, you—"

"Leave it alone." The second hiss, Evalyn recognized faintly as one of the Shadow Beast commanders. "They may weep for their dead captain. Then, they will return and finish their work. Those barrels are expected in Easthaven in a week."

Evalyn held her breath, wondering for a moment if the Shadow Beast would ignore his leader and kill the pirates anyway. But instead he snarled again, revealing dark teeth, and spun toward the fortress, the pirates a step behind.

The Shadow Commander hesitated, tilting his face toward the sky. Evalyn's pulse raced with nervous energy, bubbling through her veins.

You could do it, the voice in her mind hissed. *You could kill him. Kill him and be done with it while there's no one here to see you. You've waited for this moment long enough. This is the perfect start.*

The seconds ticked by, her eyes flitting along the docks. They were deserted. She gulped, dark fabric bunching in her grasp. Sneak up and choke him from behind; all she had to do was yank the cloak around his throat. It would be easy, over in minutes.

One day, she would be free. And when she was, she would paint the cavern walls with their blood.

Steeling herself to sneak from her hiding spot, she gripped Dax's cloak and froze.

Dax's cloak.

The image of his blood coating her hands, spilling from his body as he died flooded her subconscious.

She shrunk back. *No.* She covered her mouth, fighting to conceal the choked sob threatening to escape. *No, I won't...there has to be another way. I will not end another's life. Not again.*

The commander's footsteps echoed as he retreated.

Evalyn waited for several minutes before daring to survey the docks from her hiding spot a second time. Mercifully, they were still deserted. She shifted the barrels, finding the lightest one. Her fingers ached as she lifted off the lid and dug through salt, stinging her tender knuckles.

Three seconds and she replaced the lid, tucked safely inside the contents. The salt dug into her skin, biting and aching, the smell overpowering. She debated leaving, her fingers twitching in her lap, but footsteps echoed outside.

Her pulse quickened, fear resurfacing. With the stench of salt encircling her, she couldn't tell if the footsteps belonged to the pirates or the Shadow Beasts.

"So, this is it. He's gone."

The pirates.

"I can't wait till this is over, to be rid of those monsters."

A loud grunt, and the dock shook as they hoisted the barrels onto the ship, one after another, finally returning for hers.

Evalyn sucked in a breath, waiting for her discovery, but it never came.

"They didn't hesitate to fill this one up," the gruff voice said. Salt bounced about her, poking and jabbing as they descended what Evalyn assumed were stairs below the main deck.

The pirates set the barrel down with a thud. "That's the last of them. Now let's raise anchor. I need some time to think about what happened."

"We all do." The other one patted the barrel. "Cohen will be devastated."

With that, they were gone, the door to the main deck slamming shut in their wake.

Evalyn released the sigh as the ship lurched forward, gripping Dax's cloak, tears streaming down her cheeks once more.

two

Joseline wasn't sure what she expected from the river crossing at the Rekiv border, but violent water coursing over jagged rock through the canal wasn't it.

Fear gripped the pit of her stomach so tightly she thought she would vomit the contents of her breakfast over the edge and into the crashing rapids. She turned to Quinn. "Tell me we aren't actually crossing this."

"I know the bridge might look dangerous, but I have personally made the crossing several times." Fallon dismounted as he spoke. "This is the best spot to cross."

Joseline had no choice but to follow as the others started across.

The thick wooden boards making up the bridge floor were connected to support beams by crossed-together planks, wide enough for two horses. The bridge was secured on either side by tall poles tethered several feet away from the edge overlooking the river by long ropes staked into the ground.

But that didn't stop her heart from racing.

"It can't be worse than facing a shadow creature, can it?" Quinn's mocking tone provoked a laugh from Jenson as he passed.

Joseline glared at him. "Falling to our deaths would certainly be worse."

Quinn shrugged. "I don't know, I always thought the dive would be exhilarating."

"Yeah, sure," Jenson scoffed. Turning to her, the Demi-Fae winked, nodding to Quinn. "Fallon dislocated Quinn's shoulder as a boy to stop him from jumping off."

"I'm not surprised," Joseline muttered. "You really are an absolute idiot."

Quinn flashed that dark smirk at her. "It's not my fault you're afraid of heights and I'm not, *Joseline*."

Her cheeks heated before she could deny it, and she thrust her chin forward stubbornly. "I am not."

He motioned to the bridge with one hand, the other poised behind his back. "If you say so."

Nose flaring in defiance, she moved, *slowly,* toward the canal. The wind rushing up from the water whipped her wild scarlet curls about her face. She pushed them back with a gulp. She wished she were better at controlling the slumbering calm. Maybe then she could summon it to ease the fear. Shea sat at her feet, licking a paw, and Joseline narrowed her eyes at the fox. "Some motivational spirit guide you are," she mumbled under her breath.

Shea gave a sarcastic huff. *It's not my fault you're acting like a scared child.*

Joseline sighed, wiping a hand over her face.

"I can take Bellona," Maya offered.

Joseline blinked, handing Maya the reins with a grateful nod, but still she hung back. Quinn nudged Eclipse forward. Shea, hopping up to curl in his saddle, flicked her tail in unimpressed annoyance.

"If you're really that afraid, would you like me to go first and hold your hand?" Quinn's voice kissed Joseline's cheek like the breeze.

She turned to him, unsure if she'd heard him correctly. "What?"

Since the attack in Rivedas, things between them had changed. She wasn't sure what to make of it. They hadn't talked about that night in the catacombs, and then their hug after her duel with Maya the night before...

"If you want me to go ahead of you, I'll hold your hand—"

"Yes." She cut him off.

The first step to becoming stronger is accepting your weakness. Quinn told her something similar once; this fear was nothing different. She twined their fingers, Quinn's large hand consuming hers, and gave him a feeble smile. "Just another weakness to overcome, right?"

A hint of pride flashed in his eyes as he squeezed her hand. "That's right."

Carefully, very carefully, they stepped onto the bridge. It was sturdy, she admitted, gripping the wooden support beam.

"That's it, there you go." Quinn's melodic voice comforted her.

Another step, then another. Quinn moved at the pace she set; never pushing, never urging her faster. His fingers were white from her grip, but he didn't complain, only whispered reassuring words. When they touched soil on the opposite side, Joseline refrained from laying in the dirt and crying for joy. She tucked windblown curls behind one ear.

"Just another weakness to overcome," Quinn echoed as he pulled her away from the edge.

Their tangled fingers slid apart.

So, you've decided to join us at last. How kind of you, Shea said. Joseline knelt to adjust the laces of her boots, and the fox swished white fluff into her face. *Next time, try not to be so difficult, please? It only wastes valuable time.* Shae stretched, jumping onto Bellona, who grazed near Maya and Jenson. The mare lifted her head, nickering in greeting.

"Do you ever wonder what she'd be like as a human?" Quinn asked as they joined the others.

Joseline glanced sidelong at him. "Probably as insufferable as you."

He shot her a glare, shaking his head.

The road, which had remained relatively wide, began to narrow, the smooth dirt now rocky and littered with stones. The forest was still dense and overgrown, with several large mountain peaks visible to the west along the Badraol border. Frigid air swirled about the trees in unseen whorls. Occasionally, a small clearing shone through the treeline. Birds chirped a merry tune as the sun rose, and Joseline hummed to herself, smiling. She'd often wondered what this sort of freedom would feel like, growing up in the confines of the Citadel, but Queen Talia had always been rigorous in her rules.

Blinking, Joseline frowned. She'd hardly thought of home at all since they left, aside from her little sister Julia. Strange she should think of Corae now.

She sighed. King Nathaniel and Queen Talia, as much as they loved one another, were complete opposites when it came to her upbringing as heir. Her father, boisterous and loveable, had left the majority of her upbringing to her mother. Not that Joseline disliked her mother, but the soft-spoken Queen always favored Julia and didn't care who knew it. Even as an infant, Julia was easier to handle. She had no temper and followed every command with blind obedience, ever the sweet and pretty little princess.

Joseline, however, was very much like her father. She listened to her heart and spoke her mind, which often resulted in needless arguments. It drove her mother mad.

Talia tried her best to oversee every action, prevent any defiance, but Joseline was stubborn. It was rare to sway her once she made up her mind. Over the years, Queen Talia eventually stopped hovering, their relationship fading to tolerance. That helped, among other things.

Little Julia helped the most. Joseline adored the free time she had to spend with her younger sister, attending festivals and balls just as exciting as an hour of reading or riding. But never-ending lessons consumed them both, and as they aged, their free time waned to nothing.

Mikenna helped, allowing Joseline to lose herself within the healer's workrooms, learning whatever she could though she was never permitted to actually heal someone. Kellen helped as well...or, he had. Now the thought of her guard made her nauseous. It was Kellen who snuck her down to the barracks during one of their evening walks, and Kellen who introduced her to the feisty table of palace spies in training, all women. It was a great honor to be selected for service, almost more-so than to train for a knight's shield and jade cloak. Her aunt, commander of the forces, selected girls from a young age and brought them to live and train at the palace. They weren't her friends like Maya had grown to be, but having other young girls to spend time with who weren't prissy royal ladies was a nice change from her duties and nagging mother.

Her gaze flickered to Quinn unintentionally at the thought of the royal emissaries who had branded him a spy without understanding his true motives. Chocolatey hair blew in crazy wisps around his defined jaw, falling just above his collarbone and half pulled back from his face in a tight bun. His sun-kissed skin wasn't as dark as Jenson's, and his cheeks were in desperate need of a shave. Quinn, noticing her stare, flashed that mischievous smirk, vibrant blue-green eyes shining in the sunlight.

She turned away, fighting the blush threatening to burn her cheeks. She still hated to admit how handsome he was. She wondered what the young spies would say if they knew she traveled with him as her protector. The thought made her smile.

She was still smiling when they stopped for the day, the sunset showering the road in burnt orange light.

Quinn walked up beside her as she dismounted. "Fallon's taking Jens and Maya to scout for a campsite." She nodded absently and he frowned, taking Bellona's reins. "Everything alright?"

"I was just thinking of the palace."

That blank expression covered his face. "The palace...not home?"

"That's the thing." She followed him into the trees. "I don't miss it. I thought I would, but I almost don't even want to go back when this is all over." She shrugged, her boot catching on a tree root, her hand lashing out to brace herself against a large trunk.

Quinn laughed. "Who knows, you might even be able to look out for yourself after all I've taught you."

Joseline's nostrils flared. "I could look out for myself just fine before."

Quinn opened his mouth to reply, then closed it, drawing one of the daggers at his waist and motioned for silence. Steel glinted against his left palm where he'd unsheathed the small dagger concealed within the leather brace.

"What's wrong?" she whispered.

"Joseline, shut up."

She narrowed her eyes but obeyed, glancing ahead.

The other horses were posted to a low-hanging branch, but Fallon, Jenson, and Maya were nowhere to be seen. Even Shea was gone, and the fox never went hunting with them.

Joseline's pulse quickened.

As quiet as he could manage, Quinn secured Eclipse and Bellona's reins to a nearby tree and crept forward, motioning for her to follow. She put a hand on the floral hilt of her unused dagger, not sure what she planned to do with it. Beside her, Quinn scanned the dense underbrush surrounding the clearing and frowned.

A twig snapped to her right, and Joseline spun, a figure blurring across her vision as it darted from tree to tree, circling them. Her breath came in light gasps. "Quinn, I saw something." She took a step toward whatever it was, her hand tightening on her dagger hilt.

Quinn lunged for her. "Joseline, wait—"

Thick netting snared around them, shooting up fifty feet into the air, swinging and twisting. Joseline crashed into Quinn with a rough smack, her ankle buckling as it slipped through the rope. She bit back a cry of pain.

They were too entangled. She couldn't stand, couldn't move, and her ankle burned.

Quinn spouted a stream of curses. She opened her mouth to mutter an apology just as they slammed into a tree. Joseline cried out as her head snapped against the trunk with a loud crack, and everything went black.

three

The incessant throb in Dax's temple woke him. Then the pain. So much damned pain. It radiated through his abdomen, along his spine. But what...

Evalyn.

His eyes flashed open, and he tried to sit up, but winced, groaning. Wetting his lips, he shifted, lifting a blood-stained hand into his vision before it fell to his abdomen. To the spot where Eva had stabbed him.

But there was nothing. Not even a scar to show where the fatal wound had been.

"Evalyn?" he rasped, trying to sit once more. Nothing. He hissed, forcing stiff muscles to move against their protests. "Evalyn?"

Still nothing.

Furrowing his brows, Dax swept his gaze over the room. Someone had started a fire in the stone hearth, the embers crackling along charred wood. The bedroom windows, which he normally kept closed, were open as well, a breeze gliding in elegant turns as it danced with the crimson curtains secured to the bottom corners of the four-poster bed.

Someone had changed the sheets and his garments, though the stench of blood filled the air; the dark stains streaking the hardwood floor were all that remained of the blood he'd lost. He frowned, running a hand over the smooth skin of his abdomen.

How…Evalyn stabbed me. I know…I helped her stab me. So what in Syvi's name…

Footsteps sounded from the main room. Dax's gaze shot toward the door as the familiar mop of red curls ducked into the room. He blinked in surprise. "Cohen? What—?"

"Easy, Cap." His first mate closed the door, grinning. "You lost a lot of blood."

"Why are you here?"

Cohen sank onto the bed. "Aye, it's good t' see you too, old friend." Before Dax could ask more questions, Cohen held up a finger. "As loyal a first mate as I am, I had to come rushing back when I heard you were on your death-bed."

The comment didn't ease his confusion. "Nobody knew I was—"

"Only Naomi." Cohen cocked his head, adjusting the emerald sash slung around his hips where the ivory tunic and black leather pants met. When Dax didn't smile, he sighed. "I was on my way back already. Met up with Beck and Nim in Orira and they told me about the Fae girl."

"Evalyn." Dax turned away from him. "Her name is Evalyn."

Cohen raised an eyebrow. "Ah, so she did warm up to ya eventually. From the letters Naomi sent, I was startin' to doubt yer charm."

Dax snorted. Gods, did he miss this scoundrel. "Syvi bless you, Cohen. How you've kept yourself alive all these years is beyond me."

His first mate rolled his eyes. "Aye, and I could say the same about you, Cap. What with being stranded on land without your beloved princess."

He shot Cohen a glare. "Now you leave *Seraphina* out of this. She's the best ship in Navarre."

That warranted a chuckle. They were silent for a moment, Dax dreading the question he knew was coming. Clearing his throat, Cohen sighed. "Do you remember what happened?" Dax shook his head. "Ya should be dead, Dax."

"I know. Gods, Cohen, you don't think I realize how much blood I lost? I don't..." he pursed his lips. "I don't know."

It didn't make sense. Evalyn had stabbed him and left. He'd abandoned her, just like she always feared he would. Yet here he was, very much alive. Had someone come to heal him?

"Cap."

Dax blinked. "Aye?"

"What are ya thinkin?" He stood as he spoke, moving to pour a glass of water from the nightstand.

Dax wet his lips in anticipation. "I don't understand. Was anyone else here?" Accepting the mug from Cohen, he drank, bracing himself on the pillows with an elbow. When the cup was empty, he handed it back to his friend. "Did I...I couldn't have healed myself."

"Don't know, Dax." Cohen's gaze shifted to the door. "Naomi said you were healed when she found you. But there was blood everywhere." He paused. "I helped her change the sheets."

"Do they know?" Dax didn't have to specify who *they* were.

"They pronounced you dead, but no one's been back to do anything about it." Cohen ran a hand along the back of his neck, moving toward the closet. "It's been three days. Naomi and I have been taking turns watching, but nothing."

Panic raced through him. "Have they started...they were planning to do tests on some of the slaves. It was one of the reasons I had to get her out. Why I had to..." he gulped.

"No." Cohen shook his head, ducking into the closet for a moment before returning with a handful of clothes. "They postponed it I think, once they found you."

Good, he thought, easing to the edge of the bed. Everything ached, but he forced himself not to wince. "So, what were you two planning to do then?"

Cohen grinned, freckles wrinkling across his pale flesh. "Do ya doubt me?" he asked, helping Dax to his feet.

"No," Dax chuckled. "But the sooner we get out of here, the better. Beck and Nim..."

"Haven't returned from Easthaven yet. They aren't due back for at least another week, but I figure there are places we can hide ya or—"

The door creaked open again.

"You're awake!" Naomi said, eyes dancing.

"I am." Dax let Cohen help slide the tunic over his head though his shoulders screamed in protest. "I hear you found me."

Naomi studied the floor. "Aye."

"Thank you." He groaned slightly as he leaned forward to slip his breeches on, Cohen holding him steady. When Naomi didn't speak, he raised an eyebrow. "What is it?"

She blushed, twisting ebony hair through her fingers. "Toren's replaced you rather easily."

Dax shrugged. "That doesn't surprise me." When she didn't continue, he added, "And Elyon?"

"They have the dwarf boy in one of the torture cells with another man—Kellen, I think his name was? They brought him from Rathal." She met Cohen's eyes, then Dax's. "From my understanding, they're planning to use them as the first test subjects for their shadow magic instead of the slaves."

"Syvi guide us," Dax murmured, pulling his hair away from his face with the scrap of cloth Cohen handed him. "Is there any way we can get him out?"

"That wasn't part of the plan, Cap." Cohen took the poker where it leaned near the hearth, shifting the coals. "We could, aye, but I ain't sure if..."

"Cohen, we have to try. He's...important."

The red-haired pirate frowned, letting out a sigh. "Aye, we try then." He lifted the poker in Dax's direction. "But don't go blamin' me if we get caught, ya hear?"

"Aye, friend." Dax smiled. "I owe you."

"Bet yer arse ya do." He frowned, sighing as he replaced the poker along the wall. "Ya feelin' fit to escape?"

"As I'll ever be, I suppose." Dax ran a hand through his hair, turning to Naomi. "Where did you plan to hide us away until Beck and Nim return with the ship, little spider?"

Dax refrained from chuckling at the blush Naomi could never conceal when he used the nickname—one his father had given only to a few in his life. A nickname she'd earned three times over in the years on his crew. "There are several abandoned rooms toward the front of the fortress. They never use them for anything." She paused, glancing toward him as if waiting for his approval. Dax nodded. "I thought we could stay hidden there."

"Naomi, I trust you. The title of the Sea Dragon's little spider does not go unwarranted."

She only nodded.

"Right, shall we?" Cohen adjusted his belt, checking the cutlass was secure at his hip before giving Naomi's forehead a swift kiss. "I don't want to be out in the open any longer than we have to, and this place is still crawling with demons."

They turned to him, waiting for his command as they always had. It eased some of the tightness and confusion in his chest. His two greatest friends—first mate and secret keeper. They completed him in so many ways, and he wasn't sure he'd ever feel worthy of their friendship.

Even so, Dax said nothing, only smiled, inspecting his rooms one final time before gesturing to the main room and the stairwell waiting to lead them down into the fortress below.

It was interesting, seeing the fortress as a prisoner rather than a superior. The walls feigned constriction, as if tightening the air around them until Dax was sure it would suffocate him completely. Shadows enveloped the walls, secretive and haunting, the scent of old blood so overpowering he couldn't help but wonder if the dark stone had been painted with it in some places. It was eerie. Unsettling.

He shook his head, focusing on keeping Naomi in sight. But despite the strength of his actions, his hand continued to find its way to his stomach. To the expanse of unmarred skin concealed beneath his tunic. No matter how hard he tried, he couldn't stop thinking about the strangeness of it. The wound had been fatal, he'd made sure of that.

So why wasn't he dead? Syvi's breath, why wasn't he *wounded*? Not that he wasn't grateful for whatever magic had healed him, but it didn't stop his mind from wandering in erratic circles. Absorbed in his thoughts, he almost stumbled into Naomi as she held up a hand.

Cohen swore under his breath, catching Dax's elbow. "Cap, where's yer head at? We can't be reckless. If we get caught..."

"So be it, Cohen. There's always been a chance we would." Dax opened his mouth to say more but stopped when Naomi flashed them a narrowed glare.

After a moment, she nodded and slipped around the corner.

"Do you know where they're keeping the boy?" Dax whispered, his eyes flickering along the silent shadows.

"One of the back cells," Cohen shuddered as he spoke. "Naomi's been bringing him extra water, but...well, it isn't good."

"What isn't?"

"The situation."

"I mean, it's never been good," Dax stifled a snort.

They were silent for a moment. "Dax," Cohen began. "If we're caught..."

"If we're caught, you will let it happen."

"But—"

"Cohen. You will let it happen. You will take me wherever they ask you to, and you will stay with Naomi." He met his friend's worried hazel gaze. "Am I understood?"

Cohen looked as though he might argue, but he sighed. "Aye."

"Good."

Naomi's head bobbed around the corner before he could say more. "Come on."

The fortress was comprised of several floors, each with twisting hallways and alcoves. The towers housed the rooms of those with senior importance, the higher floors mostly bathing chambers and meeting rooms. The ground level, save for the kitchens and pantries, had been deserted for years. The dungeons made up the entirety of the lower levels, the mines easily accessible from the back doors.

Dax's rooms were secluded in the uppermost towers, which was wonderful in terms of privacy, but not in terms of a simple escape. His lack of energy didn't help either, and his stomach growled with unquenched hunger.

Dax shivered. The memory of what Narcio used to look like before the demons seized control of it sent a dull ache through his chest.

"A bit further," Naomi whispered, pulling him from his thoughts. "There's a room near the front doors that—"

"You there, stop!"

They froze.

Dax's gaze flickered to Naomi and Cohen. They moved in easy unison as they always had, as if some unspoken understanding connected them without words. Dax moved his hands behind his back, his first mate slipping a firm grip around his wrists. The captive and the captor. Yet another game to add to the façade.

Naomi blinked, turning toward the hissing voice of the Shadow Commander moments before he approached them. "Is something the matter?"

The demon snarled, Aeron's mark of power branded between his eyes wrinkling with the motion. "The pirate captain lives?" His eyes darted to Cohen, then Naomi. "Why did you not tell us of this immediately?"

Naomi cocked her head, offering an innocent smile. "We were just on our way to bring him to you."

Dax's pulse hammered in his chest, but he refused to meet his friend's eyes, instead keeping his gaze fixed on the Shadow Commander.

"I see," the demon smirked, gripping Dax's chin with a clawed hand. "Well, this is a pleasant surprise, *Captain*." He eyed Naomi, approval flickering in his soulless gaze. "Impressive, little mortal." He spun then, turning deeper into the fortress. Toward the dungeons. "Well, let's get him situated."

Don't panic, Dax thought. *Don't fight it. We'll figure it out.*

Cohen squeezed his wrist in reassurance.

"Of course, sir." If Naomi had any fear, it didn't show in her voice as they followed the Shadow Commander into the dark.

Dax tried to block out the moans of hunger. It had been easy, somehow, with Evalyn there. He'd had a purpose to stay strong. Now that strength was a distant memory. The agony of those held captive was enough to make his own fears palpable.

At the bottom of the dungeon stairs, they veered left toward the dungeons meant for interrogation. Dax gnawed on the inside of his cheek.

Don't be a fool. Evalyn endured these cells, so can you.

At last, the Shadow Commander stopped before one of the many steel doors, facing him with a menacing grin. "Well, Captain, welcome home."

The door creaked open. Cohen pushed him inside, and he let out a startled grunt, falling to his knees. He fought to keep his breath even as he clenched his fists, inspecting the room. The cell was small, the stone slick with perspiration. Several thick chains hung from the ceiling and draped along the walls.

Two pairs of chains in the center of the room were already occupied.

He didn't recognize the lean blond, his hazel eyes dull, empty. He sagged against the chains, arms secured over his head, bare chest decorated in scars. He didn't bother glancing at Dax, his breath no more than a faint rasp against cracked lips.

But the young Dwarf stared at him, open-mouthed. Dark auburn hair stuck to his forehead in sweaty clumps, his arms equally strained above his head. But unlike his companion, his eyes blazed, determination shimmering beneath eternal fatigue.

Elyon.

Dax wet his lips but didn't speak.

The Shadow Commander hauled him to his feet, shoving him toward the third set of chains and securing them around his wrists. "Seems that luck of yours has finally run out, Captain. You tried so hard, and in the end your Fae whore couldn't even obey you." He stepped away, his gaze trailing down Dax's body with a smirk. "I wish I could say I pity you, but..." he shrugged.

Dax glanced over his shoulder, finding Cohen's eyes. The redhead only winked, following the Shadow Commander into the hall with Naomi. The door slammed shut behind them. The air echoed with the remnants of the vibrations, and Dax released a shuddering sigh.

"It's really you."

He turned to Elyon, offering a weak smile. "I wish I could say it's good to see you, kid."

Elyon let out a half-laugh, trying and failing to roll his shoulders. "I thought you were dead."

"I did too."

"You know each other?" The blond boy asked, his gaze still fixed on his feet.

"Aye," Dax pursed his lips. "Sort of."

"Dax was the captain in charge of the island when I came here," Elyon explained.

"*Was* being the key word."

"What happened?"

"I was a fool. I thought...I don't know what I thought, to be honest." He sighed again, tilting his head back.

"Doesn't matter anyway," the blond muttered. "They're going to kill us."

"Kellen..." Elyon began.

"What? It's true." Kellen, the blond, gritted his teeth. "No one is coming for us."

Dax eyed him. "Always so pessimistic, lad?"

Kellen laughed dryly. "Just wait till they start torturing you. The one with red eyes, he's a monster."

"They're all monsters," Elyon said.

Dax was silent for a moment. When he spoke, his voice was softer than he hoped. "What is it they're doing?"

For a brief moment, fear flickered in Elyon's dark brown gaze. "They're making weapons. They told me once, when they were...they do things, Dax. Horrible things. Then, they heal us as if the pain never happened. But the scars..." Elyon shivered.

"What sort of weapons?" he asked, ignoring the goosebumps prickling along his flesh.

"They're breeding Shadow Monsters," Kellen replied. "Created with magic wielders and their dark, sick power. Demonic half-breeds whose bodies are filled with obsidian shards." He paused. "It's a protective stone. Yet somehow they're changing the makeup to fuel the darkness rather than ward against it. They want to create an army."

"We're their test subjects before they start experimenting on the slaves, I think." Elyon's lip trembled, his chains rattling slightly.

Well, that explains why they haven't started whatever real experiments they have planned yet.

"I wish I were dead when I'm in there," Elyon whispered.

"Don's say that," Dax said. "Life is better than death, always."

"Is it? You have no idea what it's like in there. It...it's like the monsters tear a piece of your essence from your soul and burn it into your flesh." He nodded to Kellen. "He hasn't been the same since they started."

"And how long has it been?"

"I don't know," he shook his head. "They take one of us each day. At least...I think it's each day." Elyon's shoulders shook more fiercely. "I don't want to die in here."

Kellen muttered something incoherent.

"I will do whatever I can to make sure that doesn't happen," Dax promised.

Kellen's laugh was audible that time. "Will you? Maybe it's more than we deserve."

"It doesn't matter to me who you are or what you've done, boy," Dax turned to Kellen. "No one deserves to die in the dark."

There was a pause. "And how do you plan on helping us, exactly?"

Dax's lips twitched. "My companions, the ones who brought me in here, they'll come for us."

Elyon's eyes brightened slightly. "Will they?"

"They will."

Kellen huffed, not meeting his gaze. "Well you'd better hope they come quickly, for all our sakes." Even as he said it, Dax could sense the shadow magic, could see it swirling about Kellen's body. Watching. Waiting.

four

The memories came in short bursts.

Quinn could no longer ignore the tormenting visions. They weren't *his* memories, but another's. Different, but similar, familiar.

A small cottage in the woods surrounded by a myriad of flowerbeds, the fresh smell of homemade bread wafting through the air. A girl his age, his equal in many ways though he didn't quite recognize her face.

A peaceful morning disrupted by shadowy nightmares.

The air tightened in his lungs, cutting off the vision abruptly. The pain was excruciating, the darkness no comfort.

"They still haven't woken?" A woman's voice, husky and soft.

"No, and the damned Aonani fox does nothing but growl every time I go near the fire-haired girl." The second voice was rougher, thick with the scratchy sound of a constant pipe smoker.

Pain prickled Quinn's dry, raw throat as he tried to swallow. His eyelids drooped, vision blurry, head pounding.

"They'll wake soon enough," the woman assured her companion. A fire crackled somewhere nearby, but the thicket of trees sounded otherwise dense.

Quinn wet his lips. "Water..." he groaned, squinting against the faint rays of dusk light slipping through the canopy above, vision still hazy.

"So, the big one woke first," the man said.

Quinn tried to sit himself up, his bound legs slipping beneath him. He swore as a root dug into his spine.

"Easy, now." A calloused hand gripped his jaw, holding it steady. Water dripped into his mouth, running down his chin. He almost sighed from the refreshing liquid coating his too-dry tongue and tried without success to open his eyes fully. Still the heavy feeling remained, revealing nothing more than the blurred shapes of the fire and their captors kneeling before him.

A glint of steel flashed, and he tensed. "So, care to tell us where you travel from?"

Quinn gritted his teeth, sitting up as best he could. "I don't have to tell you a Sauda-cursed thing."

A gruff laugh. "No, I suppose you don't." More water ran down his throat as the man continued, "Where are you traveling to?" Quinn coughed, and the woman pulled the waterskin back. "So that's how it's going to be?"

"Ren, stop," the woman chastised. "Our orders are to capture trespassers until Larina and Kai return, not harm them."

Quinn snorted despite the returning fatigue. "Right, because restraints and sedatives scream *don't hurt me.*"

The swift pain in his neck sent a shiver up his spine, the faint, bitter fragrance of a sleeping herb filling his nose. *Obbasia.* He cursed aloud, his body sagging to the ground. He opened his mouth, but the drowsing effects already consumed his body as it pulsed through his bloodstream.

"Sorry about that, love," the woman whispered.

Before Quinn could reply, darkness exploded behind his eyes, the oblivion meeting him once more.

※

When he awoke again, Joseline's terrified whimpering echoed beside him. "Who are you? What do you want with us?" She sounded like a helpless child...she *was* a helpless child. Panic raced through him.

She isn't hurt. Shea's voice whispered through his mind. Quinn relaxed slightly at the brush of her tail around his calf.

"Nothing you need worry yourself over, pretty little lady," Ren answered.

"Where are we and what do you want with us?" Joseline's voice sounded stronger that time.

"Rekiv, on the edge of the wastelands near the Rathal border. You needn't know more than that."

"What do you want with us?" she repeated a third time.

"Joseline, don't worry yourself with the likes of them. They aren't going to tell us anything." The words scratched Quinn's throat, and he coughed.

"Lovers reunited? How sweet." Ren's voice.

"We aren't lovers." Quinn forced his eyes open. They were still heavy, but opening them wasn't impossible this time.

Joseline sat upright to his left, eyes wide, fiery curls a wild tangle about her face. Jenson, Fallon, and Maya stirred on the other side of the fire, their hands and feet bound. It was dark, almost too dark to see beyond the firelight, but now Quinn could make out the faint outline of large tents through the trees, the sounds of horses and other voices whispering on the breeze.

He turned his attention to the woman. The dark brown fabric of her simple leather armor was worn and covered in scratches. Her long cloak pooled around her narrow frame, but she didn't appear thin or frail like someone lacking food.

She held a waterskin out to Joseline, Shea glaring at her with suspicion.

"Our orders mentioned nothing about helping them regain their strength, Freya," Ren muttered.

Fallon groaned as Freya waved Ren off. He frowned, adding another log to the fire, then striding to the others and rubbing a salve along their upper lips. Fallon went still.

"What are you doing to them?" Quinn demanded.

Ren swigged from a flask at his hip. "Just a little something to keep them asleep longer without wasting our more valuable supplies. We don't need all of ya whining, now do we?"

Freya sent him a frustrated look. "Ren."

"What?"

She sighed, standing to whisper something to him. Ren glared at her, but didn't argue, only moved to the other side of the fire and took up sharpening his small dagger. Quinn turned to Joseline. "It's going to be alright. I won't let them hurt you."

Her nose flared. "What could you possibly do to make this situation better?"

They seem harmless enough, Shea said. *Something tells me if they meant to hurt you, they would have by now. It's been three days at least.*

"I still don't trust them," Quinn muttered to the fox, adjusting his position against the tree trunk.

"So, what do we do?" Joseline's eyes filled with an expression he'd seen often in Jenson and Maya—trust, loyalty, and strength.

Quinn almost anticipated the prick in his neck this time. "We wait until they let their guard down. Then we see what information they tell us before we try to make a break for it."

Joseline's head drooped to the side when Freya administered the next obbasia injection to her as well.

Darkness consumed his mind.

five

The thin air whipped about the circular tower in a wicked frenzy, stinging Erza's cheeks. The old watchtower of Thya had once guarded the border between Rekiv and The Northlands, warding off the Northmen and their never-ending bloodlust when demons ruled the north. Now it was a half-crumbled ruin good for nothing but hosting the Shadow Games and breeding new Kitsugon for the covens. The creature's shrieks echoed in her ears as her gaze swept over Blackwing Manor on the outskirts of the village below. The dull, lifeless building reflected the dark souls of the Blackwing coven who inhabited it.

Sunlight burned her eyes, the wind dancing wisps of raven hair across her tanned skin. But Erza Stormwood was used to the stinging wind and blinding rays. She relished in them. The exhilaration of flight was unequal, weaving through clouds on the backs of massive beasts an ecstasy that sparked any young witch's desires for freedom.

With one final glance at the sweeping marshland of Rekiv and the rundown fishing village of Thya below, Erza made her way back to ground level along the outer ramp, her long, plum-colored cloak twirled about her slender body.

The Kitsugon Crowning Ceremony. Her chest fluttered at the feverish excitement of what that meant. She'd never seen a Crowning Ceremony; the last one took place when she was an infant—a helpless witchling incapable of comprehending her surroundings.

Her boots clipped against stone as she walked toward the kennels, her cloak billowing behind her. She ran calloused hands through her short raven hair, bangs brushing her forehead just above thin eyebrows.

A servant rushed past, carrying several trays for tonight's feast. "G'day, Miss," she said, her Easthaven accent thick. Erza gave a brisk nod.

The hallways were lined with sturdy cages implanted into the ancient structure, the Kitsugons' metallic stench assaulting her senses. Shrieks, growls, and the flapping of confined wings echoed off stone as she strode past cell after cell. They were majestic creatures, mysterious and dangerous. She loved everything about them.

Their bodies, foxlike in appearance, were twice the size of a large wolf, rippling with firm, dense muscle beneath silky fur. But the fierceness shone through the leathery skin along their lower legs and face. Gleaming tawny eyes and scaled snouts concealed deadly teeth, soft ears twitching toward every sound. Long tails, barbed at the tips, swished idly, the reaching expanse of powerful wings tucked carefully at their sides.

Even as a witchling, Erza had been drawn to the Kitsugon, their fierceness a flame erupting into darkness. They fueled her own ferocity, her determination.

Fearless, dominant, and loyal. Those were the Stormwood words she'd spent over a century engraving into her Elites. Though her mother never praised her, she'd been a gem since a young age. Erza Stormwood, the youngest witch in Rekiv history to ride a Kitsugon without losing control. The loyal soldier. She obeyed without question, training her coven without mercy. The Stormwood Elites were once the most feared aerial fighting unit in Navarre until the covens distanced themselves from the rest of the realm. Her fellow witchlings loathed her success for years before at last accepting her strength and potential to rule.

Except the Blackwing coven. They would never accept strength outside their own. It was why they distanced themselves from Ravencrest, why they rarely interacted with the other covens and defied whatever orders they could.

Witches by nature were heartless, soulless, born of both light and darkness. They ate the hearts of lonely mortals because it would grant them the strength of Sauda, the Goddess of Death. At least, that's what superstitious humans believed. Their fear was almost insulting.

Shaking her head, she neared the final cage, the snowy Kitsugon within as calm as her elegant rider standing outside. "You're late, Erza."

Queen Rowena of Rekiv folded her arms across a busty chest, long, dark hair a stark contrast to the pearly silks and furs clinging to her beautiful curves and narrow shoulders.

Erza straightened. "Apologies, Mother."

Daiki, the snowy Kitsugon, extended her graceful neck toward the barred door, rubbing her silver-scaled nose against the Queen's hand. The creature chirped at her rider, a light, pleasant sound.

"I hear Morana has been seen doing extra training with her flight unit." Her mother's voice was cold, calculating.

Erza fiddled with the teardrop gem chained around her neck, twirling it between her fingers. "The Blackwing heir isn't a concern."

Queen Rowena stared at her, vibrant lilac eyes piercing. "Rumors are spreading that the Blackwing coven has been even more vicious recently. The Thyan people are becoming concerned. I've heard of several deaths in Easthaven that were brutal, though the Blackwings haven't been directly tied to them, and Healer Superior Albion himself sent word to me from the Chiron."

Erza frowned, gripping her elbows. "I see. Would you like me to end the problem, then?"

"No. I trust Anwen Blackwing is capable of containing and overseeing her own coven." Her mother twirled a sapphire ring around a slender finger. Daiki ruffled her wings. "You know I expect you to win."

Erza nodded.

"A Stormwood witch has always sat on the Rekiv throne," Rowena added. "A Stormwood witch has always won the Shadow Games. Your youth compared to the other heirs does not change my expectations."

"This year's games will be no different," Erza promised.

The Shadow Games—a tournament to the death between the Stormwood, Blackwing, and Silvermist covens.

When every coven heir reached at least their two hundredth year, a set of three trials occurred to determine the new Queen of Rekiv. A Stormwood witch had occupied the jeweled throne in Ravencrest since the creation of Navarre, proving herself in stealth, wisdom, magic, and combat during each trial.

The Kitsugon Crowning Ceremony marked the start, the four-week point before the beginning competition in which the current Queen's Kitsugon's kits battled to the death—the first of two such fights during the month of Nova. A battle to determine the future queen's mount.

Queen Rowena narrowed her eyes. "I hope not." She paused before adding, "I informed the Healer Superior that we would send two Elites to the Chiron. While I appreciate the healer's training efforts, I must agree it is rather foolish to have no real warriors stationed there."

"I'll choose them myself."

Queen Rowena nodded, saying nothing as she retreated down the hall. The shrieking Kitsugon quieted as she passed. Erza waited to follow, meeting Daiki's tawny eyes. She inclined her head, blinking slowly—a great sign of respect from a Kitsugon. Erza returned the gesture and followed after her mother.

When she entered the main hallway, a venomous voice echoed behind her. "Well, if it isn't the perfect princess herself."

Schooling her expression to neutrality, Erza turned, her smile dripping fake kindness. "Morana Blackwing. What a pleasant surprise."

Morana snorted. "Oh, please, spare me your sarcasm."

Erza shrugged and continued walking. "May the best witch reign."

"Oh, I plan to." Morana licked red-painted lips, honey-blonde curls caressing her breasts and the new obsidian pendant hanging between them.

"The Goddess will decide which of us is superior, just as she decides all."

"Such a diplomatic response. Lest you forget, Odessa, Salia, Nami, and I are older and wiser." Challenge flashed in Morana's pale blue eyes.

Erza was saved from a courteous reply by another, sweeter voice. "Ages aside, she is still your princess while Rowena sits on the jeweled throne, Morana, you would do well to remember."

Odessa, one of the soft-spoken Silvermist heirs, settled the raging fire from Morana's words. Of the three covens, the Silvermist witches were the sweetest, the gentlest. It was always their downfall during the Games.

Morana scowled but said nothing, and Odessa gave Erza a smile, amber eyes kind. "I have to go," she said. "I promised Salia I'd meet her before we go up the royal seats." She waved, jogged toward the cylindrical structure's east wing housing the Silvermist coven.

"Ah, the famed Silvermist twins. Their love is pathetic. I can't wait to sink my claws into them both." Morana's crystal nails slid out from her cuticles, a shiver of longing rippling over her face before they retracted just as quickly.

Erza rolled her eyes. "Your pleasure from others pain is repulsive, Morana."

"We were born to be heartless, might as well accept that. With power comes fear, and with fear comes a lack of love. It is the way of it."

Erza shuddered at the truth behind Morana's words, but refused to believe them. She would be Queen, not Morana. Gentle yet powerful, loved by all.

The arena archway stretched above them. Stone etched with various flowers, herbs, and the illustrated evolution of the Kitsugon marked where the arch ended and the dirty sand floor began.

"Morana, where have you been?"

Despite her centuries of existence, Erza didn't think she would ever get used to the husky, hissing voice of the Blackwing coven leader. In hair and body shape, dressed alike, Anwen and her daughter could have passed for twins.

Morana met her mother's gaze, fiddling with the pendant at her throat. "I was exchanging friendly greetings with Princess Erza."

Anwen rolled her eyes. "Save your lies for those who might believe them." The coven leader nodded to Erza, making her way to the large ramp winding up the outside of the arena, Erza and Morana at her heels. The ground below was littered with spiked rock, an effort to keep any animals or unwanted people away from the tower and the supplies it contained.

The marshlands extended beyond the structure as far as the eye could see, Thya's various settlements clustered near the tower base. The Blackwing Manor glistened along the outskirts like onyx in the sunlight and the Northlands' frost-covered landscape stretched across the horizon, the snowy mountain peaks of Lake Urasa's lone island shimmering in the sun. The ramp wound higher and higher, narrowing at the top, the barrier between the jagged deathtraps no more than a copper railing and a forty-foot drop.

As they approached the final level reserved for the coven leaders and pureblood heirs, Erza nodded to the Elites stationed on either side of the doorway. Rowen, her second and cousin, flashed a wicked grin. Astrid, her third, rolled dark hazel eyes, the grip on her staff tightening. Their Elite cloaks matched hers, plum fabric fluttering in the breeze.

As the Blackwings made their way to their seats, Erza paused. "Once the ceremony is over, collect the Elites. We have an assignment."

Rowen's lilac eyes danced. "Oh good, spending all morning flying around Lake Urasa has become so dull. More Northmen rebels to dispose of?"

"Not this time." Erza could have sworn her second pouted.

"In your rooms?" Astrid asked, her expression calm as ever.

Erza nodded, approaching the seat beside her mother and fanning her cloak out behind her. Queen Rowena didn't so much as glance in her direction.

The seating in the lower balconies was littered with the coven's half-blood witches, maids, and stable hands. Erza even spotted some novice healers from the Chiron, recognizable by their cream garments embroidered with the escheca tree. Whispers of excitement wafted toward them, sunshine radiating through the open ceiling.

When Daiki entered the arena, all chatter stopped. The Kitsugon stared up at Rowena, her fellow queen and rider. Rowena smiled, and the snowy creature growled her approval, curling along the edge of the wall.

Daiki's four kits entered next, all wearing thick iron collars, led forward on long chains. The first kit, the largest, was as red as he was fierce, fiery fur and scales glowing like molten lava in the sunshine. The second male was gray with dark green scales, his thin feathered wings a lighter greenish-gray. The third was female, almost as large as the first, but her fur and scales were a blood orange compared to her crimson brother. She snarled at him as she passed, and he swished his barbed tail.

The final kit was smaller than even her gray brother. She stepped carefully, shy and timid, her eyes on the dirt beneath her paws. Her sable fur merged into scales shimmering like rainbow hematite, the sunlight reflecting hues of purple, blue, red, and gold as she walked.

The handlers removed the leading chains, hurrying out of the arena to lower the metal portcullis gate. The four kits stood watching one another, tawny eyes darting from side to side. Then Daiki roared, the command echoing off stone walls.

The large red Kitsugon wasted no time. He lunged for his gray brother, teeth snapping around his neck as the barbed tip of his tail gouged along his brother's spine. Blood ran down green-gray scales, his fur marked crimson. Gray shrieked, stumbling, and tried to fight back, but his orange sister caught his wing in her jaw. Blood spurted, dripping down his leg where she tore the wing away. His barbed tail snapped forward, finding purchase in Orange's leg even as he collapsed to the ground.

Red, looming twice his size, sank razor-sharp teeth into his neck one final time before the light vanished from those bright, tawny eyes.

Erza sucked in a breath as the larger siblings turned to their tiny, black-furred sister. But there was no fear in Black's eyes. There was challenge, strength, hope.

Orange lunged.

Black twisted, quick as lightning, and Orange stumbled into the stone wall. The arena shook from the impact. Orange turned, snarling as Black shot forward, wings secured against her sides, protected. Her teeth closed around her sister's already-bleeding lower leg, dragging her to the ground. Orange screeched, fighting to stand, but Black raked claws along her chest. Blood swelled where she opened flesh, spurting from Orange's body.

She thrashed about, her eyes flashing to her brother. But Red just stood watching, waiting to slaughter the winner.

Black took her limping sister's tail between her teeth, lashing her neck to the side and whipping Orange into the center of the arena—right toward Red.

Orange landed, screeching and bleeding, on top of him with a hard smack. They flailed, fighting to disentangle themselves, but the wounded Orange was a deadweight, unable to lift her leg or tail as blood left her body. Black sauntered toward them, challenge gleaming in her eyes as Red struggled beneath their dying sister.

Erza leaned forward, spellbound by the cunning beauty of the small Kitsugon. Black's tiny frame was a shadow to her brother clawing frantically at the dirt. Their eyes met, blazing gold in acknowledgement of the hovering defeat.

The victorious meek. Small, yet mighty. Dangerously powerful.

Red struggled a moment longer, sharp claws gouging deep grooves into the dirt, slowing as the seconds ticked by. His growls weakened as his strength did, Orange's weight crushing his lungs. At last his massive, scaled head slumped between his feet. Black flashed forward at his unspoken signal, wings and scales a blur of shimmering color. Her teeth sank into his neck, blood gushing around her jaw muscles. Red roared, the sound echoing through the open-aired ceiling, vibrating the stone walls. Her bite tightened, the sound of ripping flesh and crunching bones a faint whisper on the wind.

His fiery tail swished, a final fight to stop her. It swung around, the barbed spikes raking along her cheek and down her front leg. She snarled, fire blazing in her eyes, but she didn't release her grip, didn't back down as she yanked his neck with a final, deadly snap.

He went limp and did not rise again.

Black released her hold and straightened. A future Queen—one of two to be determined before next month's end.

Daiki approached her with a series of high-pitched chirps. She bent down, nuzzling her daughter's cheek, licking at the blood swelling there, staining her white fur crimson.

Erza released the breath, a smile touching her lips just as a scream echoed through the arena.

She was on her feet and racing down the outer ramp before her mother could give the order to do so. Rowen and Astrid remained at Rowena's side, drawing their weapons. An heir's duty, first and foremost, was to protect their coven leader. Erza might be the youngest heir, but she would die before she broke that duty.

Odessa lay crumpled to the ground halfway down the ramp, her bone-white fingers gripping the stone overlooking jagged rocks below. Tears streamed down her face, tight brown curls flying about in the growing wind.

Erza's heartbeat quickened as she knelt before the Silvermist heir, the mournful amber aura engulfing her. "Odessa?"

The older witch all but threw herself at Erza, dark plum fabric bunching where Odessa gripped her cloak. Choked sobs shook her body as she fought to control herself.

"Odessa," Erza repeated. "What happened?"

But Odessa shook her head, unable to form the words as she pointed over the edge of the ramp. Erza didn't want to know what had brought such terror to an heir, the strongest witches in Rekiv. Her pulse, normally a subtle calm, thumped violently as she inched toward the edge. Odessa's grip on her cloak tightened, the sobs loosing themselves from her throat as she buried her face in Erza's shoulder.

Stormwood heir or no, Erza wasn't prepared for the sight that awaited her.

She couldn't tell which happened first, the piercing fall or the shadowy darkness slithering over golden-brown flesh. Regardless, the witch was near unrecognizable. A large, jagged spike seared her clean through her chest, several smaller ones protruding through her throat and abdomen. From the darker shade of blood, she'd been dead before the Crowning Ceremony began. She was covered in it, the half-dried liquid coating her clothes and flesh. Her thin lips were contorted into a scream, amber eyes wide with terror, skin writhing with inky black that inched like serpents as they spread, seeping into her eyes. The darkness eroded her away, body and soul.

But despite the horrifying image and the spreading shadows, Erza knew who the witch was, why Odessa reacted like this.

It was the other Silvermist heir. Salia, Odessa's twin sister.

SIX

The brisk mountain air chilled Edan to the bone as he walked across the Chiron's inner courtyard. Mercifully, the northern snows had eased for Navarre's summer months, but with autumn upon them, the winds in Easthaven were brisk as ever and the snow would return soon enough. He pulled the thick cloak more firmly around his shoulders, the fur-lined hood a minor comfort.

"Morning to you, Master Edan." He turned toward the speaker; a young woman draped in the thin cream breeches and tunic of a novice healer, the garment's left breast embroidered with an eshacca tree. She shivered despite her boots and gloves.

"Milla, where in the name of Noria is your cloak?" Edan raised an eyebrow as the young girl stammered out an explanation, and grinned. "Go indoors. It's chilly this morning. I'd hate to see you catch another cold so soon in this weather."

Milla gave an apologetic nod, cheeks flushing as she rushed off toward the housing building on the opposite side of the open, tree-lined courtyard. Edan chuckled, scratching at the dark scruff covering his jaw, and continued toward the Chiron's main building. Heat enveloped him as he pulled open the heavy stone doors, the fire flickering vibrantly in the massive hearth splitting the grand staircase to the upper wings. Shivering, he tugged off his gloves and strode toward the eastern wing on the left side. Several novices hurried about the halls, waving and smiling as he passed.

With end of summer exams right around the corner, the halls were a hectic mess; students hurried to ask professors last-minute questions and turn in late assignments, while others rushed about to meet with study groups. Edan loved teaching new healers. The sight of young learners so anxious to succeed in their studies brought a warmth to his chest.

Lost in his thoughts, he didn't see the door opening before him as he strode around the bend toward the small staircase leading to the Healer Superior's workroom. He was rewarded with a loud squeak, papers flying through the air as the young man he collided with tumbled to the ground. Edan knelt, helping the man collect first his glasses, then the scrolls strewn about his feet.

He pushed the glasses up onto his small nose. "Master Edan!" he breathed, scrambling to his knees. "I'm sorry, I'm so sorry. I didn't...I wasn't...I'm so clumsy, I..."

Edan handed over the scrolls. "It's alright, Neirin. I wasn't watching where I was going, either."

Neirin's dark bronze cheeks flushed as Edan helped him to his feet. "Isn't it you who's always telling us to be mindful and observant of our surroundings when we leave your class?"

"It is." Edan laughed, running a hand through short-cropped black hair. "Seems I need to take my own advice."

Neirin collected the final scrolls, clutching them to his chest. "So, what brings you into the main building? I thought you said Liea and Daea were the days you reserved for the library?"

"You would be correct."

Neirin's smile widened. "A master healer, a professor, and a craver of knowledge? No wonder all the novices swoon over you, Master Edan, you're a god."

Edan chucked again. "I don't know about that, I simply like to learn and see my students succeed. As future healers, we should always crave more knowledge, especially where healing is concerned. That is our focus, after all."

"Of course." There was a moment of silence when he finished speaking and Neirin attempted to adjust his glasses with his shoulder, gnawing the inside of his cheek.

"I'm on my way to see Superior Albion." Edan eyed the armfuls of parchments. "And yourself?"

Neirin's deep hazel eyes sparkled. "I'm on my way to take these to him!" He grasped for a scroll slipping from his arms.

Edan caught it as it fell. "Don't you have studying to do?"

"I..." Neirin lowered his eyes. "Well, yes..."

"Get back to your studies. I'll take these to him."

The boy's cheeks reddened. "Would you?"

"Of course," Edan smiled. "I'd rather see you studying."

"You're supposed to say that. You only want me to pass your class."

"I want you to pass *all* your classes, Neirin," he corrected, taking the scrolls from the young student.

"I'll do my best, Master Edan!" Neirin called over his shoulder, skipping down the hall to meet a group of novices. They stared back at him, giggling and whispering, but Neirin shook his head, blushing slightly before giving one of the other boys a shove.

Edan grinned, turning back to ascend the staircase, whistling a carefree tune. The Healer Superior's door was cracked open, and Edan shouldered inside.

"Neirin, it took you long enough, child. Hopefully my request wasn't a burden." Superior Albion spoke without looking up from the worktable, his raspy voice spritely despite his age. His wrinkled hands were firm as they ground herbs within a mortar, the air thick with sage and rosemary.

"I can't speak for his ease in getting the scrolls, but I apologize for the delay," Edan replied, approaching the worktable.

Albion looked up then, his dark hazel eyes–the mark of a half-blood witch–piercing as he pursed his lips. "Edan, good. I wasn't sure my message would reach you before you left your rooms for the day."

"I slept later than usual," Edan admitted, setting the scrolls off to the side. He leaned over the Superior's shoulder, raising an eyebrow.

"Just restoring workroom stocks," he explained, shooing Edan out of the way.

Edan shrugged, folding his lean arms as he braced himself against the table. "Why did you send for me?"

The Healer Superior didn't look at him when he spoke, but his voice softened. "The Crowning Ceremony took place in Thya two days ago."

Edan's pulse quickened. "It's this year already?"

"Yes."

Edan ran a hand through his hair. "Do you think..." his voice trailed off.

"I think your sister will have no problems attaining victory. She's a skilled warrior and a merciless killer. Her Elites are the most honored and fearless witches in all of Rekiv."

"It's not Erza I'm worried about." Edan wiped a hand across his beard. "Do you think the darkness in Thya is coming from the covens or the Northmen?" Before Albion could respond, he continued, "Every day they push toward the capital with their demands for land, darkness following their every move. Shadows walk through the ports and evil forces radiate from Narcio Island in the east."

Albion's hands stopped, and he frowned thoughtfully. "When the Shadow Games are over, the Queen will send an emissary to fetch the purebloods so the new queen will have an heir."

"Are you even listening to me?" Edan tried to contain his rising anger. "We're healers, not warriors. Yet we have enemies surrounding us without any true concept of what we're up against. If the Northmen attacked us, we would be helpless to stop them. The covens must be told of the growing dangers. Thya and Easthaven are filled with so many innocent people, there has to be something we can do besides sit in the safety of our mountains."

"Is that any way to speak to your Superior, Master Edan?"

Edan cheeks heated with shame, and he reined in his temper. "No. So, what can we do?"

"I've already sent word to Queen Rowena several times with no reply." Worry wreathed Albion's tone. "Whether she is choosing to deny my warnings and demands for aid, I do not know, but she is our queen and we have no choice other than to trust her judgement. Your mother has been ruling Rekiv for centuries...she is no stranger to Aeron."

Edan nodded. "And my sister?"

"Your sister has trained to be Queen since her birth. The Stormwood Elites are the best fighting unit in Navarre save for King Reul's cadre. She's strong, despite her lack of knowledge about you."

Edan pressed his forefingers to the bridge of his nose. "If Aeron is responsible for the darkness, if the Northmen side with him, I hope she has the strength to fight him. I hope we aren't too weak to stop him."

"Oh, he is certainly responsible for the darkness," Albion said. "We can only hope now that The Order of Kynire has survived this long and can keep the promised Waeshorn Princess safe. Otherwise, the Stormwood Elites and King Reul's cadre might be the only thing standing between Aeron and Navarre."

Ignoring the flutter of fear prancing through his chest, Edan turned toward the door. His hand paused on the handle. "Do you think Kynire survived?"

Albion met his stare evenly. "I hope so, Edan. I certainly hope so."

seven

Evalyn preferred slavery to the nauseating ache engulfing her body every waking minute and the constant fear of being surrounded by water.

She wasn't sure how much time had passed—it all blurred together with the nausea, the stinging swollen lip and knuckles, the growling hunger. Her stomach clenched, bile rising in her throat as the ship rocked beneath her. Barrels banged against one another and her head screamed in protest. She debated climbing out of the barrel to attempt easing the nausea, but the choppy waters made the decision for her. She gritted her teeth against a shocked cry as she lurched forward, tumbling violently against the floor when the drum of salt collided with the wall. The lid shot off, salt exploding around her. Evalyn toppled onto her knees, crashing into the firm wood. Not trusting her legs, she leaned back against the wall, wrapping Dax's thick cloak around herself.

Shouts echoed from somewhere above. A door opened, moonlight shining down the steps and onto the salt-covered floor.

"Syvi's breath." The stocky pirate from the docks grumbled.

Evalyn covered her mouth with a shaking hand, a whimper threatening to escape. Footsteps echoed on the stairs over her head.

"The storm knocked it over?" The female pirate.

"Aye, seems that way."

Evalyn trembled as the pair scuffled around the hold, wondering if they could hear her heartbeat. Light shimmered along the walls, trapping all shadows—including hers.

"It appears we aren't alone."

Her heart dropped into her stomach.

Footsteps grew louder, rounding the stairs until she was face-to-face with the two pirates. The stocky man knelt, his watery blue eyes calm. Evalyn dropped her gaze, letting her silvery hair fall across her face.

The pig-faced woman unsheathed her cutlass, using the straight edge to lift Evalyn's chin. "How did a pretty thing like you manage t' sneak aboard *Seraphina*?"

Her throat bobbing against steel, panic rising, Evalyn flicked her gaze to the scattered salt.

The stocky man raised an eyebrow and grinned, revealing a single golden tooth. "Clever girl, aye?"

"And how, pray tell, did ya manage to escape yer chains?"

Evalyn shook her head, gripping Dax's cloak to steady her pulse. A tear threatened to fall, but she sniffed, ignoring the flash of pain as she wiped at her busted lip.

The woman narrowed her eyes. "I asked ye a question, lass."

Evalyn met her stare, eyes burning with held-back tears. The man's brow furrowed. "That cloak, it belonged to the Captain." His words broke the tears free. "Yer...Captain's little dove, aye?"

The defiant tears streamed down her face now, and she clutched the cloak tighter.

"Easy now." Deft arms encircled her shoulders, and Evalyn all but fell against his chest. The pain rippled out of her, flowing until she was sure she could cry no more. Neither one of them spoke until she straightened, rubbing reddened eyes.

"So, yer the Fae girl. The Captain talked about you often." Hesitantly, the woman held out a hand. "Pleased to meet ya. Sorry about..." her voice trailed off as the sheathed her cutlass.

Evalyn took the outstretched hand, leaning away from the stocky man who watched her with kind, smiling eyes. "I was on board this ship the night Dax saved yer life."

She blinked, taking the waterskin he offered as the woman spoke. "Do ya know, then, that he's—"

"Yes." Evalyn cut the woman off, not wanting to hear the words spoken.

"All he wanted was for ye t' be safe." The man leaned back against the wall beside her. "The least we can do is see t' that."

"Aye," the woman nodded. "Name's Nim. This old geezer is Beck." He dipped his head, a hand on his hat. "And ye are?"

She swallowed. "Eva. My name is Eva."

Nim pulled half a loaf of bread from a small satchel at her side. "Well, Eva, where ya headed to?"

She took the bread, its crust still warm. "I...I don't know." She and Dax had spent so much time planning *how* she would escape they hadn't given much thought to *where* she would escape to.

Beck stretched his legs out before him. Nim checked the staircase for any unwanted shadows, then tucked her legs beneath her, accepting the flask Beck offered. Evalyn wrinkled her nose at the harshness of rum filling the air.

"We're headed to Singaro Bay in Easthaven," Beck said. "We trade salt with the merchants there for food."

"Where is Easthaven?" She vaguely recalled the northeastern port city from Dax's maps.

"It's in Rekiv. Witch country."

The bread lodged in her throat.

Beck laughed. "Oh, don't worry, little one. They're *usually* harmless." His eyes danced as he emphasized the word.

Nim gave him a shove, shaking her head. "Don't terrify 'er, Beck." She passed Eva the flask, and she hesitated only slightly before swigging the harsh drink.

"Ain't nothin' wrong with warnin' the girl," Beck grumbled.

"The Blackwings are the nastiest," Nim said. "They kill for sport after dark but keep away from the ports most days. They reside in Thya. The Silvermists are harmless, most of 'em don't leave their gardens except to trade. But the ones ya gotta watch for are the Stormwoods. Mysterious and unpredictable those she-demons. They've ruled Rekiv for centuries. You'll know 'em by the eyes."

"Their eyes?" Eva took another bite, licking dry lips.

"Aye," Beck nodded. "Prettiest shade of lilac ya ever saw, but they're feisty, unpredictable demons, those ones."

"Stay away from lilac eyes, got it."

Beck laughed softly. "Aye, that's how ye tell 'em all apart...purebloods at least."

"Purebloods?"

"The heirs or their closest cousins mothered by the coven leaders and the purest male bloodlines at the Chiron. Stormwood eyes are lilac, Blackwings are pale blue, and the Silvermists are rich amber."

Nim stood, dusting off her breeches. "Well, if ye've finished terrifyin' her, I'm goin' back above deck. Those Shadow Beasts will come lurkin' eventually. Best tell 'em all is well before they come snooping and harm our precious cargo."

Beck put a gentle hand on Evalyn's arm. "Don't worry, little one. We'll see to it ya reach Easthaven unharmed." He started to follow Nim abovedeck, then paused, whispering over the stairs, "Best stay put though, aye? It would be the end of all our lives if the Shadow Commander discovered we were harborin' a fugitive beneath his nose."

Then he was gone.

Eva shivered, pulling Dax's cloak around her shoulders, a comfort and protection as hissing voices slithered through the cracks above.

The violent rocking of waves against the ship jolted Evalyn awake. Panic lanced through her as sunlight flooded the dark hold, but she relaxed when Beck's warm smile appeared around the stairs. He hopped to the ground, extending a hand. "This is yer stop, little one."

Eva hesitated only a moment before allowing him to pull her to her feet. She squinted into the sun, the blinding light a strange sight after so long living in the unnatural red gloom.

Beck chuckled. "Hurry now, we haven't got much time."

She met his eyes. "But where—"

"All clear you two, it's now or never." Nim's shadow loomed on the steps.

Beck reached for her, and she shrank away, but he only smiled and pulled her hood over her face. "Don't want any of those slinkin' monsters recognizing Dax's little dove, now do we?"

The corners of her mouth tugged up into a weak smile.

It was strange, the sensation of the burning sun heating her skin. Warm, sweet, and free. But she couldn't enjoy it as Nim and Beck ushered her along the deck and down the plank into the bustling port before anyone could stop them and ask questions. Only then did she dare to peek out from her hood, a small gasp escaping her lips.

Merchants of all shapes and sizes rushed along the webs of dust-covered streets, bustling in and out of shops and hauling carts down the main road. So many smells filled the salty sea air, the aromas blended together. Peasants with baskets full of goods shuffled along, acknowledging familiar faces, while seagulls screeched overhead.

But it wasn't the merchants or friendly shouts that pulled for her attention: it was the towering waterfall in the distance.

The crest of the falls poured down, almost swallowing the port beneath before it split, the thick stone walkways acting as a dam and veering the rushing water into the sea around Easthaven like a reaching embrace. Peaks stretched into the clear sky on either side of a larger domed structure, which shot downward, splitting the waterfall in perfect halves. The shimmering glass sparkled in rainbow hues, two platforms within moving in vertical lines.

Nim laughed at her wide eyes, easing her down the main stretch of road toward the distant falls.

"Welcome to Easthaven, little one," Beck said, placing a small coin purse into her hand.

"Aye, but best run along now." Nim's eyes scanned the streets. "The more distance between ye and *Seraphina*, the better. The Shadow Beasts will return from their communications any minute."

Eva nodded, turning first to Nim, then Beck. "Thank you. May our paths cross again someday, I will never forget your kindness."

"Head down the main road and up the waterfall. You'll want to head west, toward Raenya. You'll be safest there." Nim turned back to the ship.

Beck hesitated only a moment. "Remember what I told ye about the purebloods? Stay away from 'em, if ya can." Another swift nod. He gave her one final smile, his eyes wrinkling. "Until our next meeting, little one." He hurried after Nim.

Slowly, Eva lifted her head to the waterfall. She breathed, savoring the sweet, spiced air caressing her face and teasing her concealed silvery hair.

Freedom. True, pure freedom. She wanted to savor the joy forever.

For the first time in eighteen years, Evalyn took a step on her own, not dictated in any way by someone else. A tightness eased from her chest as she put one foot in front of the other, a sigh of sweet release loosening from her lips.

"Peaches! Fresh peaches brought all the way from Rathal's farmers' guild in Rivedas!"

Eva turned toward the merchant, opening the coin purse. "How much?"

He smiled. "One copper piece, Miss."

Eva fished into the purse, removing a coin, and held it out. The merchant reached for it, then froze. The stench of rot assaulted her senses as terror spread across his face.

"How...how can I help you?" The merchant stammered, his fear hanging on every word.

Shadows covered the ground before her, and the pain came rushing back. The torture, the sorrow, the fear, the death. The rotting stench engulfed her.

So, it was all for nothing. Dax's death was for nothing. I'm going right back where I started.

But before the monster could rip back the hood and expose her, a honey-coated, sultry voice said, "There you are, sister dearest. I was wondering where you'd run off to this time."

Eva dared to look up at her savior, her gaze meeting the lilac eyes of a raven-haired witch.

eight

Joseline woke to Shea's soft snarl. She shifted, the rough rope trapping her wrists at her back.

Stay calm, they're near the fire. Shea's voice in her head was a welcomed relief. The light within her flickered, the connection sparking a link to Shea's thoughts so Joseline could respond in a similar manner. She opened her eyes to find Shea curled against her thigh, chained and muzzled, but her head bowed in acceptance of the connection.

Joseline's words echoed into being as she thought them. *Do you know where we are?*

Somewhere just over the Rekiv border, they weren't lying when they said that. My assumption would be somewhere in Ebondenn.

Joseline's brows furrowed. *Rekiv is witch country…the northern wastelands.*

She glanced toward the fire. The man, Ren, sharpened a flint-tipped arrow, dirty brown hair falling across heavily-bearded cheeks. Freya stirred the contents of a large pot over hot coals, sandy blonde locks pulled back from her thin face. Neither of them noticed her.

Joseline turned back to Shea. *Did they say anything else?*

Not much. They're on guard duty for the camp. Shea flicked her tail to the narrow path. Tents loomed tall through the thick trees, the air smoky with burning fires. Horses nickered, intertwined with voices submerged in casual conversations and an occasional laugh. *They're some sort of tribesmen, I think. Warriors guarding the border or abandoners of the witch covens maybe.*

Do you think they could be the branch of Kynire Fallon was searching for?

Shea snarled, and Joseline looked up as Freya approached her.

The woman smiled, offering a waterskin. "I see you've realized we aren't on our own." She nodded toward the distant tents.

"Freya..." Ren warned, standing. She waved him off.

"What do you want with us?" Joseline demanded.

Ren pushed the arrow back into his quiver. "So, the fire-haired girl is a feisty one."

"Ren, please." Freya sighed, swigging from the waterskin herself as if to prove it wasn't poisoned. "We simply await the return of those whose command we follow."

"Oh, sure," Ren threw his hands in the air. "And while you're at it, why don't you just tell her all The Order's secrets, too?"

Joseline blinked. "The Order of—"

Shouts from the camp cut off her response, growing louder as two figures rode into view. Ren and Freya turned toward their approach.

"Quinn," Joseline murmured. "Quinn, wake up."

Mercifully, his eyes flashed open, as did the others from their spot across the fire. Fallon's silver gaze bristled with fury, but he remained silent, as did Maya and Jenson.

Two dappled horses galloped into the clearing, their riders cloaked in dark blue. Embroidered on their chests were two wolves, one jet black and one white, encircling one another around a triangle—the fire symbol.

The Elirona Sigil.

The breath stopped in Joseline's throat as the figures removed their hoods, elongated ears peeking through silvery hair.

Fae. They were Fae warriors.

The smaller one's smile reached her shining silver eyes, shoulder-length silvery hair braided back from her forehead on both sides and dyed a pale purple at the tips. A beautifully-carved staff embellished with crystals draped casually over her shoulder. They wore matching vests and pants fashioned from chestnut leather and a long-sleeved tunic beneath, but the taller one wore thin belts slung around slender hips, several expensive-looking daggers strapped there and in a scabbard at her thigh. Her hair was that same shimmering silver, braided across the crown of her head and swept back into an elegant knot at the base of her neck.

The world spun around Joseline, threatening to fall away, and Shea nuzzled her thigh.

No one spoke as the taller Fae flashed a wicked grin, standing before Fallon in two strides. The air evaporated from the clearing as she raised an eyebrow. "In all my centuries of knowing you, I never thought I'd see the day the almighty Fallon was caught off guard by a group of amateurs. My brother will never let you live this down."

nine

Quinn couldn't quite process what he was seeing as he gaped at the two Fae women before them. The taller stared at him, her gaze barely concealing her shock, blue-green eyes unmistakably like his.

Turquoise eyes are rare, unheard of in most races. They are said to be seen only in the Elirona bloodline. Gavin's words rippled through his mind and Quinn tried to speak but couldn't. He couldn't do anything other than stare.

The Fae woman wiped a hand over her mouth. "Who is he?"

Fallon sighed. Quinn turned to his mentor, not sure if he was ready for the truth hanging on Fallon's tongue. The silence was unbearable.

"Fallon, who is he?" she repeated, her voice stronger.

The truth, after twenty years.

Fallon didn't break Quinn's stare as he said, "This is Quinn, Larina...your nephew. He's Reul's son."

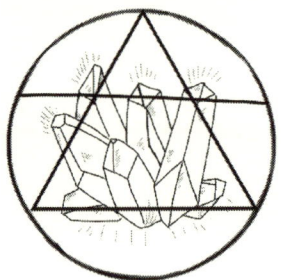

ten

Princess Julia huddled behind her father's throne unnoticed. She hadn't meant to eavesdrop—she hadn't meant to be found in here at all—but there'd been no time to run either.

The King's small council had been arguing for over an hour about how to handle the darkness spreading through Corae. Their defenses were exhausted. The demons destroyed everything, the inner city crumbling to a ghost town. Niven and the other Jade Cloaks searched for new refugees every day, and still it wasn't enough. The attacks were unpredictable, unstoppable, and her parents could only keep the people calm for so long when they had no idea how the demons were getting into the city to begin with.

Nadie and Mother tried to hide the truth from her, as did Niven and Mikenna, but she could see it from every window she walked past. Autumn was upon them; Josie had been missing since Ywone, Kellen vanishing not long after, and still Julia didn't understand any of it. For three months, the shadows swarming Corae only grew. The monsters people claimed to see in the dark roamed Julia's nightmares though she'd never seen them herself.

Everyone was terrified.

Homeless civilians piled into the Citadel's outer keep for shelter daily, their numbers never-ending. The adults tried to hide their panic, as if they thought she was too young to understand the danger, but Julia knew they were frightened. Even her father, booming orders for Niven to double guards at every watch and demanding at least two escorts at her side, was horrified. But at least he wasn't sulking in his sorrows anymore.

"Damn The Twelve! That's not good enough!" Julia jumped as King Nathaniel pounded a fist on the table.

"Your Majesty, we're trying everything we can to—"

"It's not good enough!" His voice echoed through the room, threatening to shatter the candelabra hanging from the ceiling. Julia gripped the pale green skirts swamping around her tiny legs, fighting not to shudder. The fact that even her father was unsure terrified her most. Her father was the strongest warrior she knew. He *always* knew what to do.

"We will triple all efforts, Your Majesty. We will find your daughter." Master Eldridge's voice was a hushed whisper.

"Mikenna and the healers are doing everything they can to keep our supplies stocked," Grand Master Kasia added, her voice somewhat soothing.

The sound of wood creaking prompted Julia to poke her head around the throne. The king's council was dispersing—paperwork collected, robes gathered as the elder councilors left, until only the Grand Master and Niven remained beside her father.

"Keep my daughter safe, Niven." Her father's voice was almost inaudible.

"With my life, Your Majesty." Niven bowed and left as well.

King Nathaniel was a beaten man, the defeat evident beneath the well-kept scarlet beard and royal finery. His broad shoulders slumped ever-so-slightly, and every day new wrinkles appeared on his youthful face.

"We will find her," Kasia said softly. "We'll find both of them."

Her father sighed. "When Emery and Anya disappeared, it was just a stroke of bad luck...that shipwreck ended many lives. But now their son is missing too, along with my daughter. I can't help but fear this darkness, the Langley's deaths. It makes me wonder if it was no accident after all."

"Emery and Anya Langley were loyal friends to your family since you, Emery, and Gavin Clemonte were boys. Kellen's trained to defend Joseline since he was a child."

Nathaniel stood, towering over the Grand Master though her amber gaze remained calm. "You're right." He wiped a hand over his beard. "We'll find them. We *have* to find them."

"We will," Kasia said, adjusting her forest-green robes.

"And little Julia?"

Julia gripped a small hand to her chest, ducking back behind the throne at the mention of her name.

"Julia will be safe."

The large doors opened and shut, the echo bouncing off the high arched ceilings with a dull thud. Julia took a ragged breath, then slipped from her hiding spot. She almost stumbled down the stairs leading from the throne dais, silken skirts billowing around her narrow waist constricted by a golden, embroidered corset, soft slippers light as she raced across the marbled floor.

The hallway was empty. Arched glass windows lined the walls, the afternoon sun accenting their pale orange color. Julia took off at a run toward her parents' rooms, the security of their embrace much needed. Her father would be furious if he discovered she'd slipped from her rooms without an escort.

The castle was so quiet. It put everyone on edge.

Julia turned the corner and froze.

A dark, hooded figure stood before the windows.

The light's playing tricks on you. It had to be. Her heart pounded in her chest and she took a shaky step back, reaching for the wall.

Sensing the movement, the shadow figure turned to her.

Julia took off in the other direction before she could see its face, gripping the jet pendant with a sweaty palm.

It isn't real, she repeated the words Nadie told her to say when she woke from a night terror. *It's just a dream, it's just a dream.*

Rounding another corner, Julia collided with Grand Master Kasia's thick robes with a muffled *oof*. She stared up at Mikenna and the Grand Master with an apologetic curtsy. "Begging your pardons."

She tried to rush by them, but Mikenna put a gentle hand on her shoulder. "And just where do ya think yer goin' without an escort, young lady? Somethin' tells me yer father won't be likin' that."

Julia gulped down deep breaths. "Just to my parents' chambers."

Master Kasia smiled, wagging a disapproving finger. "Lady Julia, you know your father gave specific orders to stay with your escorts. I would hate to see Niven in trouble for leaving you unattended, he's been worn quite thin the past few months."

She glanced back the way she'd come, thinking of the shadow figure. Looking up at the elder again, she nodded, putting on her best innocent smile. "I'm very sorry."

Mikenna laughed, kneeling down to meet her eyes. "I'm sure you meant no harm, dear." She exchanged a look with Kasia, then took Julia's hand, ignoring the other woman's scowl. "I'll escort her to her parent's chambers."

As they walked down the hall, Julia kept glancing behind them, expecting to meet the shadowy figure's gaze, unable to shake the uneasy feeling that something was following her.

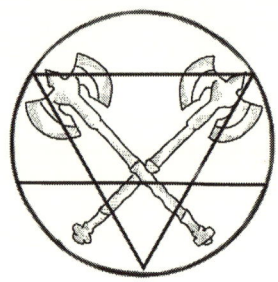

eleven

Erza hated her softness in moments it made her logic irrational. She honestly had no idea what possessed her to intervene between the demon and the cloaked girl, but she couldn't turn back now. Her body quivered with nervous energy, but she pushed it aside.

The shadowy figure snarled at her. "I don't take orders from you, she-demon."

"I understand," she sighed. "She really meant no harm." Nodding to the girl, she added, "her mind isn't all there, sadly." She sent a silent prayer to Rinoa that the girl would remain silent.

The demon narrowed his eyes, but before he could press further, a shout drew his attention toward the docks. He hesitated a moment longer before turning away. "I suggest you keep a better eye on her in the future."

"Noted, thank you."

He stalked toward the docks, Erza watching him go until he disappeared amidst the merchants, then turned back to the girl. "I don't know what you did to make enemies with such a nasty creature, but you're welcome."

"Thank you." Her beautifully melodic voice radiated with terror.

The fruit merchant, still pale with fear, held out the peach in trembling fingers. Erza took it, holding it out to the stranger. "You got a name?"

The girl reached up, pulling the thick hood back from her face. *So, Erza thought, staring at the flowing silver hair and delicately elongated ears. She's Fae. I thought I smelled one.*

The girl met her stare, turquoise eyes filled with mystery, pain, and sorrow. "Eva." She hesitated before gripping Erza's outstretched palm with a small, surprisingly calloused hand.

"Erza Stormwood. A pleasure."

Eva bit into the peach, hesitating slightly before following Erza toward the glass towers. Erza smiled to several merchants she knew, stopping in various shops. She'd come to see the silent shadows, Naoi and Fi, off toward the Chiron in an attempt *not* to think about Salia's death.

Three days, and they were no closer to discovering the cause of the Silvermist's murder. In two hundred years, Erza had never seen anything like it. She'd killed countless times, satisfied with the feeling of her crystal nails sinking into her victims, though she wasn't as cruel as her mother expected her to be. Still, she was accustomed to the sensation death brought. But nothing had ever made her skin crawl like Salia's shadow-ridden, desecrated body.

To make matters worse, Morana had begun acting…strange. She'd always been nasty, even as a witchling. But since the Crowning Ceremony, ever since Erza noted the obsidian pendant she wore, her aura changed slightly, darkness occasionally flickering in her eyes. The other Blackwings didn't seem to notice it. But Morana wouldn't let the darkness consume her so much as to kill off one of the other heirs before the Shadow Games even began, would she?

It didn't make sense.

A pure Fae trembling at everything in sight, traveling alone, and chased by demons didn't makes sense either.

Erza turned to Eva. On the surface, she reeked of salt and ash. From the way she stared in awe at the port and the approaching glass turrets shimmering with falling water, it seemed like she was taking in the world for the first time—and maybe she was.

Erza hadn't seen many Fae. They usually stayed within the borders of Dorwynn or Raenya. But those she had seen were always stoic, muscled and fierce, ready to bring down an enemy. This young girl hid her fear behind fierce eyes and men's garments bagging around her hips.

Erza cleared her throat. "So, where are you traveling from?" Eva blinked, shaking her head. Erza fought not to roll her eyes. "No backstory, then." A stray cat brushed against her ankles, and she picked the little creature up, stroking its matted gray fur.

"Sorry." Eva's smile seemed forced, pain shimmering in her eyes. "I hope to forget where I came from."

Erza raised an eyebrow, a gust of wind whipping her hair against her cheeks. "Fine." She set the cat down, and it rushed to the peach core Eva tossed in the dirt.

"Thank you."

She eased leather gloves from her fingers, cracking her knuckles. "Your past is no business of mine. But knowing what hunts you, I can't leave you on your own."

She didn't know why she said it. She had no obligations to this girl. But something churned in the pit of her stomach, almost willing her to say the words. She couldn't explain it, the need to protect this stranger, but it gnawed at her mind.

Eva frowned as Erza motioned for her to step onto the moving platform behind the thundering waterfall. "I'm not...at least I don't think..."

Erza shrugged, unable to hide her laugh at Eva's gasp when the platform began to rise, the road falling away as they rose against the current. "You could have fooled me."

"I was careful when I..." Eva cut herself off, and Erza couldn't help but wonder where she came from. "If they were hunting me specifically back there, they wouldn't have let me go. At least, I don't think so." Eva bit her swollen, bloodied lower lip.

"Well, whatever they are, they're dangerous." The platform eased to a stop, and they stepped onto solid ground.

"I know. You must think I'm really stupid." Her voice dripped with sarcasm.

The wind was stronger atop the waterfall, chilling as it whistled through the glass towers reaching into the sky. Those towers cast faint shadows along the ground, webbed with a network of roads and shops leading in all different directions amidst the rushing rivers intertwining and sliding over the falls.

Erza chuckled at Eva's wide eyes. "I never said you were stupid." She eyed Eva's clothing and led her to a nearby shop. "Perhaps a bit naïve, but not stupid."

Eva sent her a wary look, as Erza ushered her inside with a hand on her elbow. "Why are you helping me?" she asked, turning her head toward the tinkling bell as they passed through the door.

Erza shrugged, nodding a friendly greeting to the shopkeeper, and led Eva to the far wall, lined with various leather garments. "Good question. I don't usually do things for other people."

Eva opened her mouth to reply, then closed it as the shopkeeper approached them. "Miss Erza? How odd, I don't often see you without Miss Rowen."

As if on cue, her second stomped through the door, Astrid on her heels. "There you are, where did you..." Rowen stopped, eyeing Eva suspiciously. The Fae girl tensed again.

Erza ignored Rowen, turning to the shopkeeper. "Just clothing my friend here. She arrived to watch the Shadow Games this morning." The lie rolled off her tongue like honey. Humans were so unsuspecting.

Thankfully, Eva said nothing. The shopkeeper just smiled and returned to the desk, Rowen and Astrid weaving through the shelves of clothes to join them.

"So, do we get an introduction to your *friend*?" Rowen muttered tightly.

"This is Eva. She owes me for saving her life."

"You're the one who told him you were my sister," Eva grumbled.

Rowen cackled, turning to Astrid with a playful smile. "So much for not taking in strays."

Erza glared at her.

"Your mother is going to be furious," Astrid murmured.

"Why would she be furious?" Eva asked, stroking a hand over an under-bust embellished with swirling silver.

"The Shadow Games are a sacred time for the covens, a time to decide the next Queen of Rekiv. Aside from our servants, we don't let outsiders in, especially not for the competitions," Erza explained. Astrid handed Eva a loose-fitting tunic with a thin cord laced across the bust.

"What sort of competition is it?" she asked, carrying the garments behind a dressing screen.

Erza walked over to the piles of folded pants and shook one out. "The sort to decide the new queen...a fight to the death." She held up another pair of pants and tossed them to Rowen, who stuck them behind the dressing screen.

"To the death? That seems extreme."

Erza shrugged, pulling the gloves back onto her fingers as Astrid replied, "Only the strongest pureblood heir is given the honor to reign as queen. It is our custom."

"We train for two hundred years, mastering a great number of skills before we can even be considered to participate," Erza said. "The queen then reigns for one thousand years before the next competition occurs, once each heir is the required age."

Eva yanked back the curtain, biting her lip.

"Pretty thing, aren't you?" Rowen whistled, earning a shove from Astrid.

Eva had a smaller waist than Erza first anticipated, and her thighs lacked the muscle to fill out the larger pants, but at least her chest filled out the tunic somewhat. Erza eyed her, nodded, then motioned for Eva to turn with a spin of her fingers and tightened the under-bust.

Eva let out a surprised gasp. "So, you train all your lives to kill your sisters, and the winner rules until the next competition takes place?"

"The current queen has the full thousand years to rule." She tied the laces off, turning Eva to face her. "As queen, she is free to make her own decision to hand down her crown when the competition is complete, or remain queen until her rule is up."

"I'm going to fix that lip," Rowen said, stepping forward.

"She, on the other hand, never could resist helping strays," Astrid mumbled under her breath. "Especially pretty ones."

Rowen smirked then flexed her fingers, lilac light swirling in her palm. Eva pulled away, the fear intensifying in her eyes. "Hold still, it's just a bit of healing magic." She brushed her thumb along Eva's lip, the swelling and dried blood vanishing almost instantly.

Eva stared at herself in the long mirror, a sweet smile spreading across her face. "Thank you." She turned back to Erza. "That competition seems rather morbid if you ask me."

Erza shrugged. "It's just our custom, how we've always done things."

"Very lovely, dear," the shopkeeper said, breaking into their conversation.

Eva's smile widened. "How much?"

"Not a copper. The constant patronage of Miss Erza and her Elites is payment enough. I'll take those old things off your hands though if you'd like?"

Erza wondered once more where Eva came from at the slight hesitation to discard the old clothes.

"Keep the pants," Eva said. "I'll keep the cloak and tunic." She fastened the cloak on as she spoke.

The shopkeeper hurried into a back room. "That looks much better," Erza said. "Now all you need is a bath." She pushed out the door, Rowen and Astrid a familiar comfort at her sides, and checked that Eva followed them back into the crowded streets.

"So where are you taking me?" Eva asked. "Not that I'm ungrateful, but I was told to stay away from pureblood witches at all costs. I was told they're dangerous."

Erza froze, facing Eva with a venomous grin. "Oh, you absolutely shouldn't trust witches."

The girl paled, gripping the tunic to her chest.

Rowen burst into laughter. Even Astrid's lips tugged into a rare smile. Erza ran a hand through her hair and sighed. "Relax, I mean you no harm. Truth be told, I've never met a Fae before. You intrigue me."

"I intrigue you?" her melodic voice was touched with curiosity.

"You do." She flashed Eva that venomous smile again. "But I'm not the one you need to worry about."

"Who exactly do I need to worry about, then?" Eva's attempt to hide her fear was impressive, but witches were trained to pick up on auras, and hers glistened with terror.

"The other covens won't be pleased Erza brought in an outsider right before the games," Astrid explained, her fingers twining with Rowen's.

Erza nodded. "My mother will be particularly furious. She'll want me to keep an eye on you, keep you out of trouble. So, it would seem we are going to remain in each other's company, Eva."

"Your mother," the Fae girl said, "should I be concerned about her?"

Erza pursed her lips. "No more than you should meeting any other royalty."

Her eyes widened. "Royalty?"

Rowen grinned, releasing Astrid's hand to make a sweeping gesture toward Erza. "Of course, Eva, you are in the presence of a princess."

Erza gave her cousin a shove, shaking her head. "Rowena Stormwood, Queen of Rekiv." She paused, exchanging a glance with Rowen and Astrid. "I'll warn you now, there are several issues going on that have a lot of us on edge. I shouldn't be telling you anything, but if you're going to be around—"

"Don't worry," Eva cut her off with a weak smile. "I know how to keep quiet."

twelve

Larina's encampment was relatively small, but Quinn wasn't opposed to the quaintness of the small company. It allowed him space to think, to clear his restless mind. The stars above glittered in the clear sky as if dancing with their earthbound counterparts throughout the camp. Laughter echoed from Larina and Kai's fire at the center, the surrounding logs filled with smiling faces.

But Quinn relished in the solitude. Larina had been nothing but nice since unbinding them and welcoming them into her group, but it didn't give him the much-needed time to clear his head. When he said as much, Larina only nodded, the unspoken understanding in her gaze all the permission she needed to leave the fire without being rude.

Arms tucked behind his head, Quinn turned briefly toward the sound of Maya's laugh, before his gaze returned to the star's radiant glow in the sky above. Quinn envied their resilience.

He sensed Jenson's presence before his *sielapora* sat beside him. Jens offered him a waterskin, and Quinn coughed at the unexpected burn of harsh whiskey. Jenson snorted. "Everything alright?"

Quinn glared at him. "I should have known."

"You really should have," Jenson grinned. "But I thought it might help."

"Help with what?"

Jenson quirked a brow, leaning back against the tree. "You may think you can hide your feelings from everyone else, but we both know you can't hide your feelings from me."

He sat up at that, crossing long legs. "I don't know what you're talking about."

"Really, Quinn? I see the way you look at Larina."

They were silent for a moment.

"And how do I look at her, Jens?" he asked at last.

"Like you want to know her, but you don't know what to say." Quinn bit his lip as Jenson continued. "If you would stop being so stubborn, she'd be more than happy to talk to you."

"Oh? And you know that, how?"

Jenson rolled his eyes slightly. "Well, for one, she told me," he began. "And she's your family."

Quinn reached for the flask again. "*You're* my family. You and Maya and Fallon." He swigged again.

"We are," Jenson agreed. "But so is she. And that means—"

"I know what it means," Quinn snapped. When Jenson didn't respond, he sighed, his head falling into his hands. "I'm sorry, you didn't deserve that." He groaned softly, looking up. "I just…it's a lot to accept."

Jenson yawned, shifting back in the dirt. "When you choose to accept it doesn't make it the truth. It was true to begin with."

Quinn sighed again, joining his friend on the ground. "I know, Jens."

The silence stretched between them. Jenson turned, his dark gaze curious. "What bothers you so much about it? The fact that it makes you a prince, or the fact that Fallon didn't mention it?"

"Both?" Jenson chuckled. "What, I'm serious," Quinn grumbled.

"I'm sure Fallon had his reasons," Jenson said. "He would never intentionally lie to you because he enjoyed it."

"I know."

"And if it's really bothering you, just ask him. You're entitled to an explanation after he kept the truth from you." Nodding, Jenson sat up with a grunt.

"Jens?"

Jenson hummed in response.

"Thanks."

His friend raised an eyebrow. "For?"

"For always just talking through things with me. I didn't ask for your insight."

"You didn't have to ask. If I'm able, I'll always be there when you need me." Jenson flashed him a grin, pushing to his feet. "Who knows, maybe one day you'll actually come to *me* when you want to talk." He wiggled his eyebrows. "Imagine that."

Quinn laughed, shaking his head. "Maybe."

Jenson tuned to walk away, then paused. "You should come back, if you're feeling up to it." He walked away without waiting for Quinn to reply.

thirteen

It still felt surreal, strange in Joseline's mind after all these days.

Quinn—brave, insufferable, and darkly mysterious—was a prince. Son to Reul Elirona, the mythical Fae King. Heir to the Dorwynn throne.

He was another living royal child. A second source of resistance to the realm crumbling against Aeron's might.

A beacon of hope.

"Something bothering you?" Quinn asked, his fingers brushing hers slightly as they walked through the Ebondenn camp.

She folded her arms over her chest, huffing out a breath. "Nothing."

He raised an eyebrow. "You don't expect me to believe that, do you?"

She turned to him, meeting those turquoise eyes. *Elirona eyes.*

Joseline opened her mouth to reply, then closed it as they approached the Fae commander's lavish tent at the camp's center. Larina insisted they dine with her, wanting to know more about the nephew she never knew existed.

While Joseline didn't mind the meals and enjoyed the royal company, Quinn's discomfort was apparent. He and his aunt were remarkably similar, both warriors used to their orders being followed.

While it was nice they had something in common, it made decision-making over the past several days difficult to say the least.

Kai, Larina's mate, chatted with Logan—one of the captains—outside near a communal fire, Shea a purring ball of content in her arms. Logan's burgundy cloak was embroidered with the Madigan sigil, proof of allegiance to the lord who ruled over Rathal's northernmost city, but his thick tunic was a light blue, the cuffs embroidered with the fire symbol of the Elirona house. He met Joseline's eyes when they approached, bowed first to her and Quinn, then to Kai, and left.

"Did you enjoy your evening training?" Kai asked sweetly. The breeze blew thin strands of lavender hair across her cheeks.

Joseline nodded, scratching at Shea's ear as they followed her inside. Shea opened a lazy eye, then closed it, purring louder.

Quinn laughed, pulling at the tie holding back his hair. "It was nice to train alone."

Kai chuckled. "Larina means well." When Quinn opened his mouth, she added, "But I know she can be overbearing."

Before Quinn could make a snarky reply, Joseline said, "The freedom to form our own routine has been nice as well."

Smoke funneled through a large opening in the roof, a flap pulled away, but sealable in case of rain. The air smelled of stew and smoked fish, and Joseline's mouth watered in anticipation. Her evening training with Quinn worked up an appetite.

Fallon and Larina huddled together over a table covered in maps and charts, whispering in hushed voices. Jenson, his mouth full of food, grumbled something to Maya that sent her into a fit of laughter.

They look happy, she thought, daring a sidelong glance at Quinn.

They are happy. Shea replied.

Yes, but for how long?

She couldn't ponder the thought before Jenson noticed them. "Ah, the lovebirds, returned from training at last."

Joseline couldn't fight the blush that consumed her cheeks, but Quinn rolled his eyes. "You're horrible."

Larina laughed, seating herself on a low bench near the fire. "Training went well?"

Joseline nodded, laying her cloak over the log as she followed Quinn to a second bench. "I feel stronger, even in the past few days."

"You look stronger," Maya replied.

Joseline eyed Quinn slyly. "I have a merciless teacher, so that isn't surprising."

He shoved her with a shoulder, tightening his wrist blade. "It isn't my fault you're insufferable."

She scowled, wrinkling her nose. Kai sat cross-legged between Larina's knees, Shea still curled in her arms, and dipped her head back, smiling up at her mate. Larina brushed lavender strands from her forehead and kissed her gently.

Kai laid Shea in her lap, scooping some stew from Larina's bowl. "So, Fallon, have you heard from Conan?"

Fallon straightened. "No, why? Is everything alright?"

Larina put a gentle hand on his arm. "Yes, everything is fine. He just misses you."

Joseline wondered if she was the only one lost before Maya asked, "Who's Conan?"

"My mate," Fallon said casually.

Jenson nearly spit out his honeyed wine. "You have a mate?"

"I'm not an emotionless hermit, you know."

"You aren't?" Larina teased. "I thought that was all part of the Fallon charm."

Fallon, who looked as though he might actually blush, was saved from a response when Logan burst into the tent, wide-eyed. "Ma'am, a messenger from Thya."

Larina was on her feet instantly, motioning for him to come into the room. He obeyed, waving a hand to someone outside the tent. A small boy entered, his curly brown hair the same color as his skin, tawny eyes shimmering with fear. Larina smiled, kneeling to the boy's level as he approached the fire. "It's alright, Sionn, we won't harm you."

His eyes darted toward Quinn. Joseline couldn't help but smile, only imagining how the scowling, muscled warrior must appear to the child who looked no more than eight. Then his eyes darted back to Larina. "The darkness, it's getting worse."

Quinn let out a sarcastic laugh. "There's darkness all over this Sauda-cursed country, why should Rekiv be any different?"

Joseline shoved him. "Quinn, please."

Larina smiled tightly as Kai squeezed her hand. "Anything else?"

The boy licked his lips, glancing back to Logan before he continued. "The covens have gathered from the capital. The Crowning Ceremony happened the day after I left."

She shoved to her feet, swearing as she dragged a hand through unbound hair. The boy jumped, but Jenson sent him a reassuring wink and he relaxed slightly.

"Of all the times not to fiddle with silly traditions," Larina growled, pacing.

"Rin," Kai leaned against the table. "You know it isn't silly to them."

Larina swore again, pulling Kai into her chest. "But *of course* it has to be now." Nobody spoke as she took several breaths to settle her nerves, then turned back to the boy. "Thank you, dear." She looked up at her captain. "Lord Logan, see to it that Sionn gets a warm meal and a bed to sleep in."

Logan bowed, motioning for the boy to follow him out. Larina braced herself against the table, banging her hands amidst the piled scrolls, sending several markers toppling over. Joseline and the others stood, making their way to the table as well. Larina rubbed her temples. "I thought that darkness was under control."

"Maybe it's coming from within one of the covens like we first thought?" Kai suggested, running her hands over the map to smooth it down once more.

"It isn't by any means convenient," Fallon agreed. "But maybe we can use it to our advantage."

Larina eyed him. "How do you propose we do that?"

Quinn tensed beside Joseline. His fingers slid between hers, tightening almost painfully, but she didn't pull away.

Jenson tapped Thya on the map, grinning. "By sending their little messenger back with questions of our own."

The ache in Quinn's chest grew as Jenson spoke the words he knew were coming. "You can't."

But Jenson only smiled, nodding to the hand gripping Joseline's at his side. "Don't worry, Quinn. I'm sure Joseline will fight off the spiders if you ask nicely."

Quinn pulled their fingers apart but didn't laugh. "Jens, it isn't funny."

Maya put a hand on his arm. "I'll keep an eye on him."

Her response made the ache worse. "No, not both of you. I...I can't lose both of you."

Jenson shook his head. "It's just another mission, we've been doing this for years. We'll be back before you know it. This is the stuff we're trained to do. If Aeron is attacking us from the south and breeding darkness in the north with the covens, the last thing we need is to be caught in the middle."

Quinn closed his eyes and sighed. "I know."

Maya threw her arms around his neck and he pulled her close, squeezing her against his chest. "Come back to me," he whispered before letting her go and turned his attention to Jenson. "You better come back to me."

Maya nodded, smiling at Joseline then glaring at him. "*You* better take care of our precious cargo."

"Of course," he paused. "Maybe we could all just—"

"Quinn." Fallon's authority held firm.

"Get Joseline to Raenya, let us handle the witches," Maya added.

"I can help you pack your things." Quinn turned toward Freya's voice. "It's a bit colder up there along The Northlands' border. Those of us who have lived here all our lives don't mind it, but you southern babes will need more suitable clothes." With a final look at Quinn and Joseline, Maya followed Freya.

Jenson hesitated. He faced Quinn, the twinge of sorrow in his dark eyes shimmering as he held out a hand. "Until we meet again, brother."

Quinn took his outstretched hand. "Just promise me we will meet again. Promise me you won't—"

"Quinn, we will meet again." Jenson smiled. "What sort of *sielapora* would I be if I wasn't by your side when you became King of Dorwynn?"

The nervous laugh escaped Quinn's lips before he could stop it, the tight feeling dwindling. "Who said anything about being king?" He hated the way Jenson smiled as if he were only going to bed, not traveling across the country on a dangerous mission. "If you think I'd let you leave me to that fate alone, you aren't as good of a friend as I thought."

"Until then," was all Jenson said.

"Go destroy some demons for me." Quinn gave Jenson's hand one final squeeze before their grip slipped apart and Jenson followed Maya and Freya into the night.

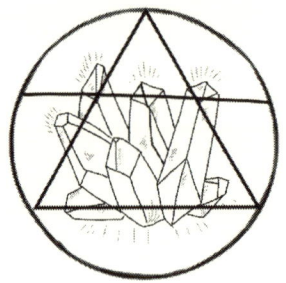

fourteen

Edan frowned at an unexpected knock at the classroom door, standing from his desk. The students glanced up from their exams, whispers echoing as Superior Albion entered the room.

"Excuse me, this exam is still in session." The chatter stopped, curious eyes dropping to the desks once more.

"A moment in the hallway, if you please," Albion said calmly.

Edan eyed the silent room. "I will know if you cheat. Not even a whisper, or that student will earn a failure marking." He slipped into the hall. "So, what warrants this intrusion?"

"You're unobservant for a master healer." That soft-spoken voice was unfamiliar. Edan met the eyes of the newcomers in the hall. The female witches wore riding leathers, chestnut-brown pants and vests, the lilac fabric of the tunics beneath crumpled from flight. They were several inches shorter than him, but their eyes and hair were the same: one cut in a short pixie fashion while the other brushed slender shoulders. Twins, if he had to guess.

"We were sent to ensure your safety by Rowena Stormwood." Again, that soft-spoken voice from the witch with the pixie hair. She extended a gloved hand where she leaned against the wall. "Fi."

"Edan." He shook her offered hand, eyeing the other witch. "And you are?"

"Naoi. We were sent personally by Erza Stormwood, we fly at her command."

"Stormwood Elites," Edan murmured, scratching his jaw. "It's an honor to meet you. Thank you for coming."

Fi's lilac eyes flicked to the classroom. "This is a bad time."

Edan narrowed his eyes at Albion. "It is, actually."

Naoi smiled, but it was Fi who replied, "We can talk later, over drinks?"

"Sure."

Fi nodded. "Good." They turned back down the hall with Albion. "See you this evening, Master Edan. Perhaps then you can explain why you look exactly like Erza."

Edan paced before the table, glancing toward the setting sun through the balcony window. It had only taken an hour of scrambling to declutter his rooms, much to his surprise. He didn't usually have guests, especially ones demanding answers he wasn't sure how to address.

He studied the tidy room, the unusual lack of books and clothes covering the floor, though the fire crackling in the hearth was normal. Wiping a hand over his mouth, he straightened a chair and coughed, then pulled at his tailored overcoat, fiddling with the golden clasps.

He jumped at the soft knock, swore, and made his way to the door. Superior Albion gave a weak smile, Naoi and Fi silent shadows behind him. Edan opened the door wider in invitation and Albion put a hand on his arm. "Thank you, Edan. I know this is short notice."

"It isn't a problem. I just don't think I have the answers they're looking for."

"We aren't deaf, Master Edan." Fi's voice sounded slightly slurred and almost amused.

He approached the table, pulling out first Naoi's chair, then Fi's. "I never said you were, did I?"

"No," she mused, reaching for the goblet of wine before her. "But you were whispering loud enough to be heard down the hall."

"Purebloods," Albion mumbled.

"That comment holds no weight, does it?" Naoi asked. "I mean, Edan is a pureblood as well."

Goosebumps prickled Edan's flesh. "How could you possibly know that?"

"Even if your eyes didn't give you away, we've been following Erza for years. It isn't hard to see the resemblance," Fi cut him off. Edan ran a hand through his hair, sighing and Fi snorted. "You even have the same mannerisms." She turned to Albion. "What I don't understand is how he has so much power. It's supposed to pass through the maternal bloodline, yet I can feel it radiating from him." She eyed him then, gaze flashing with playful curiosity.

Edan opened his mouth to deny it, but Naoi put a hand on his arm. "I've learned not to challenge her. It only makes her more passionate about the topic in question, especially when she's been drinking." Naoi eyed her sister. "And she's been drinking for at least an hour."

Fi sent her twin a narrowed glare. Again, Edan opened his mouth, this time cut off by Superior Albion. "I'm honestly not sure, it's something that's always fascinated me."

"Is that why you kept him a secret?" Fi asked.

"I kept him hidden only from the covens. He knows who his mother and sister are."

"Sister? So that explains—"

"We're twins." Edan wiped a hand over his beard. "You can speak to me, you know, I'm right here."

Fi's nose wrinkled when she grinned, resting her chin against her palm as she leaned toward him. "You don't seem to have the temperament needed for a professor. Are you always so quick to anger?"

Edan held her stare for a moment, then pursed his lips and turned away.

"Fi, stop your teasing," Naoi grumbled.

"Did Queen Rowena tell you why we sent for you?" Albion asked.

Fi leaned back, draining the wine goblet and pouring another. "Erza did, yes. Trouble with the Northmen?"

"Not exactly. We have reason to worry over the safety of our novices if they were to pose a threat though. Every day the port fills with shadows and the Northmen grow restless." Edan drank deeply from his goblet, calming his unsettled nerves.

"And you aren't warriors."

"No," Edan pinched the bridge of his nose. "If anything should happen to the students because we couldn't protect them…"

"I take back my comment about your temperament, Master Edan." Fi's voice was softer. After a moment, she turned to Albion. "So, what would you like us to do, Superior Albion?"

"Nothing, until it is needed." Albion stroked a hand over his beard. "Perhaps a few scouting missions along the border to ease an old man's worries?"

"Consider it done," Naoi sipped her own goblet.

"Very well, then." The Healer Superior stood with a resigned sigh. "Master Edan, I trust you are capable of entertaining our guests? I have several things I should be seeing to."

"Of course." Edan bowed his head slightly, and Albion let himself out.

"Darkness everywhere." Fi sipped from the goblet again.

"It appears that way." Naoi stood, eyeing her sister. "Try not to scare Master Edan too much with your drunken stupidity, will you, Fi?" Her twin only shooed her off.

Edan frowned. "You're more than welcome to stay."

Naoi smiled but shook her head. "I'm tired from traveling." She nodded toward Fi. "Watch out for that one, though, she flirts like a whore and she'll drink all your spiced wine if you don't watch her. We don't often get the opportunity to drink wine in the capital, makes her a bit…intolerant."

Fi mumbled something against the rim of the goblet, draining the remaining wine and reached for the decanter at the center of the table. Edan let out a half laugh. "Thank you for that warning."

With a parting nod, Naoi closed the door behind her.

Edan turned back to Fi, his pulse quickening despite the wall secured around his heart. "So, you're related to Erza as well." He gestured toward her lilac eyes. "Does that make us cousins?"

Fi shrugged, a hiccup escaping her lips. "I suppose it does, but our lineage is much further down. Fourth or fifth cousins perhaps?" She hiccupped again. "Gods damn it."

Edan stood, reaching over her for the water pitcher and pouring some into the empty glass beside the goblet. She traced a hand down the front of his overcoat, and he ignored the shiver it sent down his spine. "Here, it'll help," he handed the glass to her and she drank, water dripping down the corners of her mouth. Instinctively, Edan took his napkin and brushed it against her lips. Fi froze, meeting his eyes. His pulse quickened again at her stare, his stomach knotting. He frowned, sitting back and taking a sip of his own wine.

Fi laughed, her soft voice sweet as she leaned toward him, small face inquisitive. "Are you alright, Master Edan?"

"Just Edan, please."

She smiled, leaning a bit closer. "Why? Does it feel wrong for me to call you that while you flirt with me?"

Edan's nostrils flared. "I beg your pardon?"

Her stare didn't falter. "Oh, you weren't flirting, then?"

"No." He swallowed.

Fi raised an eyebrow. "You were giving me innocent doe eyes."

"I'm not a virgin."

Fi gave a half laugh. "You could have fooled me."

He sighed, forcing down the painful memories. "I'd rather not have this conversation with you."

"Because you think I'm drunk, or just in general?"

"You *are* drunk."

"I'm not." She trailed a finger down his chest. "So?"

"You really need to get laid if you think every man who looks at you wants to sleep with you."

Fi pulled back, the shock flickering in her eyes. "There's nothing wrong with harmless flirting, *Master Edan*."

The knot in his stomach tightened, fighting the words as he said them. "I think you should go." He paused. "Do you need me to walk you back to your rooms? Naoi said you've been drinking for a while."

"I'm perfectly capable of walking myself to my rooms after you've so carelessly dismissed me." Fi stood, stumbling forward.

Edan caught her just before her knees buckled, sliding an arm around her waist. "I'm sure you can." He laughed softly, whispering against her ear, "I thought you weren't drunk?"

"Careful, *Master Edan*. I might mistake your teasing for flirting." She smiled, then groaned as he moved toward the door. "So I had several glasses in my own room. Maybe I'm just a little..." her voice trailed off. "Damn The Twelve."

Edan frowned. "If you're going to be sick, I'd rather you not do it all over my clothes in the middle of the hall. I'm quite fond of this coat."

"Is that a failed attempt to invite me into your bed?"

He laughed. "That was me telling you I don't mind sleeping on the floor."

Fi's head fell against his chest. "Do you always allow women to sleep in your bed the first night you meet them?"

"I don't allow anyone into my room the first night I meet them." He lifted her into his arms, his lips twitching up into a smile as he walked toward the bed. "You must be special."

"I'm a member of the Stormwood Elite. We're all special."

Edan set her on the bed, and she squeezed her eyes shut. "I'm going to get you some more water. Don't throw up, please?"

Fi mumbled something, curling up against the pillow as he turned away. Edan shook his head. Despite all his training as a healer, sometimes he wondered why he was so nice to complete strangers. Any normal man would sleep with the witch or dismiss her. She was quite beautiful, after all.

With a sigh, he returned to the bed, sitting beside her.

"You're a good man," Fi said, taking the cup from him.

"You don't know anything about me."

"You're right, but maybe one day I'll be lucky enough to."

Edan smiled. "Get some rest. I'll show you where you can keep your Kitsugon and the best outcrops for guarding the Chiron in the morning."

She nodded sleepily, rolling away from him. Edan took an extra blanket off the foot of the bed, shifted to the soft rug, and closed his eyes.

fifteen

When Erza warned her there were issues going on within the covens, Evalyn didn't expect talk of murderous shadows whispered in empty hallways. Death, it seemed, followed her everywhere, a dark horror she couldn't escape from.

At least the ancient watchtower and the surrounding village of Thya weren't bathed in constant shadows like Narcio.

Still, she didn't completely trust the witches. Despite Beck's warnings, Evalyn didn't sense any immediate danger, but that didn't mean the danger wasn't hovering in the shadows.

Evalyn shuddered, pulling Dax's cloak around her shoulders as she moved through the halls. She knew she should move on, but her exhaustion gnawed at the back of her mind, convincing her to stay where she could at least collect some rations before she continued toward Raenya as Beck had said. *Be sensible, Eva*, she chided herself. *It won't hurt to regain some strength. Besides, the Shadow Beasts could be anywhere.*

The old, circular tower was comprised of looping hallways and so many narrow steps, Evalyn didn't believe Erza when the witch told her she'd learn her way around in no time. The Stormwood witches were housed in the north wing, Silvermists in the east, Blackwings in the south, with the Kitsugon kennels in the lower levels nearest the arena.

When Evalyn asked why the Blackwing royals didn't retire to their fortress within the Thyan outskirts, Erza replied it was all part of the Games' appearance.

The western wing was crumbling and destroyed in certain sections. The parts that remained made up the kitchens, laundry rooms, and other necessary amenities. The lower levels branched off the main structure, made up of small huts and cottages where the servants lived. The further outcropping settlements of Thya were built from the same stone as the tower, and the citizens who lived there avoided the witches at all costs.

She had yet to see the magical Kitsugon, though she read about them with her mother as a child. Their roaring cries echoed through the tower all night, and after all the horrors of Narcio, it still sent panic through Evalyn's blood.

She gnawed on her lip, prepared to admit she was lost as she turned another corner in the halls, when a corridor full of iron-barred kennels came into view. Evalyn stopped, frozen in wonder at the majestic creatures within.

Where the Shadow Beasts induced pure terror, the fur-coated, scaley-cheeked, many-hued Kitsugon evoked awe.

The door beside her shook with a snarl from its inhabitant. Her head jerked toward the creature, its long, barbed tail twitching in anticipation, dark wings folded with calculated grace and shifty, cat-like eyes glowing a vibrant tawny.

Evalyn met the creature's gaze evenly.

The midday sun glowed through narrow windows at the top of the cell, illuminating the Kitsugon's scales like a rainbow after a storm, her jet-black fur accenting the shimmering colors. She yawned, revealing sharp teeth, then blinked and turned toward the back wall, tail swishing lazily.

Evalyn blinked as well, the sudden spell broken just as quickly.

"You're a pretty thing, aren't you?" The venomous croon sent a chill down Eva's spine.

She turned, meeting the pale blue eyes of an impossibly beautiful blonde witch. Honey curls caressed her shoulders, falling just past her breasts where the laces of the sky-blue tunic ended. Her legs, covered by tight leather pants, were as slender as the rest of her, breasts popping visibly from the laces when she folded her arms over her chest. Her companion was dressed similarly with identical eyes—Blackwing eyes—her chestnut hair braided over her shoulder.

Something about them made Evalyn want to cower. Her inner fire screamed, insisting she slink as far from the blonde as she could. The pendant at her neck shimmered in the light, the obsidian power reaching for her as if blocking out the light in exchange for darkness. The feeling reminded her of the Shadow Beasts.

But Evalyn didn't give the fear the satisfaction of winning. She had escaped, and she would *not* go back there. Innocence filled her eyes as it had for so many years, schooled to neutrality as it hid the feeling creeping through her veins. A never-ending game in a world shrouded by lies and secrecy.

The Kitsugon in the cell behind her snarled as she smiled, holding out a hand. "I don't believe we've had the pleasure of meeting. I'm Eva."

The blonde snorted. "Pretty and polite? Or has Erza taught you so well in such a short amount of time?"

"Probably both," her companion mused. They laughed.

It took years of hiding her emotions to keep the shock from her face. "I beg your—"

"Eva, I see you've met Morana and her second, Lira." Erza's voice echoed with annoyance as she strode into the kennel.

"You didn't introduce me to your new pet, so I had to take matters into my own hands," Morana said, fiddling with her pendant.

"You didn't, she isn't your concern." Erza's lilac eyes flashed. "Don't you have somewhere to be?"

Morana said nothing as she stormed off, Lira on her heels.

"I hope you aren't causing problems," Rowen rounded the corner, tossing her long scarlet braid over her shoulder.

A half-laugh escaped Evalyn's lips, but the fear coursed through her, raw and uncontrollable as memories of Narcio and Toren's incessant taunting resurfaced from the encounter. *Run,* her mind screamed. *It's not worth it, get out of here.*

"Eva?" She blinked, meeting Rowen's gaze. "Is everything alright?"

Evalyn opened and closed her mouth several times. She gulped, shaking her head. "No. No, I can't..."

"Eva, they won't hurt you." Erza furrowed her brows. "They're a pain in the ass, sure, but they won't—"

Evalyn didn't wait for Erza to finish as she turned and ran from the watchtower. She had no idea where she was going, and no true sense of why she was running to begin with. But Morana's sneer filled her mind, her pretty face replaced by Toren's as if Evalyn were walking in a living nightmare, the phantom crack of his whip making her flinch.

Go away, she begged, gritting her teeth against the tears. *Please, just go away.*

Her lip trembled as she stumbled, lurching forward. Her knees stung where they skidded slightly in the frozen earth, and the sob tore from her lungs as she focused on her breathing, willing her body to remain calm.

He isn't here. Toren isn't here. Morana does even know him...

"Eva, what's wrong?" Erza's shout echoed from behind her.

Evalyn squeezed her eyes shut, shaking her head, even as she sensed Erza's presence beside her. "I'm fine, I just...I need a moment."

"You can't honestly expect me to believe that." A pause. "Look, I know you said no backstory, but whatever it is you went through is clearly troubling you. I know it isn't always easy to talk about our pasts, but if you want to, I'll listen."

Wiping her nose on her forearm, Evalyn met Erza's eyes. The witch offered a weak smile. "No offense, but you...well, you don't really seem the type to—"

Erza's laugh cut her off. "I'm not." Her smile widened. "You pick up on things rather quickly, don't you?"

She shrugged, bracing her hands on her knees. "I..." she ran her hands through her hair. "I was a slave on Narcio Island for most of my life. Let's just say learning to pick up on people's feelings helped keep me alive?"

Erza raised an eyebrow, her glance shifting toward the

watchtower. "And Morana…"

"Reminds me of someone I knew there." Erza flashed her a pointed look. "The foreman." Evalyn bit her lip. "He…he used to enjoy picking on me."

"I see."

"I just…I appreciate your hospitality and for saving me back in Easthaven. But maybe it's time I continued onto Raenya. I was told that was the best place for me to go, so…"

"I won't keep you if you wish to go." Erza began, wetting her lips. "But can I offer you some friendly advice?" Evalyn forced herself not to jump as Erza touched her hand gently. "Whether you're trapped on an island or not, the world is cruel. There will always be people who favor their anger over kindness." She paused, lips twitching slightly. "There will always be those of us who have to hide from them."

"Who…you don't seem like you'd have to hide from anyone," Evalyn admitted.

Laughing, Erza shrugged. "We all hide from something. We all have demons. Mine just so happens to be my mother."

"Your mother?" Evalyn asked.

"If she had her way, I would be a heartless monster." Erza scoffed. "I value strength, and honestly, and loyalty. I rule my Elites with an iron fist, just as I'll rule my country when I'm queen." She sighed. "But kindness and love are also things to value…things my mother finds unnecessary."

"That doesn't seem like a good way to rule, if you ask me."

"Maybe not, but my mother thinks that notion makes me soft." Standing, Erza brushed off her knees before holding out a hand.

Evalyn took it, pulling to her feet. "Valuing love and kindness doesn't make you weak, Erza."

She wasn't sure what to make of the look in the witch's eyes. After a moment, Erza smiled. "No, it does not. Just as there's nothing wrong with being afraid of the things you've gone through." Evalyn's cheeks heated. "But there are worse things in this world than Morana Blackwing, Eva."

"I don't doubt it," she whispered.

"Just take the night to think about it? You can leave in the morning if you wish." Erza paused. "But if you decide to stay, maybe we can work on something to help you defend yourself when you are on your own?"

"I'll...consider it," Evalyn promised as they started walking back toward the watchtower. Her iron shackles rubbed against her ankles, a painful reminder of the magic she couldn't use. She grimaced. "Unless you can get these off," she grumbled.

Smirking, Erza pulled up her hood against the harsh breeze. "Perhaps," she said, quickening her pace. "But I guess you'll have to stay to find out."

sixteen

The fall air swirled in crisp whorls, the woodland cottage filled with the scent of fresh bread, peonies, and frankincense. Mother always lit the incense before bed so the calming smell drifted through the small cottage at night.

It helped Quinn sleep. It helped Evalyn sleep even more. Her night terrors were worse than his.

Quinn sat up, sneaking a glance at his twin, still asleep in her bed. Her cheeks were flushed, silvery hair strewn across her face. Several strands fell over her lips, blowing about as she breathed.

Quinn hid a chuckle as he snuck from the room and into the hallway.

He crept, careful to walk where the floor wouldn't creak as he made his way around the corner and into the main room. Mother always hummed when she baked; the pleasant aroma of sweet rolls engulfed his senses.

He inched toward the front door. When Eva challenged him to a hide-and-seek rematch, she hadn't counted on him sneaking out early to get a head start. Quinn snickered to himself, tucking silvery locks behind his ears as he pulled open the door just a crack.

Slender arms trapped him as his mother whispered into his ear, "Just where do you think you're going, darling?"

Quinn's hand fell from the doorknob. "What?" he asked, wiggling to flash her his biggest smile.

She laughed, releasing him and crouching down before him. Flour filled the air as she rubbed her hands on her apron. "You know the rules, no going out alone. Besides, your sister won't be happy."

He rolled his eyes as she fiddled with his hair. "Mama…" he whined. "Please? I want to—"

"You were gonna hide?"

Quinn's eyes darted to the hallway where his sister stood, barefoot in her nightgown, rubbing groggy eyes.

He bit his lip. "No, I—"

Evalyn charged for him, her nose and cheeks scrunching up in anger, but Zaria lifted them both into her arms. "Let me go!" Evalyn growled.

Zaria just laughed, holding them close. Evalyn stopped squirming, huffing, and stuck her tongue out at him. Quinn grinned.

"Alright, my little troublemakers, you can go play until the sweet rolls are ready." She opened the door, the spring breeze stinging his cheeks. "But look out for one another. You're big now, four years old today." She kissed them both fiercely.

"Yeah," Quinn gripped Evalyn's hand as he pulled her through the door.

She laughed. "Don't be gone long now. Breakfast will be done soon."

They shuffled down the wooden porch steps and through the flower-covered yard. "Bye, Mama!" Evalyn cried.

"Be careful, my loves!" Her voice echoed through the breeze. "Be safe, and don't cross the stream!"

"Yes, Mama," they called as the cottage vanished through the trees.

The Moonswood was so beautiful, calm and serene. The air smelled of woodsy comforts and flowers, the sound of chirping birds whispering through branches in the canopy above. There was something about it, the wind rushing through his hair and Evalyn at his side that made Quinn feel invincible. Unstoppable. Their fire pulsed, mixing through blood and soul, savoring the freedom and each other's companionship.

At last they slowed, Evalyn pulling on his tunic. "You first." Leaning against the nearest tree, she covered her turquoise eyes with small hands and began counting.

Quinn launched into the trees.

Evalyn's voice echoed in the distance, but he didn't slow, didn't falter. He only ran, the freedom of his Fae senses and the wind carrying his body on wisps of air, the fire in his soul grounding him. Chuckling, Quinn veered to the side, twisting through trees to throw Eva off his trail. It wasn't until he was oblivious to his surroundings that he realized he was lost. A cold shiver ran down his spine at the shadowed feeling enveloping him. He knew these woods like the back of his hand, he'd never been lost. But this part of the wood was unfamiliar. He had no sense of direction, no idea which way to turn back, to go home. Fear ran through his veins, heating his blood. It was too dark, too quiet.

Quinn stopped, scanning the woods in search of a tree he could climb to get a grip on his surroundings. But unlike the low, easily-accessible branches of the trees surrounding the cottage, these trunks were tall, looming too high for his reach.

Be calm, *he thought as his magic began to swell.* Calm. Don't be afraid. Control the fire. You *are* the fire.

"Look what I found, a little Fae boy all alone in the woods. Frightened, are you?"

Quinn turned hesitantly toward the deep voice.

Three shadows towered over him, crawling, sharp nails digging into the earth. Their faces were shrouded in the dark gloom of the forest, but he didn't need to see them to feel the pure evil power they radiated. To smell the rotting flesh, see the dagger-sharp nails flexing, the eyes gleaming red beneath jet black fur.

He squared his shoulders, facing the snarling beasts with a fierceness of someone three times his age. "I'm not frightened."

"Oh no?" A deep growl vibrated from the second creature's throat. "You should be."

The power flickering within him warned him to run as fast as he could and never look back. But he didn't know where to go.

Quinn gulped, backing into the nearest tree. He clenched his fists, searching for some way, any way to escape. There, a sliver of sunlight between two trees.

The third creature crept forward, tail swishing above his head. "If I were you, I would run. My friends tend to kill quickly when their pray give chase. So stop staring and run."

Quinn took off through the trees like lightning, his small body weaving through them, the demons' snarls echoing close behind. The sunlight grew nearer, and Quinn pumped his legs with all his might, using any reserves of energy. Relief flooded through him for two seconds until he saw the cliff face ahead. He halted, panic rising once more.

"Looks like your little escape backfired."

"What a tasty morsel. It isn't often we find a lone Fae wandering the woods. And this one has so much power. I can smell it on his flesh."

They were even more horrifying in the sunlight. Black, mangled fur covered towering bodies, their red eyes filled with the pleasure of his fear.

Quinn bit his lip, taking a step back toward the dangerous drop. He wondered how crippling the fall would be if he jumped, wondered if Sauda would spare him.

Death hovered, unpreventable, until a soft, commanding voice said from the tree line, "Don't your kind have anything better to do than stalk innocent children?"

Before the monsters could turn to the speaker, a gust of harsh wind like a hurricane shot them into the sky. Quinn ducked, shaking as he covered his neck with his hands, rocking back and forth against his knees.

Whatever monster had done this, it had to be awful. One death in exchange for another.

The outskirts of the forest were silent for a long time. Quinn opened one eye, still covering his head in a crouch.

"Are you alright, boy?" That voice again—the voice that saved him. A hand dropped into his vision.

Quinn released a ragged breath, looking up at the man kneeling before him. Silvery hair fell past his shoulders and into bright silver eyes that matched his mother's. Fae eyes. The man smiled, the diagonal scar running along his square jaw accented by the gesture.

Quinn stared at the hand but didn't take it. "Thank you."

His savior pulled him to his feet with a brisk nod. "No need to fear me, boy. I mean you no harm."

Quinn brushed off his pants and met the man's stare. "What do you mean?"

Shock flickered in the man's eyes and he stepped back but regained his composure almost immediately. "The shadows, do they follow you?" Quinn nodded. "Where is your home? Your parents?"

Quinn bit his lip, wiping a hand across his nose. "I...I don't know. My sister and I were...but I..." Tears ran down his cheeks.

"Lost is it?" The man smiled. "That makes two of us."

A smile tugged the corner of his lips, and he sniffed. "Can you help?"

"I'll do my best to keep you safe. For now, perhaps we can be lost together."

Quinn thrust out his hand. "I'm Quinn."

The man laughed. "Fallon, at your service, Sir Quinn."

"No, just Quinn."

Another swift nod, and Fallon turned, eyeing their surroundings. "Well, just Quinn, how about we try to get unlost? Then maybe I could teach you a thing or two about defending yourself next time."

Quinn's eyes shot open.

The memory, blocked to mere snippets for so long, resurfaced. Thousands of childhood memories came flooding back like the world reappearing after a thick fog. It spread a strange ache along his temple and he sat, gasping, gripping the sheets, his bare chest covered in sweat as he wiped damp hair from his eyes. He ran a hand through mangled brown locks, forcing his breath to steady.

"Fallon was afraid you might wake in shock." Larina's voice was soft beside him.

His gaze darted to her for a moment before he inspected his tent. Moonlight streamed through the open flap opposite him, bathing his belongings in silver. He'd half-expected his mentor to be there, but Larina was alone. She cocked her head, quirking a brow.

Quinn cleared his throat. "What?"

She smiled weakly, handing him a water skin. "Fallon. He removed the remaining block on your memory while you slept. We thought it would be easier that way."

He drank, choking at the whiskey's harsh burn. "My sister?" *Gods. How could he have forgotten about Evalyn?*

Larina shook her head. "I don't know. Nobody even knew you were born. I'm not even sure Reul did."

He drank again, deeply. "We were kept secret...one my mother spent her entire life trying to protect. We never knew why. Only that it was important nobody knew about us."

"You and your sister are Reul's only living children. You are a precious gem to the world."

"It's hard to accept. Here I was starting to think I would never remember my past." He met Larina's eyes. "Joseline and I could save the world together. And if Evalyn still lives..."

Larina nodded. "Yes. Your relationship with the princess is more valuable than you know."

"We don't have a relation—" She raised an eyebrow, fixing him with a pointed look. He sighed, rolling his eyes. "Why does everyone seem to think we have a relationship?"

"Because it's obvious to everyone but the two of you apparently."

He growled, swigging the whiskey a third time. Larina snorted and crossed her legs. Quinn was silent for a moment before he asked, "What of my relationship with my father, what will that be like?"

All humor faded from Larina's eyes. "I don't know," she admitted, taking the skin. After a long time, she added, "you look exactly like him, you know. Your father. Even in human form, you look identical."

Quinn bit his lip. "Does he have a twin as well?" Larina shook her head. "What about magic?"

She smiled. "You both have a roundabout way of asking for help."

Quinn frowned. "I'm not asking for help."

"No?" Larina narrowed her eyes. "So, you don't want my help learning how to use your magic, then?"

Quinn blushed before he could stop himself. "I would greatly appreciate that, if you were willing to teach me."

"I'll do my best. What kind of aunt would I be if I didn't help my nephew?" Quinn snarled as she headlocked him, ruffling his hair.

"Can't breathe," he growled.

Larina chuckled, releasing him. "I am surprised Fallon kept it from you for so long. I'm sure he had his reasons, but..." she shook her head. "You know I'm not the only one who might be able to help with the magic."

Quinn ran a hand through his hair. "Your guess is as good as mine. Fallon has been working with me, though."

"I'm not talking about Fallon's help." Quinn shot her a questioning look as she said, "Alright, little one. He knows the truth. You can come out now."

With a soft tinkle, a tiny creature, no bigger than his palm, flew into view. He hovered before Quinn, iridescent wings fluttering as he wrung his hands together. Silver spiked hair twisted up off his forehead, revealing dazzling sapphire eyes.

"A faerie?" Quinn breathed.

"Azuri." The tiny creature nodded, glancing to Larina. Then he bowed. "Your Highness. It is an honor to meet you at last."

seventeen

She would never admit it out loud, but Eva fascinated Erza. Though she was still terrified and broken from the years she'd spent as a slave on Narcio Island, Eva had more strength than she knew—a strength that increased daily. Her calmness, heightened in the presence of the Kitsugon, made her growth even more evident. It had intrigued Erza from the start, and she almost wondered if it was part of the reason she felt inclined to help.

Never taking in strays, indeed.

Erza found the Fae girl down in the kennels every day after the Elite's morning training session, and sometimes during the evenings when she thought no one was watching. But Curra, Ysta, and Vien passed along the knowledge in their reports.

She was especially drawn to Hestia, a Kitsugon as fiery and exotic as her name. Her fur shimmered like molten gold flecked with accents of ruby, and her scales flashed burnt orange and maroon. She was deemed untrainable to ride as a kit after an incident that left five handlers dead, but Eva watched her every day, not speaking, not moving. Hestia, cautious as always, watched the Fae girl as well. Erza never said a word about it.

Today was different, though. Something awoke in Eva when Erza cut the iron cuffing her ankles, the swell of power in the room almost suffocating; Erza had never felt such a surge of magic, and the power hadn't shown itself since.

Until now.

Eva stood before Hestia's cell, hand outstretched. The Kitsugon crooned to her, extending a leathery nose toward the Fae girl's fingers. Flames tickled the tips of her silvery hair, creeping along her flesh. Her skin glowed with blue-green fire, the tendrils weaving about her head and through her hair without burning her.

She looked majestic, regal, beautiful.

"Eva." The Fae girl turned at the sound of her name, the flames vanishing. "I was thinking maybe you'd like to know how to control that fire of yours."

"That would be nice." Eva paused. "But is that something you can manage? You should be preparing for your competition."

She was right, but something kept pushing her toward Eva, insisting somehow that she watch over her. The Gods didn't push her often, not The Twelve or the Great Mother, though her connection to the Goddess Era had always been strong; but she couldn't ignore the intensity of the feeling even if she had no name for it.

"I can make time for it," Erza replied, turning down the hall.

"I appreciate that."

Erza shrugged, leaving the watchtower through a side door and entering Thya's rundown outskirts. The inhabitants shrank away as she passed, their gazes petrified. Erza ignored them, making her way to Lake Urasa, the lone island just visible in the distance. Eva's footsteps followed behind her, then froze inches away from the rowboat. "On second thought, I can't do this."

Slowly, Erza turned to face her. She looked like a rabbit cowering in fear before a wolf, her pretty face drained of all color. "If you expect me to baby you, forget it."

Eva gulped. "No, I just…" she sighed. "Bodies of water and I don't get along."

Erza frowned. "You're afraid. Fear is good. But only you can decide what to do with your fears. Own up to them and defeat them head-on, or let them control your existence."

Eva hesitated another moment, then stepped onto the boat. It rocked beneath her and she sat immediately, gripping the edges.

"Excellent, now, let go." The horrified look returned, but Erza shook her head. "No, don't give me that. Do you want control or not?" Eva gave a feeble nod. "Then, let go." When she obeyed, Erza put a hand on her knee. "Not so bad, right?"

Eva released a shuddering breath. "What if I fall in? I can't swim."

"Then you fall in, and I'll help you. How can you ever expect to get over your fears if you let them control you?" She reached over the edge, splashing water up over the side.

Eva toppled backwards on the seat, the boat rocking from the motion. "Why did you do that?"

"Eva, it's just water."

"But—"

"It's just water," Erza repeated. "It can't hurt you." Eva's chest rose and fell in quick breaths as she fought visibly to control the panic. Again, Erza cupped water into her palm, holding it out to Eva. "Didn't you have to travel from Narcio on a boat?"

Eva straightened at that. "That's different."

"How?"

"It's...I couldn't actually see the water." Hesitantly, she reached out, touching Erza's hand. "I know that probably sounds silly." The water slid between their joined palms as Erza helped her sit upright.

"Not silly. The first step is always identifying what scares you. Now, feel the wind on your face. Taste the rain, the sky. Let it flow through your bones, along your skin. Let it be one with your magic. Be at peace with it."

Erza noticed the change before she finished speaking. The calm settled over Eva, radiating from her in a sense of serene comfort. Her shoulders rose and fell, tranquility enveloping them as the breeze ruffled silver strands of her hair.

The freedom consumed her as Eva closed her eyes, her aura pulsing against the space between them. Erza watched, breathless as the magic danced on whorls of air, and for a moment, she thought she saw Eva smile.

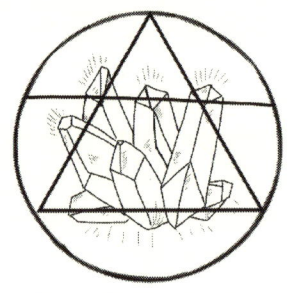

eighteen

Well, Freya was right about one thing: the air in Northern Rekiv was brutal, burning as it whispered along his skin. Jenson pulled at the cloak draped over his shoulders, grateful for the fur-lined collar as his breath puffed into the chilled air.

He shivered. Saying goodbye was easy, but physically being apart from Quinn was so much harder than he thought it would be.

"You alright?" Maya's voice jolted him back from his trance.

"What?" Jenson blinked, coughing into a gloved hand.

Sadness touched her smile. "He'll manage without us. He managed without us before."

Jenson sighed, rubbing a hand around the back of his neck. "I know. But he's my *sielapora*. Being away from him just feels…"

"Strange?"

Jenson nodded as another gust of wind sent a chill down his spine. He dreaded the snow of the coming months. Southern Rathal hardly got snow, but up north the winds alone were vicious.

He opened his mouth to ask Sionn if they were getting close when the little messenger boy pointed. Following his upheld finger, Jenson whistled, staring at the massive structure in the distance. The cylindrical building all but erupted from the ground, two columns of smaller domed buildings branching off the main one. The wall facing them crumbled in several places, the branching ground buildings accented with a plethora of huts and cottages. There were some bigger structures Jenson could only assume were an inn and tavern, but even they were run-down. The only building that stood uncrumpled was the manor on the village outskirts.

"Thya's a fishing village," Sionn explained. "We fish until Lake Urasa freezes and trade the extra in Easthaven to store food for the frozen months."

Jenson nodded, glancing to Maya. "So where do you live? I have strict orders to ensure you get home safe."

The boy opened his mouth to reply just as a honeyed voice cried out, "Sionn!"

Jenson's head turned as Maya helped the boy dismount. Jenson dismounted as well, watching as Sionn ran into the young woman's arms coming toward them from the village, her knees giving out as they sank to the ground. She held him close, stroking dark curls.

When Jenson and Maya approached, they stood, the curvy young woman fixing Jenson with a calculating look. "My brother says you traveled with him from Ebondenn and need a place to stay?"

He shook her offered hand, eyeing the knee-high boots and the defining blouse cinched around a slender waist. The fur along the collar of her half cloak brushed her dark neck. Jenson smiled. "That's right." He paused, his gaze fluttering down her chest and back up to her tawny eyes before he added, "Can you be of any assistance?"

She raised an eyebrow, her gaze sending a strange tingle along his spine as she put a hand on her hip and pointed to one of the buildings opposite the large structure. "My mama will get you settled in. Just tell her Sionn is home, will ya?"

"Of course." The sensation continued the longer he held her gaze, and Jenson released a stuttered breath, trying to ignore the tether pulling him toward her. "And if she asks who sent me?"

Her smile was as sultry as her voice, dark lashes fluttering and gaze raking over his body. "Sonya, but you needn't worry yourself with me, traveler."

"Jenson," he corrected.

"Jenson. I'm sure I'll see ya around then." She winked at him, taking her brother's hand and hurrying toward the village.

He shook slightly, the tether fading with her presence, and Maya gripped his elbow, pulling him and the horses in the direction Sonya pointed. "Honestly, you're worse than Quinn."

Jenson smirked, tearing his gaze from Sonya's swaying hips. "So, what first? It's been a long time since it was just you and me on a mission, little lady."

"It has, hasn't it?" Maya pursed her lips. "First, I need a bath and food."

"Definitely food. And after?" Jenson took the reins from her.

"After, we might as well see what we can find out about the source of this darkness."

Jenson linked their arms together. "Cutting right to the fun. I like it."

Maya laughed, shoving him as they approached the village outskirts.

As promised, the inn Sonya directed them to was hospitable. Her mother, every bit as sultry as her daughter, was delighted at the news of her young son's return. She gave them two rooms, insisting they enjoy a hot meal before they made their way upstairs. But after a warm bath, a full stomach, and an hour of asking around, they were still no closer to discovering new information. Jenson wiped a hand over his face as they walked through Thya's rundown streets, letting out a frustrated sigh. The bone-chilling breeze did nothing to relax him.

Maya put a hand on his arm. "Jens, we just need more time."

"I know that," he grumbled. "But time isn't exactly on our side."

Before Maya could reply, a familiar voice drawled, "Well, look who's all cleaned up and settled."

Jenson turned toward Sonya, the tether returning immediately. She smiled at him. "You found my mama's inn without trouble, traveler?"

"Yes, we did. Now if you'll excuse us, we have things to do, Jenson." Maya's tone flickered with annoyance.

He knew she was right, but he couldn't move, his body ignoring his mental protests. Sonya walked toward them, teeth flashing in a grin. "That so? I can give you something to do, little girl."

Jenson shook from the trance at the comment, Sonya's diverted attention breaking the bizarre spell. "It's alright, I think we'll just be going." He didn't like the feeling, whatever it was. Taking a step toward Maya, he sent her an apologetic look and linked their arms together.

Maya shrugged, the blush fading from her cheeks at the other woman's suggestive comment. Sonya gave him a defeated pout, her hand brushing against his chest as she walked past them, tracing along the deft muscle of his arm. She leaned in, her teeth sharp as she nipped his ear and whispered, "Until next time, then." Her breath crawled along his flesh even as she walked away.

"You alright?" Maya asked.

Jenson shivered, glancing down at her. "Fine," he frowned. "That was just…strange."

"Strange isn't the word you're looking for. It's enthralled. Best be careful around here, newcomer, or you might find yourself in a situation you can't get out of."

If the newcomer's unnatural beauty alone wasn't evidence of her heritage, the lilac eyes and witch mark at the base of her left ear gave the Stormwood witch away. She smirked, leaning against the stone, her arms crossed over her chest. The wind danced with the rich plum fabric of her cloak, brushing ebony strands across her forehead and neck. Her riding leathers creaked when she pushed off the wall.

Jenson opened his mouth to thank her for the warning but froze as her companion emerged from the same alleyway, her melodic voice sweeter and all too familiar. "Erza, you can't walk so fast around all the corners, I have no idea where I'm—" the Fae girl stopped abruptly when she saw them, meeting Jenson's shocked eyes. "Oh, I'm sorry to interrupt."

Jenson tensed, and Maya beside him, but he forced himself to smile and extend his free hand. "No, we were just introducing ourselves."

The Fae girl gnawed on her bottom lip, her eyes darting to the witch before she took his hand. "Oh, well, I'm Eva. It's a pleasure to meet you." Eva extended a hand to Maya, the sweet smile on her face clouded by only a twinge of fear, but Maya remained frozen, staring at the girl who was an identical, yet feminine version of Quinn.

"Jens, you're seeing this too, right?" Maya whispered, her gaze never leaving Eva.

Jenson chuckled. "I am, but you're being rude."

Maya blinked at him, shaking Eva's hand. "I'm sorry," she tucked a strand of blonde behind her ear. "You just look like a close friend of ours."

Something flickered in Eva's turquoise eyes. "Is that so?"

Maya smiled weakly, sucking on the gap in her teeth as she gripped her elbows.

Jenson turned to Erza. "Thank you for the warning about Sonya. I'll make sure to remember it, flower."

He almost reached for Maya, but Erza's voice stopped him. "In the future, you will refrain from calling me that."

Jenson tilted his head, flashing a playful smile. "What, flower?" He shoved both hands into his pockets and sauntered toward her. They were evenly muscled, lean and toned, but he was several inches taller than her. Still, she glared up at him, fists clenching at her sides.

"Yes. My name is Erza Stormwood, future queen of Rekiv."

Jenson trailed his gaze down her body once and met her eyes. Short raven strands blew across her forehead, lilac irises brimming with danger. He grinned. "Nah, I like flower better."

He nodded to Maya, and they turned to leave. "What's your friend's name," Eva called after them, "the one I look like?"

Jenson paused, debating if he should mention it at all, before replying, "It's Quinn."

Without another word, they headed back to the inn, Erza's lilac eyes burning in his mind.

nineteen

Controlling the light was harder than Joseline expected. Actually, she wasn't quite sure what she expected, but the pain prickling her spine and the sweat beading down her forehead were uncomfortable regardless. She hadn't been able to manage more than a soft shimmer of golden light at her fingertips all morning. Kai never judged, her sweet smiles and gentle approach strange compared to Quinn's usual grumbling. Shea, tail curled around folded paws, lay on a large fallen tree trunk, watching them.

Joseline wiped her forearm across her eyes, cursing her incompetence, then pulled her hair into a loose braid. "This is hopeless."

Kai smiled, tucking lavender strands behind her ear. "It isn't. Magic takes practice to master."

Joseline threw her hands into the air. "We've been practicing for three days and I can barely spark anything!"

The smile was weaker this time. "The Fae begin training their magic from a young age. To spark your power into anything after such a short time is something to be proud of."

She's right, you know, Shea thought.

Nobody asked you, Joseline pouted.

"I will say, the prince was wise to teach you meditation. That helps," Kai said. The Prince—Quinn—the title still sounded strange. "You care for him very much."

Joseline's cheeks heated. "I do not—"

"You do, but it's alright if you can't admit it. You will eventually." Kai flipped her staff into the air, the metal tip digging into the soft dirt as her hands closed around the smooth wood engraved with shimmering crystals.

Joseline gulped. "I don't know what you mean."

Kai laughed, pulling her staff up. "When I met Larina, I was like you. I denied my feelings. I...didn't think I was worthy enough to be her mate. But some things you can't deny forever."

The blush deepened. "I'm not—"

Snapping branches cut off her response. Kai spun, Shea growling, hackles rising. The sound echoed again, this time from the right. Joseline's focus darted to the noise, but she saw no movement.

Kai swore. "Kagai."

"What?"

"Kagai," Kai repeated, her grip on the staff tightening. "They're some of Aeron's lesser demons. Nasty things. They're invisible until you hit them, and their bite will sting for days."

Something shuffled along the ground behind her, but Joseline saw only the claw marks gouged through the dirt. Her pulse raced, her hand reaching for the silver blade at her hip, the feel of the flower hilt in her palm doing nothing to ease her panic.

"So pathetic, the whimpering fear of mortals." The sound echoed through the clearing.

Kai pushed her back into Joseline's. "I'm not mortal."

"No, but she is, the princess our Master needs. All alone and helpless without her pestering bodyguards."

More shuffling. Shea snarled, her tail wrapping around Joseline's leg. The princess clenched her fists. "I am *not* helpless."

A chorus of soft chuckles. "Aren't you?" The sudden prickle of sharp claws on her shoulder didn't break flesh but sent a shiver of goosebumps down her body. She straightened, fist clenching around the dagger hilt. "I wonder, what would the helpless princess do if she saw what Aeron's power could do to her beloved?"

The vision flashed briefly in her mind: Quinn's face contorted into a snarl, his beautiful eyes wild, as blood pooled from his lifeless body, living shadows crawling along his flesh. Aeron merely stood over him, his expression twisted into feral, unhinged laughter.

The light erupted from her as she screamed, the force so violent Joseline rocked back from the impact. It consumed everything, the forest around them invisible against the shimmering white. Shea stayed at her side, their auras pulsing as one with the newfound burst of the Goddess's power.

Shrieks filled the air. Dark specks streaked across her vision, vanishing one by one. The whorls of black flickered in shimmering gold around her.

It burned, the pain of the taunt and the force of gnawing magic threatening to eat her alive. She couldn't take it. The fear and the agony were killing her.

"Joseline!" Kai's voice cried out through the darkness, pulling her back.

The pain waned, the golden light sizzled, then sputtered. She was in the clearing once more, the power nothing but a faint glow at her fingertips. Shea stood at her feet, snowy fur glowing a soft, shimmering gold.

Joseline sucked in a lungful of air, relaxing. The terror, soothed by the ancient presence, still hovered in the back of her mind. Her arms and neck were covered in large and small scratches where the invisible demons' teeth pierced through flesh. She wiped away a trickle of blood from her lip, her fists clutching the dagger to her chest.

Broken from the trance, her eyes wandered to Kai, who stood gaping at her. Joseline parted her lips to speak, but no sound emerged, and she ran a hand through wild, wind-blown curls.

Kai straightened, whispering, "Goddess-blessed indeed."

twenty

The shadow whispered through the main tent, dancing along the earth in anxious anticipation. Quinn looked up from the map sprawled across the table, brows furrowing. "What in Sauda's name?" He sent Fallon a curious glance.

His mentor frowned. "I don't like the looks of that." Straightening, he moved toward the tent flap, his scowl deepening when he pushed the fabric aside.

"What is it?" Quinn asked, moving to stand beside him. The breath lodged in his throat as he took in the darkness enveloping the camp. It reached along the ground, coating the world in thick darkness that made it near impossible to see through. Shouts echoed from the surrounding tents as the soldiers shifted, preparing to move onto the offensive.

"Fallon?"

Before his mentor could reply, Larina and Kai came into view, weapons drawn, several of their captains on their heels. They moved toward the tent with determined precision, but Quinn's stare focused on the small, shaking form huddled between them, her hands clasped at her chest doing nothing to hide the blood covering her shoulders in thin scrapes.

Joseline.

Quinn's heart fell into his stomach, panic coursing through him when he met her eyes. They entered the tent, and he swept Joseline into his arms before she could protest. "Gods above, Joseline," he murmured, stroking wild curls. "I thought you said you were only going to practice just outside the camp. What in Kyaos' name happened?"

Joseline only shook her head, burying her face in Quinn's chest. Before she could say more, Larina let out a snarl, slamming a fist onto the table. Slowly, Quinn turned to face them. The only thing stopping him from marching up to Kai and demanding answers was Joseline's grip on his vest. He looked down at her, his chest tightening at the scratches along her back and hands, her green gown's flowing sleeves torn in several places.

It just made the growl in his throat deeper. "You have two seconds to explain what happened to her, or not even the Goddess will be able to help you."

Larina kept an arm around Kai's waist, leather creaking as Logan and her other commanders tightened their grip on their sword hilts. Joseline looked up at him, knuckles white.

"Quinn," she whispered hoarsely. "I'm alright." Her eyes shifted toward the others, then back to him.

He nodded, still frowning as Larina pointed to a spot on the map. "This is where you were?" She glanced toward her mate, releasing her waist to brace herself against the table.

Kai nodded, running a hand through her hair as she glanced to Joseline. "We were attacked by Kagai."

Fallon wiped a hand over his scared chin, crossing his arms. "Now there's a demon I could do without ever seeing again."

Instinctively Quinn pulled Joseline closer as his eyes flitted over the scratches covering ivory skin, his heart clenching. "Invisible demons?" Suddenly Fallon's nonsense lessons on every lesser demon in The Shadowplains didn't seem so pointless.

Shea's tail curled around his ankle. *She's alright, Quinn.*

"They attacked while we were training." Kai placed a pin in the map. "They targeted her."

"So, what happened?" Quinn asked, forcing his breath to remain calm. Azuri's weight landed on his shoulder, the faerie's presence soft and comforting.

Kai was silent for a moment before she replied, "The princess unleashed her power. She annihilated them into nothing."

Quinn glanced down at Joseline, raising an eyebrow. "You did?"

Her eyes shimmered with pain, darting to Kai before fixating on him. "They said they were going to hurt you. I...I couldn't..."

"That must explain the darkness," Quinn looked toward Logan. "Kagai trail darkness with them, right?"

Pursing her lips, Larina nodded.

"They cloaked half of Ebondenn looking for her." Ren circled his finger around the map just north of the pin.

"We should leave," Fallon said. "We've caused you trouble and overstayed our welcome."

"No." Larina rubbed her temples. "They've attacked before. It just means we move again." She waved a hand toward Logan and Ren. "Alert the others. We leave in three days. That should be enough time. We'll move west, toward Raenya. Joseline needs to get there anyway."

They left without a word.

Tension still hung in the air, though it was significantly less now. Quinn cleared his throat as Joseline loosened her grip, his arm falling away from her waist. "Any word from Jenson?"

"No. And there probably won't be." Fallon's smile didn't reach his eyes. "He'll be fine, boy."

Quinn sighed. "I know. It's just strange without him, without both of them."

"Fallon." They both turned to Larina. "I'm glad you removed part of the block on his memory. I know you don't want to push it, and you both have some things to work through." Her gaze shifted toward Quinn. "But if he really is a twin with the Elirona name, you might want to consider removing whatever blocks him from shifting. Even without his twin, the ability to transform could be greatly beneficial to us."

Questions without answers whispered along his tongue, but before Quinn could ask, Larina was gone. He eyed Fallon, Joseline's fingers brushing his in reassurance. "Care to explain what that means?" He jerked his head toward the tent flap still swaying in the light breeze. "Or anything really. You owe me an explanation by now, Fallon. I've been patient long enough waiting for you to be ready to tell me."

Fallon's stare didn't falter. "When you were a boy, I blocked your memory, as you know."

Quinn nodded, gritting his teeth. "But you removed it."

"I did, but I had to put a separate block on your magic." When Quinn frowned, he rushed on. "Even with your memory gone, you talked about Evalyn in your sleep. Your bond is stronger than I anticipated. There was too much as stake, that's why I never took you to your father. I couldn't risk..."

"Why didn't I ever question it?" he stared down at the aquamarine gem around his neck as he fiddled with it, the stone cool in his palm. "The pendant." He tangled the leather cord in his fingers.

"Correct." Fallon ran a hand around the back of his neck then along his scar. "It helped conceal your power to shift until I removed the first block and decreased the magic from growing out of control. I gave it to you after—"

"I burned down Swan Lagoon as a boy. I remember."

Fallon nodded. "And, as I said in Rivedas, it stops your Fae appearance from surfacing. As long as you wear it, you'll appear mortal."

"Right." Quinn pursed his lips, brows furrowing. "I still don't understand why you didn't tell me." *Why you didn't take me home.*

"I did what I thought was best. Your life was, *is*, too valuable...and you were only a boy. I had no idea what your life was like, only that you were already running from demons. I thought hiding the truth might give you a better chance at surviving."

"I suppose that's reasonable, right?" Joseline murmured.

Quinn let out a half-laugh, not quite sure what to make of his answer. He let go of Joseline, stepping toward Fallon. "So, is there another block that needs to be removed?"

"No, you can shift if you wish to."

Quinn nodded, not meeting his eyes. "How?"

Fallon hesitated. "I should warn you, the first change will be sudden and uncomfortable."

He raised an eyebrow. "You're the last person I'd expect to warn me about things that will cause me pain."

Sadness flickered in Fallon's expression. "I am sorry. I genuinely thought if you forgot and I raised you myself..."

Quinn took another step toward his mentor, to comfort or reassure, he wasn't sure. "It hurts that you didn't tell me. I don't know if I can forgive you just yet. I mean, it's a lot to ask someone to accept, Fallon, even for you. I'm trying, but..."

"I truly am sorry." The defeated tone was strange coming from him.

"The forgiveness will take time." Quinn put a hand on Fallon's shoulder. Azuri flew away from the motion. "But I can't really hate you for having my best interests in mind, I suppose." He chuckled softly, adding, "You did save my life after all."

"I'd be lost without this idiot," Joseline said from behind him.

"Dead," Quinn corrected. "You'd be very dead, if I had to guess."

Joseline's sweet laugh eased the tension hovering between him and his mentor. "Well, then you have my thanks for both our lives, Fallon, even if he is an idiot."

A gust of air tugged on the tent flaps, swirling stray leaves about their feet. The strong aroma of campfire and roasted ham intoxicated his senses. Overcome with its simple beauty, Fallon's voice echoed from an eternity away. Quinn blinked. "Hmm?"

"What would you like me to do?" A question filled with endless possibility—purpose, fear, risk. A question to determine so much.

Quinn drew a ragged breath, glancing at Joseline before meeting Fallon's silver eyes. "I think I'd like to know what this wolf within me is capable of."

"Small steps." Fallon said, placing a hand on his shoulder. "Focus on the magic flowing through you. Picture the wolf in your mind, become one with it."

Quinn obeyed, a bone-chilling ache piercing the base of his skull. It was sharper than he expected, stabbing and slightly painful. He hissed, reaching out for the edge of the table. Clouds of turquoise and dark streaks tangled together, blurring his vision.

The sensation jolted through him, and he gasped before he could stop it, his grip on the table tightening. The fog vanished and he blinked, meeting Fallon's eyes. "What happened?"

"Don't fight it. If you fight it, you're only fighting yourself and the shift won't happen."

Nodding, Quinn glanced at Joseline. She offered a reassuring smile before he closed his eyes again, welcoming the ache along his skull. It gripped his subconscious, threatening to choke out his air, but he gritted his teeth. *I will not faint. Not now. Don't even think about it.* Blinding light electrified his senses in response.

He stumbled, shocked and unsteady at the sensation. Fallon caught him around the waist as his knees buckled. "Easy Quinn, easy."

Cool hands brushed damp hair from his eyes, his vision still clouded. "Don't go fainting on me now, that isn't very princely."

"Joseline," he growled, "you aren't helping."

She laughed, but he ignored it, relieved she was by his side. Slowly the pain faded, and his vision returned. Joseline knelt before him, a strange look in her eyes. He opened his mouth to speak, but stopped, his eyes drawn to the long wolf's snout and sleek onyx fur covering his body.

"You look..." Joseline couldn't form the words as she reached a hand toward him, stroking it over his head and behind his ear.

Quinn huffed out a breath, fighting the growl in his throat as he rolled his eyes. Shea gave him an approving nod, swishing her tail across his snout as she walked past, rubbing herself against him. His growl warranted a laugh from Fallon. "I'll admit, I didn't expect the change would be *that* sudden. Then again, I suppose I should expect that from you of all people by now."

Quinn must have made a pathetic face because Shea said, *You can speak. Will the words into their minds.*

He let out another huff, and Joseline smiled. "Your eyes are the same."

Quinn stood, taking a step toward her on unsteady paws. *Walking on four legs is going to take some getting used to.* He tried to sit back, awkwardly tumbling to the side. *As is that.*

"Why don't you go for a run? Maybe that will help you get accustomed to this form," Fallon suggested.

Quinn whined, the sound both surprising and frustrating. Azuri seated himself on Quinn's head. "Very handsome, Your Highness. I have to say, I like this form better." Quinn rolled his eyes again, his glare stopping Joseline's laugh.

The breeze swirled leaves along the ground once more, drawing his attention to the dancing aromas, the sensation of the wind ruffling through his fur. He closed his eyes, the surrounding senses heightened as he breathed in a deep lungful of air.

It was exhilarating. His new form craved it, all of it. The wind whispered from the trees outside the tent. With one last look at Joseline and Fallon, he raced into the forest.

The wild freedom coursed through him, new and exhilarating, electrifying his magic as if it were alive. Azuri swirled around him, iridescent wings sparkling in the sunset, sapphire whorls of dust trailing in his wake. The wind beat against him, caressing silky fur. The forest called to him as it had so many times in his childhood, whispering promises as magic surged and pulsed through his blood. He pushed himself faster, muscles rippling, paws sinking into the soft earth. With a final gleeful breath, he howled into the glowing evening around him.

A shimmering ripple caught his eye to the left, pulling him toward it. Azuri paused, resting against Quinn's shoulders as he padded toward the light, cocking his head to the side as a small clearing opened before him.

Awe replaced any hesitation left in his body. He wasn't sure he'd ever seen anything more captivating. Tiny whorls of light floated through the air, dancing and twirling like faeries on the breeze. They reflected along the small pond and through the rustling patches of ferns, glistening in the setting sun.

"What is this place?"

Quinn's head darted toward the sound of Joseline's voice. Had anyone else managed to sneak up on him, he would have been irritated.

But not with her. His pulse quickened, thundering in his chest.

Never with her.

Shea curled her tail around Joseline's leg, sending him a smirk as Azuri settled on her haunches. Quinn narrowed his eyes in response and Joseline sat beside him. Turquoise mist enveloped him, swirling around his body and clouding his vision. When it vanished, he sat beside her, a man once more, his tattoo glowing. Only the slightest twinge of pain pulsed along his neck.

"Quinn?"

He blinked, turning to her. "I have no idea. Something just led me here."

Her eyes glided over the clearing, the floating lights twinkling. Her laugh bounced off them, the sound as pure as the magic itself. "Well, whatever it is, it's the most beautiful thing I've ever seen."

Unsure if it was from the exhilaration of newfound magic or the way his blood heated, Quinn couldn't look away from her. Fiery curls reflected the golden sunset like molten lava spilling around her slender shoulders. Freckles brushed like stardust along her flushed cheeks. Those forest-green eyes matched the simple dress, fabric clinging to her shoulders, flowing down her arms and out around her hips, secured beneath the corset cinched and accentuating her narrow waist. Her eyes danced with hope despite the darkness following their every move.

She was stunning. Wildly captivating.

His heartbeat stuttered, beating so violently he was sure she could hear it. He lifted a hand to tuck a curl behind her ear. She turned to him then, the words on his tongue almost frozen, but he spoke them anyway.

"No. Places like this are magical maybe, or mystical." The world slowed, the only thing that mattered her and the agonizing space between them. Quinn smiled, searching her face. "But they can't be beautiful."

The fire in her eyes blazed. "And why not?" Her nose flared slightly, her sweet voice near inaudible.

The breeze spun around them, mixing with light and fire, their magics enveloping one another. Her breath tickled his skin, their noses so close they were almost touching. Quinn had to refrain from reaching for her too soon.

"Because," he whispered, his eyes never leaving hers. "Because you are by far the most beautiful thing here, Joseline."

Whatever Quinn expected, it wasn't her grip on his tunic. He braced a hand on the ground, rocking forward as her mouth crushed his.

His pulse thundered in his chest with sweet desire. Her lips were so soft—curious, willing, gentle. The energy swirled around them, sparking and humming as a small moan escaped her lips.

He'd wondered for a long time what kissing her would feel like, but nothing prepared him for the reality. It was pure magic, beyond anything he expected it to be.

When they broke apart, Joseline's dancing eyes met his. Her throat bobbed with each breath, but she never looked away. "You think I'm beautiful?" She brushed hair from his face, her eyes flicking to his mouth once more. "And just how many women have you fed your sweet nothings to?"

"Quite a few," he admitted. "But none of them as special as you." He tucked another runaway curl behind her ear. "I've always thought you were beautiful, Joseline." He cupped her face in his hands, sending a blush spreading over her cheeks.

With that, he tangled his fingers in her hair and covered her mouth with his. Her lips were just as sweet, warmer now, the energy heating his blood as she leaned into his body. He ran a hand down her back, hers sliding up his chest, linking behind his neck. Time stopped, the air humming with an electrifying lullaby only they could hear, the ancient melody synchronizing with their racing heartbeats.

Quinn let out a gasp at her unexpected grip on his hair, her mouth smiling against his. He breathed in her scent, the lilac notes intoxicating. Faster and faster the wild breeze spun, their bodies entangling with one another. Quinn tightened his grip on her waist, all but dragging her small body against him, moving his hips with hers. Her moan jolted energy through his blood as he caressed her back with roaming hands.

More, his mind begged. His body throbbing, heating. *More.* She arched slightly, her body pleading with his unspoken promises.

No, he thought, coming to his senses. He broke away, gripping her shoulders gently. "Joseline," he murmured, his eyes searching her face before he pressed a kiss to her temple. "Not yet."

She blinked, her gaze flickering over his chest before she curled into him with a nod. She stroked delicate fingers along his neck, toying with the leather cord holding the pendant, tracing the ink of his tattoo. "Are you alright?"

Quinn laughed, biting his lip. "More than alright."

Joseline's finger danced over the swirling ink on his neck, the touch sending delighted shivers along his spine. "I think I've known that would happen for a long time. I just needed to stop hiding from my feelings."

He swirled lazy circles on her bare shoulder, his chest rumbling with a chuckle. "I've never been good at admitting my feelings. But with you..." He kissed her temple again. "It's different with you. It's always been different with you. Even when I couldn't admit it, I knew it would be. And now...I've never felt that way with anyone, especially not from just a kiss."

"*Just* a kiss?" Her lips brushed his, sweet and gentle. Still, his heart somersaulted from the pure exhilaration. "Well, *I've* never even been kissed."

"I am well aware of that," Quinn mused, still fighting to calm the soft ache as she shifted to sit beside him, their movements syncing to balance one another. He toyed with a curl and she hummed, her head resting against his chest.

"Personally, I've yet to determine if I trust anything you say when it comes to girls, given your ravenous reputation."

Quinn snorted. "I can't blame you, I suppose."

They were silent for a long time, the breeze whispering promises through the forest on glittering moonbeams. His heart trembled suddenly, and Quinn wished they could remain blinded by the magic forever, never returning to the looming darkness.

As if sensing his thoughts, Joseline sighed. "What now?"

Quinn bit his lip, brushing soft fingers along the cuts covering her shoulders. "Now, we go back to reality. We keep going, get you to Raenya. We take it one day at a time."

Joseline nodded but gripped his tunic when he tried to stand. "Whatever the future holds, whatever happens with Aeron, we do it together." Her eyes shimmered with a thousand promises. A hope for a brighter future, a better one.

"We've always done it together," Quinn said. "Even before we knew the truth about me."

She pulled him forward, their lips meeting fierce and strong. "Promise me, Quinn. Promise."

Quinn tangled his fingers in her hair, lifting her face to search her eyes. They swirled with emotion, love, determination. He would never let that light fade from her eyes. "You have my word. Together, always."

He said no more, and they sat listening to the blissful serenity, the moonlight above showering them in stardust.

twenty-one

Edan allowed himself one final moment to admire his reflection before nodding and reaching for his cloak. He smoothed a hand along the embroidered overcoat, midnight blue shimmering faintly with silver. Fastening the cloak at his throat, he closed the balcony doors then crossed the room to slip on his boots. He released one final sigh before straightening and turning the knob.

Answers. They needed answers. The library was the most logical place to start searching for them. Slipping into the hall, Edan let out a startled gasp, nearly colliding with Fi where she leaned against the wall outside his door. It clicked shut behind him. "Noria be damned, you could announce your presence, you know."

She snorted, crossing her arms. "We need to talk."

Edan frowned. The shadow twins hadn't spoken to him since they arrived several days ago. Curse Noria, he'd barely seen them in the halls or during meals, and all he could think of was the way Fi's teasing made his pulse race. Even now, the traitorous emotions threatened to surface, but he locked them away.

"What about?" He began walking, not waiting to see if she followed.

"Naoi and I just returned from a scouting patrol along the Northlands' border."

That explained why he hadn't seen them. "And?" He ran a hand along the railing as he rounded down the staircase to the main level, robes flapping in the breeze.

"The Northmen are preparing to march. Here or toward Ravencrest, I don't know."

Her words froze him. "What?" He could barely breath, his blood chilling in fear. "How do you know?"

"I've fought them before, seen them prepare for battle. And usually when an army is gathering their forces in war camps along their borders, it means they're planning to march." She favored her left hip. "So, *Master Edan*, what do you plan to do?"

Edan continued walking, striding off the final step and into the main courtyard. "I don't know," he murmured.

With exams officially over, the courtyard was littered with students preparing for Malonas, the festival acknowledging the fall equinox on the twenty-third of Nova. The eshacca trees, rare fauna that maintained their leaves year-round, were beginning the change from summer green to fall gold.

"Master Edan!" Neirin approached, holding up two banners, one deep red and one a shimmering dandelion. "Which do you prefer?" His eyes fluttered down Edan's chest for only a moment before returning to his face. "They're meant to be the flags lining the bonfires at the festival."

"What color do the eshacca leaves turn to honor the fall harvest?" Edan asked.

"Gold."

Edan smiled. "Then I think the gold would be more fitting for the occasion, don't you?"

"Yes, yes, of course." Neirin blushed and hurried away, ebony curls blowing about his face.

"He likes you," Fi murmured.

Edan coughed. "I'm sorry, what?" The heavy stone doors to the library groaned when he opened them.

Fi smirked. "That boy, he likes you."

"I'm not blind," Edan shook his head. "But I'm his professor, and

I'm not interested in affairs that could cost me my job. I do enjoy it." The doors swung shut, the soft lamplight significantly duller than the sunshine.

"I am curious, though."

Edan let out an exasperated sigh, crossing his arms and facing her. "About?"

"About the non-virgin claim you made," she purred, and his eyes flickered to the surrounding bookshelves for fear of listening ears. "I enjoy flirting with you, Edan. You're amusing when you're flustered."

His temper lashed out before he could stop it, and he pushed her back against the wall, his grip holding her hands over her head. She let out a small gasp, challenge flaring in her eyes. "Your flirting, sweet Fi, is obnoxious. I was in love with someone, a long time ago, and he died. He died because I was too weak to save him." Edan released her hands and she straightened her vest. "Satisfied?"

The challenging gaze faded slightly when she passed him, slender curves swaying. "For now, but not for long."

"And if I told you I'm no longer interested in such relations?"

Lilac shimmered as she eyed him, trailing her gaze down his body as if she could smell the heat coursing through him. "I wouldn't believe you for a second."

The truth in her parting words sent a ripple of longing down his spine. It had been years since someone awoke that longing. He sighed, following her to where she crouched halfway down the aisle, brushing her fingers along the aged volumes.

"This library is ancient," he said, smiling at her jump.

"I see that," she breathed, standing. "Are you looking for anything specific?"

He strode past her, eyeing the books. "I think so. It's been ages since I've read it, but I believe there's a way we could shield the Chiron."

"You mean a barrier spell?" She jogged to catch up.

Edan frowned. "Sort of. It would dome the building, make it completely invisible so only those who know of the barrier could find it." He paused, taking out a large book, then continued on. "If memory serves me correctly, it should be impenetrable as well."

"That would be very useful."

He nodded, scanning the higher shelves. "Hold this?" He didn't bother checking if Fi took the book as it slipped from his hand, pulling a ladder toward him. Several rows up, he let out a pleased grunt, removing another smaller tome.

"Naoi is with Superior Albion," Fi said once he was on the floor again. "Should we go to them?"

"These should be a good place to start," he muttered to himself. "I'm not sure how much time we might have. First, we need the approval of the other masters. Then, I can start searching for the rest of the volumes." He examined one of the spines. "This one should have several more in the field…I know there are others, but it will be a challenge to find them. Neirin should be able to help, the boy might as well be a master librarian." He began walking, startled by Fi's grip on his arm. "What?"

"Should we go to them?" she repeated.

Edan blinked. "Yes, that's where I was going."

She pursed her lips, favoring her left hip again. "You love it in here."

The comment took him by surprise. "What do you mean?"

"In here," she gestured to the bookshelves reaching the ceiling. "Your eyes are shining. You look relaxed, at peace. That's how Erza looks when she flies."

Edan laughed. "I told you, Fi, you don't know anything about me." He continued toward the main doors.

"I'd like to."

He rolled his eyes. "I'm sure you would."

"You know, I've never had a man I flirted with deny me." She glanced at him sidelong, fluttering her lashes. "Especially not an attractive man."

"Sounds like your ego could use a rejection."

"Forever?"

His mouth twitched, the smile threatening to surface. "Maybe." He pushed the door open, relishing in the chill prickling his flesh. "I need to protect my students first."

"You're sure about this, Master Edan?"

Edan shook his head, leaning against Superior Albion's worktable. "No, I'm not sure about any of it."

"It wouldn't hurt to look into, right?" Fi asked, still skimming one of the thick tomes from the library. "What have you got to lose?"

Albion was silent for a moment. "Nothing," he sighed. "We need to consult with the other masters before we try anything, though."

"Of course," Edan agreed.

"I'll request their presence at a meeting then. For now, we can do no more, I'm afraid."

Edan recognized the dismissal, Naoi and Fi following him out of the Superior's chambers. They were halfway back to his rooms before Fi spoke. "Do you think the masters will agree?"

Edan ran a hand through his hair. "The masters can be...fickle. I don't know what they'll say."

"But you're a master, too," Fi pointed out.

Edan laughed. "Yes, but I was raised to be heir by Superior Albion himself. The other masters were not, and some of them don't always approve of me. So knowing it was my idea..."

"Convincing them might be a challenge," Naoi finished.

Edan needed to think. He needed to meditate, to clear the emotions gripping his mind. They were suffocating, and the painful memories resurfacing every time he so much as glanced at Fi did nothing to ease his growing frustration.

Waving farewell to Naoi, he ignored Fi as she continued to walk with him toward his rooms. At last he sighed, his hand pausing on the handle. "What do you want, Fi?"

She linked her hands behind her back, fidgeting. "I..."

"What?" he growled.

"I'm sorry."

Edan frowned. "For?"

She wrung her hands, studying the floor. "For the flirting. If...if it really bothers you that badly, I'll stop. I just don't get to do it often with men who fight it, that gets rather dull."

Edan swore, slipping his fingers beneath her chin. "I'm not angry about it, Fi. I just haven't had someone do it so openly in a long time."

"Since the man you loved?"

The firm wall around his heart refused to budge. "Yes." His fingers fell away.

She met his eyes. "If you need to talk about it, I could..."

"Not right now," he interrupted. "Maybe someday."

Fi smiled, and turned to go.

"Fi?" She faced him again. "For the record, if my past were different, I probably wouldn't fight it as much either."

Her eyes danced. "Someday, Master Edan. For now, meet me in the courtyard tomorrow morning. I want to show you something."

Edan watched her go, folding his arms across his chest and leaning against the door as she swished her hips. Then, smiling, he let himself into his room.

"You know, most mortals think that Kitsugon are just a myth. That they died out centuries ago." Edan laughed nervously, eyeing the deep blue creature stalking around the outer wall, barbed tail twitching in anticipation.

Fi's eyes blazed with amusement. "Most mortals are dull and boring."

He gulped, smiling weakly as the Kitsugon watched him. "So what exactly are we doing?"

She trailed a lazy finger down his spine as she walked past, sucking on her bottom lip. "Riding, of course. Why do you think I told you to wear something more casual?" Fi stroked the creature's snout, the scaled edges along her face narrowing into various points around her head.

"If you think I'm getting on that thing, you're mistaken."

"She won't bite...not unless I tell her to." Fi nipped the air in his direction. "Isn't that right, Endra?" The Kitsugon chirped in agreement, tawny eyes narrowing on Edan.

His pulse quickened. "I'm not…"

"A witch who's afraid of heights?"

Edan gritted his teeth. "And what if I am?"

"How pathetic," Fi mused, adjusting the clasps of her riding leathers.

"I'm not pathetic…lest you forget, I wasn't raised a witch, Fi." He stalked toward her, prepared to yank her around and meet her eyes, but she turned and braced a hand against his chest as if she expected the movement. "Then why don't you climb up there and show me how *not* pathetic you are, *Master Edan*?"

His pulse quickened, and he could have sworn Endra chuckled. "Fine." He gripped her azure fur, the Kitsugon adjusting slightly so he could hoist himself into the saddle on her back.

A second later, Fi jumped up, her backside pressing against him. "Don't get too excited now," she crooned, wiggling herself into his chest.

"You're ridiculous," he murmured, ignoring the flash of heat that rippled through him as she fastened the riding buckles. "I really don't think this is—"

Endra's sudden lunge cut off his words, and he gasped, wrapping his arms tightly around Fi's waist. She laughed, grinning back at him. "Do you trust me, Edan?" she called above the roaring wind and flapping wings.

"Not in the slightest!"

"Perfect. Use your instincts then."

"I don't—"

But she turned back to Endra, massive wings beating on either side as the creature rose higher into the clouds. "Fly, girl," she said, stroking the Kitsugon's ears. "We need to scare him a little."

Edan refused to look down, his stomach flipping somersaults. "No, no, you don't need to scare me at all. I'm perfectly alright with not being scared."

She pressed her shoulders back, meeting his eyes. "Come now, Master Edan, where would be the fun in that?"

Edan opened his mouth to reply, but cut off as Endra bunched her haunches and dove toward the earth. Edan fought down a scream, squeezing Fi's waist tighter as his eyes slammed shut. His pulse thundered, his heart beating so violently he thought it would burst from his chest.

"Edan, it's alright," Fi whispered, her voice surprisingly soft. "Open your eyes, this is the best part."

His pulse slowed ever-so-slightly. Carefully, he opened one eye, then the other, the breath lodging in his throat. He wasn't sure where to look first—the distant sea, the majestic beauty of the frozen Northlands, or the clouds dancing around them. The fear faded slightly, replaced by awe at the sheer loveliness of the world. A world he'd never seen like this—couldn't see like this from the ground. The salty wind caressed his skin, the sea shimmering like blue crystals on the horizon. It rippled through his hair, the chilling cold all but forgotten, a minor sacrifice to the exquisite freedom. It was pure beauty.

Edan considered looking down, wondering if he'd imagined the centuries of fear, but the nervous shiver stopped him. "I'm still not looking down," he murmured. He shook his head, fists bunching as he snapped his gaze upward.

"This is my favorite part," Fi breathed. "No matter where we fly, what we're sent to do, the view above the clouds is always breathtaking."

Edan didn't trust his voice, the wall around his heart rippling just slightly. "And if you were sent to kill?"

"Even death becomes beautiful from up here."

The wall hardened again. "Death is never beautiful."

Endra glided through the clouds, dipping and weaving along the currents. Fi sighed, turning away. "You would be such a different ruler from your mother."

"Am I wrong?" he asked, his voice stronger.

"No, you aren't."

He sighed. "It doesn't matter anyway. I'll never be a ruler. I don't want to be."

"Nobody wants to rule, Edan."

Again, her comment took him by surprise. "Not even Erza?"

Fi laughed then, guiding Endra north. "*Especially* not Erza." She paused for a moment before adding, "You two aren't so different, you know."

Before he could reply, the thick smell of smoke coated his lungs. Edan frowned, peering over Fi's shoulder.

The camps along the Northlands border stretched on for miles. Large campfires filled in holes around clusters of tents, the air echoing with gruff shouts and neighing horses even from this height. There must be at least five thousand troops, as if the Northmen had gathered all their clans in a call to war.

"There's so many of them." Panic filled his chest.

Fi nodded. "I've never seen them all gathered like this. The Elites have dispatched troublesome Northmen before among the varying clans, but this many..."

"That's not common?"

"No, they normally can't stand one another and fight amongst themselves." She veered Endra east, following the line of tents.

Edan searched for something, anything that might be able to help them prepare for the possible attack, a hint of what the vicious clans were planning. But he was no general; he knew nothing about battles and demons aside from the stories he'd read as a boy or the ones Karo, the master storyteller, whispered around the hearth on cold winter nights.

Something rippled in his vision along the shore. "There," he pointed, Endra following his finger.

The Northmen moved through a small mountain pass, carrying what looked to be heavy bundles into small boats. They were all similar, a black flag waving at their masts—two crossed scythes, their long hilts circled in black to form an X in the center.

Edan's blood went cold. "They aren't all attacking the Chiron. They aren't all marching on Ravencrest, either."

"How do you know that?" Fi asked, narrowing her eyes.

"Because," Edan pointed again, this time out over the Terboia Sea, "Narcio Island is that way. Whatever they're loading into those ships, they're taking to Narcio."

"Then we should go scout it." Fi urged Endra forward with a click of her tongue, but Edan yanked on the reins, his hands shaking. "Are you out of your mind?"

She glared back at him. "What are you talking about? It's just scouting, that's what I'm here for."

"Aeron's henchmen rule Narcio. They enslave healers there and torture them."

Fi tried to take the reins back, but Edan kept his grip firm. "Edan, Noria be damned, let go!"

"I'm not going there." The panic rose in his chest, memories flooding through his mind as he fought desperately to push them back behind a mental wall. "Fi, if you want to get yourself killed, then fine. But take me back to the Chiron, *now*."

The shake in his voice must have convinced her. She stopped fighting his grip on the reins, letting him guide them. Endra flew straight and true, her wings beating occasionally to maintain their height. The wind rushed past them, soothing him, calming the nerves and the pain.

"The man you loved, what was his name?" Fi's voice was so soft, Edan almost didn't hear it above the rustling breeze.

"What?"

"What was his name?" she repeated.

Edan's lip quivered slightly, the wall spilled open, only for a second, images flooding into his consciousness: Those dark hazel eyes shining with so much life, so much love, fading in death against the cold snow. The sweet smile and square cut jaw that haunted his dreams. The innocence they'd lost together, and the death he hadn't been able to stop.

Foolish. Damn The Twelve, they'd been so foolish.

He shut the wall before the tears could fall. "Kiran. His name was Kiran."

"A ray of light," Fi whispered its meaning, leaning back against him with a smile. "He sounds like a ray of light to you."

Edan's chin trembled. "Yes, he was."

They said nothing else as they landed outside the Chiron's outer wall. Fi unclasped the buckles and slid to the ground, Edan following her on unsteady legs.

"There you are, we've been looking all over for you!" Naoi ran toward them, Neirin and Milla at her heels.

Edan eyed the young students, folding his arms. "You really shouldn't drag them into business with the masters."

"Superior Albion asked us to help her find you," Neirin said. Milla nodded in agreement, and Edan shrugged, starting toward the gated archway leading into the courtyard. "Well, I'm here now, what is it?"

"The masters agreed to meet," Naoi said. "Your presence is required in the council room."

Edan glanced over at Fi, his chest still fluttering from both the personal information he'd shared and the exhilaration of flight. She was right, he hadn't wanted to come back down. Edan pinched the bridge of his nose. "Well, I suppose we should get this over with then." He didn't wait to see if they followed him inside.

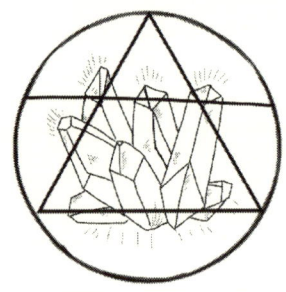

twenty-two

There was no sense of time in the shadows.

Dax's throat had long gone dry with the desire for water. He just hoped, for Elyon's sake, Cohen and Naomi actually had a plan. The Shadow Beasts slipped in and out of the room like wraiths, coming for either Elyon or Kellen. When they returned, the boys were hollow, eyes glazed over in inexplicable torment from whatever they'd gone through.

But never him.

Dax wasn't sure if he should be glad or worried. Regardless, it did nothing to ease the constant uncertain anticipation that hung in the air.

He eyed the young man beside him, wetting his lips. "So, Kellen, is it?"

Kellen blinked. "That's right."

"What's your story?"

Kellen shrugged, his gaze falling to the floor. "It's not worth telling."

"Everyone has a story worth telling."

He laughed at that. "Not me. I'm done trying to fool myself into believing I'm worth anything." He paused, and Dax said nothing, sensing there was more. "I'll...I'll never be strong enough to help her," he sighed. "I'm too weak to save her, or Elyon, or anyone. I don't even know who I'm trying to fool anymore." Defeat rippled through Kellen's voice.

"Who?" Dax prompted.

Another pause. "My mother. The whole reason I agreed to help the cursed monsters in the first place is because they hold her prisoner. At least, that's what they told me."

"What of your father?" he asked.

Kellen laughed, the sound laced with grief. "My father was a stronger man than I'll ever be."

"Why do you say that?" Dax twisted his neck slightly, hissing when it released a soft crack.

"He...he would never break his vows. He took them seriously to his death. But I couldn't even do that." Again, Dax waited for him to continue. "I was a knight of Rathal. Personal guard to Princess Joseline. I swore to protect her with my life."

Dax raised an eyebrow. "That's rather impressive." Kellen let out a half-laugh. "And did you? Protect her, I mean."

"No." Kellen hung his head. "I betrayed her, and it backfired." He sniffed. "The hope that I can save my mother is all I have left. I have to get to her before—"

"Don't let them hear you talk like that," Dax whispered. "They'll kill her for sure if they hear you."

Kellen gulped. "How do you know?"

"Because that's what they do. They take your worst fears and use them to destroy you." His chest clenched.

"I take it you know from experience?"

"Aye," Dax nodded. "They destroyed everything I loved. And now they're going to use me to hurt the only one I kept trying to protect."

The door creaked open, cutting off Kellen's response. Dax lifted his gaze as Elyon stumbled into the room with a groan. The demons restrained him, but before they could retreat, a sharp laugh echoed from the doorway. "So, it is true."

Dax clenched his jaw. *Toren.*

The foreman sauntered into the room with a crooked, dirty smirk. "I heard you were dead. I must admit, I was rather disappointed. But here you are, alive and well." He paused, scowling up at Dax. "Too bad that little bitch ended up being useless and running away. I would have loved to—"

"Shut your mouth," Dax seethed.

"Or what, *Captain*?" Toren challenged. "Are you going to fight me?"

"I said, shut it."

Toren straightened, making himself as tall as possible, though he only came up to Dax's chin. "You can't do anything to me, that's what you hate the most, isn't it? I could sit here and say whatever I want, and there's nothing you can do about it."

It took all his effort to restrain himself.

"She was rather pleasant to look at, wasn't she?" Toren ran his tongue along his teeth. "Quite the figure, for a slave. Tell me, what was she like? I've always wondered what a Fae woman was capable of in bed—"

The crack of their skulls colliding echoed through the chamber when Dax headbutted him.

Toren stepped away clutching his nose, spouting a stream of curses. Dax refused to groan, but his vision blurred slightly from the impact. *Gods above, that was stupid.*

"Sauda be damned," Toren groaned, clutching his nose.

So worth it, though.

It was an effort to remain calm, but Dax focused on his breath, clenching and unclenching his fists. "Don't talk about her like that."

"Enough of your bickering, mortals." The new voice came from the hallway. Elyon and Kellen stiffened as Dax stared up at the newcomer. He grinned back with crimson eyes, their color a stark contrast to the pallor of his skin. He ran a tongue along his lips, biting a long-clawed nail. Like the Shadow Beasts, Aeron's mark branded the flesh between his eyes. He cocked his head to the side, looking first to Dax, then Toren, still clutching his nose. "Quite the firecracker, aren't you, *Captain*?"

"What business is it of yours?" he retorted.

"Listen to you!" he laughed. "So confident and demanding."

"I'm not demanding anything. But I'm not afraid of you, Akuma."

The demon's eyes widened. "Well, now. It's been ages since once of my playthings actually knew what I was." He bit his lip, stepping toward Dax. "How exciting."

"I suppose."

"Oh, I think I'm going to enjoy playing with you, Captain," he smirked, revealing pointed canines.

Dax snorted. "Whatever you say, filthy blood demon."

The Akuma smacked him. "Now, now, be nice. I know you've been rather lonely, what with these two getting all my attention." He paused, running a hand along Dax's chest. "But you've earned a turn, don't you think?" He turned to Toren, scowling. "You will leave him alone, rat."

"As you say," Toren mumbled.

"You two," he said, stopping before the Shadow Beasts guarding the door. "Bring me the Captain first thing in the morning."

The door slammed shut.

"Now you've done it," Elyon hissed. "That demon is a monster."

"I'm not afraid of him," Dax replied.

"You should be," Kellen murmured.

"Maybe. But I refuse to let the dark consume my sanity."

He only hoped that thought would last.

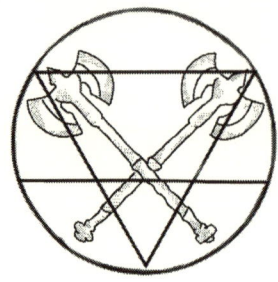

twenty-three

The effort to breathe was unbearable as she fought to swim toward the surface. The water engulfed her, almost blinding.

She'd survived though. She survived even when everyone else around her died. They always died, always left her broken.

But not Quinn. Somewhere, he survived. He was alive.

She wondered if he knew she was, too, if he dreamed of her as she dreamed of him. Why hadn't he come back to them? If they'd been together...

"Listen, if you aren't going to focus, don't waste my time. Rowen doesn't like being in charge of training." Eva blinked at Erza's annoyed tone. "Sorry."

Erza ran a hand through her hair and sighed. "It's fine, just, are you alright? You've been distracted since—"

"Since two strangers told me they know my twin brother, who I assumed was dead for the past twenty years, and then just walked away?" Eva barked a sarcastic laugh. "How am I supposed to feel?"

Erza was silent for a moment. "Do you want to talk about it?"

Eva bit her lip, resting her chin in her hands. "There's nothing to talk about. We were together, then he was gone; we never saw him again."

Her chest tightened at the memory. She'd searched for Quinn everywhere that day before returning home alone. Her mother loved her, she knew that, but part of Zaria died the day Quinn disappeared.

"I'm sorry, I can't imagine what that was like for you," Erza said. "The closest thing I have to siblings are my Elites."

Eva shrugged. "It's alright, it was a long time ago."

"It still hurts though." Erza squeezed her hand, the touch strange and unexpected, yet comforting.

"Of course it still hurts." She released a shuddering sigh. "He was my other half. With him gone..."

"But he isn't gone." Erza smiled. "Maybe you could go with them when they leave."

Eva's chest fluttered. "With Maya and Jenson?" She ignored the light blush that spread across Erza's cheeks at the mention of Jenson.

Shrugging, Erza stood, not flinching as the small boat rocked uneasily. Eva, however, gripped the sides, water splashing onto her boots, soaking the wood. "Gods above, don't do that."

The witch raised an eyebrow, a grin spreading across her face. "Don't do what—this?" Before Eva could object, she was falling, submerged beneath the freezing water as she toppled over the side of the boat.

Panic engulfed her, horror resurfacing as she clawed at her liquid captor. It choked her, filling her lungs as she flailed through the dark, desperate to reach the surface. She gasped as the watery prison released her, only to submerge her once more.

Then she was back inside the boat, soaked and shivering. She sucked in air, her stomach clenching, mind willing her panic to calm. Eva closed her eyes, a hand on her racing heart.

"That is quite a flight response you've got there." Eva scowled at Erza, who chuckled. "I wouldn't have let you drown, you know."

Eva wiped soaking hair back from her face, shivering as a gust of icy wind danced along the lake. "You can't imagine what that was like." She smeared a hand across her nose, sniffing.

"No, but I also learned at a young age how to face my weaknesses head-on." A flicker of sadness flashed in Erza's expression. "Two hundred years old, and I'm the youngest heir in the covens. My mother refused to let age be a weakness."

Eva bit her lip. "What happened?"

Erza frowned. "I had an older sister."

Eva waited for her to continue, wringing the water out of her skirts.

"About a hundred years ago, we had a...disagreement. My mother said we could either move past it and forgive one another, or duel over it. It was a stupid, pointless fight, but my sister...I was always the better fighter."

"Did you kill her?"

"I didn't have a choice."

"We always have a choice."

Erza shrugged. "It doesn't matter. I've since become stronger. The Stormwood Elites are more sisters to me than she ever was. It's...it's always been that way even before I..."

Unsure what else to do, Eva put a hand on Erza's knee. "Thank you for sharing that with me."

Erza straightened, shaking her head. "I don't usually talk about it. My mother's always said witches aren't meant to form attachments. It's just a pointless emotion. Some would even say we're incapable of love, that we're born without hearts...that's why we eat them for fun." She scoffed. "Sometimes, when I see the pain emotions bring people, I almost let myself believe her. It makes you weak."

Eva's brows furrowed, and she pursed her lips. "Is love a weakness if it gives you something to fight for?"

Erza smiled. "No, I suppose you're right."

Cocking her head to the side, Eva said, "I don't mean to pry, but it sounds like you have very different views from your mother."

"We've never gotten along. For as long as I can remember. Her views...I will create a different world than she has. I will have my people's love and respect from more than just fear. Otherwise, I wouldn't feel worthy of calling myself their queen." Sighing, Erza shrugged. "My point in bringing it up to begin with was, fear can still be a powerful tool if you allow it to fuel you. Guide your power with the fear of your enemies rather than letting it control you and you might surprise yourself."

"I think I can manage that." Evalyn closed her eyes, breathing in through her nose, out through her mouth. Her heartbeat slowed, one with the world around her as she honed and focused the energy humming through her veins.

She jumped when Erza reached for her hand. "Good, now, imagine your fears in your mind. Picture them." Eva didn't panic this time, even when Erza took their combined hands and dipped her fingertips into the lake, the boat rocking ever-so-slightly. "Imagine those fears are rippling further away at your command."

The fire heating beneath Eva's skin pulsed, bubbling with each word. It tingled her flesh, calming and soothing as she pulled it up from the caged magic within her.

"The further away the ripples move, the less terrifying they become. They're *your* fears, Eva, no one else's. Don't let them control you."

The seal locking the well of power snapped, collapsing in on itself as if it had never been. The flames surged, rising behind her eyelids, threatening to consume her, but Evalyn shook her head.

No, the voice in her mind whispered. *You cannot destroy me with fire. I am the fire. And I refuse to be your prisoner.*

The flames roared in defiance, but she didn't back down, didn't cower. Images flashed in her vision: her mother's lifeless body. Quinn, smiling and happy at her side. The cottage burning. Dax, young and daring, pulling her from rushing waters. Dax, bloody and dying by her hand. Elyon kneeling before the foreman's whip. Naomi, the servant girl who taught her so much.

Faces she didn't recognize piled into mass graves, the shadow monsters, those they tormented, the blood-red moon. The vow she made to burn that fortress to the ground, to save those she'd left behind, those she hadn't been able to help before she helped herself.

Eva opened her eyes, the raw, blinding power glowing at her fingertips. Flames danced in her palm, pure and unbound wildfire. They flickered softly, wavering with her lack of complete control, but they were pure and vibrant—blue fire, the hottest, the deadliest. It calmed her rage and surged through her, magic sparking into the air around them, encompassing the boat in a shield of living flame, the water shimmering with aquamarine steam.

twenty-four

Erza had left Eva dried, fed, and in her rooms under Rowen's watchful eye over an hour ago, and she was still in shock. She hadn't expected Eva to actually conjure anything. The shield would most likely have broken upon any real impact, but she'd done it.

She walked briskly through Thya's streets, rounding the corner into the main square. The opening ceremony was in a week. Of course, her cloak would rip now when she was expected to wear it. The deep purple fabric blew in the wind behind her as she made her way toward the tailor's shop. Villagers crowded the main walkways, the smell of fish engulfing her from cart-loads of the day's catch. She did her best to smile, but uneasy sidelong glances followed her nonetheless.

Erza suppressed a sigh. No matter how hard she tried to be friendly, there was always someone afraid of her. They'd gotten better in recent years, but her people's fear always frustrated her. She couldn't blame them, not really—not when they looked at her and saw her mother's cruelty. Still, it irked her.

Stupid, superstitious fools, she thought, rounding another corner. She smiled at a merchant, and he looked away instantly, the cart behind him creaking as he quickened his pace. Erza sighed. *If only they could realize I have no interest in becoming my mother. But they're too afraid of me to try.*

"Miss Erza!" The high-pitched cry echoed from a secluded dead-end and she looked up at Sionn, a weak smile tugging on the corners of her mouth. At least not *everyone* was afraid of her. She knelt before him. "Hello there, little man."

He grinned, pointing behind him to a small group of children huddled around a pile of damp logs. Erza's heart clenched. Sionn was the only one who wore a cloak, the others shivering against the harsh breeze. She wished, not for the first time, that the Blackwings cared more for their people. When she was queen, she would change that. "Need some help, huh?"

"Yeah, Sonya went to go look for some dry wood, but she's been gone a long time." He crossed his arms and frowned. "Probably sidetracked with some man."

Erza chuckled, twining her hands around one another, her magic sparking at her fingertips. The current pulsed within her, and she ran a hand along the pile of wood. The fire flickered, brought to life and rising through the wood as she willed it. Several dry twigs buried beneath the heavy ones sparked, crackling with lilac embers before the orange flames consumed them.

"Thank you," one little girl rubbed her hands together, stepping toward the fire.

"It's my pleasure," Erza said.

Sionn gripped her hand as she turned to leave. "Good luck in the competition, Miss Erza. We all know you're gonna win."

"That's the plan." She paused before adding, "Tell your sister I said to keep her urges under control, will you? We don't want her scaring visitors away. Thya gets so few of them."

She brushed a hand through her hair as she made her way to the main road.

"So, I hear you're talking about me, flower."

Erza nearly ran into the brick beside her. Her eyes shifted to the roof and toward the pleasant tenor voice she hadn't been able to get out of her head since she'd first heard it.

When she didn't respond, Jenson grinned, landing before her with cat-like grace. His thick burgundy tunic buttoned up his chest with silver clasps, the only hint of color in his otherwise black garments. His worn boots were slightly splattered with mud, as were his black leather gloves. The beautifully-carved longbow hung off one shoulder. "Is that a yes?"

Erza narrowed her eyes and crossed her arms. "I've been doing no such thing."

Jenson flashed a smirk, raising an eyebrow. "No? That isn't what I heard."

She opened her mouth to make a smart reply, then closed it. "I don't know what you're talking about. Now, if you'll excuse me." She brushed past him and around the corner.

"It's alright if you were, I don't mind."

Erza rolled her eyes, facing him again. "It has nothing to do with you. Sonya... she tends to scare travelers away before they can feel welcome. Especially when they're..." her voice trailed off.

"Especially when they're what?" His words lingered in the space between them.

Erza pursed her lips, favoring her right leg. "Look, Jenson, I don't have time for your teasing." She glanced down at his mud-covered boots. "Why don't you go back to whatever puddle you were jumping in and leave me alone?"

His laugh made her heart flutter as much as the playful look in his dark brown eyes. "Do you always get so riled up when you're nervous, flower?" He took a step toward her, and she retreated, her back pressing into the cold stone sending a chill up her spine. Jenson braced a hand above her head, his eyes never leaving hers.

What in Nova's name was going on? She couldn't actually be nervous.

"I mean, is that right? I make you nervous." Jenson's breath tickled her cheek, but he didn't touch her, his smile teasing against his bronzed russet skin.

Erza released a breath, refusing to look away from him. "I don't get nervous."

"And I don't enjoy teasing women I find attractive, yet here we are, both doing things we say we don't do."

"Well, stop doing it, then." Erza pushed against his chest, walking briskly away from him, away from the intense heat surging through her from his gaze. Screw him, he'd already wasted too much of her time.

"I'll stop if you let me accompany you to wherever you're going."

Erza rolled her eyes, but didn't halt. "You expect me to believe you have any interest in what I'm doing?"

They turned a final corner before reaching the main road. He kept up with her quick pace. "Do you want the truth?" She sent him a glare, and he chuckled. "You're having problems with a dark power you can't explain. Maya and I are here to figure it out."

Erza stopped at that. "What?"

Jenson raised an eyebrow. "Darkness. You know what I'm talking about."

"You seem pretty trusting of what I say about it," she observed, picking up their pace again. "I'm a stranger. For all you know, I could be the cause of the darkness."

Jenson laughed. "I don't trust a damn word that comes out of your mouth, flower."

She paused before a small shop, the open sign hanging half off the hinges in a dirty window. He reached past her, and she held in the smart reply as he opened the door.

At least he was a gentleman.

"Miss Erza, what a surprise!" the shopkeeper rasped.

Erza undid the golden clasp of her cloak, draping it over her forearm. The air symbol—the triangle cut in half by a horizontal line—glimmered lilac in the dim light. "I need this fixed." She laid the torn section of fabric on the counter. "It seems Morana and Lira overloaded the resident Blackwing seamstress for the next month, and I don't have time to travel to Easthaven or Ravencrest. My second gave me your name."

The old woman smiled, wrinkles sprouting around her eyes. "Ahh, Rowen. She's one of my frequent customers. Travels all the way from Ravencrest, or so she tells me."

"So, can you help me?" Erza tapped her nails against the counter, glancing at Jenson.

The woman took the fabric in her arms and nodded. "Of course, it shouldn't take long. Will you and your lover wait here, then?"

Erza coughed, refusing to give Jenson the satisfaction of blushing. "We are not lovers. You have no place to assume such things."

The woman blustered an apology before retreating into a back room concealed by a hanging curtain.

"I'm making you blush already? Impressive, even for me." Jenson leaned back against the counter.

"You must have quite the reputation." Glancing at him, she added, "I thought you said no more teasing."

Jenson held up his hands. "I did. My apologies." There was a moment of silence before he said, "So. The darkness." His pleasant voice was just touched with concern.

She eyed him. Part of her wanted to lie, easy and painless, but the other part of her trusted him. That was the part that terrified her. In two centuries of life, she'd never trusted anyone other than her Elites. Yet here she was, her heart reaching for the stranger, calling to him as if they'd know each other for years and believing him when it made so much more sense not to.

With a sigh, Erza ran a hand through her bangs. "A few weeks ago, we had a death in the Silvermist coven. I've seen a lot, but I've never once seen something that terrified me. Her death terrified me."

She'd hardly talked about Salia with anyone, not even Rowen or Astrid, whom she confided everything to. The Shadow Games were a week away and nobody was closer to figuring out the grotesque murder than when Odessa found her sister's body. Erza worried for the Silvermist witch once the games began...once Morana got her claws on her.

"What terrified you about it? If you don't mind my asking." His warmth at her side stopped the chill from prickling her flesh.

"The shadows." There was no hesitation in her words. "The shadows covering her. They were alive."

Jenson swore, running a hand through onyx hair as he pushed away from the counter. "We need to talk to Maya."

"We?" She shook her head. "I can't just...I have things to do." Her mother would be furious if she wasn't at dinner. She'd already missed it several times this week for Eva's training, and she promised to be there tonight with the other heirs.

The seamstress pushed through the curtain, handing her the cloak. Erza shook it out, checking the work before murmuring her thanks and tossing her a silver coin.

"Maya needs to hear this, too, whatever you have to say." He held the door, smiling as she brushed past him and clasped her cloak at her throat once more.

"Did you not hear me when I said—"

Jenson put a finger to her lips. "Don't worry. It doesn't have to be long." Erza rolled her eyes as he removed his finger and headed for the inn. "Besides, it'll give me a reason to see more of that pretty little face, flower."

Jenson was surprised Maya didn't make a fuss when he knocked on her door with the Stormwood witch—she'd made quite the fuss after their first encounter. But one look at him had her opening the door and locking it again behind them, a flask of honeyed whiskey in her hand.

He hadn't meant to eavesdrop. Noria curse him, he hadn't meant to follow her at all. But he couldn't fight the pull of her presence. Erza was...intoxicating, to say the least, and he wasn't one to fight his urges. Jenson didn't get intoxicated easily anymore. Erza didn't strike him as someone caught off guard by much either, not by desire or worry.

So when she'd mentioned the living shadows, her eyes failing to hide the fear, he couldn't stop the goosebumps prickling his skin. They'd never seen anything like that. Even in all Fallon's books, all they'd encountered in recent months, he'd never seen mention of shadows being *alive*.

"Let me get this straight," Maya said. "The shadows actually moved. Spread like snakes, thin lines moving across her face?"

Erza, cross-legged on the bed, nodded. "It was...odd. I've never felt anything like it besides one other time."

"Which was?" Jenson swigged the spiced whiskey, the burn in his throat settling his nerves.

She hesitated. "It was a few weeks ago, in Easthaven, when I found Eva."

Maya glanced at him, biting her nails. "Eva?"

Erza ran a hand through her short raven hair. "She won't say much about where she came from. Gods above, she hardly says much of anything."

"But?" Jenson prodded.

"When I found her, she was approached by this shadow demon. I couldn't see his face, but I know he was a demon. He stank like one." She reached for the flask.

"But the darkness here, the feelings, they've been going on since before Salia's death...before Eva was here," Maya clarified.

"Yes," Erza sighed. "I don't understand it."

"Neither do we. If we did, we wouldn't be here asking questions." Jenson tried to smile. It all sent a strange ripple of ease along his spine. Erza stood. "I still don't understand why it matters to you. I know you're trying to help, but it's our business." She shook her head. "Sorry, that's not what I...it's strange discussing coven business with outsiders."

"We appreciate it."

"Right, well, I have to go." She made her way to the door, then paused. "When you leave, you should take Evalyn with you. She can't stay here. And if you know her brother..." she trailed off.

Jenson stood as well, blocking her path, and she glared up at him. "Era's whip, Jenson, I can open the door myself."

He smiled. "Be careful, flower."

Erza rolled her eyes, attempting to push past him, huffing as she collided with his chest. "I'm always careful. I don't need a guard dog, I've been trained in combat since I was born, and I could rip your throat out before you take your next breath."

"You never made me think otherwise." When she opened the door, he gripped her arm. Before she could protest, he added, "If you hear anything about Aeron or the Shadowplains, *anything*, come find me immediately."

Erza cocked her head, smirking. "Is that a command?"

"More like a plea."

With a brisk nod, she vanished into the hall. When the door closed, Maya leaned against the wall behind him. "Enjoy teasing her, don't you?"

He grabbed the flask from her, taking a long swig. "No, she makes it easy." He kicked off his boots, launching himself onto the mattress. "Besides, I tease everyone."

She laughed, crawling up beside him. "You've never teased me like that, nor any girl I've ever seen you flirt with either." She folded her arms, resting her chin on her forearms.

Jenson leaned on an elbow. "Do we have to talk about this?" He didn't understand the attraction himself, whatever it was, and he was in no rush to have a full-blown conversation about it.

"You don't wanna talk, fine." She took the flask, pointing it at him. "Just promise you won't let any feelings block your judgement."

He glared at her. "My feelings block…? I'm not Quinn, you know."

Maya laughed. "No, but you can at least admit you find her attractive, can't you?"

Jenson raised an eyebrow. "Attractive? She's the most beautiful woman I've ever seen."

"Yeah, beautiful, older, and way out of your league." Jenson gave her a shove as she swung herself around, kicking the bedframe and draining the flask before hoping off the bed. "Come on, lover boy. If we're going to drown ourselves in the darkness, I think one night of drowning in whiskey and spiced wine first won't hurt anyone."

Jenson reached for his boots. "Just don't come running to me when you're still drunk in the morning."

"If I recall, you're the one who was still drunk last time." Maya skipped toward the door, carefree and childish. "Let's go! Don't wimp out on me now."

Jenson laughed, shaking his head and pulling the door shut. His chest tightened suddenly, wondering how long before they'd be this free again.

twenty-five

The attacks were becoming more frequent. Nothing serious, but the Kagai trailed their every move. They'd moved north to get *away* from the pesky demons. The constant shift in position wasn't out of their way, but moving only seemed to make it worse.

Joseline straightened her back, eyes fluttering beneath closed lids as she focused on the breath. In through the nose, out through the mouth.

The sounds around her echoed faintly. So close, yet an eternity away. The nickering horses hitched just outside her tent, the shouts of soldiers exchanging positions on guard duty, the clash of steel giving away those training before the evening meal.

Birds cried from the surrounding trees, though the forest was significantly less dense now than it had been in Rathal—the Redhorn mountains and Rekiv's frozen wasteland strange. Shae's tail thumped lightly on the ground beside her.

The thoughts passed through her subconscious, dancing like leaves on the breeze. The uncertain future all but forgotten as she allowed her mind to relax. The meditation was second nature, soothing and flawless where it had once been frustrating.

Steadying herself, Joseline found the magic dwelling within her, the aura of essence calling to her, begging for her attention. *Slowly*, she warned, reaching forward with a phantom hand.

The golden light floated to her in answer. Opening her eyes, she blinked, inspecting the orb of power flitting in her palm.

Her lips twitched into a smile.

Joseline, I'm hungry. Shae's voice in her mind broke her concentration. The orb vanished. *You've been at this for hours. You can take a break to eat.*

Joseline sighed. *You can go eat something yourself, you know.*

I could, she replied, stretching back on her haunches. *But if I do, there would be no one here to make sure you eat as well.*

Shrugging, Joseline stood, brushing off her breeches. While she was grateful for Kai's borrowed dresses, she had to admit the leather armor was a comfort she wasn't sure when she'd become accustomed to.

She pushed out into the evening light, weaving through the scattered tents with Shea padding at her heels. Everything was so different, so real for all of them. So many unknown fragments falling into place—Quinn's heritage, the darkness coming from Rekiv. Yet Maya and Jenson's absence still put everything off balance. As if a piece to the puzzle she'd grown accustomed to was now missing. Though Quinn would never admit it, he struggled with it. Not that she blamed him, Quinn had never been good at voicing his feelings—except for her.

Just the thought of their kiss in that meadow sent a pleasant tingle along her spine. The first of many, many kisses.

Are you ever not thinking about him? Shea grumbled.

Joseline furrowed her brows. *I'm not—*

You can't hide that doe-eyed look. You are totally smitten. It's disgusting.

Joseline rounded Larina's tent before she could spout out an excuse. The fire circle just outside the looming flap crackled, the thick logs around the open flames occupied by the captains and Kai, Quinn, and Fallon. Laughter echoed through the smoky air.

Quinn caught sight of her, standing and closing the distance between them. Her heart hammered as he wrapped an arm around her waist, his lips covering hers, warm and demanding. Joseline braced a hand on his chest, smiling when he broke away. "Why hello," she breathed, ignoring the chuckles from the others.

He ran a hand through her hair. "Hello."

Her blush deepened, and she nodded toward the iron pot hanging over the fire. "It smells delicious." Their fingers tangled as he led her toward the others.

"Rabbit stew. Turns out, Kai is quite the cook." He leaned down, his whisper tickling her ear as he added, "That, or she does a lot of praying to Ryneas."

The thought of Kai praying to any of The Twelve, especially about food, made her laugh. Kai looked up at her, grinning through a mouthful of bread.

"So, Joseline," she shifted her attention toward Larina when the Fae spoke, "you seem to be coming along in your training." She nodded in the direction Joseline had come from. "You're even meditating by yourself now?"

Joseline accepted the steaming bowl Fallon handed her. "Once I opened up to myself, the magic got easier."

"You're going to be a little Maren in no time!" Kai exclaimed.

Joseline pursed her lips, swallowing the bite of stew. "Who's Maren?"

Logan laughed across the fire. "You're the Princess of Rathal, but you don't know who Queen Maren was? The Waeshorn Comet?"

She fiddled with her curls, shaking her head. "I only know she was an ancient Queen of Rathal. My mother always believed magic was folly. She wasn't very keen on my learning about magical fantasy over how to maintain crop shortages or keep the peace. Most of those stories were locked away in the capital…Rathal hasn't spoken of those myths in centuries."

"Well maybe not in Corae, but in Adoa, our storytellers told all the old tales. My father, Lord Madigan, insisted." Logan gave her a close-lipped smile.

"I think Queen Talia believed in actions over words. After centuries of peace, she insisted the stories were meaningless to prevent panic or fear," Fallon explained.

Joseline nodded. "Foolish, if you ask me. Why stop the telling of stories with the knowledge and potential to help save Navarre?"

Quinn chuckled beside her. "Says the one who wanted nothing to do with them several months ago."

Joseline rolled her eyes. "Tell the story, Logan. I was always fond of stories."

He cleared his throat, laughing nervously as he ran a hand through his sandy hair. "It was more an observation than a story. She was the last mortal queen to possess magic. She died a martyr in the Second Demon Wars three hundred years ago to protect her children and the Waeshorn bloodline."

"You're forgetting the faeries," Larina said, her gaze fixating just past Quinn's shoulder.

Joseline turned to look at him but saw nothing. "Faeries aren't real."

Quinn raised an eyebrow. "You were the one led into the woods by Pixies, who now has an Aonani fox as a companion aren't you?"

Kai laughed. "Of course they're real. Queen Maren was one of the only mortals in Navarre history who could see them."

Joseline's eyes widened as a faint tinkling filled her ears. Her pulse quickened, and she turned toward the sound, toward Quinn, but there was nothing.

She returned her attention to Kai. "What about the Faeries?"

"Maren helped my sisters, Iona and Nara, rescue them from The Shadowplains," Larina said. "In return, they vowed to help the promised princess of legends."

Despite her excitement, Joseline frowned. "I don't understand. Why would my mother hide this? The servants talked, and I spent all my free time in the libraries searching for ancient texts, but I never found anything about them."

Larina crossed her legs. "We believe Aeron's henchmen kept Rathal in the dark. Maybe they stole any books, snuffed out rumors to prevent panic from spreading. Fallon mentioned your guard was a spy? Maybe there were others you didn't know about."

"They only need you to bring Aeron back, so they could have easily concealed the history from you," Kai agreed.

Joseline reached for Quinn's hand as Kellen's face flickered in her mind, his blond hair and bright smile never straying far from her side. A pawn to hide the truth. They were right, she could only assume there had been more as well.

Quinn squeezed her fingers. "You've gotten so much stronger since we left Rathal."

"It's irrelevant. A few months of training won't be enough," Fallon said. "Aeron is too powerful. He's ruthless, he's had centuries to prepare."

Kai looked first at Fallon, then Quinn before her eyes settled on Joseline. "That might be true. But with the Goddess's strength, the protection of The Twelve, and her loyal warriors, she has a chance. Besides, she can skin shift with Shea; it's one of the abilities of the Aonani."

Shea wrapped her tail around Joseline's calf as she turned to Quinn. Eyes wide, he opened and closed his mouth several times as if unsure how to respond. At last, he bit his lip, brushing a curl away from her face. "Can you?"

Joseline fiddled with her hair. "I suppose? I...I did it once when we were attacked, I think..."

The wildfire in Quinn's eyes blazed. "Show me."

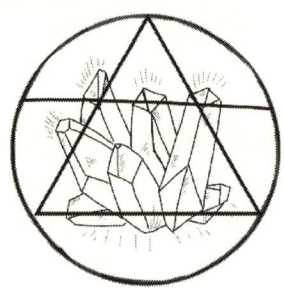

twenty-six

Edan leaned against the long council table, pinching the bridge of his nose and trying to remain calm. The only thing he hated more than council meetings were the ones that lasted several days, where no one could agree on anything. His nerves deteriorated by the second, grating against his thoughts. They'd been arguing over what to do for *three* days. With each one that passed, it took more effort to keep his temper under control.

"I still say the Northmen won't attack us," Master Serrell repeated for the tenth time. "They've never attacked before. Why cause panic when none is needed?"

"They have no reason to, we're a humble people," Master Karo agreed, flashing Edan an apologetic smile.

Edan shrugged. Of all the masters, Karo and Zarin were the only ones who completely approved of him. At least some of the others had begun to agree as well. Either the Master storyteller had spoken with them, or they'd finally seen his point. "As I explained before, it would only be a precaution. If we're wrong, then we have nothing to worry about."

"And if they're right, we can go on living in peace without risking our lives." Master Rouland stood, long ivory robes twirling about him, his gaze fixed on Fi and Naoi. "I favor this."

"I second that," Master Jeremias stroked his long, brown beard, folding his hands neatly before him on the table. "If it's something that will protect the students and keep them calm, what have we got to lose?"

Master Zarin said nothing, only picked at a loose thread of the lilac-and-gold embroidery accenting the cuff of his robes. He hadn't said anything since the first day, mustering a weak hello but not meeting Edan's eyes. It did nothing to ease the tight feeling in his stomach that twisted every time he saw the master. They'd been friends once, good friends, and Zarin's silence always bothered him.

Superior Albion looked to Master Ansell and Master Ballin, but they averted their eyes. "We will need a final vote today," he said, his tone calm as always. "Without a warning as to if and when the Northmen could strike, time is not on our side."

Edan huffed into the hands covering his mouth. Of course Ansell and Ballin wouldn't say anything on their own. They followed Master Nichol's every word like loyal puppets.

"We all know the covens have never thought highly of us," Nichol himself spoke up. "They care about nothing but keeping to their sacred matriarchy intact and ignoring us unless it's to continue their bloodline. Queen Rowena is cruel. We spend our time training young healers and helping the people of Rekiv, and all they can do is keep to their ridiculous traditions, kill their own sisters, and pretend we don't exist." Master Nichol glared at the twins and spat, "I say we decide on our own, but send them on their way."

Fi snarled, taking a step toward the old man, but Naoi held up a hand. "You should be thanking us. Without our scouting, you wouldn't have known there *was* a threat."

Master Nichol barked a laugh, stroking a hand over his greying beard. "It wasn't me who sent the request, she-demon."

Fi snarled again. "You have no room to talk, you're a witch, too. You all are."

"I'm not a horrid, entitled pureblood who thinks she can prance around demanding whatever she likes." He folded his hands in his lap, his expression collected, but Edan sensed the nerve the older master struck. Pure hatred gleamed in Fi's eyes.

Edan shoved up from the table, slamming his fists against the wood. Mugs and scrolls rattled, candles sputtering. "Enough!"

The room went silent.

"I suggest you think carefully about what you say next, Master Edan," Albion whispered from the head of the table.

All eyes watched him. Edan swallowed his disrespectful reply. "What is the point of this?" No one spoke up. "What is the point of any of this bickering? We aren't fighters, none of us. We train our students to *heal*, to help others, to be kind. Yet we sit here arguing about whether or not we will show them that same kindness and help them when they need us?"

Master Nichol chuckled. "I always knew taking you in would be a bad idea. Too much power for your own good, pureblood."

"This has nothing to do with my bloodline, Master Nichol. This," he gestured to the council, to Fi and Naoi, "this is about Navarre, about the students whose lives we promise to protect. This is about us showing them the same kindness we teach them to bestow on others. How can we expect them to take those lessons to heart if we refuse to give them a chance to *live*? This stopped being about bloodlines and covens a long time ago."

Master Nichol glared at him. "Always so considerate of your beloved students, aren't you?"

The council room chilled instantly.

"Now, let's not bicker amongst ourselves," Master Zarin began.

Edan's chest tightened as he fought to keep the temper under control. *Every damn time.*

Master Nichol's lip curled. "Aren't you, Master Edan?"

"Nichol..." Master Jeremias warned.

"Tell me, did you consider giving Kiran any kindness when the two of you decided to—"

"Master Nichol, that is enough." Superior Albion's tone was authoritative and final.

Edan clenched his fists. His nails dug into his flesh, a painful attempt to stop his shaking. He wished Fi and Naoi weren't here; he wished he couldn't feel the other masters' eyes, waiting for what he would say next. His fingers curled and uncurled tightly, unspoken emotions beating violently against the mental wall.

Master Nichol smirked, knowing he'd hit his mark. He stood, Master Ansell and Master Ballin mimicking him without a word. "I don't care what you all decide. My interests lie with the protection of my students. At least I *truly* have their best interests in mind."

The soft click of the door sounded like an explosion in Edan's head. He slouched against the chair.

"He's always known how to get under anyone's skin," Master Rouland offered softly.

Edan opened his mouth to speak, but Master Zarin interrupted him, dark hazel eyes calm. "Edan, you know none of us blame you for Kiran's death."

He laughed, taking a long sip of water, though he longed for something stronger. "You can't expect me to believe that. You of all people have every right to."

Master Zarin smiled weakly. "He was a handful, and once he made up his mind, there was no stopping him." He paused. "But I know how much you loved my brother."

"Can we not talk about it, please?" His voice sounded like a strangled whisper. Fi still watched him, though he avoided looking at her.

"A vote." Superior Albion stood. "Those in favor of enacting the wall?"

Slowly, all hands raised. Edan let out a relieved sigh.

"Then it's decided." The masters stood one by one, collecting their papers and leaving until only Albion, Zarin, and the twins remained.

"I meant what I said. The sooner you stop blaming yourself for something you couldn't have stopped him from doing, the sooner you'll be able to forgive yourself, Edan," Zarin said. "You've done right by him, tried and tried to make it right. The students love you, worship the ground you walk on."

"Zarin, please, just..." Edan begged, fighting the tears swelling behind his eyes.

But Zarin continued, putting a hand on his shoulder. "Superior Albion made you his heir for a reason." He glanced to the head of the table and was rewarded with a nod. "Master Nichol has always been jealous of that, always wanted to see you fail, to replace you. But you've proved yourself a better man again and again. The darkness will only consume you if you let it, and Kiran would have wanted you to find the light."

With that, Zarin left, the room silent in his wake.

A moment later, Edan pushed through the door. He needed to be alone. The sweltering anger was hot and itchy against his skin, clawing for release. The memories threatened to suffocate him like they always did when he let the wall down.

Edan took one look around his room and banged a fist against the wall, screaming, as if that would make the pain go away. He stomped over to the worktable, shoving everything onto the floor and flipping the table over. Then he kicked at the wood for good measure, cursing when a sharp pain exploded along his toe.

He screamed again, the sound strangled, and tore the neatly-folded quilts off the trunk at the foot of his bed. He snatched the bottle of spiced Rekivian whiskey from his bedside table, relishing in the harsh burn, and whirled on the closet, ready to rip everything off the hangers, but froze when he caught sight of the small, pillared balcony overlooking the snow-covered mountains.

Kiran loved that view.

Edan swore, swigging deeply from the bottle before he ripped at his tunic, the layers of fabric scorching against his burning flesh. With a frustrated cry, he yanked on the overcoat, several clasps clanking against the wooden floor as the stitching ripped. Two seconds later, the tunic lay crumpled near the end of his bed.

Edan swung his legs through two small pillars, resting his forearms on the edge of the balcony. He breathed, drinking again, forcing the raging anger to calm.

The darkness will only consume you if you let it, and Kiran would have wanted you to find the light.

In the seclusion of his room, he couldn't hold back the tears.

Hatred, fear, agony consumed him, pouring from his eyes, down his cheeks. The breeze churned from the mountains, the snowy peaks so strong, so solid. He'd been that strength once, and now his anguish tore him apart.

He almost didn't hear the door creak open, but he refused to turn toward the noise. He didn't care. "I'm sorry," Fi began. "Your door was open, so I thought…"

Edan banged his head against the balcony ledge, a groan escaping his lips as he dragged a hand through his hair, pushing his face against his bicep. "Go away." He swigged the whiskey.

She only whistled, no doubt inspecting the damage he'd done to his room. "Quite the temper you have."

"Fi, don't." He needed her to leave before he gave into her flirting for his own stupid, selfish desires. "I want to be alone."

"Nobody wants to be alone when they're miserable, they only tell themselves that so no one will see them cry."

Edan swore, a shudder rippling through him. Goosebumps prickled his flesh from the cold air, but still the heat raged. He drank again, cursing when the last drops emerged, and tossed the bottle to the ground far below. Shattering glass echoed in its wake.

Wood creaked behind him and he turned to see her leaning against the doors. He straightened, facing her, and she eyed him, gaze flickering over the lean muscle of his stomach before finding his eyes again. "Am I wrong?"

He wanted to push her back against the wall and kiss the words out of her mouth, kiss her until the heat and anger and pain melted into oblivion. And he hated himself for it.

"Why don't you do it?" she prompted. "If it'll make you feel better about yourself, Edan, then kiss me."

Damn her to The Twelve for knowing what he was thinking. Damn it all.

He pushed himself against her, burying his lips in her neck as he gripped her waist. She arched to meet him, letting out a delighted moan, her fingers digging into his shoulders. Her skin heated beneath his mouth, pulse hammering in her throat, and she ground her knee along his inner thigh, the heat intensifying. Her crystal nails slid free, tracing lazy lines along his sculpted biceps. He shivered, pushing them harder, teeth nipping at her ear. She moaned again, gripping his hair.

The darkness will only consume you if you let it, and Kiran would have wanted you to find the light.

He stopped, the words echoing in his head.

"What's the matter?" Fi breathed.

His chin trembled when he met her eyes, and he swore, trying to push her away.

The crystal nails prickled his flesh, holding him firm, but he refused to meet her eyes. "Edan, I don't know what happened with Kiran, and I'm not asking you to tell me. But whatever it is, it seems like you're the only one who still hates yourself."

"I do hate myself." He'd never said it out loud before.

"Why?"

"Because I could have stopped him!" His temper broke free, unable to hold back the words any longer. He banged a fist against the wall above her head, but she didn't flinch. "I could have stopped him, and I didn't."

His knees buckled beneath him and he slid to the ground, shaking in anguished rage. Fi sat with him, holding him as he cried and it eased some of the tightness in his chest. After several moments Edan sighed, pulling her close, desperate for warmth now that his temper had begun to cool.

"I loved a man once. Era be damned, I would have followed him anywhere," Fi whispered. "Queen Rowena cursed me for being weak, told me if I didn't stop seeing him she would exile me from the Elites." She laughed. "Erza didn't like that, she insisted we were hers to command and any issues Rowena had with us must be discussed with her first. They didn't talk for a whole week."

Edan looked down at her. "What happened?"

"He died." She snuggled into his shoulder, her nails swirling along his back.

"How?"

Fi laughed, shaking her head. "Oh no, you don't get to hear my sob story until I get yours."

Edan chuckled at that. "Fair enough."

She pursed her lips, narrowing her eyes. "We should get you inside though, you're freezing."

"I don't mind it," he lied, wanting an excuse to keep holding her.

"That's fine, but you're going to catch a cold." Her crystal nails brushed along the patch of hair trailing down from his navel and he inhaled. "We wouldn't want that."

Edan uncurled from her warmth, pushing to his feet. "No, I suppose not." He offered her a hand. She took it.

"Do you need some help with..." her eyes scanned the remnants of his temper outburst.

"I think I'll be alright." He approached the closet, pulling a thick tunic over his shoulders with a shiver and tucking it into his breeches. He wasn't looking forward to the looming winter.

Fi shrugged and knelt to pick up the table. He raised an eyebrow, crossing his arms expectantly. Her nose scrunched up and she held her breath, but before he could help, it was standing again.

Edan chuckled. "I believe I said no."

"You did, but I'm bored. Besides, I still don't think you're ready to be alone."

"I think I'm a grown man and I can make that decision for myself." He reached for one of the unfolded quilts.

"Oh, you are? I had no idea. What with the temper tantrums and all..." It took four steps to cross the room and yank her against him, and she let out a surprised gasp. "Now, *Master Edan*, is that any way for a respectable professor to behave?" She tapped his nose.

"I must admit, you make acting like a respectable professor extremely difficult."

Fi looked up at him through dark lashes. "Do I?"

He kissed her witch mark—the air symbol tattooed behind her left ear. "Very much so." When he moved away to pick up the scrolls from the floor, he could have sworn she pouted.

"So, the council agreed to try the spell." She bent down to help him, swishing the large feather plume through the air.

"Yes."

"When will they start?"

Edan paused, running a hand through his hair. "Honestly, I'm not sure. I still have to find the other book first."

Fi placed the empty inkwell on the table, setting the quill beside it. "Any idea where it might be?"

"Some." Edan frowned, leaning against the worktable. "But several students might have a better idea."

"Will they ask questions or spread rumors about what the books you need might pertain?"

"Not if I ask nicely. I am a favorite professor, you know."

She gave him an incredulous look. "I'm sure you are."

Edan rolled his eyes. "I'll speak with them." He pushed away from the worktable and started for the door. "You and Naoi meet me in front of the library tomorrow morning."

She followed without asking any more questions, but paused in the doorway, looking up at him. "Of course, *Master Edan.*"

"See you in the morning."

Fi winked, then left without another word.

"Nova help me," he murmured. "She has Kiran's sass."

He reached for his cloak, fastening the clasps before slipping into the hall and heading toward the student's wing. If anyone could find the final volume they needed, it would be Neirin.

twenty-seven

One week. If all went according to the original plans he'd made years ago, they would be bidding Narcio farewell in no more than a week. Dax sent a silent prayer to Syvi that his cell mates could withstand the darkness that long.

He laughed softly, the anticipation of the Akuma demon's threat sedating the air with nervous energy. So, this was their "shadow testing"—taking the soul apart in small fragments and repurposing the energy without the wielder knowing. Despite their explanation, Dax hadn't wanted to believe it, couldn't believe it was possible. Not until Kellen returned to their cell the previous evening, incoherent and swathed in dark, whispering shadows. They filled his eyes, swarming about his expression numb and unreadable.

He shuddered, grateful Evalyn managed to escape.

"Do you regret not going with her?" Elyon rasped.

Dax turned to the Dwarf, his chest tightening. "Aye, but it was better this way."

It was safer this way.

"You cared for her," Kellen said. "She has to know why you couldn't."

Dax ignored the tear that betrayed his emotions, wishing he could scrub the evidence away. "She knows. Asking her to kill me was one of the hardest things I've ever done. But it was the right thing." He adjusted his shoulder, gritting his teeth against the dull ache. "I just hope it was worth it. I hope...I hope I didn't send her to her death."

"She's okay," Elyon cut him off. "She's a fighter, a survivor."

The door creaked open. Dax frowned at the Shadow Commander leaning against the stone frame, his eyes drawn to Aeron's mark of power seared into the flesh on the demon's forehead—the symbol separating commanders from their subordinates.

"Well, *Captain*? I think it's about time we let you in on the fun." He grinned, motioning two other Shadow Beasts into the room.

Dax smirked, showing no sign of fear as they sauntered toward him. "Just make it quick, will you? I'm growing rather fond of these chains."

The answering slap echoed across his cheek, metal rattling as one of the Shadow Beasts gripped his chin. "Shut your mouth."

Dax let out a choked laugh, nostrils flaring. "But why would I? It's the only weapon I have left."

"You're a pathetic excuse for a mortal, you know that, don't you?" the Shadow Commander drawled.

Dax rolled his eyes. "If you're going to torture me, can you get on with it? I have a long day of wallowing in self-pity planned."

Kellen snorted, and the Shadow Beast whirled on him. "Do you want to take his place, traitor?" Dax could have sworn Kellen's chin trembled. The demon snarled at Dax. "And you, shut your mouth. You don't have power to demand things from us anymore, *Captain*."

Dax hissed involuntarily, their sharp nails digging into his biceps and dragging him down the dark halls without a reply. No matter what happened, he would fight it. He wouldn't allow his memories to be the reason they hurt her.

I will not be your downfall.

The words echoed though his mind as they flung him face first onto a cold stone table stained with old blood. Whether it belonged to Elyon, Kellen, or another unlucky victim of their torment, he wasn't sure. The vile stench engulfed his senses all the same.

A dark form came into view as they bound Dax's hands and ankles, a leather bit dangling from the creature's clawed hand. He glared up into the Akuma demon's red eyes and scared face.

"Captain," he purred. "I'm so honored to have you join me at last. I've heard so much about you."

"Save me your lies and do your worst. I'm not afraid of you, blood demon, and I'm not going to tell you anything."

The demon laughed, gripping his hair and forcing his head up. "And here I was, about to tell you I wouldn't use this." He held up the bit. "One more chance, I'm feeling generous." He let Dax's head fall, blood streaming from his nose as it smacked against aged stone.

Dax wasn't prepared for the excruciating agony as dark shadows assaulted his mind. He pushed against them, trying desperately to shield the private memories. But with each moment his strength slipped, until at last Eva's vision shimmered in his subconscious.

"There she is," the demon purred. "I'm surprised, most don't last longer than a few seconds. She must be special for you to keep me out so long."

Dax gritted his teeth until his jaw ached, jerking against the restraints. "Leave her alone. She's nothing to you."

The Akuma chuckled as darkness gripped Dax once more. Memories flashed too fast. Things he'd long tried to forget.

Evalyn seated before the hearth, flustered and beautiful, their faces inches apart.

Tears streamed down his face, his heart clenching as the memory clouded and vanished.

Dax grinned down at a soaking child huddled on his deck, half-drown and terrified. She narrowed her vibrant eyes, turning away from him.

Darkness, then another memory.

Fear pulsed through him.

No, he thought, jerking against the restraints, fighting with all reserves of strength. *Not this.*

But the memory clarified as if sensing his panic.

Dax leaned against his desk, *Seraphina* swaying steadily beneath him. He held a hand over his mouth, the other wrapped around his chest as he stared out the cabin window. The stars shimmered beautifully on calm water.

The door clicked shut and he turned, meeting Beck's eyes. "Well?" he breathed.

"She's asleep." The stocky pirate assured him, stopping beside the crystal bottle of rum. He uncorked it, pouring two glasses and making his way toward Dax. "Do ya know who she is?"

"Of course I know," Dax snapped, taking the glass. The harsh liquid soothed his shaking nerves.

"Aye. So, what do we do, Captain?"

A question he had no idea how to answer. Dax closed his eyes, sighing. "I'm open to suggestions."

Beck laughed, scratching at the stubble along his jaw. "Is this a jest? The Sea Dragon is caught off guard by a little girl? You'll never hear the end of it from Cohen."

Dax ran a hand through his hair. "She can't be more than six, Beck. Gods, she's a child. How do I protect a child?"

"I don't have an answer to that, Captain."

Another sigh as Dax finished off the rum and set his glass down on the tray. "Taking her to Dorwynn could be a bad idea. From the look of those clothes, she might not even have come from the capital...I have to protect her."

"Do ya?" Dax frowned at Beck, giving him a sharp nod. "An' how do ya plan to do that?"

He folded both arms across his chest. "I...there's something about her. Something I can't place. I just have to help her no matter what that means."

"Aye, there's something about 'er alright, she's—"

Dax silenced him with a wave of his hand. "My father would have helped her."

Beck stood beside him now, watery blue eyes kind. "Aye. But he's gone." He paused before adding, "so tell me what *ye* want us t' do, Captain, an' it will be done."

Dax bit his knuckle, nodding once before he said, "We take her with us. I'll deal with the monsters, make up some excuse. She can hate me all she wants, I'll find some way to protect her as best I can. If she's there, at least I can try to keep her safe."

"Will ya help 'er escape, should opportunity arise, or conditions grow too dangerous?" Beck asked.

"I'll tell her what I can, keep her alive. Then, when she can escape, I'll help her. I may not know what I'm doing when it comes to children, but I'll try." He reached for the rum, pouring a fresh glass. "Go find Cohen, will you? It seems we have quite some planning ahead of us."

Beck smiled. "Aye, Cap."

The memory vanished as blood filled his mouth, choking him as his head slammed into the table. Sharp nails dug into his flesh, the demon's snarling face dropping into his blurring vision.

"Where is she." His voice dripped venom.

Dax gritted his teeth, refusing to betray her. *I will not be your downfall*, his mind echoed. "I don't know what you're talking about. She stabbed me and ran."

The grip on his shoulder tightened. "Don't lie to me. What did you do?" the Akuma roared. "Do you have any idea how valuable that girl is?"

Dax spat and the demon turned away, hissing. A rippling calm coated his body in response, smooth and gentle, like the waves of the deepest blue seas. The feeling was strange, overbearing almost. But it numbed the pain spreading through his head.

"Pathetic mortal. Did you think we wouldn't smell a rat?" Pain sliced across his cheek, blood swelling where razor sharp nails cut flesh. "Did you honestly think we wouldn't know you were planning something?"

"Clearly not," Dax deadpanned.

He could endure it. He *would* endure it. Evalyn and the others held captive here had endured much worse for years. The calm sensation shuddered as if in agreement.

The Akuma's slap brought him back to reality. "I can see into your mind," he cooed. "But it's pointless. You're never leaving this place." He chuckled. "Not alive anyway."

Before Dax could think up a reply, a hissing yelp sounded from somewhere to his left.

The Akuma snarled. "What in Aeron's name is the problem?"

"This one's hiding something." The voice sounded feminine, but still masked with that same hissing darkness. "I can't merge his essence with the shadows. I can't touch his soul."

"What do you mean you can't?" The Akuma frowned. He turned to Dax, gripping his chin painfully. "He's mortal, he's disposable."

Dax gave a half-laugh, the taste of his blood salty and bitter.

The female came into view. She knelt before him, flashing a smile with razor sharp teeth. Dax tensed as her serpentine emerald eyes narrowed on him.

A Nyokiaa.

He gulped, shivering as the snake demon hovered over his shoulder, trailing a long nail delicately down his spine, thick shadows swirling about her naked chest. "Mmm, so handsome, isn't he?" Her companion scoffed, but she continued. "*Too* handsome for a mere mortal."

"What do you mean?" the Akuma snarled, clearly unimpressed with her vagueness.

But the Nyokiaa knelt before the stone slab, meeting Dax's eyes. She licked her lips, the forked tongue sliding over ashen flesh. "Your kind really are as stupid as they say, good for nothing but merciless torture." Again, the Akuma snarled, but she ignored him, eyes still fixated on Dax. "What's the only race lesser demons can't touch?"

Dax flicked his gaze toward his torturer, unsure what she meant. The Akuma's eyes widened. "I thought Aeron and his children killed all the Demi-Gods in the second Demon Wars? Rounded them up for a public execution. I thought it was strange that the Fae girl didn't kill him, but I never thought…"

"Of course you never thought, you're incapable of intellect," she purred, caressing Dax's cheek.

He forced himself not to pull away from her touch.

"So who's—"

"He's Syvi's son. I guess not all of The Twelve had birthed a child yet. Funny, I always expected the sea goddess would birth a daughter."

The blood pulsing through him froze. "What?"

Her lips curled back from her teeth. "You didn't know?"

Dax gulped, gritting his teeth. *So that's why Evalyn couldn't kill me?*

"So, what do we do with him?" the Akuma questioned.

The Nyokiaa stared at him as if he'd just asked the stupidest question. "We can't take control of his soul," she replied, standing. "That doesn't mean he's incapable of torture. We'll simply have to wait for the master's return so Aeron can kill him."

Her companion flashed an inhuman grin. "An immortal victim." The look in his crimson eyes made Dax's blood run cold. "Eternity is a long time to suffer." As if to prove his point, he drove his nails into Dax's shoulder. He snarled, blood swelling in his mouth where he bit his tongue to keep from screaming.

Dax clenched his fists, nostrils flaring. "We'll see who's laughing when we escape," he murmured, bracing himself for the onslaught of darkness.

twenty-eight

The fluttering in Erza's chest at the thought of seeing Jenson again infuriated her. Rowena insisted emotion was an illusion for the weak that witches were immune to, yet here she was, heart racing at the thought of meeting those dangerously playful eyes again.

"Are you nervous?" Eva fiddled with the clasps of her new cloak.

"No, I just hope they aren't busy." Erza ran a hand through her hair as the inn came into view. She needed to be back in an hour for the opening ceremonies; she had plenty of time, but she didn't need to be worrying about Eva during the first contest. If Jenson really did know Eva's twin, it shouldn't be an issue for him and Maya to watch her for a few days. Rowen and Astrid would have other things to worry about during the contest, she couldn't burden them with watching the Fae girl as well.

She flashed a smile to the innkeeper before pulling Eva up the stairs. "Don't look so panicked, it's going to be fine," Eva said.

"Who said I was panicked?"

"If they're busy, I can look after myself."

But Erza shook her head, banging on Jenson's door. "I'd feel better if you were with someone else."

"Maya," Jenson's voice echoed from within the room, the door jerking open. "I told you I would—"

Erza couldn't fight the blush that exploded across her cheeks. Jenson blinked in surprise, a hand still frozen on the door while the other braced against its frame. She fought the urge to trail her eyes down his half-naked body, the trousers unlaced along his hips, deft, sculpted muscle still glistening from the remnants of a recent bath.

He pushed his dark hair from his face, raising an eyebrow and wetting his lips as he smiled. "You aren't Maya." His hand fell away from the door and he ushered them in. "I must say, flower, I'm pleasantly surprised."

Eva nudged Erza and she tore her gaze away from his chest. "Right, well, I have a favor to ask."

Slowly, Jenson tied the laces of his trousers, still smiling. "Oh?"

Erza scowled, folding her arms. "I don't have time to—"

"You're the one stumbling over your tongue, flower, not me." His voice was a purr, soft and taunting.

Damn him.

Erza gritted her teeth. "Look, I was just wondering if you could watch Eva for me."

Eva rolled her eyes. "I already told you I don't need to be watched over. I survived years in the Narcio dungeons on my own."

Erza ignored her. "With everything else going on, I can't." Her gaze wandered over the muscle rippling along Jenson's back and the intricate detail of the tattoo covering his spine before he pulled a dark navy tunic over his shoulders and tucked it into his pants.

Her heart hammered as he shoved his hands into his pockets and sauntered toward her. She couldn't look away when he leaned forward and whispered, "For you, flower, anything."

Erza took a step back, eyes darting to Eva. "Thanks." She paused at the door. "Try not to flirt with her, she's fragile."

He laughed. "And you aren't?" Before she could respond, he added, "No need to get jealous, my jests are only for you."

She turned on her heels and left, her stomach twirling in violent somersaults the entire walk back to the watchtower. For once, she didn't try to impress the villagers with pleasant smiles, her face twisted into a scowl.

Damn him. Damn him for messing with her head.

"Well don't you look...distracted." Erza wanted nothing more than to strangle the Blackwing heir for her icy, sarcastic tone. Her gaze found Morana leaning against the wall of the corridor to her left. She cocked her head. "What is it? Someone on your mind?"

Erza scowled. "No, mind your own business."

Morana's lips curled back to show her teeth. "You might want to get those emotions under control, Princess. I'd hate to see anything happen to you out there. Three days is a long time, *accidents* could happen."

Something flickered in Morana's pale blue eyes, echoing the faint pulse of the strange obsidian pendant hanging between her breasts. Erza almost missed it, the glimmer so sudden; but it pulled at her, the odd, uncomfortable feeling creeping along her spine.

The darkness. Could it actually be coming from Anwen and her daughter?

She fought to keep the fear from her voice as she said, "Everything alright, Blackwing?"

The darkness flickered again, but Morana only grinned, brushing a hand along Erza's shoulder as she passed. The action sent a ripple of discomfort through her blood. "Mind your own business, *Stormwood*."

Then, she was gone, approaching the archway leading toward the assembled group waiting to escort the heirs to the island on Lake Urasa. But Erza wasn't worried about the challenge. Her body shivered without warning, paralyzed by the strange presence, every bone screaming to turn tail and run. She gritted her teeth.

"Erza?" Astrid's cool voice echoed down the corridor.

She turned, her face schooled to neutrality as Astrid walked toward her, clad in dark colors that matched her skin, her long hair braided back along her spine, accented with golden clasps. Rowen matched her pace, their tangled fingers swinging loosely between them. The bottom of their cloaks moved as one in the breeze.

"We received word from Naoi and Fi," Astrid said.

"And?" Erza raised an eyebrow.

"They reached the Chiron. The Healer Superior and several of his masters have been helping them."

"Anything else?"

Rowen's lilac eyes shimmered with amusement. "Nothing unusual. Fi is swooning over one of the young Masters."

Erza laughed, some of the tension easing from her chest. "Nothing unusual is right."

"His name is Master Edan. He's a handsome young healer."

Erza shrugged. "I don't care what Fi's playthings look like."

Rowen hesitated, looking as though she might say more, but stopped herself. "Be careful out there."

They walked into the open air, pwusing before joining the others who had gathered. "You know I will be. Everything is taken care of?"

"You'll only be gone a few days, you know," Astrid chided. "We're more than capable of handling things."

"I'm aware. I did make you my second and third for a reason."

"Oh, I thought that was because I'm your cousin and you have to like me?" Rowen teased.

"Just watch your back out there," Astrid said softly. "Morana's been acting…off. And the more time we have to spend here with them, the more I'm starting to suspect something is off with Anwen. It does seem likely that a problem this large would stem from the coven leader herself."

Erza's mind flashed to the pulsing gem at the Blackwing's throat. "I know."

Rowen gripped her arm harder than necessary, and she growled, but her second didn't flinch. "No, you don't. While you've been off practicing novice magic with Eva, it's gotten worse."

Erza pinched the bridge of her nose. "My mother would insist I whip you for talking to me like that." She paused, releasing a groan. "You know I won't do that, but Rowen, we've talked about this. Besides, I can't just accuse Anwen Blackwing of being a murderer without solid proof."

Rowen sighed. "I didn't mean it like that. I like her, I do. But she's distracting you. Either her or the Demi-Fae you sent her off with instead of your own Elites."

Erza slapped her for that, hating herself instantly. The sound echoed only slightly in the wind, but Rowen didn't flinch despite the red mark forming over her cheek.

"Anwen's been watching Eva." Astrid's remark caught Erza off-guard, but still, she didn't apologize.

"That makes me even happier with my decision." She ran a hand through her hair. "Jenson and Maya know her brother. I'm hoping they might take her with them when they leave. They won't let anything happen to her."

The Blackwing leader made her uneasy, and she suspected the leader of being responsible for her daughter's dark aura. The further Eva was from Anwen, the better.

"Do you want us to keep an eye on them?"

Erza pondered the thought but shook her head. "Jenson seems more than capable." She ignored their raised eyebrows and added, "Anyway, I need you here. I sent her with them for a reason. I don't need your attention distracted as well. The Elites need to be ready should anything happen."

"You still suspect—"

"Yes." Erza cut Rowen off before she could finish, glancing toward the boats for prying ears. Anwen stood in the Blackwing boat, Morana at her side; the thin layer of shadow coated them, visible even from this distance. "It's only gotten worse since Eva arrived, since I saw those...things in Easthaven. I haven't said anything to my mother yet because I want to be sure, but just be ready."

Rowen and Astrid kept her pace as they continued. "Just try not to get yourself killed out there, will you?" Rowen said. "I hate the thought of not being at your side. Besides, I don't think I could handle being commander in your place."

Erza raised an eyebrow, giving Rowen a shove. "I don't plan on dying."

"Erza, come here." Her mother's voice clawed for her attention; she stood on the dock near the bow of their narrow ship, her eyes trailing over Erza as she approached. Queen Rowena slipped two fingers beneath Erza's chin. "You will not disappoint me," she said, glaring at Rowen and Astrid's joined hands and stepping onto the boat.

Erza remained where she was, staring down at her reflection in the water. Black leather covered her thighs, blending with the boots lacing up behind her knees. The thick lilac fabric of her tunic rippled, stopping halfway up her forearm and lacing across her chest. The black leather vest dipped to a slight point at her navel, clasped with silver fastens up her chest and cinched at her sides, the tunic visible beneath. Leather gauntlets coated her forearms, and several belts slung around her hips, accented by various daggers and clasps. Her rich purple cloak billowed behind her as a gust of wind pierced her cheeks.

She truly looked like a coven heir today.

She set her jaw, giving her reflection a satisfactory nod, then stepped onto the boat.

Three days of remaining on the island with no other rules but the prohibition of their magic. Survive, or die.

They reached the shore in half an hour, the snow-dusted mountains towering above them. The light snow covering the ground crunched beneath her boots as she stepped onto solid land. Daiki soared amidst the clouds, her massive form shadowing the snow.

"She's so majestic, just like your mother," Odessa whispered from beside her.

Erza turned to the Silvermist heir. Her amber eyes had remained a constant state of red since her sister's death, her light-brown, freckled cheeks always stained with tears.

"She is, isn't she?" Erza lifted her gaze. "Are you going to be alright out there?"

"What do you care if I'm distracted? It'll make things easier for you, won't it?"

Erza turned to her, frowning. "You should know by now I'm not one to slaughter innocents."

Odessa's smile made her chest tighten. "I know." She hesitated, eyes drifting out to the water. "Kill her slowly for me, when you do. She deserves it." Then, she was gone, her deep green cloak flowing behind her as she hurried to catch up with her mother.

The words echoed in Erza's head as she stepped into line beside the other heirs, their unspoken alliance lingering.

"Heirs of Rekiv," Rowena's voice carried on the wind, a deadly melody, "this day marks the official start of the Shadow Games. The first contest of three to challenge your cunning, strength, will, bravery, and power. Rekiv must be ruled by all five traits."

Erza stood at attention, the perfect soldier, Odessa to her left, Morana and her older sister, Nami, to her right. All eyes focused on the Queen. The others who gathered to watch the games begin were silent, Daiki curled on the ground behind Rowena.

"This is your vow, your oath. Show no mercy, fight for your coven's honor as is an heir's duty. A witch's bond to her coven is eternally binding, never to be betrayed. A witch's mark is her vassal from the day she receives it...never forget that." Erza touched the witch mark tattooed behind her left ear.

Rowena gestured to the looming golden gates behind her, to the mountains reaching into the sky. "For the next three days, you'll remain here, alone. Your task: survive on instinct, your knowledge based solely on your mortal skills. The use of magic of any sort will result in disqualification and death. Those alive in three days' time will continue with the next challenge. Those dead, well..."

Rowena looked at Erza, then stepped toward the gate. Raising a hand, she formed a circle in the dirt between the golden arches. The runes glowed against the snow, weaving and swirling about one another.

"May the best witch win, *Princess*." Erza refused to shiver at the venom in Morana's tone.

"Step into the circle to reach your starting point. You'll each be transported to a different side of the island." The lilac circle of runes pulsed as Rowena spoke.

Morana pushed her slightly, stepping up first. The shadow in her eyes flickered as she vanished in a cloud of shimmering dust. Nami followed.

"Best of luck," Odessa whispered, straightening. The dust shimmered and she, too, was gone.

Erza forced the shadows from her mind, chin high. She stepped into the circle.

The sensation was instant, painless. Not even a second and the mountains enclosed her, the lake at her back. Snow drifted around her ankles, swirling in whorls on the breeze. Her cloak fluttering about her on the icy wind.

With a satisfied huff, she flexed her fingers. *Slow*, she thought. *Cautious*. All she had to do was stay out of sight. She wasn't *expected* to kill, only remain alive.

So she wandered, honing her mind into survival mode. The first day dragged on, and she collected what food she could until at last the sun dipped toward the horizon. She almost didn't sleep at all, but found an unoccupied cave. She searched the back in the dim light, relieved to find a small stream running through the rock and no unwanted companions.

But when she settled between two grooves in the stone, sleep wouldn't come for hours. Jenson's face flickered in her mind, those dark chocolate eyes and long lashes taunting her. *Damn The Twelve*, she groaned, wiping at her face as she finally drifted off. He was going to be the death of her.

The bone-chilling scream jolted her awake.

Sunshine streamed into the shallow cave, golden-red hues reflecting off the snow outside. She inched toward the entrance as a second scream echoed over the mountain peak above her.

Erza crouched, crystal nails sliding out, digging into the earth, the cold no more than a nuisance as she climbed. A sickening crunch chilled her blood as she neared the top; a metallic stench tingled her senses, followed by a dark presence that crawled along her skin.

Blood covered the mountainside. It splattered the snow, pooling around Nami's lifeless body.

Morana knelt over her sister, bloody crystal nails sinking into the earth above her body, tangled in dirty blonde hair. Nami's petite form sprawled about, limbs mangled, twisted as if her ankles snapped when she tried to crawl away rather than fight. Blood streamed from behind her head, hand marks smeared across her cheeks and imprinted into her throat.

The sound of crunching bones tore Erza's attention toward Morana, still crouching over her sister. The Blackwing heir lifted her head and moaned, smiling faintly, eyes closed and blood oozing through her lips, dripping down her chin. Nami's chest was ripped open, ribs cracked and pulled away to reveal her inner organs. Her heart gone.

Erza kept her gaze on Morana, as the Blackwing heir opened her eyes, the once pale-blue replaced by a shimmering, soulless black.

Erza ducked out of sight, heart racing.

The noise continued, and Erza covered her mouth. Careful to mind her footing, she retreated down the snowy slope and sprinted into the small patch of trees, launching behind the first trunk.

"Well, I suppose it's about time someone else noticed something was wrong. She's been coated in darkness for months." Odessa's hiss drifted from the next tree over.

Erza spun on her, dagger poised to attack, and the Silvermist held up her hands. "Relax, I mean you no harm, I…I was looking for you."

She quirked a brow but remained silent.

"I…I thought we might form an alliance." Odessa dug a hand into her bag. "I have food."

"What makes you think I want your help?"

Odessa's eyes darted up the mountain. "That."

Erza frowned. "If I agree, we don't speak of it after—"

"We don't speak of it," Odessa promised. "I know I'm not going to win, but I don't care to be mauled by a demon witch either." She held out her hand.

After a pause, Erza took it. "I can respect that." She smiled. "Well then, Silvermist, let's keep each other alive." She walked away from the mountain, not waiting to see if Odessa followed.

twenty-nine

There was freedom in the black wolf's form, a serenity Quinn couldn't quite explain. His training with Fallon and Larina continued, and having a true hold on the wildfire coursing through his veins and Azuri's constant support relieved some of the mental uncertainty.

But this freedom was something else.

Turquoise shadows enveloped him as he stood from his wolf form, running a hand through the hair he'd left unbound. The magic electrified his fingertips.

Azuri landed on his shoulder, inspecting the small thicket. "You're getting quite good at that, you don't wince anymore when you shift."

Quinn laughed, the sound growing more genuine with each passing day, as he leaned against a thick tree trunk. He pulled a knee up to his chest and plucked an apple from his pocket. When he held it up to Azuri, the faerie shook his head, sapphire eyes narrowing slyly. "So, when are we going to talk about your sister?"

Quinn glanced sidelong as the creature perched on his shoulder. Azuri rested his chin on his knees, cat-like eyes and mouth wide in a smile. Shrugging, Quinn bit into the apple. "I'm not sure there's anything to talk about."

"You're twins. Can you sense her? Sometimes there's a connection like that."

"I dream about her, sense our memories together sometimes. It's hardly more than that." He took another bite, juice spurting from his lips. "But she's alive. I think I'd know if she wasn't."

Azuri nodded. "What about Joseline?"

Quinn's grip on his knee tightened. "What about her?"

The faerie held up his hands. "Oh, nothing." When Quinn glared at him, the sly smile intensified. "She doesn't need you at her side anymore, not constantly. She's gotten much stronger with Kai's help in her magic training."

"She has, but that was always the intention." Quinn straightened a little, tossing the apple core into the nearest tree. It broke in half, rolling on the ground. "I'm proud of her."

Azuri hovered before his face, wings shimmering. "You two have a special bond."

Quinn met his gaze, fiddling with the pendant at his throat. "I know."

Something flickered in Azuri's eyes. "I'm curious, what it was like when you two met? When a Fae meets their *sirdispora*—"

"We don't need to talk about that," Quinn interrupted him, shoving to his feet. "I know what a mate is."

Azuri's laugh echoed through the trees. "It's a good thing. Not every Fae even meets their mate. You're lucky to have met so young." He crossed his arms, wrinkling his nose as he leaned closer. "Besides, having her around helps. I know you're lonely."

Quinn frowned. "Who said I was lonely?"

"And here I was, thinking you were past not talking about your feelings." Azuri sighed, leaning back. "You miss Jenson and Maya, you aren't sure how to talk with your aunt, you want to know where Evalyn is, you don't want to think about being royalty or having those obligations, you—"

"Alright!" Quinn whirled on the faerie. Wildfire glowed around his hands and along his tattoo, the pendant cool against his chest. "Gods, Azuri. No, I don't want to think about any of that. How can I?"

Quinn turned away before Azuri could see him cry. Blinking in surprise, he scrubbed at his cheeks angrily. Of course, he wanted to see

Evalyn again. Since the moment he remembered her, she was constantly in the back of his mind. But there wasn't anything he could do about it.

Quinn sighed, running a hand through his hair as the glowing flames calmed, fading from his fingers. "Azuri, I'm sorry."

The faerie's wings shimmered in the light before he came into view. "It's alright."

Quinn shook his head. "No, I shouldn't have yelled."

"True. You have quite the temper when you let yourself slip. Careful, or you'll end up standing in the ruins of a forest fire."

"I already burned a building down once, it's fine." The silence echoed for a long time, Quinn never breaking Azuri's stare. Then, the faerie laughed, wrapping his arms around his stomach, his tiny body shaking. Quinn's lips curved into a smile, the tension between them easing.

"I was wondering where you'd snuck off to with that pretty little princess of yours, Son of Dorwynn."

Quinn spun, coming face to face with the Shadow Commander they'd faced in Rivedas—the one who'd told him Joseline was being attacked. Aeron's mark, etched into the flesh between his eyes, was a stark contrast to the pallor of his skin.

Panic gripped his stomach. *She's safe*, he assured himself. *She's unharmed back in camp with Kai*. Still, he snarled, teeth flashing as he unsheathed the dagger at his wrist, another flicking in his hand. "And I was starting to wonder if we'd actually seen the end of you. Tell me, demon, why haven't you attacked us again while we've traveled?"

"The Master is still weak. So he's decided it best not the draw more attention to ourselves than necessary; our presence is rather obvious. So he's chosen a more…subtle approach."

"You mean the Kagai?" Quinn growled.

He glanced at Quinn's dagger, his gaze neither confirming or denying to accusation. "Are you going to fight me, bastard?"

Quinn lunged forward, dagger slicing toward the demon's chest. He missed, but the long nail caught on the leather cord around Quinn's throat. He gagged, fighting to get away, clawing at the pendant, gasping for breath.

The cord snapped, the pendant falling to the ground.

Raw power rippled through him, shifting and beating through his veins, along his muscles. He hissed, gripping his stomach and stumbling back, swallowing a cry. It burned, viscous tingles pulsing and crawling along his flesh. He doubled over, hair falling into his eyes.

But it wasn't the usual dark brown. The strands, sweaty against his face, shimmered silver in the afternoon light.

It stops your Fae appearance from surfacing. As long as you wear it, you'll appear mortal. Fallon's words echoed in his mind.

The commander charged, snarling.

Quinn stepped to the side, his Fae senses humming, swirling together. It was even more exhilarating than the first shift, his speed and reflexes increasing tenfold. Magic thrummed within him, the blue-green fire twirling itself around his blades as he moved. Quinn grinned at the demon, a feral growl rumbling in his throat.

The commander lunged again, hissing. This time, Quinn launched himself over the demon's head and kicked its shoulder, the blow sending the creature skidding across the ground. Quinn pressed the heel of his boot into its neck, the Shadow Commander writhing and spitting, tearing wildly to get free. Quinn dug his blade into its spine, and the demon roared.

"I won't let you hurt her." Quinn released his hold, kicking the creature onto its back and kneeling on his chest.

"Sometimes, I wonder if Aeron is right," the commander hissed. "If the Fae really are the monsters."

The dagger at his wrist slashed across the Shadow Commander's throat. Dark blood splattered Quinn's face, bubbling and pooling. Quinn's chest heaved as he leaned forward, whispering, "I am not a Fae bastard. I am Quinn Elirona, Prince of Dorwynn and Reul Eliorna's heir."

He stood, brushing the hair back from his face, his fingers gliding over delicately pointed ears.

"It's nice to hear you say that out loud." Azuri landed on his shoulder.

Quinn lifted the Shadow Commander's chin, blue-green power swirling around his fingers as the body writhed in flame, then crumbled to ash.

He paused before the pendant. His nose flared slightly at the soft crunch as he slammed his heel into the crystal. When he lifted his foot, the remnants shimmered in a million pieces. He closed his eyes, sighing as the breeze ruffled through his hair.

"Well, it's true, isn't it? It's time to stop fighting the truth. Fighting it won't change anything." Quinn squared his shoulders, not bothering to turn back to the pile of ash blowing away into the breeze.

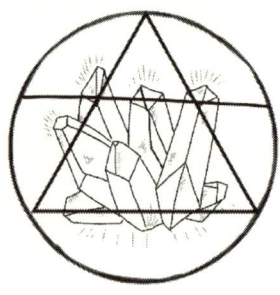

thirty

It had been two days since the heirs were taken to the lone island to complete the first challenge, and Evalyn tried her best not to think about Erza. Whatever happened now was out of her control. Rowen told her one of the Blackwing heirs was dead; she hoped it was Morana, but doubted the witch clouded in darkness would go down so easily. Their first meeting still made her shiver.

"Hello?" She blinked, Maya's hand waving before her face. "Sorry, what?"

"Ugh," Maya puffed out a sigh, pursing her lips with furrowed brows. "I *said*, what's this past you won't talk about?" She paused, her stern expression softening. "I want to know you. Quinn's like a brother to me."

Evalyn crossed her legs on the wide-lipped stone fountain they sat on. The small basin was long dried out, nothing but leaves and pebbles remaining on the inside. She fiddled with the end of her braid. "That doesn't make you a sister to me. I don't know you."

They both looked up at the sound of Jenson's laugh. She liked Jenson, his carefree kindness a relief to all the horrors she'd been through. Despite his teasing when Erza was around, he had a way of comforting Evalyn without trying, his presence soothing and gentle.

"I thought you two might be hungry, and these smelled delicious."

Jenson held the fold of dough, sweet smelling cream, and strawberries toward her, its aroma mouthwatering. "Crepes?"

"Everything smells delicious to you, you ravenous pig," Maya grumbled, reaching for the crepe.

Evalyn's lips twitched into a smile.

"Thank the Gods we didn't scare her emotions away. You haven't smiled all morning, I was starting to worry." Jenson sat beside her.

The smile faded. "I'm sorry. You're both very kind, I'm just…"

Jenson put a hand on her knee, and she jumped slightly. He pulled back, but said, "It's alright."

She bit her lip, then lifted the crepe to her mouth.

"He does that too," Jenson murmured. "Bites his lip like that."

Evalyn met Jenson's dark eyes, smiling again. "Still? Our mother always used to yell about it, told him he'd chew his entire lip off if he didn't stop."

Maya laughed. "Honestly, I'm surprised he hasn't yet."

They finished the crepes in silence. Evalyn watched a few villagers pass the alcove, guilt hammering in her chest as they shivered in scraps of old clothes while she sat bundled in warmth. She knew all too well the mistress of cold.

Crows flew overhead, their caws deafening. Clouds covered the sky all morning, and the small outlet they occupied—surrounded by brick walls on three sides—was the perfect funnel for the chilly wind. It stung her face, biting with invisible fangs. But Evalyn ignored it, unable to think about anything but the questions taunting her. She finished the warm breakfast, collecting herself before she turned to Jenson. "Can…can you tell me about him?"

Jenson leaned back on his hands, long legs stretching in the dirt as he tilted his head toward her. "What do you want to know?"

Everything? Anything. What did he do? What was he like? What sort of man had he become in the past twenty years? But a thought slipped from her mind before she could stop it. "Why didn't he come back? Does he even remember I exist?"

Maya sucked on her gapped teeth and gave Jenson a nod. "He…" Jenson wet his lips. "He couldn't. He had a block put on his mind by

Fallon, the leader of Kynire...our organization. He's the one who found Quinn. Demons almost killed him, but Fallon rescued him and started training him to protect himself."

"So, he's a warrior...a fighter?"

"I would say survivor is more accurate." Eva smiled at that. "He talked about you in his sleep a lot, so Fallon blocked his memories of being Fae...and of you. He was raised a mortal with no idea what he really was."

"He talked about me in his sleep?"

Jenson nodded, his smile kind. "You two were close." Not a question—a gentle observation.

"Yes," she whispered. "I tried so hard to forget him. Especially once..." She gritted her teeth, painful images flashing through her mind: the island, the dead bodies of her loved ones, the eighteen years of chains and suffering.

She put a hand to her mouth, the sob escaping violently before she could stop it. *Damn it. I will not let the darkness consume me.* Evalyn brought a knee up to her chest, hugging it, burying her face into Dax's cloak. The tears streamed down her cheeks. So much sorrow, so much agony. Yet hope lingered amidst it all. If she could get to Quinn...

She looked over at Maya and Jenson, rubbing her red eyes as Jenson put a steady hand on her back. "If you don't want to talk about it, you don't have to."

But Eva shook her head. *Confront the darkness. Face the fear head on.* "When...when I was six, I watched my mother murdered by shadow demons. I ran and was rescued by a pirate captain who took me to Narcio Island where I was forced into slavery, to mine obsidian for eighteen years." They both sat still, listening and watching. She rushed on before she lost the nerve, "I waited, I trained when I could. Then, about three months ago, the pirate captain took me under his wing, into his bed. But he never..."

Her chest tightened at the thought of Dax. His smile, his dark blue eyes, that deep, silky voice. She didn't fight the tears that time.

"You love him?" Maya's tone was sad and understanding.

Eva's nose flared as she met Maya's eyes, gripping Dax's cloak. "I don't know. Maybe. Yes?" Her lip trembled. "It doesn't matter anyway."

"Doesn't matter? Of course it does."

"No, it doesn't." She closed her eyes. "I killed him so I could escape." Dax's bloody body on the oversized bed flashed in her mind.

"I'm so sorry, Eva," Maya's voice was tight, like she understood every ounce of pain.

Sighing, Evalyn stared up at the snowy Kitsugon circling the crumbling watchtower. "Sometimes, I wish I could just make it all go away, shed my skin and become something different, something strong and fearless." Her blood hummed as she thought it, magic she'd been working to control rippling along her flesh. A massive white wolf danced through her mind, so real she was sure it towered over her. Glancing up, there was nothing but the sky and the Kitsugon disappearing behind the stone watchtower. She huffed, the sound more animal than human.

"Eva?" She blinked at Jenson's voice.

Turning to them, the image of the wolf vanished. "Yes?"

Maya stared at her with wide eyes. "You...you were a wolf. You shifted into a wolf."

Evalyn sucked in a breath. Her mother always said Fae had the ability to shift, but she'd never thought of actually *trying* to shift. "I was picturing a white wolf in my head."

Maya pursed her lips. "How much control over your magic do you have?"

"It doesn't just explode, if that's what you're worried about." She twirled the braid around her finger. "I've been practicing control with Erza. I can make a shield if I focus, but nothing more."

Maya stood with a satisfied nod. "That decides it." Jenson raised an eyebrow. "I'm going to scout for a place to practice. At least we can teach her some more self-defense." Without another word, she was gone.

When Maya was out of earshot, Jenson sighed. "You can't be too hard on her for trying."

"What do you mean?" Eva traced her fingers over the cold stone.

"She's always had a thing for Quinn. She'll never admit it, but she does."

Evalyn bit her lip, putting two and two together. "Trying too hard to be friends."

He nodded. "She has a rough past, too. Sometimes, she doesn't come across…she means well."

She smiled weakly. "That, I can understand." They were silent for a long time. "Can Quinn shift into a wolf?"

Jenson frowned thoughtfully, crossing his legs. "I don't know. He just found out he was Fae when we left."

Disappointed, Evalyn swung her feet over the ledge, bracing her hands beside her and kicking the stone. So many questions swarmed her mind. She opened her mouth just as Jenson stiffened beside her.

"Well now, this is a surprise." The sultry, hissing voice prickled goosebumps along her flesh. "I was wondering when I'd get the chance to meet Erza's honored guest."

Evalyn met the elegant woman's eyes. She looked like Morana, but older—blonde and busty, with curves made to drive a man mad. The coven leader, Anwen Blackwing.

She smirked down at them, her tongue gliding over pale teeth in a teasing gesture. But there was an uncomfortable darkness to her, as if it sucked out the light from around her. It was like the Shadow Beasts, only worse; but Evalyn didn't cower in fear.

I will not let the darkness consume me.

"What are you doing here?" Her voice was strong, like her will, like her mind. She wasn't a slave anymore, she was free. And she would cower from darkness no longer.

"I'm merely enjoying the view of my village, no harm in that, is there? It is quite a lovely day for a stroll." Anwen held up a basket of grapes, popping one into her mouth. Her eyes shone with malice, shadows flickering amidst pale blue as she turned her gaze to Jenson. "And you, the Prince of Dorwynn's *sielapora*, you don't even know what power dwells within you." The darkness deepened. "How pathetic."

Jenson stood beside her now, his fists clenching and unclenching at his sides. Evalyn stepped forward. "What are you doing *here*, with us?"

"Eva, careful," Jenson warned. "There's something not right about her."

The shadows flickered in her gaze again and Anwen laughed, the sound just as horrifying as the Shadow Beasts. "So, the archer has a brain after all. Well, no use in hiding it, then, is there?" She brushed a long nail against her lips. "My true name is Adria, daughter of Aeron and Princess of The Shadowplains. And my father wants you dead, Evalyn Elirona."

thirty-one

Princess of The Shadowplains.

Panic coursed through Jenson, fierce and rippling, but he forced himself to remain calm for Eva's sake.

Aeron's daughter.

"What's the matter, half-breed? You look surprised," Adria purred, trailing her eyes down Jenson's body.

Evalyn spoke before he could respond. "Why would Aeron want to kill me? I haven't done anything to him."

Adria's laugh dripped with malice. "You don't even know who Aeron is, do you?" Another laugh. "You poor, sheltered little princess, do you have any idea who you are?"

Jenson moved toward Eva, his hand reaching back for the quiver he'd left in his rooms. *Damn it. Stupid.* "You aren't going to touch her."

"Aren't I?" Crystal talons gripped his throat in a heartbeat, cutting off his air, and Adria lifted him off the ground as if he were no more than a rag doll. "But hurt her? Never. Aeron wants her alive."

Adria scoffed, dropping him. Evalyn rushed to his side, but he shook his head, glaring at the demon princess. "You'll have to go through me first."

"I believe I just did. Though I didn't expect the last healer of Norah's bloodline and one of the sole survivors of the Southern

Continent's massacre to be so pathetic." Adria turned away.

Jenson lunged forward, but she flicked her wrist dismissively smashing him into the fountain's stone lip, his side screamed in protest—yet it was the side facing Adria that burned in agony, the side she'd stuck with dark magic. He winced, gritting his teeth.

"That sweet mouth is going to get you killed, half-breed." She turned to him, the darkness illuminating her grin. "And we wouldn't want that. Whatever would your prince do without you?"

An agonizing shudder rippled through Jenson and he bit back a cry, gripping his side, muscles spasming as he tried to stand.

"You have the wrong person. I'm no princess." Eva shook beside him, but her voice remained calm, strong.

Adria laughed. "A little princess who doesn't know who she is and a worthless refugee who denies his gifts. Maybe I should just kill you now, after all." She frowned, rubbing a finger over her lips lazily. "Alas, that would raise too many questions." She turned away. "Enjoy your freedom while you can, little princess."

Jenson tried to call out, to speak, to move, to do *something*, but the agony paralyzed him. Black sprayed across his vision as invisible claws raked up his side. He sank to the ground, his feet giving out beneath him.

"Gods, Jenson," small hands slipped around his waist as Evalyn whispered frantically in his ear, "can you help me a little here?"

He could barely nod as Maya's shouts echoed through the alcove. The strange shadows enveloped his mind. Evalyn's grip weakened as he sank back to the ground. She swore.

Foggy, he tried to speak, Maya's name barely passing his lips as the darkness consumed him.

He couldn't stop shaking. His body convulsed, engulfed in blinding intensity that clawed along his flesh, inky snakes hissing and tightening.

Small hands gripped his temple as he thrashed, sturdy and sure. "Jenson, I swear to the Goddess and The Twelve, if you die on me, I'll go into the Nightlands and drag you back myself," Maya's tone, though sarcastic, radiated with fear.

He opened his mouth to mumble a reply but shuddered with another lance of pain shooting up his left side. His words came out a jumbled slur.

"So wake up, damn it. If you die, Quinn will kill me, too."

Jenson tried to laugh, but it came out hollow and raw. Blood coated his tongue, almost choking him, the agony clawing out from the space behind his ribs.

Then, abruptly, it lessened.

"I've almost got the poison out." Another voice he didn't recognize. "If he can just hold on a few moments longer..."

Jenson, Darling. The third voice, he hadn't heard in years—not since his mother dove on top of him as a shield, their house crumbling to the ground, crushing her with its weight. *Open your heart to the light. You are a healer of great value...it will save you. Control it, use it to heal others as its power now heals you. Norah's blood runs in your veins, my son.*

The clawing darkness screamed, refusing to give up its hold, but something tore it away. He cried out, no more than a whisper as he arched against the bed.

Then, blackness.

thirty-two

The second day of the trial passed uneventfully, and Erza started to wonder if she'd imagined the whole encounter. But Odessa's sleeping form beside her reminded her of the horrible reality she'd witnessed.

Only one more day to stay away from Morana, or whatever demon possessed her. The thought of those soulless black eyes sent a shiver down Erza's spine. They'd managed the first two by sheer luck, keeping to the scarce clusters of trees to hunt and returning to the cave Erza had found to sleep. Odessa's soft breathing filled the cavern instantly, but Erza remained awake. Her nerves too jumbled to rest.

Yawning, she bit into the squirrel meat they'd roasted the night before, her gaze never straying from the cave entrance.

Odessa moaned softly beside her, eyes fluttering open. "We're still alive."

Erza cocked her head. "We are."

"Good." Odessa reached for her waterskin. "I dreamed she found us."

"There's still time."

Shivering, the Silvermist stood. "I'd like to avoid that. It's hard enough to manage the energy to wake up without..." she trailed off.

They were silent for a moment before Erza spoke. "How are you holding up?"

Odessa shrugged. "I'm not, but I wouldn't expect you to understand." She met Erza's eyes, then added, "Everyone knows you and your sister weren't close. Not like Salia and I anyway."

Birdsong echoed from outside, and Erza stood, stretching her arms over her head. "Right, well, we should probably go get something more to eat." Snuffing out the embers of their small fire, she checked her weapons.

"You ate all the food?" Odessa frowned.

"Not all of it." Erza held up the small satchel of berries. "But I couldn't sleep." She didn't like the pity that filled Odessa's expression. "You didn't see what I saw."

"I wasn't judging you."

Erza strode out into the sunlight without replying. Odessa followed her, her gaze shifting to the snowy slope beside them. The surrounding mountains were quiet, save for the chirping sparrows flitting about the leaves. Erza held up a hand for Odessa to stay silent as she pulled a dagger from the strap along her thigh. Nodding Odessa kept her gaze locked on the peaks as they crossed the open space to the trees. Once under the woodsy cover, she hurried off in search of more berries while Erza hunted, and she sent a silent prayer to Era for the Silvermist coven's skills in foraging.

She'd almost tracked the flock enough to attack when a faint rustling sounded behind her. Erza froze. She shifted slightly, scanning the trees for Odessa, but she was alone. Her pulse quickened, and she scanned the surrounding trees for a low-hanging branch, launching herself upward into the first one she found.

She climbed swiftly, her crystal nails a welcomed support. Several moments passed as Erza focused on the ground below, wondering if she'd imagined the noise.

But Morana's form came into view below her. "Where are you, Stormwood?" she called. "I found your little cave, the whole thing reeks like your disgusting perfection." She snorted to herself, her nails sheathing and unsheathing as she flexed her fingers. "Where are you? We're running out of time. They'll be coming to fetch us at sunset."

Erza focused on her breathing, her gaze fixated on Morana. *Don't look up. Please, don't look up.*

Even as she thought it, Morana's head tilted slowly.

Panic raced through her as the memory of Nami's body filled her vision, and she tried to angle herself further to the side of the trunk to avoid Morana's inescapable gaze.

A loud screech echoed from the other side of the island and Morana's head snapped toward the disturbance. She let out a cackle of laughter before sprinting away. Erza let out a sigh of relief, sagging against the trunk. Her head fell back against the bark as she tried to calm her racing heart.

"Erza?" Odessa's whisper came several minutes later. "Erza, where are you?"

"I'm here," she answered, beginning the descent. Odessa stopped abruptly as she dropped to the ground. "One more moment, and I might not have been."

"The birds promised to help," Odessa smiled, her gaze flitting toward the direction Morana had run.

Erza blinked. "That was you?"

Shrugging, Odessa held up a full satchel of berries. "It's always been a Silvermist specialty to speak with animals. I asked if they could help us."

"You saved my life."

Odessa tossed a handful of berries into her mouth. "And you've saved mine several times. Shall we call it even?" Erza nodded. "Good. Now all we have left to do is keep away from her until sundown." She glanced up at the sky, pursing her lips. "By my guess, I'd say we've only got a few more hours to go since we...rather, I slept late." Smiling, Odessa popped another berry into her mouth. "Shouldn't be too hard."

"No, not too hard." Erza couldn't help but smile. "Right, well, thank you again."

"Don't mention it, Stormwood. Just do us all a favor and stay alive."

Erza nodded. "I think I can do that."

"Good." Without another word, Odessa turned toward the water. "Are you as good at fishing as you are at hunting? I do love fish."

Laughing, Erza followed the Silvermist.

thirty-three

Joseline didn't ask Quinn what happened in the woods. She didn't care. But whatever it was, it did nothing to ease the constant fluttering in her chest at the sight of him.

He looked like a god; like Kyaos or Yvaos, majestic and beautiful. His hair, now silvery-white, shimmered like starlight when he moved. Joseline longed to run her fingers through the silky strands. His eyes pierced through the starlight that fell into them, the scruff once coating his jaw a mere memory, the delicate point of his ears captivating.

"Hello, is Joseline there? I'd like to speak with her, please." He waved in front of her face, and she blushed, shaking from the trance. The teasing look in his eyes softened in a way it only did for her. "You were staring at me again."

The blush deepened. "Was I?"

He nodded, reaching across the space between Bellona and Eclipse to squeeze her hand. "But I don't mind." He smirked. "I like the thought of you thinking about me."

Joseline frowned. "You're insufferable."

Quinn laughed. "Always." Pulling away, his expression hardened once more. "Your training with Kai is going well."

"How would you know?" she asked, flashing him a sidelong glance.

He bit his lip. "For one, she told me. But I noticed—"

"Spying on me?"

Quinn's response was cut off as Larina called their small company to a halt. Several dismounted, thankful for the rest, but Joseline's skin prickled with a familiar discomfort of an oncoming attack. From the look on Quinn's face, he felt it too. The horses nickered, prancing nervously on the confined forest path.

They made their way toward Larina. She nodded to them, cautious eyes darting through the trees. "You feel it as well?

"What is it?" Joseline asked.

"More Kagai," Kai spoke without hesitation. "But they aren't alone. Whatever is with them, it's ancient. The horses have been spooked all afternoon."

A soft growl rippled from Quinn at her side. "Damn them. Why can't they show themselves?"

As if on cue, a voice said, "Looking for me?"

The speaker, a lean woman with ashen gray skin and coal black hair, leaned against a tree further up the path. She wore no clothes, but thick shadows and long hair covered her body. Joseline paid no mind to her nakedness, her gaze drawn to the slit emerald irises instead. The woman smiled, revealing a double row of thin, sharp teeth, her forked tongue dancing over them.

Startled gasps filled the air, and several horses pranced in anxious discomfort. Joseline's pulse quickened, her hand reaching for her dagger. Metal swished through the air as several others did the same, but Larina held up a hand, motioning for them to stop. Her eyes never left the woman. "What is it you want, demon, and where are your little friends?"

The demon gave a pout, batting dark lashes. "Come now, Daughter of Dorwynn. Must we speak in such negative terms? It's insulting."

Larina didn't hesitate. "Where are your friends, *Nyokiaa*."

Joseline shivered, leaning toward Quinn. "Nyokiaa?"

"A snake demon."

Joseline frowned. "But she doesn't—"

"Don't let the shadows deceive you."

She opened her mouth to reply, but the Nyokiaa's voice pulled for her attention. "There now, a little respect isn't too much to ask for, is it?"

"What is it you want?" Larina demanded.

The Nyokiaa clicked her tongue against her teeth, shaking her head, and pushed off the tree. The shadows moved with her, swathing her as she sauntered forward.

The light hummed within Joseline, begging for release. But she focused on breathing, keeping the magic at bay.

"I only wanted to see how your journey to Raenya was going...that and a little revenge, that's reasonable, isn't it?" The Nyokiaa smiled, her eyes finding Joseline's, then Quinn's. Joseline ignored the twang of jealousy as the demon's eyes slithered over Quinn's body, lingering on his tattoo and the deft curves of his biceps. "You two have been very mean."

"I would be careful about what you say next, demon," Quinn warned, daggers hanging loosely from his fingers. For a moment, Joseline wondered if he would shift.

The Nyokiaa gave a sarcastic laugh. "You've murdered countless of my kind, destroyed my little friends' families, and *I* must be careful what *I* say, Son of Dorwynn?" Serpentine eyes narrowed, her nose twitching. "How dare you."

The air shifted, darkness seeping around the leaf-covered ground as footsteps scurried around them.

The Kagai.

Panicked whinnies and creaking leather filled the air as they braced themselves for the attack. Fallon scowled at Quinn, but Larina and Kai were silent, their eyes meeting hers. Joseline blinked, confused, until Shea curled her tail around her ankle.

You can do it again, the fox said, her voice calm. *Your magic wants to be free. Trust it. Trust yourself.*

Joseline shook her head. *But I can't. I don't—*

Trust me.

The darkness swarmed around their company now, the familiar scuffle of the little demons' footsteps echoing through the trees.

"I think perhaps I'll start with the children of Dorwynn," the Nyokiaa murmured. "The heartbreaking cries of the promised one will be almost as enjoyable as her torture."

At that, Joseline squared her shoulders and took a step forward, any hesitation vanishing from her mind. "No."

The Nyokiaa's eyes darted to her. "No? Hah, you foolish girl."

Darkness surrounded Joseline, clawing at her, biting and stinging, as the Kagai swarmed with reaching hands. Quinn's voice echoed an eternity away, distant though he stood right beside her.

Trust yourself, Joseline, Shea whispered. *Trust the power within you. You were meant to do this.*

"You will not harm us." Joseline knelt, palms in the earth. *Focus,* she begged. *You can do this. You can control it.*

She half expected nothing to happen—then the blinding light shot from her fingers, spreading and weaving in cold soil. It moved in whispering tendrils, electrifying the living darkness, feeding off the sound of the demons' agonized shrieks. One at a time, they flashed, vanishing into nothing even as they fought to run, to get away from the light they couldn't fight.

"That's not possible!" the Nyokiaa wailed. "It's too soon for your power to be this strong!" Light flooded over her, tranquil and soothing despite the cries as it overpowered the darkness. The demon screamed, her flesh consumed by pure magic, the glow radiating along her skin. She thrashed, trying uselessly to throw the light from her body, but the power only intensified, binding her tight until she threatened to explode.

Joseline smiled. "You tell Aeron I am no one's plaything. If he means to steal my country from me, I'll be ready. I'll fight with all my strength. And I will never stop until I send him back into the darkness where he belongs."

The demon's anguished cry slowly faded, the darkness dimming until all that remained was a thin fog shimmering with pale, golden light.

thirty-four

Erza's entire body ached as she climbed the final steps to her rooms with heavy feet. After three days of avoiding the blood-crazed demon dwelling within Morana, her exhausted senses craved rest. Cold, and caked in sweat, she wanted nothing more than to bathe, change into a skimpy silk nightgown, and sleep for a century.

But at the sight of three Elites, one at the top of the stairwell and two at attention on either side of her doorframe, their dark skin shadowing them just outside the torchlight, the exhaustion faded.

Ysta, Curra, and Vien relaxed slightly when they saw her, but Erza frowned. She'd left her rooms empty, there was no reason for Rowen to have posted guards. Unless...

She forced her expression to remain neutral. "Report?"

Vien leaned against the wall, flipping a throwing star with a gentle flick of her wrist. "There was a...situation."

"What sort of situation?"

"Nothing here," Ysta assured her. "In Thya."

"Is Eva alright?"

Vien's face was an unreadable mask. "Not Eva, Jenson. The pretty Demi-Fae."

"I do know who he is."

Vien nodded, then went back to flipping her throwing star and eyeing the stairwell with her brooding dark hazel glare.

Curra added, "We didn't tell your mother."

Erza frowned again, her hand on the knob. "Why not?"

"We figured you would want to inspect things for yourself first."

"You figured correctly," Erza said, and pushed into the room.

Jenson lay in her bed, tucked into the far corner, shirtless and motionless. Maya sat cross-legged beside him, chewing on her fingernails. Eva paced before the window, a breeze blowing the long curtains into the room. Rowen and Astrid knelt near the hearth, feeding thick logs to the fire and whispering in hushed voices. Her second wrapped her arms tightly around her waist, her skin ashen, looking shaken as she did only after a serious healing. Astrid knelt beside her, stroking her back. But when Erza shifted her attention to Jenson, nothing seemed out of sorts.

She coughed, letting the door slam lightly behind her. All four women turned toward the noise, Eva jumping more than the others. Erza's gaze landed on Rowen, who took three seconds. One to sigh, one to stand, and one to brush the ash from her palms onto her loose-fitting grey pants. Astrid said nothing, but remained close by—a silent comfort. "Anwen attacked Eva and Jenson by the old fountain in Thya a little over a day ago."

Erza turned to Evalyn. The fear radiated off her, but she kept her shoulders squared, the wildfire surprisingly calm.

"Are you alright?" Erza inspected her for any injuries.

"I'm fine." She turned to the bed. "But Jenson, when she—"

"She *is* the darkness, Erza." Rowen's voice was strong, sure. "It's as we feared."

Maya's half-laugh cut Erza off. She squeezed Jenson's hand, not looking at them. "You say *darkness* like it's a mere inconvenience to you."

Rowen snarled, stepping toward the bed, but Astrid caught her, an arm around her waist. "Am I not the one who helped you heal him? Maybe I should just finish him off while he's weak and helpless, you ungrateful piece of—"

"Rowen, stop," Erza ordered.

Her second sighed, tossing her long scarlet braid over her shoulder, and the tension eased. Before returning to the hearth, however, Rowen added, "He's a healer, Erza. An extremely powerful one. I don't think he has any idea, but when I was healing him...something awoke. It was a light I've never felt before, something ancient. It quite possibly saved his life from whatever demon poison Anwen infected him with."

Erza nodded, moving to sit beside Maya on the bed. Without the snarky remarks and teasing smile, Jenson looked so small, so pale despite his bronzed complexion. Sweat beaded along his forehead, his eyes moving in feverish nightmares behind closed lids. Erza ran a hand through her hair, opening her mouth to speak, but Eva's whisper stopped her. "Adria said she was Aeron's daughter, a princess of The Shadowplains. What does that mean?"

The question was so quiet, Erza's blood ran cold. "She said what?"

"Aeron's daughter," Astrid repeated. "You heard her right."

Erza closed her eyes, suddenly dizzy. A demon princess. Of course, it made so much sense. The growing darkness, the change in Morana right after the change in her mother all those years ago, the constant unease around the Blackwing coven. The shadows she sometimes saw flickering in their eyes. Their increase in bloodthirsty delights. All at once, everything they didn't understand was clearer.

Three hundred years had passed since the Second Demon Wars. How long had the demon princess been in control of Anwen's body, of Morana? How long had she kept them all shuffling blind in the darkness of her web?

Jenson coughed, moaning slightly, and Erza turned to him. "Flower, you're here. I was just dreaming about your pretty face." His playful voice was weak and raspy, but he smiled. "Do I look as pretty as I feel?"

Erza couldn't help but smile back. "You look like you had a death match with Sauda and lost."

Jenson laughed, then winced, gripping his side with his free hand, Maya's knuckles going white in the other. Erza caught her breath when the blankets slipped down his chest. Inky tendrils spread across his side like a tangled spider web, thin and uneven, sprouting from just above his hip and reaching along his coppery flesh. The ends had begun to fade, now a dark purplish grey compared to the jet-black of the rest, as if the poison had been stunted from spreading. But the resemblance was undeniable.

Salia's death. Less grotesque, but all too similar.

It was Anwen. Or rather, Adria, the demon princess controlling her body.

Erza focused on breathing, her head falling onto her knees as she forced the panic out. *Witches are heartless, emotionless, cruel.* Her mother's words echoed in her mind.

Emotionlessness be damned. She'd been fighting that her whole life.

"You alright?" Jenson asked. "I know I don't look great, but I didn't think it was bad enough to kill you."

"No," Erza shook her head, lifting her chin to wipe a hand over her mouth. "Era and Nova guide us, none of this is alright."

"Even the Goddess couldn't help us right now," Rowen sighed. "I'm going to gather reports. Would you like me to give them to you tonight or tomorrow?"

Erza waved her away. "I'm too exhausted to deal with anything else tonight. Tell Ysta, Curra, and Vien they can go. We'll be fine."

Astrid said nothing as Rowen gripped her hand and reached for the door. "Until tomorrow. Thanks for not dying on me out there."

With a nod to Maya, Erza made her way to the bathing chamber, motioning for Eva to follow. When they were alone, she asked, "What else is bothering you? And don't tell me nothing, I can sense your aura."

Eva sighed. "It's just something Adria said."

Adria—Anwen Blackwing. It would take some getting used to, calling the coven leader by that name.

Once the water steamed from the faucet, Erza stripped, sighing as she peeled sweat-soaked clothes away from her flesh. She was too exhausted for formalities, and Eva didn't comment on her nakedness. "What was it she said?"

Eva almost smiled as Erza sank into the porcelain tub. She

moaned, relishing the deep heat soaking into her bones as she dunked beneath the water. When Erza resurfaced, Eva replied, "She called me Evalyn Elirona. The last name seemed important, but I don't…" she trailed off.

Erza reached for a wash rag and the bottle of jasmine-scented lather, scrubbing her skin and scalp raw. "Elirona is the royal house of Dorwynn, the Fae people."

Eva's brows furrowed. "So, she thought I was a member of the royal Fae house?"

Erza shrugged, breathing deeply before she dunked beneath the water once more. When she emerged, she stood, reaching for the robe hanging over the hook near the door. "Is it an impossible thought?"

"Well, I suppose not. Just a strange one."

Erza walked to the small mirror over the sink, brushing her fingers through her hair before picking up the comb. "There are far stranger things in the world than reality, Eva."

Eva gave a half laugh. "Would you like my rooms? I don't mind if you prefer your own space."

Erza shook her head, reaching for the thin silk gown hanging on the bathroom door. "What I want is my own bed. I'm willing to sacrifice half of it for a wounded traveler." With that, she hung up the robe and yanked open the door.

Jenson and Maya spoke in hushed voices. Erza ignored Jenson's wide eyes and the flutter it birthed in her chest. "Maya, why don't you go with Eva? Sleeping in a bed will do you some good, and I'd feel much better if she wasn't alone." When Maya's eyes flickered to Jenson, Erza smiled. "Don't worry, I'll call for you right away if anything changes."

The girl frowned, but stood, eying Erza's gown. "Better watch yourself around him if you're going to dress like that."

"I doubt he'll try something when he can barely laugh. But if he does, I promise you he'll regret it."

Maya laughed, following Eva out the door. "Good," she called over her shoulder. "He needs a woman like you to tell him no."

Erza shook her head, smiling. As soon as the door closed, however, her pulse quickened. She cleared her throat, slipping into bed beside

Jenson.

"Don't worry, flower. I'd never dream of taking advantage when your mind is so frazzled." Jenson's teasing barely masked the pain in his voice.

Erza ran a hand through her hair, adjusting the pillows. "Oh, that's reassuring, I was worried."

He laughed, then hissed, his face twisting in pain. "I wouldn't, even if I wasn't on death's bed. I would never do that."

Erza rolled onto her side, narrowing her eyes at him. "Death's bed? Gods, have you always been so dramatic?"

He smiled weakly. "Someone has to be, with the world ending. Besides, if it weren't for my dramatics, would I ever see you smile?"

Erza blushed before she could stop herself, turning away at the red flowering her cheeks. "I do smile, you know."

"Not as often as a pretty flower should."

The blush intensified. "Can you stop teasing for once?"

Jenson was silent for a long moment. "I'm sorry, I don't…it helps me not think about…"

Erza's chest tightened, guilt flooding through her. She turned back to him. "Jenson, I'm sorry."

She jumped when he took her hand in his. His skin was smooth, but clammy, long fingers twining with hers. She didn't move, didn't pull away when he squeezed their clasped hands, their fingers falling to the space between them.

"It's alright," he sighed, closing his eyes. "Let's just get through tonight. After that, we can worry about everything else."

Without another word he drifted off to sleep, his chest rising and falling peacefully. Their hands remained clasped, unmoving. But despite her exhaustion, Erza couldn't sleep no matter how hard she tried. Fear and pain engulfed her. Thoughts swarmed through her mind in violent circles—her country, the future of her Elites, her coven, Eva, even the man beside her. But the truth about Adria, hidden for centuries beneath a dark façade, worried her the most.

This attack was a mere warning, and Adria almost killed him. Next time, Erza had a feeling the demon princess wouldn't be as generous.

If that were true, they couldn't afford to waste any more time. Her coven was in danger. Her *country* was in danger. Time was a luxury they didn't have.

She'd have to talk to her mother.

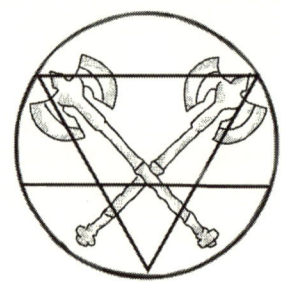

thirty-five

"I found something!"

Edan looked up from the book he'd been skimming, quirking an eyebrow as Neirin skipped toward them from the back stacks of the library. Fi hopped onto the table, swinging her legs while Naoi pulled her hair into a small braid.

Neirin set the book down eagerly, dust flying through the air as leather contacted wood with a soft thud. He blew the remaining dust off and beamed, wiping his arm across his forehead. "I was starting to think I'd never find it."

"You and me both," Naoi yawned.

Edan rolled his eyes, resting his chin on his hand. "So?"

Neirin's grin deepened. "It's an old spell book. Master Nichol said once that…" he paused, tucking onyx curls behind his ear and examining the floor.

"Master Nichol said what?"

He looked up at Edan through long lashes. "Master Nichol said once that the Chiron housed all the old spell books, the ones Aeron used to…to destroy Navarre the first time he attempted to rule, during the First Demon Wars."

"And let me guess," Fi said, leaning over him to tap a finger on the cover, "this is one of those books?"

"It is!" Neirin squeaked excitedly. "The Dorwynnian king sent them here for our protection."

Edan laughed at the boy's glee. "Well done."

Blushing, Neirin wrapped his arms around his waist and glanced down again. "It wasn't difficult to find. I just wasn't sure where the archives were, so it took a bit to track down those shelves, but..."

Neirin trailed off when Edan put a hand on his arm. "Neirin, I'm proud of you. I knew you would find it, that's why I asked for your help."

The blush intensified. "Thank you, Master Edan."

He smiled, glancing over at the twins. "So, shall we?"

Fi gripped the thick leather cover, pulling it toward her. The pages were crisp and stained, several corners ripped or folded from years of use. Thin ribbons secured on the inner spine were tucked into various pages, which cracked slightly with each movement.

"That's not good." Naoi frowned at the words. "Unless you have a student up your sleeve that can read ancient Dorwynnian, or you're also a master linguist."

"I can read some Dorwynnian," Neirin admitted. "But nothing in the ancient language."

Sighing, Edan flipped through more pages, hoping foolishly that they might find something in the common tongue. It figured that they would find what they were looking for only to be unable to translate it.

Turning the page again, he paused, staring at the illustration. Something about the swirling shadows and the creatures standing within them made his skin crawl. They stood around a hole in the earth, various runes littering the ground at their feet. Through the hole, the faint outline of swirling demons swarmed, ancient and forgotten: Shadow Beasts, Kagai, Nakoiyaa, Akuma, Spindelen, creatures he didn't even know the names of. Holding hands, the demons standing around the hole smiled, eyes glinting in the dark wind, shimmering a blue-green rimmed with black.

A portal.

"What is that?" Neirin whispered.

Edan took a breath, wiping a hand over his mouth. "Nothing good."

"They're demons." Naoi turned to her sister.

Fi's eyes widened, her face pale. "No," she breathed. "Look." She pointed to the picture. "They're...Fae."

Edan saw them then, the delicately-pointed ears hidden beneath dark hair. His blood chilled.

"I don't understand," Neirin said. "I thought the Fae were...why would they be standing around a portal to The Shadowplains?"

"I don't know," Edan admitted. For Neirin's sake, he hoped his voice sounded stronger than he felt.

The boy backed away from the table, shaking slightly. "I..."

"Neirin, it's alright."

"Is it?"

Edan had no real answer for that. Still, he replied, "We will protect you."

"Can you promise me?" Neirin looked more like a scared mouse than a strong-minded student.

"To the best of my abilities, yes. I would give my life to protect you, all of you." The words knotted Edan's stomach slightly.

Neirin smiled weakly. "I trust you." His hand gripped the clasps of his robes, bunching the ivory fabric at his chest as his eyes flickered back to the book. "But I can't...I'm no help anyway." He turned to the door, pausing to add, "Put that wall up, Master Edan, please." Then he was gone.

"He's terrified," Fi said, watching the door click shut as a gust of wind blew through the library.

"He should be," Naoi added.

Edan didn't look at either of them, his eyes stuck on the picture. It didn't make sense. The demons were Fae, but Dorwynn had been the main line in the fight against Aeron since his first rise to power. King Reul's own father, King Elcan, had died during the Second Demon Wars trying to end Aeron's terror aided by the mortal queen, Maren. Yet these monsters...

"Edan?" He looked up numbly. Naoi tapped the page. "Do you know anyone who could read this?"

He shook his head. "I...I don't know." He scratched his jaw.

"Superior Albion needs to see this. And Master Karo." He pointed to the Fae-eared demons. "Karo might be able to explain something." Forcing his hands not to shake, Edan closed the book.

"Then let's go find them." Naoi stood, making her way to the door. Fi lingered, inspecting him. He gave a weak smile, stepping toward the door, but Fi put a hand on his arm. "Edan, it will be alright."

"Will it?"

Fi's gaze shimmered with hesitation. "It has to be."

"Are you two coming or not?" Naoi called, holding open the door.

Fi gripped his hand, twining her fingers with his. The contact sent a shiver up his arm, and he tensed. She paused for a second, pursing her lips, then stood on her toes, giving his cheek a swift kiss. Before he could gape at her, she pulled him toward the door.

"Fi..."

"Don't overthink it."

The chill air swirling through the central courtyard felt colder than usual. A flock of birds flew overhead, swarming the main building's high turrets, the bells ringing through the sky. Edan sighed, walking toward the sound, clutching the book to his chest. It weighed heavily against him, but he held it nonetheless.

It will be alright, he told himself. *It has to be alright.*

Albion, Karo, and the twins took the evening meal in Edan's rooms, an unbearable, chilled silence following their conversation. Edan's hearth provided no warmth as they sipped on honeyed wine and ate spice cakes. The cinnamon dough prickled along his tongue, sweet but slightly bitter.

No one spoke. The book lay open on the rug, the picture glowing darkly in the crackling flames.

Edan lounged on a settee, elbows resting on his knees, swirling the wine in his goblet. Occasionally he glanced up, avoiding the picture pulling for his attention. Beside him, Fi flexed her fingers, sheathing and unsheathing her crystal nails. Naoi leaned against the settee on the ground.

"So, the truth about this. That's what you want?" Master Karo gestured to the open book from his seat on the lipped stone hearth.

"Can you read it?" Superior Albion asked.

"I can." Master Karo rubbed his temples. "Though I must admit, it's been a long time since I read ancient Dorwynnian. This bit of history isn't typically a story that's told. Most races have forgotten it alltogether."

Edan looked up at the storyteller. "Bit of history?"

Master Karo emptied his goblet, dragging a hand through dark auburn hair, then pointed to one of the demon Fae within the circle. He was handsome, eyes shimmering with hunger, his head cocked to the side, watching the others around him. "That is Aeron."

"What?" Fi narrowed her eyes.

"No," Edan shook his head, swallowing the lump in his throat. "No, Aeron was a demon who found a way through the portal to our world."

Master Karo sighed. "That is the lie the first storytellers told to prevent the rise of panic."

"Aeron was Fae?" Edan breathed.

"Yes." Master Karo stood, pacing before the hearth. "Some say he was the first Demi-Fae, mothered by the demon queen herself. Others think he allowed his soul to be consumed by the darkness in his greed for power." He sighed again, staring down at the book. "I'm afraid that's all I know. King Reul and the storytellers of Dorwynn might know more. They might have other secrets their people have kept hidden."

"What sort of secrets?"

Karo stroked his beard. "I'm not too sure. Possibly information about The Twelve's ancient relics." He turned to them. "The relics, otherwise known as the weapons of the Gods, have resurfaced several times throughout our history. Each time, the weapons choose their master, just as the Goddess chose which of her children would wield them at the beginning of time."

Fi leaned forward. "Is that all they are?"

He nodded. "Era's whip, Yvaos's daggers, Syvi's cutlass—the weapons resembling a select few of The Twelve. But I haven't heard of their resurfacing since the Second Demon Wars."

"May Riona and The Twelve guide us," Albion whispered.

"Is there anything we can do?" Edan barely registered his own voice. "Is there any true hope to stop his return?"

"First things first," Albion stared at Master Karo. "Tomorrow, we gather the masters and put up the wall."

"And then?"

"Then, we—"

"What does this say?" Edan wasn't sure when Fi had stood and moved toward the book. She crouched before it now, fingers rushing along the cracking page she'd turned to. Unreadable words lined the margin, scribblings that looked to be ingredients bulleted near the bottom corner. In the center was a beautiful drawing of a flower stem. The white petals almost glistened off the page, shimmering a faint shade of light blue. Several little berries were clustered at the flower's center in the same shade.

Master Karo frowned. "Those are an ancient plant, the Goddess's sacred flower. They used to litter the countryside, blooming everywhere. But they were long ago extinct anywhere other than the Crystal Palace in Dorwynn thanks to shadow magic. They're called *liwotta krina*...Mercy's Moonberry in the common tongue."

"What do they do?" Edan asked, draining the remnants of his wine and coming to kneel beside her.

"Infused with the Goddess's power, it was once said that Noria used them to ward off darkness from The Shadowplains to protect Rathal. Her Demi-God daughter, Norah, the mortal Goddess of Healing, learned to use the berry juice to heal wounds from shadow magic and demon poison. All her healers on the Southern Continent wore pendants with dried flower petals as a protection charm. The gardens in the healer's guild were the most exquisite Navarre had ever seen."

"Until the Southern Continent was overthrown by Aeron's henchmen, and everything was destroyed," Naoi mumbled.

"But do you know why it was overthrown?" Master Karo asked. No one spoke. "Because Aeron feared these flowers. They're one of the only things capable of stopping him."

Edan looked up, confused. "Aeron can be stopped by a flower?"

"Oh, no." Master Karo laughed. "But Noria was the Goddess of Healing. So even when she gave up her immortality to marry Alaric Waeshorn, their bloodline was fused with her light, capable of healing even the strongest darkness. So, Norah's descendants, the healers from the Southern Continent, there's a good chance they might have the knowledge to use this to stop him."

"No one survived the massacre in Moslica though," Fi said.

"Perhaps," Master Karo mused. "Even without her bloodline, they're still powerful flowers." He tapped the page. "If we were able to get our hands on them, something tells me this spell would be quite useful."

"What does the spell do, Master Karo?" Albion asked.

He was silent for a moment, then said, "It reverses the effects of The Shadowplain's dark obsidian. It heals darkness and wards against evil."

"You mean, it wards against Aeron," Edan murmured.

Master Karo only smiled.

thirty-six

They'd been training for hours and Joseline still showed no signs of tiring. Quinn grinned at Azuri where the faerie perched in a nearby tree, then lunged. It was an effort to refrain from using too much speed, his body still not quite used to the increase in Fae abilities. But Joseline's progress was so impressive, he wanted nothing more than to help her grow.

They twisted and moved around one another, light and fire swirling, churning rhythmically. Punch, block, repeat. Her footwork was impeccable. Quinn towered over her, but she met his eyes fiercely.

Months ago, she'd been weak and helpless. Fierce and stubborn, but helpless. The woman standing before him was strong, mentally and physically. Lean muscles rippled beneath her thin tunic, her grip on her dagger relaxed and natural. Green eyes gleamed with determination and challenge.

Quinn twisted his fist toward her side. Joseline just barely avoided him, but she didn't falter. Sweat dripped into her eyes, her chest rising and falling as she lunged again and again. She never hit her mark, but each strike brought her closer than the last. Quinn blocked her easily, his eyes drawn to the beauty as she moved, the breeze ruffling her hair, the freckles spattered across her face.

Pain, sharp and surprising, lanced across his cheek, and he

stumbled back, brows knitting together. He touched his face, blinking at the sticky blood staining his fingers.

Joseline stared at him, her face beet-red. "I...Quinn, I'm so sorry...I didn't mean...are you alright?"

"I'm fine."

She reached for him hesitantly. "You're bleeding, Quinn. Gods, I..."

He pulled her into his arms, crushing her against his chest. "I'm fine." He chuckled. "You distracted me enough that you actually managed to hurt me. You should be proud."

Joseline lifted her hand to stroke his cheek, brushing soft fingers just below the cut along his cheekbone. "I didn't mean to."

Quinn gripped her hand, shaking his head. "I'm alright, it's just a scratch. It'll heal in an hour."

She pursed her lips. "But I—"

"Do you have any idea how adorable your blush is?" He ran his fingers through her loose braid. "It could drive a man crazy."

Joseline sucked on her lip. "You drive *me* crazy, idiot."

Quinn smiled, his eyes flickering down to her mouth. She eyed him, fluttering her lashes, then yanked on his tunic. He smirked against her lips, relishing in the sweet warmth of her kiss. They stayed like that for a moment before Quinn pulled away, still pressing his forehead against hers. "It's strange, you not needing me to look out for you anymore."

Joseline braced a hand on his chest. "I changed a lot this summer." She traced the outline of his tattoo, the delicate point of his ears. "We both have."

He opened his mouth to reply, but a paralyzing tremor of fear lanced through his body. Quinn let her go, stumbling back; Azuri was at his side instantly, a soothing calm on his shoulder.

"Your Highness?" Azuri whispered.

He shook his head, gritting his teeth just as Evalyn's vision flashed in his mind. He saw *through* her, staring at the beautiful woman radiating with darkness, pale blue eyes flickering with shadows. Evalyn was unharmed, but panic coursed through her—the same panic he felt.

Then Jenson flew through the air past her, crumpling against a lip of thick stone.

Evalyn rushed to him, and he moved, wincing in pain as he gripped his side.

The image vanished.

"Quinn, in the name of The Twelve, say something. You're scaring me." Joseline knelt, her grip tightening on his bicep.

He didn't remember falling to the ground. He bit his lip, forcing the breath to remain even.

Jenson is fine, get a grip on yourself. He's fine, and he's with Evalyn. They're together. He took Joseline's offered hand. "Everything is fine." He gave her cheek a quick kiss, then pulled her toward Larina's tent.

"Why don't I believe you?" She eyed him suspiciously. Azuri snorted.

"I'm fine, really." He paused, frowning, not quite sure how to explain what happened himself. "I just need to talk to Fallon."

"Alright..." Joseline murmured, tugging him toward the main circle of tents. "Let's find him." Quinn didn't follow, the space between their hands going taunt. "Quinn?"

"I...can I talk to him alone? I...you should be training." Joseline frowned. "I'm alright, I just think this is something I need to do alone."

Before she could protest further, Kai walked by with a small hunting party, two rabbits hanging from the rope over her shoulder. She beamed at them. "How's the training going?"

"Joseline actually managed to hit me," Quinn mused.

Kai whistled. "Impressive. It took me years to hit Larina." She quirked a brow, noting the tension between them. "Something wrong?"

"No, Quinn just had something he wanted to talk to Fallon about." Joseline smiled weakly. "Any idea where he might be?"

"He was talking with Larina before I left."

"Thank you," Quinn turned toward Larina's tent, then froze. "Joseline, can—"

"Don't worry," she kissed his cheek. "I'll help Kai." She glanced to the Fae woman. "If you need help, that is?"

"I will never turn away another pair of hands."

Smiling, Quinn headed toward Larina's tent. His mentor looked up when he entered. "What is it?"

Damn the old man for always being able to read his face. "Is it common for a twin's connection to be so strong I can...*see* them?"

"What's this about?" Larina asked, shoving her hands into her pockets. "Did you see Evalyn?"

Quinn nodded. "I think so. But it wasn't like I was watching her. More like I was living her emotions *through* her. Is that possible?"

"I'm not sure," Fallon admitted, turning to Larina. "Have Iona and Nara ever experienced anything like that?"

"Now that you mention it, yes." She reached for the steaming mug on the table, gripping it in both hands. "What did you see?"

"Jenson is with her. He was attacked by...I don't know. It was a woman, but Evalyn was terrified. There were shadows in her eyes..." Quinn breathed deeply, forcing the panic down. "I need...please I need to go to him."

"I can't let you do that." Fallon's authoritative tone was final. Quinn bit his lip, meeting his mentor's eyes. "I know you want to help him, and your bond with Jenson has always been strong. But you can't leave Joseline." He opened his mouth to argue, but Fallon continued, "You have to trust him."

"I do trust him, but why can't I just..."

"Quinn, Joseline needs you."

He gripped his sides, focusing on keeping his breath calm. "If something happens to him and I'm not there to protect him, I'll never forgive myself."

"Jenson is strong enough to take care of himself, you know that. Protecting the princess is the objective here."

Quinn bit his lip again to stop it from trembling. "I know."

Fallon turned to Larina, who cleared her throat. "It seems to me your telepathic connection with your sister is strengthening." Larina pursed her lips. "This is the first time it's happened?"

"Since we were children."

"Right, well, we'll keep an eye on it for now." She set the mug down. "Jenson didn't strike me as weak, Quinn. If I've learned anything from being around my brother, it's that we must trust those whose lives we value most to take care of themselves without us." With that, she left.

"She's right," Fallon said. "Try not to dwell on it. Once we get Joseline safely to Raenya, I promise we will find him before going anywhere else, alright?"

Quinn nodded. "Thank you." But Fallon only smiled, following Larina into the growing evening light.

thirty-seven

The darkness threatened to consume them all. Even though it couldn't fully control Dax like Elyon and Kellen, it crept through his mind and tortured his subconscious in dark, greedy tendrils, threatening to pull away his memories.

"It doesn't affect you, not like it does us." Elyon's whisper was near inaudible.

"No, but I can still feel it." Dax paused, his gaze sliding to the Dwarf boy. "You can see it, in your eyes sometimes." When Elyon didn't respond, Dax sighed. "Is it painful?"

"No," Elyon replied, the hesitation flickering in dark eyes, the only indication of his lie.

"I just don't feel in control of my own body. It's like I want to do one thing, but the darkness wants to do another," Kellen whispered. He hadn't said much of anything lately.

Dax sighed again. "My comrades will be here any day now. When we're free of this place, I might know somewhere we can search for a cure of sorts."

"Of sorts?" Elyon shifted toward Dax, his chains rattling. "Someplace unpleasant, I assume?"

"I'm not sure, to be honest," he admitted. "I've only sailed by it myself."

"And where is this mysterious sanctuary?" Kellen rasped.

"I wouldn't call it a sanctuary."

"Well?"

He grunted, rolling his wrist against the unforgiving steel. "The Isle of the Gods."

Elyon sucked in a sharp breath. "It's real?"

"Of course it is, it's a string of islands along the southern peninsula of Dorwynn, said to be one of the most sacred regions of Navarre. Second only to Moslica on the southern continent."

Excitement flashed in Elyon's eyes, but a disruption in the hall cut off his reply.

Dax's gaze flickered to the door. He should have expected Toren to come back, yet the foreman's presence still irritated him. "I see you're as horrible at following orders as ever, Toren."

The stout man snorted, his tongue tracing browned teeth. "You have no room to talk really, seeing as you're the one in chains and I am not."

"Yet here you stand, still jealous of me somehow." Dax wanted the man to deny it, but the admission danced through his gaze. "I wonder, why is that?"

"Shut up," he spat, shoving Dax backward. "You think you're so high and mighty, Sea Dragon? Look at you."

Dax quirked a brow. "Do I?"

"You've always thought you were better than me."

Dax blinked. "That's not true, Toren."

"It is. I know it is. Ever since they named you in charge instead of me, even though I was the one who obeyed without question. Every time, it was me, and you and your pathetic pirates still reaped the rewards because this was your home island. It makes me sick."

Dax could sense his companions' tension beside him, but he met Toren's gaze evenly. "If it makes you feel better about yourself to hate me, I won't stop you." He sighed. "But it was never my intention to make you feel that way."

"Shut up!" Toren screamed, his fist rocking Dax's jaw to the side.

Dax smirked before he could stop it. "Feel better now?"

"No." He punched Dax again. And again.

Dax let him, focusing on breathing between punches, on letting his body move with Toren rather than against him. He would endure this. No matter how easy it would be to kick the shorter man in the chest, he would not resort to violence.

"Well, are you just going to stand there?" Toren seethed. "Say something!"

"What is it you want me to say? That I hate you? That you're despicable? That I wish you dead?"

"Something, anything. Say anything." Toren begged, the hesitation all to audible in his voice.

"I don't hate you, Toren."

Fury filled his gaze. "You're a liar. A filthy, rotten liar, and I should kill you where you stand and be done with it."

Dax opened his mouth to reply, but the clink of unsheathed steel froze him. Blood splattered his chest when the blade protruded through Toren's body. The foreman coughed, dark liquid bubbling about his lips as he stared down at the blade. His eyes widened in shock before he collapsed to the ground, his limbs convulsing uncontrollably until he lay still.

Cohen stood before him, head cocked to the side as he grinned. "Sauda's breath, what a pain."

Elyon let out a startled gasp beside him, small face going pale. Dax smirked, shaking his head.

"Doin' alright, Cap?" Naomi asked from her watch near the doorway.

He eyed Toren's body, pursing his lips. "I've wanted to do that for a long time. But thank you."

Cohen ran a hand around the back of his neck. "Aye, sorry bout that."

Dax only shrugged. "You did what had to be done. He shouldn't have been here anyway." He found Naomi's gaze. "Did anyone hear him?"

Naomi slipped into the hall. Sighing, Cohen let out a groan. "Suppose I should get him somewhere they'll find him, yeah?"

"You already planned to kill him?" Elyon whispered.

Cohen eyed the young boy with a calculating look. "Not...here exactly. But we improvised." He winked.

Naomi returned. "All clear." She met Cohen's eyes for a moment before her gaze shifted to Toren's lifeless body. "We should probably get that lug somewhere they'll find him, though."

Cohen smirked. "Like I just said."

Dax nodded. "As far from here as you can manage. We don't want to run into any unneeded complications when we make a break for it."

Cohen saluted. "Leave it t' us, Cap." He braced himself, hauling Toren over his shoulder with a grunt. "Rinoa's arse, he's a heavy bastard, ain't he?" A smile brushed his lips at Elyon's chuckle.

Naomi hesitated before following Cohen into the hall. "Beck and Nim should be back with *Seraphina* any day now. We'll be out of here soon enough."

Kellen sniffed, his eyes opening slightly. "How is it we're planning to escape, exactly?"

Dax's mouth twitched. "We're going to walk through the front gates with my towers of the main fortress burning behind us."

Cohen popped his head back into the cell. "That's the plan, anyway. Come on, love, I need yer lookout expertise."

Shaking her head, Naomi walked passed him, pressing a kiss to his cheek. She turned back to Dax for a moment, her eyes kind. "We'll get you out of here, Dax." Her gaze fell to Elyon and Kellen. "All of you." Then she vanished into the darkness.

thirty-eight

"Then enlighten me, woman, I'm damn close to going out there and finding her myself!" Julia cringed at the anger in her father's voice. She glanced at her mother, fiddling with the jet pendant at her throat.

Queen Talia sighed. "Nathaniel, please. They're trying as hard as they can. Letting your temper get the best of you isn't going to bring Joseline back."

He ran a large hand through his thick scarlet curls. "I don't know what else to do. For years we've denied the stories of our ancestors, denied the possibility that Aeron could ever return to our world. Now his shadows torment our citizens and haunt our every move. Our people cower in panic, unsure if their own rulers have the capability to protect them, and twice now our captain of the guard has vanished in thin air. I don't know what to do, Talia."

Julia reached for her father's hand. "It's okay. Josie is as stubborn as you. Wherever she is, she's alright."

His booming laugh eased some of the tension from the room. Mother squeezed her hand. "*Almost*, not quite." She gripped her husband's hand as well. "We'll get through this."

Julia hoped so. She hadn't seen the shadow figure since that first sighting, but the unease followed her every move.

"You can ask the assassins," Talia added. "Sometimes my sister sends her spies to train in The Redlands with them."

Julia glanced toward her father. His thick brows furrowed thoughtfully. "She did mention that in the last council meeting. I'll talk to her. I've heard good things about Kasen."

There was silence for a moment before her mother went on, "Then there's the other option."

Nathaniel shook his head. "They are a myth I'm not sure I believe despite whatever else I hear."

Julia straightened. "You mean the Fae?"

Her parents turned to her, smiles kind. "Yes, dear."

"Anya always told us stories about them, about Dorwynn. She said it's beautiful, and their warriors are…" her voice faded, sadness taking hold as she thought of Anya. Nadie was gentle, but Anya had been a second mother to her. They never knew what happened to her and her husband; Kellen hadn't been the same after his parents disappeared.

Her father's smile weakened. "I miss them too, sweetheart."

"Do you think Kellen is with Josie?" she asked.

"I don't know, child. I have to believe he would have brought her home if he was."

Julia fiddled with her hair. "Could the Fae help find them? If they could, you should ask them."

Nathaniel touched her shoulder. "I will do everything in my power to bring your sister home safely."

"Good." Pushing back from the table, she hugged her parents with a firm squeeze.

"Goodnight, dear." Her mother gripped her face, giving her forehead a kiss. "Stay with Niven in the hallway."

"Yes, Mother."

Shadows danced along moonlit halls as she walked with Niven to her rooms, neither of them speaking. The days grew shorter now that Kyaos was upon them. The tension grew heavier the closer they got to her chambers, but only Julia seemed to notice it. The stone hallways were colder than usual, the shadows alive as they moved in the torchlight, and she clenched her fists.

The tension was strongest right outside her rooms.

Julia gulped, but forced herself to smile and curtsy to Niven before opening the door. "Nadie, I'm back!" The dark swallowed her words.

Strange, she thought, stepping into the sitting room. *Nadie usually has the candles lit.*

Coming into her sitting room, Julia froze.

The figure from the hallway stood before the cold hearth, its smile glittering like rusted steel. It gripped Nadie from behind, one hand covering her mouth while the other pressed a sharp nail to the elderly woman's throat. Her pale blue eyes were wide with terror.

"See," It whispered into Nadie's ear loudly enough for Julia to hear, "I told you she'd come." Its dark eyes met hers. "Little princess, I'm so pleased to meet you."

Julia shook, frantically thinking of how to get Nadie free without harm. Niven had taught her a few combat skills, but she was no trained warrior. *Don't just stand there, do something! Help her, don't be a fool!*

The figure laughed as if it could read her thoughts. "Oh please, precious, there's no need for that."

Julia's eyes never left the figure. "What do you want?"

Its smile prickled goosebumps along her flesh. "Nothing too drastic."

Nadie jerked her head away, "No, Princess, don't listen to him. He's a demon, he—"

The figure's grip tightened, his nail digging into her throat warranting a gasp of pain.

"Stop!" Julia cried. "You're hurting her."

"I only want you to come with me," he murmured. "A...friend of mine wants to meet you, that's all. He needs a *favor*."

Her eyes darted to Nadie. She had to protect her people, always. Joseline would. How could she call herself a princess if she whimpered in fear when their lives were threatened?

Julia clenched her fists. "If I come with you, will you let her go?"

Nadie shook her head, and Julia gulped, the question lingering between them. "Yes," he said at last. "If you come willingly."

Julia gave a sharp nod. He pushed Nadie forward, reaching for Julia's waist in the same movement. She slammed into his chest, shadows enveloping her small body. The last thing she saw of her chambers was Nadie crying out, reaching for her, as the shadows swarmed around them.

thirty-nine

Soft chirping whispered through the open window on the fall breeze, calm and soothing. For a moment, it kept the dream alive, the false hope that yesterday was just an illusion.

But blinding pain lanced along his broken ribs with each breath, pulling him back to reality. Jenson winced, bracing himself to shift upward on the pillows, but a sigh from the bed beside him kept him frozen.

He blinked, glancing over at Erza. He hadn't expected she'd still be here. Her warmth radiated from tanned flesh, a peaceful comfort at his side. Her silky coal hair sprawled across his bare chest. Her cheeks and nose were flushed a light pink, her chest rising and falling in sleep against his shoulder. Her hand still gripped his, the other wrapped around his bicep. She moaned softly, snuggling against him, and her lips puckered.

Jenson refrained from chuckling, not wanting to wake her. She looked so innocent, so different from her waking counterpart. Tempting and exotic. She moaned again, the strap of her gown slipping from her shoulder as she moved, the fabric pulling taut across her breast.

Jenson's cheeks heated and he averted his eyes, frowning. Gods, what was the matter with him? He lay beside a beautiful, half-naked woman and blushed like a naïve boy? What kind of spell had the damn witch cast on him?

He steadied his breath, squeezing her hand lightly, and she mumbled something inaudible into his bicep. Jenson laughed, then hissed at the pain in his side. "Flower, wake up, or I'll have no choice but to believe you're mumbling sweet nothings to me."

"Tell yourself that, Jenson, if it makes you feel better." She yawned, stretching her hands over her head, the motion lazy as she arched her back against the bed.

"Nothing makes me feel better but staring at your beauty." His eyes fluttered down her body.

Erza frowned, propping herself up on an elbow. "You just can't help yourself, can you?"

He flashed a playful smirk, winking at her. "Around you? Never, apparently."

Erza rolled her eyes, sitting up to run her fingers through her tangled hair. "No wonder you're such a lady-killer. Common mortals love a man who can make them laugh."

Jenson narrowed his eyes. "Who said I was a—"

Erza put a calloused finger to his lips. Those lilac eyes flickered to his throat, smiling at the thumping pulse she could no doubt see there. "Oh, please," she teased, brushing his onyx hair from his eyes almost timidly. "I can practically smell the pathetic women on you."

"Does that bother you?"

He watched her hand trail down his body, sending delighted shivers along his spine. "Don't be ridiculous. I don't have emotions. I'm a heartless witch, remember?"

Jenson laughed, then winced. She inspected his face while her hands pulled down the sheets to his hips. He winced again when her hands touched the shadowy bruising along his ribs. "You know I don't believe that for a second. If that were true, I wouldn't make you so nervous."

Erza frowned, leaning over him. Her breasts dipped, and his eyes fluttered down before he could stop himself. She quirked an eyebrow, slipping cool fingers beneath his chin and lifting his gaze from her chest. Her skin was soft where it brushed the spidery web of inky tendrils. "You don't make me nervous."

"Don't I?" He traced a lazy circle along her forearm, and she jumped.

"Damn it, Jenson, please."

He raised an eyebrow. "I thought I didn't make you nervous?"

Erza's hands froze over his broken ribs. "Magic is hard enough when your mind *is* focused." He opened his mouth to speak, and she cut him off sharply. "Do you want to be healed or not?"

She pressed her hands to the bruise. He gritted his teeth, preventing the next wince, and nodded. "So, how much do you train your magic?" he asked, vaguely recalling the whisper of his mother's voice.

Her hands glowed lilac, a thin layer prickling his skin; cool like a kiss of hushed wind spreading through his bones. Jenson didn't try to fight the sigh that slipped through his lips, when the ache released.

"It depends on what path you choose to pursue in your training," she replied.

"Is there anything uncommon? Talking to the dead, or necromancy?"

Erza shot him a glare. "Those aren't the same thing, Jenson. Communication with the dead is actually quite common if there's a strong enough bond. Necromancy is a forbidden dark magic."

"I see." Jenson said nothing else, watching her fingers trace over his ribs. As she worked, the black web of bruises shrank, lightening to his skin's normal bronze. But Erza paled too fast for someone with years of control.

Jenson yanked her hands away from his abdomen, the color returning to her cheeks almost immediately. "Erza, stop, you're no healer. You're hurting yourself."

"I know my limit, thank you." She tried to pull her wrists from his grasp, but he refused to let her go.

"No, you don't. You may know your limit with normal healing, but nothing about this is normal. You have no idea how strong the darkness is. I don't need you exhausting yourself for my sake. You have other things to focus your energy on."

Erza glared at him for a moment before nodding. Only then did he release his grip. She slipped from the bed in silence, the silk gown brushing her upper thighs as she rummaged through the armoire for clothes and closed the bathroom door.

Jenson released a deep sigh, resting his head against the pillows. This was even worse than they could have imagined. The shadows and demons were *everywhere.*

The thought of Aeron rising to power terrified him. The thought of their failure terrified him. He wanted to be hopeful, but they were running out of time.

I meant what I said, darling. You have more strength than you know.

Jenson's eyes widened, his chest clenching at his mother's unmistakable voice in his head. He opened his mouth then closed it, unsure how to respond.

Her laugh echoed in his mind. *It's alright, don't be afraid. I'm not able to hold the connection long. You are capable of so much, if you're willing to learn how to use the healer's light within you.* She paused, her voice tinged with sorrow. *I'm so sorry darling, I didn't mean to hide it from you.*

Jenson glanced toward the bathroom door. "I wasn't imagining things. It really was you I heard."

It was, but just as I granted you the hidden knowledge of your power, I also must give you warning. Darkness may overpower the light, that is certain. Only those whose hearts are pure may rain their light down in turn to cover the darkness.

Jenson frowned. "I don't understand."

Joseline will be strong, with time. But you contain the purest of healing magic. The strength of the first healer, the Demi-God Norah's blood runs in your veins as it ran through mine, as does the Fae fire that ran through your father's. I used the last of my strength to shield you before I died, but when Adria struck you, the shield vanished, reawakening your healing gifts. The shield saved your life.

"You aren't making any sense, Mother."

You are a Demi-Fae, blessed with the blood of light and fire, heir to the fallen healer's guild in the south, and sielapora *to the Prince of Dorwynn. You hold a great potential, and a great threat to the darkness.*

Jenson frowned. "I know we're *sielapora*. Fallon told us a long time ago."

Kindred spirits are beautiful and rare. You and Quinn have a special bond, a special connection. The door to the bathing room opened. *Rowen, she's got a gift for healing, the* sielapora *to the witch who holds your heart. You'll learn quickly once you start, but she's the one who can help you.*

Without anything else, her voice was gone. Jenson said nothing of the conversation, only smiled at Erza.

"I'll send Rowen to stay with you. Her specialty is healing, so if you experience any more pain, she can help. Don't do anything reckless like try and go anywhere, will you?"

"When you asked me so nicely?" Jenson teased, "I wouldn't dream of it."

Erza rolled her eyes. "Wonderful."

"Where will you be?"

Her hand paused on the door. "I need to speak with my mother."

"About me?" he pressed.

Erza's expression remained emotionless. "It doesn't matter, Jenson." She turned the handle but didn't pull, as if she expected him to press her.

He straightened a bit to a sitting position. "Erza, I was sent to find out what darkness was growing here. Yesterday, I was attacked by *Aeron's daughter*, who's been playing at coven leader for centuries. We're all involved in this now, whether you want to admit that or not. So keeping me in the dark, shutting me out, it isn't going to help a damned thing."

Erza's eyes brimmed with a dangerous rage he usually saw only when he talked back to Quinn. But Quinn was his leader. Erza wasn't.

When she realized he wasn't backing down, she sighed. "Try not to torment Rowen too much." Her voice softened as she let herself out.

Jenson hissed, and brought himself slowly to a sitting position. His side burned in protest, but the inky web had waned, the pain dwindling further thanks to Erza's help. He moved his legs over the edge of the bed, biting back a cry.

If he was going to be any good at healing others, the least he could do was fight through his own pain.

forty

Wind whistled through the circular, dirt-covered arena, warm sunshine beaming through the open ceiling. Evalyn gritted her teeth, the turquoise barrier shimmering faintly before her as Astrid launched another gust of air. The air dissipated, then vanished.

Astrid quirked a brow. "May the light of the Goddess and The Twelve bless us all. Your will not to lose control is insane." She didn't try to keep the awe from her voice, something Evalyn didn't think the dark-skinned witch showed lightly.

The other Elites halted their morning training to look at her. Ira and Zea gave her swift nods then continued their duel, each with a hatchet in both hands. Vien smirked, throwing stars dangling from agile fingers, and Curra's dark brown eyes danced with pride. Eva fiddled with her hair, studying the ground.

Rowen grinned, motioning for Ysta, Soren, and Azar to pair off with Maya, before skipping over to them and wrapping an arm around Astrid. "I told you, didn't I? She'll never be a true fighter, sure, but for someone who was never even able to practice…"

Astrid let out a low whistle. "I didn't expect you to mean it so literally."

Eva blushed. She'd always thought years in chains would weaken her control over the wildfire once she was free. She never imagined it would actually *strengthen* it.

"After all this time, you don't trust me?" Rowen pouted, giving Astrid's cheek a swift kiss, eyes dancing playfully when they met Eva's.

Astrid threw another gust of wind toward her, thinking to catch her off balance, but again Evalyn brought up the shield. The funneled gust sputtered and died against it. Several feet away, Maya twirled a staff around her slender body, parrying with Soren. She paused, flashing Evalyn a wild grin, the gap in her front teeth barely visible.

Rowen tightened the long tail of hair atop her head and pursed her lips. "Now, I want to try something new." Astrid frowned as Rowen rushed on, "Maya told me you almost shifted."

Evalyn sent Maya an annoyed smile, which Maya returned with an apologetic shrug. "It wasn't that big of a deal, really."

Vien paused mid-strike. "Not a big deal, are you joking?"

"Do you realize how useful shifting could be if you control it as well as that shield?" Curra agreed.

Astrid almost smiled. "Maybe it's not a big deal to you, Evalyn, but it is a unique Fae ability. Almost all the strong shifters were wiped out with the Demi-Gods during the Second Demon Wars aside from King Reul's cadre. So it's worth learning to control."

"Not to mention, seeing someone shift would be wicked," Rowen added, sticking her tongue out at the teasing shove from Astrid.

Evalyn crossed her arms, biting her lip. "But I don't want to...I don't even know where to start."

Rowen's lilac eyes simmered with the challenge. "Try just imagining the shift. Picture yourself changing in your mind. Isn't that what you did before?"

Evalyn gulped but nodded. She closed her eyes, all too aware of the chill pulsing through her as the well of slumbering power flared, the already visible magic reaching up her sides, clawing for freedom. It roared hungrily, but Eva gritted her teeth, maintaining the control.

I will not be your prisoner.

"Incredible," Maya breathed.

Carefully, Evalyn opened her eyes, the remnants of turquoise smoke swirling about her. When it cleared, she stared down at two large paws, white as snow. Her eyes widened.

"I honestly didn't expect that to work on the first try." Rowen wiped a hand around the back of her neck.

"Maybe it was luck?" Soren suggested.

Evalyn's heart fluttered with pride, but her words came out as a satisfied huff. Rowen and Maya blinked simultaneously, then threw their heads back in fits of roaring laughter. The other Elites turned to them, Azar snickering as Ira and Zea snorted in unison. Even Astrid cracked a smile.

"So, no talking when the wolf is out," Ira said, pulling her hair back to expose the shaved left side of her head.

Astrid shrugged. "I don't know of any animals that can physically talk anyway. Even the ancient Aonani foxes of the Goddess could only communicate telepathically."

Maya approached her, holding out a hand. Evalyn eyed her warily, large white tail swishing back and forth in the soft dirt, but she sniffed her outstretched fingers.

"Can you fight in this form?" Maya asked, scratching behind Evalyn's ear.

No, Evalyn whined. *I don't—*

Rowen crossed her arms, favoring her right hip as Astrid walked over to the others who had gone back to practicing. "We can always try." Rowen pointed to the middle of the arena. "Let's see if your control is as strong in this form, shall we?"

Before Evalyn could whine again, the scent of jasmine and lemon verbena filled her nose. Her gaze shifted toward the open arch leading to the hallway as Erza approached. The worry evaporated from her expression as she caught sight of Eva.

"So," Erza mused. "I see the training is going well?"

Evalyn opened her mouth to huff, snarling as pain lanced through the base of her neck. The turquoise fog swarmed about her. When it cleared, she was human once more. Her legs crumpled beneath her, cramping when she tried to move, but she forced herself to stand.

"I can shift," she breathed, giddy with excitement. She brushed the dirt from her crimson gown and tugged at the thin leather belt slung around her waist. The golden tassels at the ends jingled slightly from the movement.

Erza laughed, though the twinge of worry still filled her tone. "I can see that."

Evalyn gave her an inquisitive look, but it was Rowen who spoke. "What's wrong?" The Elites stopped practicing, drawn in by the question.

Maya stepped forward. "Is Jenson—"

"He's fine, Maya," Erza cut her off. "I just need Rowen to watch him for me."

Eva laughed before she could stop herself. "Something tells me Jenson doesn't need a guard dog."

"You can say that again," Maya muttered.

Rowen raised an eyebrow. "The famed Erza Stormwood, lost her heart to a wounded Demi-Fae?"

Soren, Ysta, and Vien chuckled at the remark, but Erza's glare stopped them. "No, I just want to make sure the poison doesn't get worse. You're my *sielapora* and a strong healer. I trust your judgement."

"Of course." Rowen left without another word.

Erza turned to the others. "Astrid, Vien, with me. Soren, Azar, stay with Maya and Eva. The rest of you, humor me and do another perimeter check?"

"Anything specific to look for?" Curra asked, sheathing her scimitar at her hip.

Erza shook her head. "I just want us ready. Now that we know the darkness *is* Anwen, who knows when she might strike?" Curra and the others made to leave, but Erza added, "I mean what I said. Scout the usual circles around Thya and the watchtower. You see one toe out of line from *anyone* and you report to me. *Immediately.*"

"And where are we going?" Astrid asked.

"I need to speak with the Queen," Erza's voice echoed as they vanished down the hall.

Evalyn watched them go, Soren and Azar positioning themselves near the arena entrance, and cleared her throat. "Maya," she breathed.

"I...I know what the others said. I know they were trying to help, but I don't want to fight. Not like that."

Maya faced her, smiling weakly. "I know."

Her pulse quickened. "You...you do?"

"Sure," Maya approached her, giving her an amused look. "You've been through a lot. You've...you've watched people die."

Evalyn bit her lip. "I have, but, so have they."

"It isn't the same," Maya shook her head, placing a gentle hand on her shoulder. "They've killed people. Trained in combat from a young age, but you...you've watched people suffer. Good people, people you cared about."

Her lip trembled involuntarily. "I don't mean to be useless," she breathed. "I...I used to think I wanted that. That I was strong enough to take down those who would oppress the weak. But now..."

"Eva, there's nothing wrong with not wanting to fight."

Evalyn met Maya's gaze, the younger girl's grip on her shoulders gentle. "There isn't?"

"No," Maya smiled. "And it doesn't make you weak either. It takes strength to make that decision for yourself."

She hung her head. "I just don't want to be useless." Sighing, she hugged herself. "When I was captive on Narcio, I used to dream of the day I would break free and kill my oppressors. I needed it. I craved it." She let out a weak laugh. "But now, seeing the beauty and goodness in the world I...I want to be a part of that beauty. I don't want to be the reason someone else suffers."

Cool hands lifted her chin and Evalyn met Maya's eyes, their green depths swirling with pride and understanding. "It takes a strong heart to admit that. You have more courage that you give yourself credit for."

Her lips trembled, but she managed a smile. "Yeah."

"And I promise, you won't get any crap over not wanting to fight from me." She smacked Evalyn's shoulder lightly. "But that's not to say I can't at least teach you how to defend yourself in case you need to."

"You did promise me you would," Evalyn said.

Determination flickered across Maya's expression. "I did." In response, she gripped Evalyn's dress, hiking it up under her belt then tightening the leather around her waist, exposing her thighs up past her knee. "We don't want that to be in the way though. I'd hate to see such pretty fabric ripped."

Without warning, Maya's leg shot up, missing Evalyn's cheek by half an inch. Evalyn stepped back, frowning, and Maya twisted her elbow toward her ribs. "Maya, wait, what am I—"

The smaller girl never stopped moving. Duck, weave, spin, punch. She circled Eva, always an inch from her face or side. Evalyn let out a gasp when Maya actually tapped her lower spine. "So, are you going to start moving, or am I training myself?" Her breath whispered in Eva's ear.

This time when Maya spun, Evalyn brought her forearm up to block the swing at her nose. Their eyes met for a moment, and Maya smiled, moving her fists down toward Eva's stomach. Again, Evalyn blocked her.

"That's much better," Maya said, shifting on her feet as she waited for Evalyn to follow her movements. "We can work on breakaway maneuvers tomorrow. For now, I'm just curious if you can keep up. I promise you an attacker won't stop for you to catch your breath whether they're demon or human."

Nostrils flaring, Evalyn mimicked her, a slow smile spreading across her face.

forty-one

"Focus," Quinn growled. "You can do this."

Joseline narrowed her eyes, wanting nothing more than to slap the annoyed look off his handsome face.

Shea huffed. *You could just punch him, that'll shut him up.*

Right, because nothing says determination like breaking my hand on abs of steel, Joseline replied.

"Your problem is you aren't focusing," Logan said. "Begging Your Highness's pardon."

She clenched her fists, smiling weakly at the lord who reminded her of Kellen in so many ways. "I am trying."

She breathed deeply, nostrils flaring as the prickle of magic electrified her flesh, surfacing from the well within her. Her eyes flashed open in excitement. But no sooner than she did, the golden shield enveloping her simmered and died. She kicked at the dirt, scowling.

"No, you need to stop thinking about Quinn and start worrying about yourself," Larina commented.

The blush heated Joseline's cheeks before she could fight it.

"She doesn't think about me all the time." Quinn grumbled. He lounged on a fallen tree trunk, bracing himself on his forearms, watching her training proceed.

Kai raised an eyebrow. "Just like you don't think about her?"

Larina snorted. "Like father like son. Reul can't admit his feelings either."

Frowning, Joseline crossed her arms. "I just can't do it. You're Fae. You're born with magic. My body may be getting stronger, but I'm not capable of this. I'm no witch."

"I would be tempted to believe you," Kai smirked. "But I've seen you do it before." A pause. "And I know you've been practicing on your own."

Joseline didn't like the look that followed, passing between Kai and Larina. She opened her mouth to say as much when Larina lunged for her nephew. Shock flashed across Quinn's face as she twisted his arms behind his back, Kai's dagger pressed against his throat.

Panic coursed through Joseline, boiling her blood. "Are you crazy?" she shrieked, flinging her arms toward them. Blinding light erupted from her fingertips, and startled gasps filled the air when it cleared. Joseline blinked.

Anyone within a five-foot radius of Quinn had been knocked to the ground. Horses shied away from their riders, and saddlebags lay sprawled on the ground, their contents half-emptied. Some of the soldiers scrambled to clean up the mess, while others stared at her, wide-eyed and shaking.

Quinn growled, spinning to Larina. "What in Yavos's name was that about?"

Larina shook her head. "Interesting. Your power is tapped into your emotions."

Joseline glanced toward Quinn, still fuming beside her. "Is that a good thing?"

"Yes, and no. The control must be impeccable." She paused before adding, "Now, use that to control the light." Her gaze flickered to Quinn. "Use your fear of losing him."

Joseline opened her mouth to say she wasn't afraid of losing him, but quickly swallowed the lie. She *was* afraid. They all knew it, thanks to that display.

Joseline closed her eyes this time, letting the truth consume her.

If controlling the power was what it took to defeat Aeron, she would do it. Her people, her country needed her.

The realm needed her. To keep Quinn and the others alive, she would do anything, even give her own life. She released a breath and opened her eyes.

Only it wasn't *her* eyes she saw through.

Confused, she shifted her gaze, the breath pausing in her throat as she took in her surroundings. The world towered above her, the earth soft beneath her padded white paws and silken fur. A sense of awe and inexplicable pride filled her.

She had *merged* her essence with Shea—both spiritually and physically.

She cocked her head, one ear drooping to the side. It was strange, seeing the world from the ground. The breeze ruffled through Shea's fur, through *her* fur, leaving her bare and exposed.

You did it. Quinn's voice echoed in her head and she looked up. He'd shifted into his wolf form. Even he loomed over her, his onyx fur dark and masculine.

You look riveting, he admitted slyly.

Seriously? She huffed, walking toward him on unsteady legs and breathing in his scent. Despite the change and the crisp fall air around them, it was still him—pine and frankincense and utterly Quinn.

Joseline smiled, the feeling strange on Shea's lips. Still, she let out a soft chirp, arching her back and rubbing against his side.

The chuckle rumbled his entire body. *I want to show you something.* Quinn nuzzled his nose to hers, caressing her cheek with his. She leaned into him, nodding.

Quinn shot past her, streaking through the trees like black lightning, his massive form no more than a shadow.

Shea, if you're still here, please don't kill me.

Shea's sarcastic laugh echoed in her mind. *I'm still here, don't worry.*

With a swift nod to Kai, Joseline ran after Quinn. The wind ruffling her fur was exhilarating. She breathed deeply, absorbing the scents and sounds of the forest as she caught up with him. His eyes danced when they met hers, the joy reflecting her own.

In that moment, she knew she could do anything as long as she was by his side.

One look at Quinn, and I knew I would follow him to the ends of the earth. Maya's words echoed in her mind. She might have laughed at them once, but now they were solid and binding.

Quinn howled into the night, echoing her bliss. She followed his lead, consumed by the true freedom.

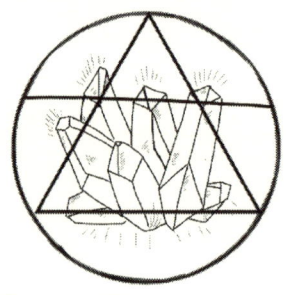

forty-two

With the Master's collective help, the wall went up without effort. The students hadn't noticed any difference, and the spell didn't interfere with their weekly trips to the port in Singaro Bay. But Edan couldn't stop worrying.

Neirin, though he said nothing of the book, cast nervous glances at him every time they passed in the hallway. Part of him hated himself for worrying the young man, but without the book, the wall wouldn't be in place. The students wouldn't be protected.

Their protection was all that mattered.

"I know what it is!" Fi exclaimed, bolting up from where she lounged on his settee.

Edan raised an eyebrow at her. Naoi turned to her sister. "I think I've figured it out as well. I knew they looked familiar."

"I'm sorry, I'm confused," Edan frowned.

"The Moonberries. I've seen those flowers before," Fi tapped a finger against her cheek. "I've been trying to figure out where I've seen them since the wall went up last Daea."

"Are you planning to share with the class?" he prodded.

Fi chortled. "You're such a professor."

Edan rolled his eyes. "Well?"

Twisting chest-length onyx hair into a braid, Naoi said, "They aren't extinct everywhere but Dorwynn."

Fi grinned, nodding at her twin. "Queen Rowena keeps some in her personal garden at Ravencrest."

Edan's pulse quickened. He gripped the back of the settee. "We need to collect some." He glanced between the twins. "If we could add them to our stocks here, if Master Karo could translate the recipe for that potion..." he pointed to the closed book on his worktable.

"Good luck getting Queen Rowena to let you into her private gardens," Naoi muttered.

But Fi's eyes sparkled. "Well, maybe if *Edan* asked her, she would agree." She bit her lip, eyelashes fluttering.

Edan's heart clenched. "You want *me* to speak with my mother."

Her smile spread slowly. "I do."

Naoi crossed her arms. "You, Vien, and Rowen just love getting into trouble, don't you?"

Fi shrugged. "It'll be no trouble at all."

Edan gave a nervous laugh. "You do realize I've never *met* my mother? She told Superior Albion to kill me when I was born, and he didn't." He ran a hand through his hair, walking out onto the balcony, letting the cool evening air soothe his heating skin. "Erza doesn't know I exist."

"Maybe Erza is the one you should speak to, then."

"I don't feel like being considered for grotesque murder, thank you." Edan didn't look at her when he spoke.

"Fi," Naoi began, "maybe you should leave—"

"It's alright, Naoi, I'll talk to him."

Naoi said nothing else. With a soft click, the door closed behind her.

Edan sighed. "Fi, I really don't think that's a good idea."

He sucked in a breath when she came to stand beside him, their fingers brushing together. "Are you afraid?"

He turned to her. "What kind of stupid question is that? My sister and mother are vicious murderers, of course I'm afraid of meeting them."

"You know," she reached up to stroke his cheek, "you really

shouldn't be so upset about it."

"I'm not—"

"You are." Fi smiled, and he swallowed the growl. "And you shouldn't judge people before you know them. Erza isn't a murderer."

"Isn't she?"

"No. You just don't want to meet them and then feel obligated to stay. You don't want to feel torn between them and your students."

Edan opened his mouth, then closed it.

Fi chuckled. "Oh, please, it's written all over your face." She leaned against his shoulder. "Master Edan, the novice healer's self-proclaimed god, protector of the innocent."

He scoffed, tilting his head against hers. "I'm still not used to this."

"Used to what?" Fi looked up at him then, her eyes glittering with confusion.

"Being touched," he squeezed her hand. "At least not like this." Fi looked as if she might make a flirtatious reply but he squeezed her hand tighter.

"How long has it been since…" her voice trailed off.

"Since Kiran died?" Fi nodded. "Over a century." He waited for her to laugh, but she just watched him, her expression filling with sadness. He turned away. "Go on, Fi, laugh."

"I'm not laughing at you for having a kind heart, Edan."

His cheeks heated. "Surprising, I thought you of all people would."

"Guarding your heart after it was broken shouldn't be something to make you feel sorry for yourself. It only proves how kind you are." Fi smiled. "I think you'd be a great ruler."

"I don't want to rule."

"Your people would love you, if you treated them half as well as you treat your students."

"I don't know anything about ruling a country. Besides, Rekiv's never had a King before. The people wouldn't accept me even if I wanted to." Fi was silent, watching him with a strange look in her eyes. "What?"

"Nothing, just…I can see why Kiran loved you."

The blush exploded across his face. "Fi, we've been doing so good about not flirting and—"

"I wasn't...I wasn't flirting."

He raised an eyebrow. "Weren't you?"

"No. I was being serious." She studied their twined fingers. "You're a good man."

He coughed, pushing away from her to brace himself against the railing. "Your flattery won't earn you any kisses, you know"

Fi laughed. "If I wanted to kiss you, I would do it. I'm rather enjoying just watching you squirm."

Edan chuckled. "So, are you going to come with me to find those flowers, or am I expected to face my mother and sister on my own?"

"You *are* going, then?"

"I think I could handle it, if you go with me." His heart pranced slightly.

She eyed him, releasing a half laugh. "Sure, Master Edan, I'll go with you."

"You will?" He fought to keep the thrill from his voice.

"Try not to be too excited," she winked. "Now that the wall is up, we would be safe to leave soon."

"I can talk with Superior Albion about it in the morning."

Fi nodded, then looked up at him through her lashes. "So, what do I get for being your loyal escort?"

"Nothing."

Fi pouted. "Nothing? That doesn't sound fair."

He shook his head. "I don't give handouts, ask any of my students."

"So if I wanted something I would have to take it myself?"

Edan shrugged, turning back toward his room. He didn't expect the yank on his overcoat or the shock as her soft lips pressed against his. He let out a startled breath, taking a step back. "What in Noria's name was that?"

Fi bit her lip, trailing a finger along his collarbone as she walked past him. "Don't overthink it."

Edan caught her arm, his pulse racing. *Damn her.* "May all The Twelve curse you if you assume I won't overthink that."

Fi winked again, then started for the door. "Then do, I won't stop you."

"Your efforts to break the wall around my heart are amusing," he called after her, still slightly out of breath.

She twisted her head, lilac eyes sparkling. "I'm doing no such thing, *Master Edan*. You're doing that all on your own."

"You really do have Kiran's sass."

Fi laughed. "Good, you could use some sass to calm that anger of yours."

"I'm not always angry, you know."

"See you in the morning, Edan." Fi let herself out.

Edan ran a hand through his hair, whistling as he eyed the book on the worktable. *Tomorrow,* he thought, catching his gaze in the mirror before undressing and sliding into bed. *Tomorrow, we might get some answers.*

Endra let out a series of pleasant chirps, ruffling indigo wings when she caught sight of Edan. Fi turned toward him, then doubled over in laughter. Edan narrowed his eyes, hefting the satchel further up onto his shoulder. "What?"

Fi just shook her head, turning back to the straps she'd been adjusting on Endra's saddle.

The frown deepened as he looked down at his clothes. He hadn't worn anything ridiculous—thick chestnut breeches tucked into boots that matched his coat, the tunic beneath a deep grey with swirling navy accents. A black belt was slung across his hips, matching the heavy fabric of the cloak draped around broad shoulders. He'd kept the hood up, an added layer of protection from the cold stinging his face.

"Oh, would you stop looking at yourself like that? Endra was just excited to see you is all," Fi said, her voice light with humor.

Edan released a sigh, shaking his head as he walked toward the Kitsugon and her rider. He was starting to wonder if the Elites slept and bathed in their riding leathers. In the month he'd gotten to know them, he never saw them in anything else.

"Found your calling at last I see, pureblood." Master Nichol's voice froze him in place. He turned slowly, focusing on the anger threatening to rise. The elder master wore the usual plain robes, his hands concealed beneath long, draped sleeves. Masters Ansell and Ballin stood behind him, silent and obedient as ever.

Edan opened his mouth to reply, but a soft voice said, "Master Nichol, Superior Albion wishes to speak with you." Nichol faced Zarin, glaring, but made his way back into the courtyard.

Edan gave a weak smile. "You don't need to stand up to him for me *all* the time, you know. I'm not a boy anymore."

Tawny eyes shimmered with amusement. "Don't fool yourself, Edan. You can't control your temper around him and you never have."

They were silent for a moment before both men laughed, deep and calming. "Sometimes, I don't like how right you are, Zarin."

"You're nervous."

Zarin was always able to see right through him. "A little, but this is for the best. I have to believe that, regardless of what my...what my mother might say or do."

Zarin ran a hand along his ebony-bearded jaw. "You're stronger than you think."

Edan laughed. "For the dangers we face, I don't think I'm nearly as strong as I need to be."

"Maybe not, but then again, we never know our true strength until we need it. Kiran knew your strength even when you didn't." Nodding toward Fi, he added, "So does she."

"My nose itches when people are talking about me, you know," Fi called over to them.

Edan ignored the light blush heating his cheeks. "Try to keep Master Nichol under control for me, will you?"

Zarin smiled. "Of course. Karo, Rouland, Serrell, and Jeremias are on your side in this. Even if it doesn't always seem like it, they do accept you."

And they don't blame you, either. The unspoken words lingered.

"Good, I'm glad." The air whipped heavy gusts of wind about them, and Edan looked up as Naoi's burnt-orange Kitsugon circled above them. "I should probably go."

"May the light and the strength of Rinoa and The Twelve guide you, Edan Stormwood."

"Keep the students safe for me," was all Edan said before turning toward Fi and Endra.

His bag thumped against his thigh, the book within a reminder of what they searched for, the picture concealed within the reason they needed to find it. The promise of what they might lose if they failed a constant weight on his chest.

"Ready, *Master Edan*?" Fi asked.

"As ready as I'm going to be," he replied.

"Any day would be lovely," Naoi shouted down. "It's a two-day ride back to Thya, don't forget." Her Kitsugon let out an approving cry and they took off, the harsh wind vanishing with them.

"Patience is a virtue," Edan grumbled under his breath as Fi climbed into the saddle. He took the hand up she offered him.

"Not in this case, unfortunately." She buckled the straps around them both, turning to flash him a wild grin. "Shall we, Mister Stormwood?"

Edan's lips twitched. "I think I like Master Edan better."

She planted a quick kiss on his cheek. "Master Edan it is, then." She leaned over Endra's neck. "Fly, girl."

Try as he might not to think about the ground falling away below them, Edan's grip tightened around Fi's waist as it had during that first flight. At least this time he didn't shut his eyes. His heart fell into his stomach with a strange combination of terror and awe.

Fi laughed, the sound rattling the wind dancing around the Chiron's turrets, their peaks no more than a distant blur as they left the school behind.

forty-three

Julia's feet dragged painfully with each step, the thick cloth blinding her eyes. Fear filled every crevasse of her body, the demon's grip on her waist painful as it moved them through the dark. Another choked sob escaped her lips.

"No use crying, little princess," the vile voice hissed in her ear. "It'll do you no good."

Julia sniffed, jumping as a door creaked open and the rough grip thrust her forward. Her dress ripped, and she stumbled, her knee burning where it scraped cold stone.

"There now, that's better." Someone tore the burlap satchel off her head. Before she could look up at the monster, the shadow figure slammed the door.

A gust of wind echoed through the dark, and she shivered, tears running down her trembling bottom lip.

The darkness was consuming everything. Whether the council cared to admit it or not, it took Josie. It took Kellen, too. And now, in her foolish attempt to save Nadie, it had taken her as well.

"Princess Julia? Gods forbid it, is that you?"

Julia's head shot toward the raspy voice of a woman huddled in the corner. Julia blinked, her eyes adjusting to the dim. "Who's there?"

The middle-aged blonde crept toward her. "May The Twelve

bless you, child, how...are you hurt?"

There was something familiar about her, the tired hazel eyes beneath the dirt and blood coating her skin. A nasty gash ran down her left arm, and her hands were bound. But there was a comfort, a security at the sight of her nonetheless.

"Anya?" Julia whispered.

Nobody ever knew what happened to the royal nursemaid and her husband, and whenever someone asked Kellen what happened to his parents, he always changed the subject. But here she was.

Anya's throat bobbed, a weak smile touching cracked lips. "Yes, little one, it's me."

Julia gulped. "I'm not little anymore, I'm eleven now." Anya's smile widened, and she continued, "What happened to you, why did you leave us?"

Sadness filled her expression. "Aeron." Anya's eyes searched the darkness as if she expected the long-forgotten demon king to appear when she spoke his name.

"I don't understand." Wind whipped through the alcove, thickening the stuffy air.

"His henchmen came to my husband, demanding he use his position with your father to gain information. They killed him when he refused." A sob escaped her lips. "Then they took me, demanding Kellen..." she couldn't finish, tears running down her cheeks.

"They used Kellen to get close to Josie."

Anya nodded, sniffing. "I don't think they have her, though."

The worry in Julia's chest lightened briefly. "And Kellen?"

"I don't know. They won't tell me anything. I can only hope he's alright."

Julia shivered. "What do they mean to do with us?"

It was a long while before Anya looked up, eyes full of warmth and kindness. "Your guess is as good as mine. But whatever it is, I won't let them hurt you. You won't be alone anymore."

Before Julia could reply, an icy chill circled the room and Anya's eyes went wide in fear. Julia searched the darkness, for the source of Anya's terror as a laugh echoed through the shadows. The fear she'd forced away at the sight of her nursemaid returned.

"Don't lie to the child, pathetic woman. Of course she's going to be alone."

Julia didn't hear her own scream as the nightmare stepped out of the shadows behind Anya. Blood pounded in her ears, blocking out everything as the enormous creature gripped Anya by the hair and lifted her off the ground. Tears streamed down her face, her pleas inaudible as the nightmare slit Anya's throat in one slow, graceful movement.

Blood spurted everywhere, coating her skin and clothes in hot, sticky liquid. The creature dropped Anya's lifeless corpse to the ground, her head falling onto Julia's lap. Julia shook uncontrollably, panic overtaking her.

It's just a dream. A horrible dream.

The creature knelt, lifting Julia's chin with a bloody nail. She met its eyes, forcing her breathing to settle, the stench of blood and steel consuming her senses. Even in the darkness, the glowing eyes watched her, radiating evil. But the beast merely twisted its head, cocking it to one side with a smile. "Hello, little princess."

forty-four

"I see. You're certain of this?"

Erza stood at attention, hands poised behind her back. "Yes, Mother."

Queen Rowena nodded slowly. "Anwen will be dealt with when the time is right. No reason to cause panic in the middle of the Shadow Games."

Erza frowned. "But she's responsible for Salia's death. She must be held accountable. It's our duty as Rekiv's rulers to bring her to—" Her mother's glare cut her off, and she grumbled, "as you wish."

Queen Rowena nodded again, looking down to her paperwork. "As for the travelers, you realize what an asset they could be to us? A lost Dorwynnian princess and the last of Norah's sacred healers, whether they know their strength or not, are powerful allies."

"I do."

"Good." Rowena pushed up from her chair, gown sweeping around her. "And have you heard anything from your Elites at the Chiron?"

Erza followed her mother across the room where she shut the balcony doors. "No, but they're due back here with a report any day now."

"Good. Anwen will be dealt with," Rowena said with her back

turned. "Once you win this competition, and are named my heir, you will return with the travelers to their people, learn what you can as Rekiv's official heir. But until then, you will not let my decisions cloud your judgement during tomorrow's competition, is that clear?"

"Yes, Mother."

Sweat beaded down Jenson's neck as he fought to boil the water in the bowl before him. Steam wafted into the air after a few moments, and he grinned.

"Yes!" Rowen clapped. "You're a natural!"

He leaned back, chuckling. "It's in my blood, I believe is what you said?"

The red-haired witch rolled her eyes, glancing toward the hearth ablaze with a fire *he* created. Maya and Eva leaned over a book on the thick bear-skin rug before the flames. "Norah's healing gift is in your blood. She was the Demi-God child of King Alaric Waeshorn and Noria, the Goddess of Healing."

"Right." Jenson wiped a hand around his neck, still not quite comprehending the new knowledge.

Rowen gave him a little shove. "Believe it or not, you're getting good. It's like you don't even have to try, like your body just knows what to do."

"You mean my blood knows what to do," he corrected.

"I hate to admit my envy, but there is power in godly blood, Jenson." Biting her lip, she motioned to Maya. "Time to try something else."

He glanced over at his young companion, who whispered something to Eva. The Fae girl nodded and returned her attention to the book sprawled on the rug. "Are you a master healer yet?" Maya asked, walking toward them.

"No, but I'm being promoted, I think?" He raised an eyebrow at Rowen.

Maya cocked her head, hands on her hips. "Promoted after only three days? Fallon might even be impressed."

Jenson let out a half-laugh as Rowen spoke. "I won't deny you're doing well." She held up a hand. "But real injuries are not as simple as boiling water or lighting fires. Concentration is of the essence, and sometimes that's a luxury you aren't given in a dire situation. Not only must you attempt to remove pain if you lack the herbs to quell them, but you must also sew the wound shut."

He shrugged. "Sounds easy enough."

She shoved his chest, and he toppled backward out of his chair with a surprised yelp, his side screaming in protest. Rowen held out a hand, helping him to his feet. "*That* is exactly what happens to those who say it's easy without understanding the danger."

Maya stifled a giggle. "Jenson, your reflexes are lacking."

"It isn't something to joke about," Rowen warned. "Unexpecting reflexes are one thing. But telling yourself the mental control being a healer requires is easy, only invites a catastrophic burnout." She turned to him and added, "And the burnout, if left unchecked, will kill you."

Jenson met her eyes evenly, refusing to let the flicker of uncertainty show. "I don't need a lecture about avoiding a burnout. Just show me what to do."

"It's more than simply avoiding it." Rowen reached for a dagger from her boot, slicing it along her palm. As she spoke, she used her other hand to stitch the wound closed, faint lilac twirling about her fingers like a thread as she waved them over her hand. The skin knitted closed in response. "You have to know *when* the burnout is coming. Knowing yourself and what you hope to accomplish by visualizing it in your mind." When she met his gaze again, there wasn't even a scar where her palm has been bleeding moments before.

"Stop talking and show me."

Rowen's eyes flickered with the thrill of his determination. She didn't break their gaze as she held out a hand to Maya. "Might I borrow your wrist?"

Jenson quirked a brow. "What are you—"

"Scared?" Rowen challenged.

"No, I just...what if..."

"Oh, I'll be fine. Stop being a baby," Maya grumbled.

"But what if I can't heal you?" The doubt danced through his mind, his pulse racing slightly at the thought.

"I hope you won't let me die without trying."

"You can do this. You were born to do this, whether you knew it or not." Rowen didn't give him a chance to argue as she sliced the blade along Maya's wrist.

"Wait, but what do I do?" He tried to keep the shudder from his voice, fists clenched so they wouldn't shake.

"Stitch the wound." When he frowned, she added, "It's like stitching a wound the old-fashioned way, only the thread moves from your magic. Visualize it. Demand it to happen, and it will."

The hesitation crept along his spine, taunting him. Jenson stared at his palm, trying to focus.

Maya watched him, her eyes avoiding the blood pooling along her flesh. "I know you won't let me die."

Pure panic flooded his body, and Jenson reached for the healing light fluttering within the well of his power. But he couldn't grasp it. His essence danced just out of reach, tingling when the shimmering gold brushed his fingertips.

His pulse quickened as he shifted his attention to the cut on Maya's wrist. It wasn't deep, but it was still bleeding steadily. Maya tapped her foot absently, but she held her free hand under her wrist to catch the blood as it dripped.

He gritted his teeth. *Come on, Jens, stitch the wound. It can't be that hard.* He shook his palms, breathing deeply. *Come on,* he repeated. *You can do this.*

"Jenson..." Maya hissed, running her tongue over her teeth.

"Focus," Rowen warned.

Jenson's nostrils flared, and he dug his nails into his palm to keep from shaking. The glow flickered in his fist as he reached for the magic within his subconscious.

"There you go, that's it!"

He furrowed his brows, opening his palm. The light hovered above his open hand, bobbing and weaving faintly, but it didn't move. His breath grew ragged, heat flushing his cheeks, but he refused to give up.

"Come on," Jenson groaned. "Why isn't it working?"

Rowen waved her palm over Maya's wrist, the thin lilac thread knitting broken flesh.

His hands fell away, and he sighed, pinching the bridge of his nose. "I don't understand," he said into his hand. "What...what did I do wrong?"

Rona handed him a water skin and he gulped down the cool liquid. "Nothing, Jenson. It isn't easy to grasp the first time even for those with such natural potential." Her smile was kind as she twisted the tip of her braid absently.

"So I'm not a failure," he asked.

The red-haired witch laughed outright. "No, you aren't." She smirked. "Honestly, I'm impressed. When I first started, it took me ages just to start a fire. Which, need I remind you, was a success on your second try."

Jenson smiled at that.

"Don't be so hard on yourself, Jens." Maya reached for his hand, squeezing it gently. "You've always focused on what you can't do rather than seeing what you did."

Rowen folded long legs beneath her on the chair, glancing to where Eva still knelt over the book, her finger brushing parchment as her lips moved silently. "Aeron better watch out. The Elirona twins have quite a strong court forming at their backs."

Jenson exchanged a look with Maya. "Just the Elirona court?" He ran a shaky hand through his sweaty hair. "I doubt Erza would be turned away if she proposed an alliance."

Rowen stared at him for a long time before she replied, "You're right. I don't think she would."

forty-five

They were still in their animal forms when Quinn woke. The air was crisp for early Nova, winter just around the corner, and with it, the exciting preparations of Mabonas and harvest season.

Quinn uncurled himself from Joseline's small form, stretching, his paws padding against soft earth. The camp was quiet, smoking fires long abandoned in the hopes of much needed sleep. The moon was a pale crescent in the sky, crickets chirping from beneath scattered trees. The terrain had begun to change again; the Redhorn mountains looming tall to the west along the Badraol border, and Rekiv's half-frozen marshes sprawling the barren expanse to the east, the trees of Farowa Forest a thinning clump around them.

With a sigh, Quinn yawned, resting his muzzle against his massive front paws.

"Are you alright?" Azuri asked, perching between his ears.

I'm worried.

"Admitting your feelings? How unlike you," Azuri teased.

Quinn growled. *I'm serious. We hold the fate of Navarre in our hands.* He glanced to where Joseline lay. *What if after all this we can't stop him?*

Azuri's small fingers in his fur were oddly comforting. "I don't know if you've noticed or not, Your Highness, but your strength is growing. Your *court* is growling."

Quinn stiffened. *I don't want to talk about—*

"I know you don't. But it's true nonetheless. Your sister lives. You *sirdispora* grows stronger every day at your side. Your *sielapora* is ever loyal to you, and you're surrounded by trusted warriors."

The breeze picked up, prickling a chill down his spine. Quinn sighed. *It's just a lot to take in.*

"Of course it is," Azuri agreed. "But you're doing well."

Quinn huffed. *Not like anyone gave me much of a choice.*

The faerie's laugh was like the tinkling of bells.

Quinn? Joseline's soft hum danced toward him on the breeze.

He padded toward her, pressing his muzzle into her fur, breathing in the soothing scent of lilacs. *I'm here, Joseline.*

She purred, forest eyes bright. *I'm cold.* To prove her point, she stood, arching her back as she rubbed herself against him.

Quinn chuckled. *It is rather chilly, isn't it?*

Very. It's almost as cold as your heart.

He swished his tail across her face. *My heart is perfectly warm, thank you.*

Joseline's eyes danced, tail swaying as she made her way toward her tent. *Oh, come on, idiot. There's a few hours left until everyone wakes. I'd like to spend them as warm as possible.*

In the same tent?

She turned back to flutter her eyelashes at him. *Do I scare you, Quinn Elirona?*

Quinn chuckled. *You don't think I'm going to take advantage of you?*

No, you're too respectful for that sort of thing. She continued walking. *Besides, I'm sure if you tried, Fallon, Larina, and Kai would put you in your place.*

Quinn shook his head, trailing after her.

forty-six

Reality and fantasy blurred together. Blood pooled around him on the stone slab, his own or others', Dax wasn't sure. Nothing was certain but the pain.

The horrid, blinding pain.

It tore him apart, burned him alive from the inside despite the calm, phantom water pulsing through him. The Demi-God essence given to him by his mother, Syvi; the mother he never met.

The Akuma flipped a dagger in one hand, pacing lazy circles around the table. "Let's try this again." He paused, the tip of his dagger pressed against Dax's sternum. "Where is the Fae whore."

Dax focused on the breath, blocking out his torments. He would not say anything no matter what they did to him.

He would not betray her.

"I don't know."

Hissing, the Akuma trailed the dagger down Dax's body to his navel, slow and lazy. Steel sliced through flesh, and he arched against the stone swallowing the agony.

"Where *is* she."

Dax gritted his teeth. "I don't—"

Fresh blood coated his teeth, dripping down his face from his nose where the blood demon struck him. Another strike and the hilt of his dagger slammed into Dax's side, knocking the breath from his body. Dax gasped.

"Tell me!" the Akuma snarled, banging his fists against the stone. Dax shook his head.

The throbbing spread across his face, his eye aching as it swelled. The demon looked as though he might stab him out of frustration, but the rage calmed and he relaxed, smiling.

"Fine, half-breed, don't tell me. I have no need to rush. We have time." He ran a nail down Dax's cheek, blood swelling from his touch. His face moved closer, his expression lazy, and he licked the fresh cut. "We have all the time in the world."

"I will not be her downfall," Dax gasped. *I will not,* he repeated, even as the shriek of pain erupted from his chest.

The blood demon knelt before him, his vile breath whispering in Dax's ear. "No," he purred, smearing the blood across his cheek. "But she will be yours."

Dax blocked out the sound of steel scraping stone. He blocked out the sound of his rasped screams and the pain as the demon tore apart his flesh—Evalyn's image the light piercing through the looming darkness to keep him sane.

I will not be your downfall.

The promise shone like a beacon through the shadows encompassing his heart.

I will not be your downfall.

He said it over and over, gritting his teeth, his mind overwhelmed with blinding, unrivaled agony.

I will not be your downfall.

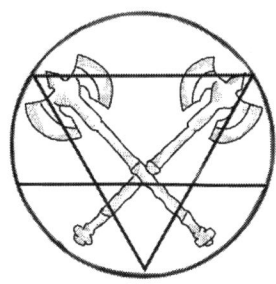

forty-seven

Ten minutes.

That's how long Erza had left to correctly order the golden chalices filled with poisoned wine on the table. But she couldn't focus. Her mind was a mushy jumble of fear, confusion, and uncertainty. She ran a hand through her bangs, fighting the urge to glance up at Anwen—Adria, Aeron's daughter—perched beside Queen Rowena in the royal box.

She'd killed Salia in cold blood. Killing another witch without reasonable cause was of the highest crime. And Odessa...the Silvermist heir would never fully recover from her twin's death. Even now, standing at the table beside Erza, she was incoherent, unfocused. She'd gotten worse since their alliance during the first challenge. Downcast amber eyes filled with silent anguish, and her short, dark curls jutted in every direction, the bags under her eyes evident despite her dark complexion. She was a scared doe staring down the hunter's arrow with no fear of the looming death that awaited her, numbed by the irreversible grief of her loss.

Erza was surprised they'd survived the trial on Lake Urasa at all.

The crone overseeing the competition tapped her crystal nails on the table beside her as the hourglass on the pedestal continued to empty. Gritting her teeth, Erza eyed the chalices again.

Five poisons, one water. Label the goblets from least poisonous to most deadly within the time frame. When the hourglass emptied, she drank the one deemed least poisonous. The challenge was harmless enough—if you were right.

Erza swore under her breath. Three left.

She knew herbs and poisons like the back of her hand. Basics in herbology were always mastered at the beginning of a witchling's training journey. The first part of this challenge—labeling various herbs and their uses—had been so easy. Yet here she sat, unable to clear her head enough to focus, unable to erase her mother's scowl from her mind.

Morana rearranged the cups to her right, smiling viciously, once-blue eyes shimmering black. She'd hardly seen the Blackwing heir since...Erza shuddered.

"Two minutes."

Wiping a hand over her face, Erza reviewed her options. Nexim's Thorn sat on the far left. Ingesting the juices of the plant's deceptively-beautiful thorns rewarded one with a week of itching rashes around their mouth and along the tongue—uncomfortable, but not deadly. Aersyn was next. While death was inevitable if not dealt with, the effects were immediately recognizable and easily treatable. The Eospia Venom of the deathly Northlands viper, if not treated immediately, could kill within hours if you were lucky. If you were unlucky, within minutes.

That left Waevyn, Fellephyn's Tears, and water. Odorless and colorless, Fellephyn's Tears would kill within hours as well. Waevyn would cause severe indigestion. Erza placed the bitter-smelling Waevyn between the Nexim's Thorn and the Aersyn, then reached for the remaining two goblets.

She couldn't focus. So much more was at stake now than a stupid competition, a ridiculous crown she didn't want. So much more than being heir and taking the Rekiv crown. Everything she'd worked for was miniscule and insignificant compared to the uncertain future.

She sniffed one of the remaining goblets though it was pointless.

"One minute."

Erza's pulse quickened, her mind swarming with distracting

thoughts, but she gritted her teeth and refused to let the panic show. She sniffed them both again, at last placing what she hoped was Fellephyn's Tears at the far right.

"Hands back."

The crone eased to her feet, her cane puffing up small clouds of dust when it shuffled along the ground, rich green skirts dragging behind her. She approached Odessa's table. "Drink," the crone ordered. Odessa obliged without hesitation, the dull look still in her eyes.

So empty. So broken.

The Silvermist heir lifted the leftmost goblet to her lips. At first, nothing. Then she turned a splotchy red, doubling over with a cry of agony as the Waevyn worked its way through her system.

No one rushed to her aid. Odessa's mother watched from the royal box, her eyes filled with a similar sadness as if neither of them truly cared that she'd failed. Odessa remained standing, gripping the edge of the table, her face contorting with pain.

The crone motioned for her to leave. The wrong choice without the resulting death still meant disqualification.

The crone moved to stand before Erza. "Drink."

Erza found her center, forcing her pulse to calm and her fingers not to shake as she lifted the cup to her lips. The cool liquid ran down her throat. She breathed, waiting, watching as the crone inspected her, observing her for the extremely dilated pupils that would indicate the presence of Fellephyn's Tears.

The seconds seemed like an eternity.

When nothing happened, the crone smiled, moving toward Morana. Only then did Erza dare to look up at her mother. Rowen, Astrid, and the rest of her Elites stood behind the queen; warriors ready to defend at any moment.

"Erza Stormwood. Morana Blackwing. In one week's time, on the fifteenth of Nova, you will duel to the death. For the crown, for your covens, for your honor." With that, the crone was gone.

Erza turned toward the archway leading out of the arena, concealing her shuddering sigh. One final challenge.

It's almost over. The nonsense is almost over. Then we can worry about the more important things.

She braced a hand on the railing of the western stairwell as Morana's hissing, inhuman voice said from behind her, "So, it's just you and me. I can't wait to see the look on your sweet little face when I bash in your skull and pull out your heart."

forty-eight

No matter how many times Edan told himself everything would work out, he couldn't quell the violent hammering of his pulse as the old Thyan watchtower appeared on the horizon.

It's fine. His grip on Fi's waist tightened. *Everything is going to be fine.*

"For a pureblood, you sure don't mask your fear well, Master Edan." Fi's voice danced on the breeze, light and teasing.

"I wonder, would you survive the fall if I tossed you?" Edan grumbled.

She smirked back at him. "You wouldn't. You like me too much."

"Do I?" Edan murmured into the witch mark on her neck, relishing in the heat prickling her skin.

"You said yourself, I have Kiran's sass…which, I'm assuming, was something you liked about him." She batted her long eyelashes. "And where would you be without your lovely escort?"

Edan chuckled, but Endra's loud chirp cut off his response. He looked over at Naoi, who grinned and signaled the dive.

They spiraled toward the ground, Endra keeping her wings tucked against her sides until they were dangerously close to the earth. Fi let out a delighted whoop, even as Edan squeezed her tighter.

Endra landed with a graceful prance, shaking her massive head. Fi unclasped the buckles, sliding to the ground with a soft thud. Edan dismounted as well, albeit much less gracefully.

The crumbling tower loomed overhead, the faint cries of other Kitsugon echoing through the wide archways making up the lower levels. Endra butted her snout against his outstretched palm. "This is where they're bred, right?"

Naoi nodded, unstrapping her bags. "Yep, there's a kennel beneath the keep in Ravencrest, but only the Elites and the Queen house their mounts there."

Edan ran a hand through his hair, grip tightening on the satchel slung across his chest. "So, now what?"

Fi twined their fingers together, the flirtatious gesture calming his racing pulse. "We figure out when you can meet with Queen Rowena."

He stopped her as she tried to walk forward. "*When* we can?" He frowned, forcing the looming anger away. "This can't be a matter of *when*, Fi. The lives of innocents might depend on us finding those flowers."

"Your mother is *Queen*, Edan. And she isn't exactly the type you can waltz up to and demand things."

"Well, that is going to change." Edan wiped a hand over his mouth, closing his eyes against the temper threatening to surface. "Fi, we can't..."

"You're back!" Edan looked up at the unfamiliar but pleasant voice. Blonde curls bounced around the slender young witch's shoulders as she approached them, her hazel eyes shimmering with the same excitement Fi's always did.

"We did promise a monthly report to Erza if we stayed that long," Naoi commented.

"I know. I thought I saw you circling, but the others didn't believe me." The blonde threw herself at Fi, gripping her shoulders tightly. "Missed ya."

"I missed you, too, Soren."

"No, she didn't, she only wants you to think that." Another unfamiliar voice. This witch's skin was a rich bronze, her eyes matching Soren's.

Fi released Soren to glare at her. "Vien, your sarcasm is never appreciated."

Vien smirked, her eyes flicking toward Edan. "So, you're Erza's mysterious twin?" He gave a swift nod.

"You look just like her!" Soren squeaked.

Edan couldn't help but laugh. "She doesn't know I exist."

"But you know she does." Vien raised an eyebrow.

"The Healer Superior insisted I knew where I came from."

Naoi spoke before Vien and Soren could question him further. "How far are they into the games?"

Even Soren's expression turned solemn. "The second challenge took place this morning. The duel will be between Morana and Erza."

"We expected that, didn't we?" Naoi replied, unstrapping Fi's bags from Endra's saddle.

Vien nodded. "The others are doing afternoon training with Astrid and Curra."

"And Erza brought back a Fae girl from Easthaven the day you left. She's been teaching her magic. She…she's really sweet. Shy and quiet most of the time, but sweet."

Fi burst out laughing. "Erza? She doesn't bring home strays."

"True," Vien crossed her arms, favoring her left hip. "But the girl was being followed by demons."

Edan's blood ran cold. "She *what*?"

Soren and Vien looked as though they might not speak again, but Fi said, "You can talk around him, it's alright. Learning what we can about demons is part of the reason we brought him back with us."

"He isn't the only visitor, either," Soren crossed her arms. "A pair of travelers named Jenson and Maya, they came from the Kynire camp in Ebondenn to investigate the darkness as well."

"Do we know for sure yet where the darkness is coming from?"

"It's Anwen."

Fi rubbed her temples. "Of course it is."

Edan held up a hand. "I'm sorry, who's Anwen?"

"The Blackwing coven leader," Fi sighed. Endra nuzzled her arm in comfort. "The Blackwings have been causing problems for centuries."

"I know them," he said. "They cause a lot of problems in Easthaven as well."

"But it's worse than Erza thought," Vien whispered, glancing around to make sure they were alone. "She's Aeron's daughter."

The picture of dark Fae and an open portal to The Shadowplains flickered in his mind. He rubbed his shoulder, the satchel strapped there suddenly heavy. "I need to speak with my mother about obtaining some of those flowers, *now*."

Fi didn't look convinced. "I already told you, we have to see when—"

"Fi, we don't have time." He gestured toward the others, then gripped his satchel, holding it up slightly as if to remind her what was concealed inside. "*Aeron's daughter?* We're already running on sheer luck." He dropped the satchel, the book banging against his thigh.

He made to step around Vien and nearly collided with another witch, this one with long scarlet hair braided down her back. He hadn't even heard her approach.

Her lilac eyes met his. Edan blinked when she grinned, holding out a hand. "Well hello, cousin."

"Hello?" he replied meekly, his gaze flickering to the arched doorway behind her.

"In a hurry, are we?"

Edan let out an impatient huff. "Yes, actually."

"I'll walk with you."

He frowned. "Thank you, but you don't even know where I'm—"

"I do, you're going to see Queen Rowena. Erza's with her now."

Fi chuckled, her hand trailing up his spine, and he ignored the delighted shiver that followed. "Edan, meet Rowen, Erza's second."

Edan eyed the scarlet-haired witch. "A pleasure."

"Likewise."

He turned to Fi, glancing over her shoulder at Naoi. "Right, well, I'll see you later, then."

Fi gave a little pout, running a finger along the scruff covering his jaw. "You're going to leave your escort just like that? Do you even want to see me later?" She batted those eyelashes at him again.

Fighting another shiver, Edan rolled his eyes. "I'll be sure to let you know how it goes if I make it out alive."

Fi looked as though she might say more, but Rowen interrupted, "Erza will be waiting for a report once she learns you've returned."

Without another word, Fi led Endra into the watchtower, Naoi and her Kitsugon following. Vien and Soren brought up the rear as they entered the kennels, Soren skipping happily.

Fi turned back, calling out, "Be careful with him, Rowen. He's a bit fragile." She winked when he scowled.

Rowen laughed. "I must admit, I'm impressed. Fi doesn't usually keep interest in men longer than a week."

He snorted. "Not for a lack of trying on her part. I think she likes my temper, which is...strange. But it probably has something to do with the fact that I don't give her what she wants."

"You can resist her?" Rowen pursed her lips. "That's a feat in itself."

Heat flushed his cheeks. "Let's just say I've never..."

"Say no more." Rowen slipped a hand through his arm, moving them toward the watchtower. "Come on, cousin. I want to hear all about life as a Chiron Master." She looked up at him. "From healer to healer."

Edan nodded, his lips twitching into a smile.

"Well, I for one think Master Nichol sounds like a royal prick," Rowen declared.

Edan couldn't help but laugh as they ascended what Rowen promised was the final flight of stairs to the Queen's rooms. "He certainly is."

They hadn't stopped talking the entire walk, erasing the fluttering nerves at the thought of meeting his mother. It was different...nice. Not just with Rowen, but Fi, Naoi, even briefly with Soren and Vien. He felt at home with them, welcome. It eased a tightness in his chest that had lingered since Kiran's death.

"What?" he asked, realizing Rowen had spoken.

She smiled, freeing her arm from his. "We're here." She motioned to the door ahead, embellished with a golden knocker. "Are you ready?"

"No?" he admitted, wiping a hand over his mouth.

"Just breathe."

Edan nodded, lifting his hand. But before he could knock, the door swung inward. He sucked in a breath.

He wasn't sure what emotions he'd expected when he met his twin, but the intuitive awareness warmed his core. Two halves broken apart and rekindled in kindred recognition. She was his height, with black hair brushing along her neck and leveling with thin eyebrows. They had the same angled jaw, but her features were softer, those wide lilac eyes the only indication of her shock.

"Who's your friend?" Erza managed, turning her attention to Rowen.

Rowen grinned. "Master Edan, from the Chiron. He just got back with Fi and Naoi."

"I see." Erza ran a hand through her hair, the bangs falling just above her eyes as she met his gaze. "And why have you come here, Master Edan?"

"Erza, go collect your reports. I'll see to our new guest." The silky feminine voice came from within the room.

"As you wish." Erza eyed him, cautious and curious, but stepped into the hall. "Rowen, you let anything happen to the Queen…"

Rowen gave a small nod. "On my honor, Erza."

Without another word, she was gone, dark plum cloak billowing behind her. Edan watched her go until the silky voice spoke again. "Well, come in and let me look at you then."

Edan turned to Rowen, who held the door, offering no more than a weak smile. Then it clicked shut behind him and he swallowed, bracing himself as Queen Rowena turned.

The resemblance between the three of them was uncanny. Queen Rowena was clearly older, with higher cheekbones, but if he'd ever doubted his heritage, seeing her before him now eased any doubts from his mind.

Rowena gave him a calculating, judgmental look with narrowed lilac eyes. "So, it appears my orders to have you killed were ignored."

"It appears that way, yes." Edan hoped she couldn't hear his hammering pulse as she circled him.

"And you're doing well, I presume?"

Edan forced himself to keep still except for the straightening of his shoulders. "I'm Superior's Albion's heir."

"Well indeed," she scoffed.

"You never told Erza about me."

It wasn't an accusation, but her eyes narrowed even further. "Why should I have? You should be dead."

"But I'm not."

Queen Rowena eyed him keenly, unsure if he was being pert. "No, you aren't."

Edan released a breath. "I was hoping to discuss something with you."

Queen Rowena stared into the fire. If she'd heard him, she made no indication of it. "This predicament is quite perfect actually." She faced him, crossing her arms. "Your sister will be traveling to Ebondenn for me after she's won the final trial. I hate to return to Ravencrest without a Stormwood heir at my side. But you are also an heir."

"And?" Edan fought against the temper threatening to surface when she flouted his question.

"You'll return to Ravencrest with me."

Edan froze. "I'm sorry, what?"

She faced him again. "Did I stutter? You'll return to Ravencrest with me, serve as heir in her place should something happen to me."

Anger heated his flesh, and he found himself longing for Fi's soothing touch. "I'll do no such thing except on my own accord. I am a Master of the Chiron, and I should be treated as such whether I'm your blood or not."

The slap of her hand against his cheek echoed through the room. "Perhaps Superior Albion allowed you to speak to him in that disrespectful tone, but I am your Queen and you will watch your temper when you speak to me, or you won't speak to me at all."

It was all Edan could do to keep the temper from unleashing.

She scoffed, waving a dismissive hand. "Erza is so obedient, I suppose one of you would have to have your father's temper." Her lips twitched slightly, and for a moment Edan thought she might smile. "Rowen will show you to a vacant room. After you've settled yourself, you might as well meet your sister. She'll only ask more questions otherwise."

Rowen opened the door behind him as if sensing the dismissal from the hallway. Edan couldn't hurry from the room fast enough.

forty-nine

"See that?" Fallon pointed to the mist looming before them. It shimmered oddly in the light, rippling against the sun.

Joseline nodded, staring at him quizzically.

"Raenya," he murmured. "We're almost there."

Her heart drummed with nervous excitement. They were so close. The frozen marshes made travel tedious to say the least, but seeing that mist made the fabrication of her imagination dull.

She could barely contain her excitement at the promised security that awaited her. Kai laughed at the head of the column, staring down at Quinn, who padded beside her mare in his wolf form.

"I am glad he talked to me about his vision with Evalyn instead of just charging off, but maybe he's having a harder time adjusting to Jenson and Maya's absence than I thought." Fallon said suddenly.

Joseline gave him a weak smile. "I know he misses them, but he seems alright most of the time. He's strong."

"You make him strong, Joseline."

She blushed. "I have so much to thank him for." The wind rustled from behind them, scattering fiery auburn hair across her face. "I just hope it's enough."

"It will never be enough, not really. But how can we hope to win if we give up before we try?"

Joseline blinked at the strange flash of doubt. But then, Fallon had seen Aeron's destruction before. He'd been alive, had fought in the Second Demon Wars, had lost loved ones. She tucked a loose curl behind her ear. "You're right."

They rode on in silence for a moment more. "You give the people hope, you know."

She followed his gaze to the entourage behind them. The company had seen better days. Battered and beaten through years of fighting demons the rest of Navarre refused to believe in, demons she hadn't believed in either before Ywone's end—but not broken.

Joseline opened her mouth to speak, but sudden shouts from the front of the column silenced her. Fallon snapped to attention, motioning for her to stay behind him as they made their way to the group.

Raenya's shimmering doorway remained ahead. But it wasn't the glowing light that caused the panic. It was the shadowy figure approaching from the distance—from the Redhorn Mountains.

Every muscle in her body tightened, months of training vanishing from her memory. She was no longer a warrior in training, no longer a beacon of hope, but a naïve princess escaping her city, overcome with an inexplicable pull toward a demon king's spirit swathed in darkness. A deep, haunting voice echoed in her memory, Quinn screaming her name as Rathal's wall crumbled.

How? She was here, alive and well. He needed her soul to return to power. The figure standing before them wasn't...it couldn't possibly be him.

Nevertheless, here he was.

Shea uncurled herself from Joseline's lap, Quinn snarling at Bellona's feet while Fallon, Larina, Kai, and Logan formed a protective half-circle around her.

"So, it appears the she-demon spit truths after all." The too-perfect voice purred, chilling her blood. "I half-expected my trek here to be a useless waste of time."

Closer and closer he stepped, until at last he appeared as more than shadows. He was so dark. Black trousers decorated with various belts and straps all sheathing an assortment of weapons. The layers blurred together, so Joseline couldn't tell where the black tunic ended and the long, black coat began, dark swirls embellished by Aeron's mark of power—the crossed scythes.

There was no light in his eyes, the blue-green iris rimmed with black, the darkness threatening to spill onto his pale skin. Etched into his high cheekbone was a teardrop scar, the flesh beneath shimmering molten gold. When he smiled, the life vanished from her body as if he'd pierced through her soul. Sweat dripped down her neck. "My sister is having so much fun with your friends in Thya, I couldn't resist the urge to have some fun of my own. After three hundred years, the Dwarfs have become so dreadfully boring." His grin radiated death.

"Who are you?" Larina's voice was every bit a general demanding answers, firm and strong. Kai had already notched an arrow to her bow.

He fixed his gaze on Joseline. "Who do you think I am, Princess Joseline?" Before she could respond, he held up a hand, tapping his chin. "You know, I heard something not too long ago about another princess...a little one with raven hair, stolen from her home by the darkness." The grin widened. "You wouldn't happen to have any relation to her, would you?"

For a moment, Joseline thought her heart stopped. Any warmth left in her veins chilled.

Julia.

"What have you done with her?" Joseline's voice came out as a choked whisper.

The others looked at her, confused. Yet Joseline saw no one but the shadowy man before her.

"What have *I* done? Why, nothing. I spend all my time with my loyal subjects in Badraol."

Fallon frowned. "You are responsible for the Dwarfs' disappearance?"

Joseline shook her head, every thought blurring together. "You aren't him."

He chuckled. "Him? You mean my father?"

Father? He was Aeron's *son*?

"My father has yet to return to us." He paused, his eyes never leaving Joseline's. "But soon, all that will change."

"I'm not going anywhere with you." She hoped her voice remained calm.

The demon laughed again, warranting a snarl from Quinn. "You are not, but your sweet little sister..." he picked at his nails lazily, shrugging.

"The young princess is nothing to you." Fallon's voice was stern. "Joseline is the one you need."

Aeron's son shook his head, eyes widening in amusement. "That is where you Children of Dorwynn are so very wrong."

"Wrong how?" Larina demanded.

He grinned. "The soul of the promised princess is required, but *only* to return his full magical power. With Joseline's soul, he will be invincible. The fire-haired beauty will become an empty shell, a slave to do my father's bidding. But she does not have to be the sacrifice. The sacrifice only requires a descendant from Alaric Waeshorn's bloodline."

Sacrifice.

"What?" Joseline fought to remain in the saddle as her head spun. Bellona shifted uneasily beneath her.

"Such a sweet thing, I hear. My father's Houzo guards her himself. He says she smells delicious...her fear is intoxicating."

No, her mind screamed. *Please, not Julia. Anyone but little Julia.*

"Let her go." Magic tingled her fingertips.

He grinned again. "Oh, it's too late for that. But maybe he'll let you see her corpse...if you're lucky."

Joseline wasn't sure when she started crying. Wasn't sure when she tried to race toward him or when Quinn shifted to hold her in his arms as she screamed. "You can't do that! Please, you can't, she's a child!"

She struggled uselessly against Quinn's hold, fighting like a madwoman to free herself and launch toward the demon prince. But Quinn held firm.

"A useful child," the creature purred.

Her eyes burned with tears. "Please..." she whimpered.

But the demon only bowed, winking at her. "I'll tell the beastie to pass on your hello." The shadows closed around him, swirling, opening into a dark void. "By the way, Princess, you should stick to groveling in the future. It suites you."

Then he was gone.

Joseline sank to her knees, staring at the spot where the demon prince stood moments before, any hope of seeing Julia again swallowed with him.

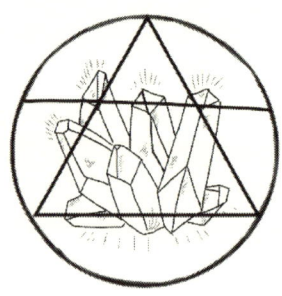

fifty

The warning gong rumbled from somewhere overhead, startling Dax from a restless sleep. The hallway outside echoed with shouts and rushing footsteps until at last there was silence.

"Sounds promising," Kellen murmured.

Dax eyed him. The soldier looked horrible, the deep purple bags under his eyes a mercy compared to the ruination of his lower back. Whatever dark magic the demons used to rip apart their flesh, they always healed them. Yet the scars, though painless, remained.

"The extent of that excitement has yet to be determined," Dax replied, more to himself than to Kellen.

"Meaning what?" Elyon rasped.

Before Dax could reply, the door creaked open and Naomi slipped inside. "Anything worth sharing?" he whispered.

Naomi pulled long raven hair into a high bun. "They found Toren's body."

Cohen closed the door behind him, grinning. "It's about time."

"It's been three days," Naomi mumbled, producing a set of lock picks before setting to work on Dax's chains. "Beck and Nim are stationed at the dock, we just need to get to the ship." The chains clicked free and fell to the ground. She moved toward Elyon, towering over him by several inches though she herself was rather small.

"What about the sea monsters?" Elyon frowned. "I...I thought there were demons in the water that would rip a ship to shreds."

"Aye, there are." Cohen patted his shoulder. "But don't worry. We have a ship they won't touch."

"They'd better not," Dax grumbled, rubbing at his wrists. When Naomi finished with Kellen's locks, he motioned toward the door. "Shall we?"

The group crept into the hall in silence, and it took all of Dax's will not to let his panic show.

He didn't have time to worry about the slaves who remained. He didn't have time to wonder if everything would work out, if the eighteen-year-old plan would hold strong.

The ruse had held up this far. Naomi's innocent act, Beck and Nim's obedience, Toren's death. One of his men to raise the alarm and find the body once Cohen disposed of the foreman, Dax's oblivion to the truth of Evalyn's heritage. The Shadow Commanders summoned to find Toren's corpse.

All for Navarre, for the future protection of the realm.

Of course, he *had* hoped Evalyn would actually kill him. He hadn't counted on being a Demi-God or falling...he wouldn't think about her. He couldn't. Not now.

They had one chance. One chance, and then they'd never have the opportunity again.

At least Elyon and Kellen were able to walk on their own. The darkness made seeing their way through the dungeons more challenging, the dim crimson moonlight seeping through high barred windows no help at all. Dax stumbled, gritting his teeth as Cohen's grip tightened around his waist. "You alright there, Cap?"

Dax's narrowed glare silenced him.

The walk that lasted no more than five minutes felt like an eternity. Dax's chest tightened at the rattling chains of the slaves echoing down the final corridor. Two sets of dungeons. One for prisoners of the mines, and another, the ones from which they had come, fueled by less pleasant actions.

He blocked out the moans of hunger, blocked out the clanking chains, and the soft whimpers of pain as the staircase leading to the main fortress yawned before them. Naomi held up a hand, and they stopped, hiding in an abandoned alcove of crumbled stone. Several Shadow Beasts rushed by, their hissing shouts harsh whispers in the stale air.

Elyon cast a nervous glance toward him, and he hoped his smile was reassuring. Dax had never realized how small the Dwarf boy was, how frail. He wished, not for the first time, that he would have looked after the young Dwarf more.

"All clear," Naomi whispered from the top of the stairs.

Elyon and Kellen went up first, Cohen bringing up the rear with an arm still holding him upright. Dax was breathing heavily by the time they reached the top, but he gave Cohen a nod. Naomi jerked her head to the left, and they moved along the wall.

The shadows were brighter in the main fortress, but only a little. Torches lined the damp stone, bolted high above their heads, illuminating their position along the entire length of the hall.

Nobody spoke as they followed Naomi, occasionally ducking around corners or halting in a dark patch between torches, Cohen keeping a careful eye on the space behind them. Only two more corners, and they would be at the main hall.

Just a little further...

"You really are an arrogant fool if you thought you could get away with this."

Panic and pain lanced through him at the sound of the Akuma demon's voice.

"We already have gotten away with it." Naomi replied, her soft voice strong.

"Oh, have you?" the Akuma raised an eyebrow as footsteps echoed down the hall to his left.

Dax half expected more demons to appear around the corner, but it was his own men. He shot a narrowed glance toward Cohen, who shrugged, grinning. "What?" His eyes flashed to Naomi, dancing playfully. "We tweaked yer plan a bit. Hope ya don't mind, Cap."

Dax wanted to smile, wanted to be proud, but his chest ached. He knew Cohen well enough to know what his friend was insinuating.

"Hah, you think you can stop me? Mere mortals?" The Akuma challenged.

Dax ignored the demon, watching his friend. "Cohen, you don't have to."

Cohen only flashed a smile, releasing his hold on Dax's waist. "Aye, I do." He paused. "I would have stayed with you until the end, Cap. I...you've always been a brother to me."

He returned the smile weakly, gripping Cohen's arm. "I know, friend."

"Naomi, keep him safe," Cohen turned to her. She looked as though she might speak, but Cohen reached out a hand to cup her cheek. "I love you," he whispered.

Her eyes brimmed with held back tears. "I love you too, always."

Then, Cohen drew his cutlass, eyes wild as he launched himself at the demon. Steel met claws as they rushed on, the echo of the skirmish ringing along stone as they moved away from it.

The main hall was empty, the front doors crumbled and useless as they had been for years. Ash-filled air kissed his cheeks, and Naomi pushing through rust covered gates as the harbor stretched before them. Crimson shimmered through the clouds above, engulfing the blood red moon.

The ship came into view, *his ship*, resting, waiting in the docks. Beck and Nim stood by the lowered plank, shifting anxiously. Beck rushed forward when he saw them, slipping an arm around Dax as he stumbled. He turned toward the fire burning bright and steady from Dax's towers in the upper fortress, his graying brows furrowed.

"Cohen isn't coming." Beck's voice was a whispered confirmation beside him, pulling only slightly for his attention.

Dax shook his head, wincing as he stumbled up the plank.

"Aye," Naomi sounded as though she might cry, but refused to let the tears fall. "We always knew there was a chance not all of us would."

Nim hefted the anchor, and *Seraphina* slipped through the dark waters in silence, propelling them further from the dock. Dax turned back to the burning fortress.

A beacon of hope.

A show of weakness.

"Dax, come on. We need t' get ye cleaned up." Nim spoke from behind him.

"Go see to the young ones, I can wait."

She narrowed her eyes at him. "Cap, ye—"

"Nim, I said I can wait. Has it been so long that you forget to respect your captain's orders?"

With a sigh, Nim rolled her eyes. "As ye say."

Dax remained a moment longer, flames shimmering in dark eyes.

I'll find you, Eva, and then, I'll never let you go. We'll burn Aeron's Shadowplains together, little dove, for all he's put you through. I promise.

Then, he turned, smiling at Nim where she leaned against the doorframe of his private quarters. He brushed a hand against the dark wood, kissing the sea dragon pendant he kept hanging from the frame as she slipped an arm around his waist. Flames glistened, dancing in the night sky behind them.

fifty-one

"I thought you would have come to find me by now."

Edan turned at the sound of Erza's voice, the breeze soft as it whispered along the arena's upper ramp. She wore the same plum cloak and riding leathers as when she left Rowena's rooms, her witch mark near-invisible amidst the onyx strands of hair. She quirked an eyebrow at him, crossing her arms.

"I didn't want to bother you when other things demand your attention."

Erza stopped beside him, releasing a half-laugh. "Things other than discovering I have a twin I never knew existed, you mean?"

He couldn't help but smile. "Like discovering you have a twin or like fighting to the death for the sake of a silly tradition?"

Her nostrils flared. "So, Edan," she took a step toward him. "Am I the monster you thought I was?"

Edan tensed. "I—"

Erza waved a dismissive hand. "Don't bother lying to me, Fi told me. And there's no reason to be angry with her, she reports everything to me." Her expression softened only slightly. "*Everything*."

Edan ran a hand over his beard. "I must admit, sister, you aren't what I was expecting."

"Well, brother, maybe you shouldn't judge people before you know them."

Something inside him fluttered, more than the ease and security he'd felt since arriving here. He couldn't place it, but it didn't need an explanation. It was comforting, soothing all the same.

"I don't blame you for anything, you know." Erza reached a hand toward him, hesitated, then pulled back. "I don't know what my knowledge of your existence would have changed anyway."

"Nothing." Edan sighed. "I get the feeling it would have changed nothing."

Erza nodded. "I'm…glad to have you here. Shocked, but glad." Her smile seemed out of place, as if she didn't do it often. "I know we've only just met, but there are things I feel we should catch up on."

"We'll have plenty of time. Just…promise me you won't die today."

Her mouth twitched. "Only if you promise me you'll somehow convince our mother to like you and get those flowers you need."

Edan chuckled, turning out to watch the snow blowing through the distant mountaintops. "You have my word."

"My Elites will protect you, should anything happen. I don't want *you* dying on *me* either." They were silent for a moment before she added, "Will you be at the competition today?"

Edan blinked, turning to her. She met his eyes evenly, her face emotionless. "I didn't think it would be wise to give you another distraction. Do you want me to be?"

Erza shrugged. "It doesn't matter to me."

Edan reached for her, then pulled back, narrowing his eyes. "If it does, I'll be there."

"No, it's alright. If something happens, I don't want you to be caught in the middle."

"Are you expecting something to happen?"

Erza ran her hands through her hair. "I honestly don't know. I wouldn't doubt it, but…" She faced him. "Just get those flowers, Edan." She retreated down the ramp, leaving him no choice but to follow her. "Whatever it takes, whatever she demands. I know she can be difficult."

"I will," he said, catching up to her.

"Good. Navarre's survival might depend on them."

Evalyn panted, fighting the exhilaration as blue-green smoke engulfed her vision. When it cleared, she was standing again, wiping sweat from her eyes as she settled back into human form.

Clapping echoed from behind her, and she turned toward the noise. Despite spending the past month in their presence, it was still strange and inspiring to watch the Elites train. With Erza busy preparing for her competitions, Rowen and Astrid led afternoon training, so Eva, Jenson, and Maya had no choice but to join them. Having the Elites' approval and encouragement filled her with a sense of pride.

"I must admit, I'm impressed. I sure hope Quinn's been practicing his shifting as hard as you, or you're going to put him to shame." Jenson, finally well enough to be up and about, walked toward her.

She pursed her lips, running a hand through her unbound silver hair. "Thank you. But I'm not interested in beating anyone. Beside, from what you've told me, he seems too stubborn to give up without a fight."

Maya laughed, nudging Jenson's shoulder. "Even if he was, this one wouldn't let him get out of control."

"You have to love the perks of being a *sielapora*, don't you?" Rowen chuckled, adjusting a strap on her thigh.

Eva took the waterskin Naoi offered her, gulping it down greedily. The fair-skinned witch smiled impishly.

"We should go," Astrid's remark seemed more directed to the Elites, her eyes shimmering molten gold. "The final duel starts soon, and we're expected to guard the Queen."

Rowen nodded to the others, and they collected various weapons littering the dirt before entering the hallway. The wind pushed them toward the outer ramp, the chill burning Eva's cheeks. Naoi and Fi remained to guard the arena entrance with Astrid's dark-skinned cousins, Ysta and Curra. The others followed them up to the royal balcony.

Evalyn's pulse quickened the closer they got. As if sensing her unease, Maya and Jenson took a step closer to her, a harmless movement, yet natural, as if they'd done it countless times before.

They probably have for Quinn, she thought. *It shouldn't be surprising that it would comfort me as well.*

Rowen's voice carried back to her. "Don't worry, Erza's a warrior. We've been training together for two centuries. She knows what she's doing."

"She was born to be Queen," Vien agreed, winking. "She'll be fine."

Astrid gave a sharp nod, her fingers brushing against Rowen's. "And if Anwen—Adria—tries anything, we'll handle it." She glanced at the Elites around her. "Together."

Eva nodded, and they entered the upper levels through the thick plum curtain. She glanced toward Queen Rowena, her face solemn as ever, and curtsied. The Queen raised an eyebrow, but said nothing, turning her attention to the open arena below where Erza and Morana entered.

Eva bit her lip, sitting between Jenson and Maya as Rowen, Astrid, Vien, and the others took up their defensive stances beside their Queen. Daiki circled above their heads, perching on the flat, crumbling expanse with a massive shake of her white-scaled head. Beside her, the black Kitsugon curled in contempt, hematite scales shimmering vivid hues of blues, purples, and greens in the setting sun.

The mount of a future Queen.

A heavy, black fog coated the arena below. Eva frowned, glancing toward the others, wondering if she was seeing things, but Rowen's scowl validated her concerns.

She gripped the fabric of Dax's cloak, from fear or for comfort, she wasn't sure.

Erza, clad in simple chestnut riding leathers and Stormwood purple, radiated strength and splendor. But it wasn't Erza who worried her.

Standing at the other end of the arena was Morana. Jenson and Maya tensed, Maya whispering, "A Shadow Beast?"

Eva didn't need to acknowledge the truth, didn't need to deny it. Because it wasn't Morana's pale blue eyes—Blackwing eyes—that filled her vision. They were dark, soulless, and brimmed with shadows.

fifty-two

Emptiness consumed Joseline's being.

They had Julia. They had her baby sister locked in some dungeon, alone and terrified, and Joseline could do nothing to help her.

Another tear ran down her cheek. She didn't bother wiping it away. Shea, curled against the bedrolls scattered around her, whined, rubbing against her knee. Joseline stroked her fur absently, unblinking.

The tent flap rustled. She didn't look up. "You know, this is exactly what he wants."

Joseline didn't move. She hadn't moved since they put her in here. She couldn't sleep. None of it mattered.

"Joseline, talk to me." Quinn's voice cracked slightly.

Another tear fell. Honestly, she was surprised she still had tears to shed.

Quinn sat beside her, Shea moving to make room for him in the private tent. Joseline's nose flared, her eyes too swollen to close as he slipped calloused fingers beneath her chin. "Joseline, please."

Joseline opened her mouth, then closed it, unable to form the words. The breath slipped through her lips, shuddering and harsh.

"Joseline..."

"She's only ten, Quinn. No, eleven. It's Nova, she turned eleven in Kyaos. I missed her birthday. I never miss her birthday," she breathed.

"She's only eleven."

A shiver ran up her spine as he tucked a curl behind her ear. "We'll find a way to help her."

Shivering again, she surrendered, leaning into his warmth. He wrapped strong arms around her, pulling her against his chest. She breathed him in, pine and frankincense, safe and soothing. "Can you promise me that?"

He didn't answer.

She wiped her nose, sniffing. "What kind of ruler am I if I can't protect my own sister?"

"An honest one, who tries to save everyone even when they can't."

She nuzzled against the crook of Quinn's shoulder, her arms wrapping around the hard muscle of his waist. "He said they were going to sacrifice her." Joseline looked up at him. "I can't...we can't...I told her I'd always be there for her."

"We will do whatever we can to save her. That, I can promise." He touched his lips to her forehead.

You've got company, Shea said as Kai's head poked into the tent.

"How are you feeling?" she asked, tucking her lavender hair behind elongated ears. "Up to eating with the rest of us today?"

Quinn raised an eyebrow, aquamarine eyes filled with a kindness he reserved only for Joseline.

"You don't have to, nobody is forcing you," Kai added, bending to pick up Shea as the fox curled around her ankles. "Larina just wanted me to remind you we're still entering Raenya tomorrow, so—"

"I'm doing better," Joseline lied.

Kai's stormy eyes narrowed, not entirely convinced, but she smiled weakly before ducking back out with a purring Shea.

"Are you sure?" Quinn untangled his arm from her.

She laced their fingers together. "Of what?"

"That you're alright."

Joseline shook her head. "No. But there's no need to worry them. It would be pointless to go after her before I'm blessed by Amber Falls anyway, right?"

"Right."

She pulled him from the tent, their hands still clasped. "So, Amber Falls first."

"Then, we'll find a way to try and help Julia. We'll do everything we can." He squeezed her fingers, stroking light circles over her palm as they made their way to the main fire, his promise lingering along her flesh.

fifty-three

The darkness coated Erza's flesh as she entered through the carved archway, white knuckles gripping her spear, her eyes shifting, adjusting in the growing dimness.

Why was it so dark? It was midafternoon. Even on a cloudy day the sky was still visible through the open roof. But the unnatural fog had her squinting to find Morana crouched in the dirt across the arena.

Erza sucked in a breath. The Blackwing heir looked demonic, her eyes soulless and dark as she grinned at Erza.

She glanced up, finding Daiki beside the small, black Kitsugon, their tawny eyes shimmering, unblinking, judging. Queen Rowena braced herself against the railing, staring down a too-perfect nose. Rowen and Astrid stood a step behind and to her right, Eva sat between Maya and Jenson, his dark eyes dancing despite the blank look on his face.

She inspected them all, silent and calm, before turning her gaze to Adria. There was hardly a witch left within the demon possessing the Blackwing's mind. Once pale blue eyes rippled with shadows that shimmered faintly along her flesh, her movements cold and rigid. It still shocked Erza that seeing the truth had taken them so long.

But Adria was no fool, and she'd manipulated them all.

Erza almost didn't hear Daiki's earth-shattering cry signaling the start of the duel. She could have sworn Jenson jumped, and she smiled.

"What a childish mistake, starting the duel of your death unfocused," Morana taunted.

Erza bared her teeth, twirling her metal-tipped staff in her hand as she turned; but Morana was gone. She tensed, then bit back a cry of agony as pain exploded across her left thigh. She stumbled, blood swelling, running down her leg as she whirled, searching for Morana in the mist. Again, she was greeted by nothing. "Only a coward hides in the dark," Erza hissed.

Cold sweat ran down Erza's neck as she felt Morana at her back. "Oh, lighten up, Princess. I'm only playing with you a little. It's more fun that way." The laugh that followed made her skin crawl.

Erza clenched her teeth and launched her elbow backward. The responding crunch of bone wasn't satisfying enough.

Morana growled, wiping at the blood pouring from her nose. Challenge gleamed in her eyes, and Erza grinned, ignoring the agony along her thigh.

They circled each other. Erza gnawed on the inside of her cheek, forcing herself not to limp, not to show weakness as she searched for an opening.

There.

She ducked, crystal-embedded wood an extension of her arm as Morana surged toward the place where Erza stood seconds before. Erza's fist contacted her ribs, then gripped her wrist, helping her fall over the staff. Morana landed with a hard thud, and Erza seized the moment to rip away part of her tunic, wrapping it tightly around her upper thigh to stop the bleeding. But before she could pick up her staff, Morana tackled her to the ground.

Pain exploded along her skull as Morana's weight crushed them both into the dirt. Erza snarled, clawing to free herself, but Morana held her firm. Erza couldn't look away from the Blackwing's shadowed eyes.

Morana lowered her head to Erza's ear. "I'm going to take great pleasure in killing you, Erza Stormwood. Then, I'm going to kill all those you hold dear."

The shriek almost erupted from her throat as the demon dug a sharp crystal nail into the wound on her leg. Dark spots prickled her vision. "I'm not going to die that easily," Erza gasped.

"No? But that handsome half-breed will, I'm sure, as will that helpless brother of yours." Pale blue smoke curled around her fingers, the color of Morana's magic—another part of the façade.

Erza rolled on her good leg, breaking free from the demon's grip and stumbling to her feet. She lunged for her staff, bringing it up between them.

The imposter witch laughed. "You expect to stop me with a piece of iron-tipped wood? My power is ancient."

But Erza stepped toward her. The air swished around the wood as it dipped and weaved, the crystals infused into the wood refracting against the faint light. "I was born a Queen, and I won't die a coward."

The iron tip of her staff sliced flesh, and Morana hissed, slinking away from it. "You're no queen, you're merely a princess reaching for an impossible crown. There's only one master of this world, and he bows to no one."

The fog swirled about Erza's feet, weaving, twisting around her. Then it tightened, blocking out her air. Gasping, Erza nearly dropped her staff, and with a snarl Morana shot forward.

Erza hefted her staff just in time to block the slashing claws, the fog's phantom grip loosening. They broke away, circling each other. Morana lunged again, toppling them to the ground, lashing against the staff between them. It groaned from the impact for a split second before snapping completely. Erza's eyes widened as the splintered wood fell to the dirt.

"Pity," Morana grinned. "We all fall to the darkness sooner or later. It resides in all of us."

So many emotions swarmed Erza's subconscious—hatred, anger, fear, love. She held back tears, refusing to show weakness. "My grandmother gave me that staff."

"Oh? I thought witches weren't sentimental?" Morana licked her lips. "What are you going to do about that now?"

Erza surged toward the demon, her pulse quickening, blood boiling. The air shimmered at her fingertips as her crystal nails slid free, snaking around her palms. She struck, her magic lashing out in a swift gust of lilac wind; Morana dodged it, but Erza struck again.

And again.

The shimmering wind raced through the arena, gusting like an uncontrollable cyclone around her as the anger grew, blowing away the darkness. The demon's smirk vanished when it threw her to the ground. She crawled away from Erza's approach, but not quickly enough.

Erza knelt, picking up half of the splintered staff, the metal tip glinting, the smooth shaft a minor comfort in her hand. It glowed, lilac twining along the splintered end, mending and molding. The metal rippled, thinning and elongating. Air swirled, mixing with fire, earth, and water as Erza subconsciously willed the elements she'd spent years mastering into existence, forging a new weapon. They lashed together like a whip of lilac lightning when Erza cracked her wrist, twisting about her calves.

The arena fell silent.

She stared at the weapon in her hand. Era's whip— a relic of the Goddess of War and the Hunt. One of The Twelve, the one from whom her name stemmed. A weapon of the elements gifted to her by the Mother Goddess to fight the darkness.

Slowly, Erza turned her attention to Morana. The Blackwing still lay, staring, trembling on the ground.

With a final cry, she lunged, but not fast enough even with the blood-thirsty demon raging inside her. The shimmering whip wound around her throat, dragging her to the dirt, the metal nimble and malleable. She gagged, struggling against the constricting cord.

But Erza only saw the demon beneath. She stepped along the dirt, kneeling beside Morana. "The darkness may bow to no one, but neither do I. So you can tell your precious god I decide my own fate. I will not succumb to the dark, and I will not die by your hand or his. Not today."

She thrust her crystal nails into Morana's chest.

Morana shrieked, arching off the ground. The shadows vanished for only a moment from Morana's eyes, the pale blue visible once more. "Erza," she choked, gripping the whip. "Erza, thank you."

Erza frowned. "Another trick, demon?"

But Morana shook her head, gasping. "No," she coughed, her skin paling, lips turning blue as she struggled for air. Tears swelled in her eyes. "Thank you, for setting me free." Morana shuddered again, blood pooling from the wound, bubbling at her mouth before she went limp.

Only then did the pain in her leg overcome the adrenaline. Erza gritted her teeth, pulling her hand away, nails digging into the sand as she fought to keep the agony from her face. Blood welled, oozing between exposed muscle and flesh as she struggled to her feet. The whip curled itself around her wrist, snaking along her flesh to her forearm, then froze. Erza gaped, twisting her arm to inspect the accessory, then smiled despite herself.

The soft thud behind her pulled her attention back to reality. She turned, face-to-face with the young Kitsugon shimmering like raw hematite.

Lilac eyes met gold, and everything faded away—the pain, the fear, the confusion. Nothing else mattered but her and the beautiful creature walking toward her. Erza met her stare evenly, her breathing shallow as she watched, waited. The Kitsugon stopped just out of reach, a question filling those tawny eyes.

She held up a hand, blood dripping down her forearm. The Kitsugon's eyes narrowed, but only slightly, before she sniffed, first Erza's outstretched hand, then the weapon concealed along her arm. Time stood still, witch and Kitsugon spellbound by the unspoken connection and acceptance. Then the creature blinked once, bowed her head, and pressed her snout into Erza's palm.

Her blood warmed, exhilaration overpowering at the bond rippling through her. Erza leaned forward, touching her forehead to the black scales. *Mine. This beautiful creature of darkness is mine.*

"Sauda," Erza whispered the name.

The Goddess of Death. An end, that like all things, was still beautiful. The Kitsugon opened her eyes.

"Your name is Sauda." Erza couldn't imagine it being anything else.

Sauda pulled away, a soft croon vibrating from her throat, then pushed her snout toward Erza once more. Only when they pulled away a second time did Erza allow her gaze to meet her mother's.

Queen Rowena still stood with hands braced on the balcony. Daiki let out a roar, the sound echoing through the arena. Then the Queen's mouth twitched into a smile unnoticed to anyone except Erza. But the internal satisfaction was enough.

Sauda chirped, crouching her front legs. An invitation. Erza's pulse quickened as she reached out a hand, stroking the coal fur, and hoisted herself onto Sauda's powerful shoulders.

Then they were flying.

Erza relished in the exhilaration, the wind caressing her face like a lover's touch. She never felt as free as she did in the air; she almost groaned when they landed along the ramp outside the royal seats, the flight not nearly long enough. With a sigh, she opened the curtains to face her mother, refusing to limp on her wounded leg.

The small crowd clustered around the Queen—crone advisors and her Elites along with the other coven leaders. She didn't allow her gaze to flicker toward Eva, or Maya and Jenson, but she could sense them watching as well.

"Erza Stormwood." Queen Rowena's voice filled the arena, ringing off every crevasse. Erza lowered to one knee on her uninjured leg, a hand braced on the ground. She bowed her head respectfully, pride swelling in her chest as her mother whispered, "My daughter."

"Yes, my Queen."

"You have proven your skills in more ways than one this Nova, and the Goddess for which this month is named has shown you blessings, as have her sisters. Era, Goddess from which you are named, grants you mighty weapons," she gestured to the whip now coiled at Erza's forearm, "and Eona, for her desires stirring within your own heart." Rowena took a step toward her. "You have displayed strength, cunning, perseverance, all things worthy of a Queen. From this moment forth, I name you, Erza Stormwood, my heir and successor, future Queen of Rekiv, and protector of our land. Rise, my daughter."

Erza stood, their gazes holding for a brief moment before Rowena turned toward the curtained doorway.

That was when Adria struck, lunging for Queen Rowena's exposed back. But the Elites were ready. Rowen and Astrid moved as one to block the demon's path, Ira and Zea on either side of them. Soren's twin blades shimmering with lilac wind, Vien's throwing stars hanging from her fingertips. Daiki snarled from her perch on the stone turret above just as Sauda did. Erza's fingers twitched, the whip uncoiling from her wrist and snaking around Adria's forearms, securing them behind the demon's back. She shrieked, trying to yank away as her flesh burned.

Only then did Rowena speak, without bothering to face Adria. "You should know, demon, how foolish this attempt was. You were never going to get far." She glanced sidelong as Erza. "Prepare her for escort to the dungeons at Ravencrest. We leave in the morning." She waved a dismissive hand, exiting the arena. The Silvermist coven leader and the crones followed her in silence.

Rowen and Astrid exchanged a look; then Astrid bound Adria, iron shackles sizzling against the demon's flesh.

"Fools," Adria snarled. "Aeron will end you all. There will be nothing left of your pitiful realm when the darkness consumes it. Then, we shall thrive, feeding off the light within your souls."

"Aeron will do no such thing." Erza wasn't sure when Jenson had stepped forward, but she was glad to have him at her side.

Adria loosed a horrid laugh. "He will, half-breed. Not even Norah's light," she eyed Erza, "nor the new witch queen, nor the Children of Dorwynn can save that wretched fire-haired princess you so blindly follow." Jenson's jaw clenched as Adria spat at him. "The Goddess and her twelve children combined couldn't protect her from Aeron's return. Even now, he holds captive the other daughter with Waeshorn blood. You will all fall to the darkness."

At a nod from Erza, the Elites escorted Adria away. Only then did Erza shiver, unable to ignore the truth of her words. Her knees buckled, and she didn't fight the arm Jenson slipped around her waist. "You need a healer," he whispered against her hair.

Erza frowned even as her vision blurred. She tried to push him away, but she could barely lift her arms. "I'm fine. Don't let my mother see you, traveler."

Jenson's chest rumbled as he laughed. "You're full of shit, flower."

Her snarl must have come out as slurred mumbles, because he laughed again, lifting her off her feet and cradling her against him. "Everything will be fine, for now." The rock of his step lulled her into oblivion.

For now, she thought, her head falling against his chest. *But how long is that?*

fifty-four

"Jenson, you have to get some sleep eventually."

He glanced up at Rowen, wetting his lips. "I'm fine."

Even as he said it, his eyes drooped.

"You aren't fine." Rowen pulled up a chair beside him, eyeing Erza's unconscious form, so peaceful amidst the infirmary sheets. "And if Queen Rowena saw you doting on her like this she would never let Erza live it down."

"I don't care," he growled. "I just wish I could help. But I can't. I'm useless."

Rowen snorted. "Useless, huh? So dramatic."

Jenson smiled at that. "Maya would be the first to say it's one of my charms." He sighed, letting his head fall against his bicep.

They were silent for a moment until Rowen cleared her throat. "Have you thought about using your gift?"

"Of course I have," he chided. When she didn't respond, he sighed. "Sorry, that came out a little too harsh."

"It's alright," Rowen put a hand on his forearm. "You're worried about her, there's no rule that says you have to hide that."

"Except the stupid idea that you all have to show no feelings to be strong."

The silence stretched stronger that time.

At last, Rowen said, "Queen Rowena is the only one who truly believes that."

Jenson kept his gaze focused on Erza. On the tightly bandaged thigh uncovered by the quilt concealing the rest of her body. "What if...what if it's infected or..."

Rowen shrugged. "What if it is? Do something about it."

Jenson glared at her. "You already know I can't do it."

"No," Rowen shifted to face him, raising an eyebrow. "I know you failed once, on your first try no less, and now you're giving up."

"I'm not—"

"Aren't you?" Not a reply. A challenge.

Jenson frowned, slipping his fingers from Erza's. He gulped, rubbing his hands together and concentrated on the magic swirling in his core.

It glowed an iridescent gold, humming gently as if waiting for him.

Simple, he thought. *Heal the wound.*

Heal her.

Jenson closed his eyes, pulling air into his lungs, sensing it fill his chest. His fingers tingled slightly, eyelids twitching in response.

Heal her, he repeated. The breath slipped through his nose.

He envisioned the wound bending to his will, torn flesh knitting closed as he demanded it. His fingers danced rhythmically through the air, guiding him, but still he kept his eyes closed.

A moment later, the tingling faded.

"Jenson," Rowen whispered. "Look."

His eyes fluttered open.

The bandage had opened slightly. The wound beneath, gone. Jenson held in the gasp. "I...I did that?" he asked, turning to her.

Rowen flashed a knowing smirk. "I told you to stop doubting yourself."

He could only manage a half-laugh in response. But his gaze remained fixed on Erza's thigh. On the now unmarred flesh broken and inflamed only moments before.

Rowen nudged him, and he turned to face her, pride gleaming in her eyes when he met her gaze. Jenson rubbed his hands together, unable to shake the awe away as his lips twitched into a smile.

fifty-five

Joseline was in a daze, a trance she couldn't break out of. Fear clouded her smile, looming in her eyes when she thought he wasn't looking. Quinn wasn't sure if the others noticed. Fallon, maybe, but the others didn't know her like he did, couldn't see the pain behind those beautiful eyes.

He glanced up at her, Bellona looking down at him with a snort. He preferred his wolf's body these days, not quite used to the constant energy pulsing through his new Fae form. Besides, Eclipse didn't mind the absence of a rider, and Azuri lounged along his haunches, humming quietly. Sunlight glinted along the clouds, hues of orange and cranberry blinding their party as the sun rose in the sky.

"Quinn, I can feel you staring at me."

He opened his mouth to deny it, but he *was* staring at her. His ears twitched when he huffed. *I know you aren't alright.*

"What do you want me to say?" The fire flared slightly in her voice.

Nothing. He looked ahead, the veil of Raenya shimmering along the shoreline of the Jesma Sea.

"Don't do that."

Quinn furrowed his brows, eyes narrowing at her. *Do what?*

"Shut me out."

He glared. *I'm not—*

"Yes, you are." Her eyes softened, flickering with pain. "I...I thought we were past that."

Quinn growled at Azuri's tinkling laugh. *She's right, you know.*

The growl deepened, and he shifted, blue-green smoke curling as the wolf's form faded. Once human, he gripped Eclipse's reins and swung himself into the saddle. The stallion let out a surprised neigh, shaking as he adjusted to Quinn's sudden weight.

They were silent for a long time before Quinn dared to meet the fire radiating from her glare. "I'm sorry, I didn't mean it like that. I don't know what I expected you to say."

Joseline pursed her lips. "If you meant your question to be rhetorical, just say so, idiot."

Quinn's mouth twitched into a half-smile. "We will do whatever we can to save her, but we need to save you first."

The company stopped ten minutes later per Larina's orders, and she gathered her commanders. "Only those of Fae heritage may enter with the princess." She gave Logan an apologetic look, and he shrugged, running a hand through his hair. "Kai, Fallon, Quinn, and Joseline should be enough. Besides, seeing both Joseline and Quinn will already be a shock to the citizens."

Kai laughed, stroking Shea. "This one isn't moving anytime soon." Shea yipped in agreement, and Joseline laughed, the sound less forced than over the last two days.

"Of course, Shea as well. The Aonani foxes do dwell in Raenya, I'm sure she'll be welcome."

They split up, Larina making her way through the ranks, Kai seeing to the horses, while Logan conversed with Freya and Ren. Fallon approached them, eyeing the misty shimmer. "I was only a boy the last time I came here…a tour of Navarre for Reul after he was crowned king."

"What was it like?" Joseline asked.

"Beautiful." There was no hesitation in his reply. "One of the most beautiful places in Navarre."

Quinn raised an eyebrow. "Don't turn into a reminiscing elder just yet, old man. It doesn't suit you."

Fallon glared, but said nothing, shaking his head as he walked toward Kai and their horses.

"Are you ready, Princess?" Larina's voice was soft behind them.

"Are we ever truly ready to accept our fate?" There was no fear in those green eyes now, only excitement and nerves.

Larina inclined her head, a smile spreading across her face. "No, we are not. But when faced with doubt, the stars have a funny way of shining brighter, even when it would be easier for them to dim." She glanced at the space between them, their fingers silently reaching for the solid comfort. Her smile widened. "Listen to the stars, Princess. They will always guide you home."

Then she was gone, silver shimmering behind her as she walked toward the veil. Her cloak billowed in the breeze, a hand reaching out toward Kai as her mate stepped to her side, Shea still sprawled in the crook of one arm. Without so much as a glance over her shoulder, Larina held up a hand. The veil parted for her, beckoning them inside. The Fae pair were majestic, radiant. It made something clench in Quinn's chest; not pain, but awe.

"You're just as beautiful as them, you know." Joseline murmured, nudging him.

He turned to her, that same awed look shimmering in her eyes as they trailed down his body. He smirked, exhilarated by the fire dancing in her gaze.

Fallon chuckled, walking past them. This time, the veil parted on its own, some internal lock unclicked by Larina's initiation. Quinn didn't realize how fast his pulse was racing until Joseline's soft touch calmed the raging flames, their fingers twining. "Together," Quinn whispered. It had become a motto, a promise.

They took a cautious step, Joseline's grip tightening. He could feel her pulse against his thumb, sense the fevered excitement rolling off her body in waves. The smell coated his nostrils, lilac and windstorms, her scent as intoxicating as the lightning and flower blossoms it reminded him of.

Only a few more steps.

"Together," Joseline repeated.

She squeezed his hand. "Quinn, what if..."

"Don't." He stroked his thumb across her wrist.

Joseline stared at him, hesitant and unsure, but strong. She'd gained so much strength since Ywone, the spring start of their journey an eternity away rather than a few summer months. The once frail and helpless princess stood proud, toned with muscle, her fingers calloused from training. Freckles littered her face, as wild as her unbroken spirit, hair kissed by flames.

Quinn tried again, the comforting words strange on his tongue, but she looked like she needed them. "Don't...doubt yourself."

Her face shone with understanding. "Quinn, awkward attempts at comforting pep talks don't suit you."

They both laughed, releasing some of the tension.

"Together," he repeated—an eternal, binding promise. "We do this together, whatever it takes. We started into the darkness together and I'll be damned by all The Twelve and the Goddess herself if I leave you to the darkness alone." The smile spreading across her face was the most relaxed on he'd seen in days.

"We will fight and keep on fighting. We will protect innocents, destroy demons, and never give up until Aeron is sealed away forever. The darkness will fall, and we will remain strong. Together, we will coat the world in starlight."

Tears brimmed Joseline's eyes. But she nodded, squeezing his hand one final time, and stepped into the shimmering veil.

No amount of curiosity could prepare Joseline for the sheer wonder of seeing Raenya with her own eyes. She froze, the breath caught in her throat, her eyes widening as if that would help her absorb everything faster. Quinn, still gripping her hand, froze as well.

Rolling, grassy plains covered with flowers danced along endless seas of green; tulips, lavender, jasmine, and peony engulfed her senses, among countless others. A small fortress stretched along the horizon in the distance, sunlight gleaming against marbled stone in vibrant golden rays. Trees littered the hills, in random clusters offering shade from the sun.

It was slightly warmer than the frozen marshes they'd come from, as if the breathtaking country was in a perpetual state of spring. Birdsong echoed across the plains, some ducking into high branches where hungry chicks waited, others weaving along the peaceful breeze. Deer, rabbits, and squirrels dotted the hills, oblivious to one another as they went about their daily business.

The light flickered within her, drawn to the crystalline pillars standing guard around the plains. There were twelve of them, presumably one for each of Navarre's gods. They shimmered, raw yet contained, the tops opening into four clasps, their clawed grip wrapped loosely around a glowing golden sphere.

Joseline's pulse thrummed at the sight, echoing as if that protective power resembled the light residing within her.

She walked in a daze, Quinn's hand never leaving hers, the others only a step ahead. The further they ventured into Raenya, the stronger the sensation within her became. The belonging, the connection to this land and its glorious splendor. She was meant to be here—the Goddess's power surging through her didn't need to scream it at her. She already knew.

There were houses hidden within the massive hillsides, their vibrantly-colored doorways the only indication they were there at all. Some reached toward the sky while others stretched along the horizon; there were even some with little gardens enclosed by picket fences, flower boxes lining the windowsills.

The eternal spring glistened everywhere, even before they entered the heart of the country. Flowery shrubs lined the cobblestone paths in hues of purple, blue, pink, and white. Honeybees danced between the blossoms while butterflies and hummingbirds waltzed with the soft breeze. Branches arched above, covering the path, shielding them from the sun.

Kai turned back, laughing at their wide eyes, and winked, her smile kind and playful.

Finally, the echo of rushing water consumed them. Though Joseline braced herself, she could barely contain the gasp as they broke through the trees.

Enormous raging waters tumbled down from the cloud-kissed, moss-coated mountains into the golden pool below. Amber flowers circled the peak, a crown of nature fit for a goddess. The mountain circled the pool with outstretched arms, an inviting crescent. Near the peak loomed two small caves like eyes, their entrances illuminated by gold.

But it wasn't the crescent embrace or the glowing eyes or the flowered crown that threatened to stop her heart. It was the water.

The Amber Falls.

The water tumbled between the eye-like caves, shimmering in the afternoon sun, glistening like molten amber. Joseline ignored the tear that fell from her cheek, the beauty consuming her.

Quinn's grip on her hand pulled her attention away. She blinked, forcing herself back to reality as she followed his gaze.

The creatures of long-forgotten legends surrounded them on all sides. A haven for half-breeds and forgotten races—that's what Raenya was. Her gaze followed them, eyes wide with awe: Demi-Fae, the white foxes of the Aonani who eyed both her and Shea, centaurs, creatures that appeared human but rippled with raw power, then vanished into the growing crowd as one creature or another—shifters.

The sheer beauty of it took Joseline's breath away. Fresh tears wet her cheeks as Quinn brought her close, his arm around her waist. She leaned into him, and Shea purred at her feet.

Joseline smiled up at Quinn, and for a moment, she thought the movement was no more than a trick of the light; but then, blurred light cleared, the iridescent wings shimmering just above Quinn's shoulder becoming visible.

A faerie.

The tiny creature met her stare, silvery hair and sapphire eyes bright. He blinked, as if surprised she could see him, then grinned, revealing slightly-pointed canines. Joseline let out a choked laugh and turned back to the other assembled creatures. She could see them all, iridescent wings gliding between shadow and sunshine, airless and so tiny beside their counterparts.

Only those with the purest of hearts may see faeries. The words echoed in her head.

She looked up at Quinn and found that for once, he was at a complete loss for words. When she turned back to those assembled before them, the creatures did something she never expected. One by one, they nodded, and bowed.

In all her life, Joseline had never imagined these beautiful beings were real. The things of myths and legends, yet visible right before her eyes, bowing to her as if she was the almighty Goddess herself.

She wished Julia were here. Her sister would be ecstatic to see the glory of the living fairytales she adored so much. The thought made her smile.

Princess Joseline Marie Waeshorn.

Joseline blinked, meeting the pale blue eyes of the massive Aonani fox walking toward them.

Mortal blessed by the light of the Goddess and chosen protector of Navarre. It is our greatest honor to welcome you into the sacred country of Raenya. The creature met Shea's eyes, radiating warmth. *And you, little one. Well done.*

Shea turned away, her ears twitching. *It was nothing, Shina.*

Shina chuckled. *It seems my daughter hasn't lost her plucky touch.*

Shea let out a frustrated huff. *Thank you, Mother, for that clarification.*

Joseline laughed as several other races made their way toward her. A faerie with iridescent wings and bright golden eyes; a shifter with skin covered in tattoos rippling with raw magic; a Demi-Fae with ever-so-slightly pointed ears half as noticeable as the delicate, elongation of Quinn's pure Fae extremities; a half-man, half-wolf whose tail swished lazily behind him; a centaur with a vibrant green mane.

"Joseline," Quinn whispered beside her. "At least close your mouth if you're going to stare like an idiot."

Heat exploded across her cheeks, but she obliged. There were just so many of them. So many unknown, forgotten races, all beautiful, fascinating.

"Thank you," she managed, hoping her voice sounded stronger

than she felt. "For the warm welcome."

Shina turned to Quinn. *And you, Son of Dorwynn and Reul's heir, have done so much to get her here unharmed.* She bowed. *You, too, deserve great praise.* Quinn looked as though he might open his mouth to speak, but Shina spun toward the pool. *Come, we have much to do.* She eyed Fallon and the others before walking toward the shore.

Even if Joseline didn't feel compelled to follow the great white fox, she would have, her curiosity piquing. Quinn followed as well, engulfed in aquamarine fog when he shifted. Joseline sent him a questioning look, but he only huffed, trotting ahead of her to walk beside Shina. The silver-haired Faerie landed on his haunches, winking back at them.

He's fine, Shea promised. *Just overwhelmed.*

Quinn doesn't get overwhelmed.

Everyone does, at one point or another. Shea's ears twitched. *Besides, how could he not be? This is a lot for anyone to take in.*

Quinn let out a warning yip, stopping Joseline inches from the water's edge. She froze, sending him a grateful smile.

Princess Joseline. Shina's whimsical voice pulled for her attention, her eyes kind. *Are you ready, child?*

Her pulse quickened, prancing against her ribs in nervous flutters. "What do I do?"

Shina bowed her head to the pool. *Simply kneel where the land meets the water, and drink.*

Joseline gulped but nodded, her eyes darting to Quinn. He rubbed against her calf, a soft rumble of encouragement vibrating her leg. She sucked in a breath, fists clenched, and stepped toward the shoreline. Kneeling in the dirt, she allowed her gaze to flicker up to the caves glittering with molten gold; then she cupped her hands, dipping them beneath cool water. She hesitated as she brought them to her lips, pulse still prancing.

It's alright, I'm right here. Quinn's words echoed in her head, calm and soothing.

She gave him a close-lipped smile. "I know, I just...what if, after all this..."

His tail curled around her feet. *You can do this.* He sent her a wry look. *After all we've been through, this is what you choose to let frighten you? It's only water.*

Joseline laughed, sending him an equally wry look, then lifted the water to her lips.

Instantaneous light exploded in a circle around them, the sensation so bright Joseline had to close her eyes. Power rippled through her, tingling along her flesh. Heat and cold electrified every sense, prickling her spine. Then, as quickly as it had started, it stopped, the earth and water still around her.

"Open your eyes, my chosen daughter."

Joseline blinked at the beauty of the unfamiliar, immortal voice. After several moments to calm the power coursing through her, her eyes opened, settling on the majestic forms in a crescent moon around her, bending their formation with the Amber Falls.

The Goddess and The Twelve.

Beautiful and shimmering, they hovered slightly above the pool. The Goddess smiled, pale skin sparkling like stars, twining within the long hair tumbling over shoulders and breasts. Her gown a sheer burgundy, illuminating the bright gold of her eyes like an eternal flame. Her children filled the space around her on either side, all dressed in colors of their elements, the royal houses they protected, or the months that shared their name.

Riona and Sauda, the twin Goddesses of life and death, swathed in revealing aquamarine and crimson silks, leaned against one another. Kyaos the Wise wore scholar's robes of billowing ivory, while his spring sister, Ywone, Goddess of Beauty, stood to their left. Joseline let her eyes linger slightly on the Goddess for which her birth month was named, a small smile spreading on her lips when Ywone returned the gesture.

Noria's kind smile consumed her petite, rich bronze face, her healer's robes billowing about her. Syvi was dressed in chestnut leather pants and vest; her cunning indigo eyes, hidden behind ebony curls, electrified Joseline much like the seas she was Goddess of. Ryneas, the summer God of trade and wine, watched her curiously, his smile genuine, and lifted a wine goblet to his lips in a toast.

Era, the Goddess of War, smirked, the famed whip coiled around her wrist glowing a faint gold, while Eona, Goddess of love and desire, fluttered long eyelashes, a smile creeping across her full lips. Nova resembled every element of the moon she was Goddess of, her dark skin shimmering as if infused with starlight, tattooed along her forehead, neck, and shoulders in swirling patterns.

Malous stood with arms crossed, draped in his precious gold at wrists and throat, the soft clink of glittering jewels echoing softly. Yvaos, God of Strength, eyed Quinn with an approving grin.

Joseline wasn't sure she was breathing. She gulped, opening her mouth to speak, then closing it abruptly. Quinn snorted, and she blushed, studying her hands in her lap.

"My child, do not be afraid." Joseline looked up as Ywone stepped forward. Her golden hair tumbled about a youthful face, rosy cheeks the same color as her lips.

"I...I don't..." Joseline trailed off.

Ywone knelt before her and lifted Joseline's chin. "There's nothing for you to fear here."

Joseline fiddled with her curls. "I just don't know what it is that's expected of me now."

Ywone helped her to her feet. "You already know the answer to that."

"I know, but I—"

"No." Noria stepped up beside her sister. "We cannot tell you what to do, for it is only in your hands that your destiny can truly be seen." She met Joseline's stare with an expression that reminded her strangely of Jenson—their eyes the same deep brown, their hair tousled onyx, their skin that same beautiful, radiant bronzed russet.

Quinn growled at Noria's response, and Joseline knew her glare echoed his anger. "You can't even give me some guidance?" she asked. "How am I supposed to stop Aeron if I don't—"

"The keys and the relics." Yvaos and Kyaos spoke in unison as they stepped forward.

Era chuckled, shaking her head. "You two just can't help it now. You've become so good at reading each other's thoughts."

"They've never been able to help it." Syvi sounded bored, despite the smirk on her red lips.

Yvaos and Kyaos rolled their eyes simultaneously, warranting yet another laugh from the others.

Joseline couldn't help but smile at the exchange, their mundane teasing easing some of the fear pulsing through her. Quinn, however, remained tense.

Kyaos noticed it as well. "You can relax, Son of Dorwynn, we mean her no harm."

Quinn narrowed his aquamarine eyes, but mercifully didn't growl. Instead, he let out a resigned huff and laid himself at Joseline's feet.

Yvaos crossed his arms, turning back to Joseline. "So, the keys."

She nodded. "What are they?"

"A failsafe. A final protection of the realm if those blessed with this power before you were unable to stop Aeron. If brought together, their unique power and knowledge will be of great value…a power you'll need to bring together if you wish to stop Aeron for good."

"Always so cryptic with your wisdom, brother," Nova scoffed.

Yvaos raised an eyebrow in amusement.

Joseline frowned, ignoring Ywone, Kyaos, and the twins as they crouched to speak with Quinn in hushed voices. Her impatience flickered, but she bit the inside of her cheek to fight a smart remark.

"Something bothering you, Princess?" Syvi pursed her lips.

"Yes, actually."

"Seems her temper is as fiery as her curls," Era murmured.

Joseline crossed her arms. "No, I just—"

"Enough, all of you." The pool went silent when the Goddess spoke, all eyes drawn to her. She stepped forward, glaring at her daughters, though her smile was kind when her gaze fell on Joseline. "Aeron's power grows stronger and you allow your fear to consume you. Fear for yourself, your country," the Goddess's eyes flickered to Quinn, "those you love."

Joseline nodded.

"Your sister."

Her chin trembled. "Yes," she admitted. "But I don't want to cower from him."

"No, it appears not."

More silence.

"So how..." Joseline paused only for a moment. "How do I stop him? If what you say is true, if I am the last hope for my country, then how do I make sure we succeed? What are these keys you speak of and how do I find them?"

Quinn stood at her side once more, his secret discussion with the Gods over. She reached for his warmth, her fingers weaving through his dark, soft fur.

"The relics were scattered after the First Demon Wars, hidden and lost since the original lock was created," Ywone said.

"But they're closer now," Noria assured her. "They've shifted over time so when the time came to make themselves known, they would be ready to unite the keys once more. Their essence searches for the relics, always. Two you already have, and four more you must attain."

"You couldn't give a *yes* or a *no* answer, could you? Or tell me where to find them?" Joseline asked sheepishly.

The Goddess flashed an apologetic smile. "To connect the realm, you must first connect the keys. Only together will you be strong enough to stand a chance of defeating Aeron for good."

The light radiating from them dulled slightly, and the Goddess reached out to touch her cheek, a jolt of their connected power rippling through her. Uncertainty gripped Joseline's chest. "But what do I—"

"Find the keys and their relics, my daughter. Send Aeron back to the darkness. I fear it is too late for him to ever be saved." The Goddess faltered, her form shimmering a moment longer.

The bubble of light enclosing them faded, Fallon, Larina, and Kai becoming visible on the other side further up the shore.

Find the keys and their relics.

"But how..." Joseline's voice trailed off and she stumbled back, suddenly dizzy.

Aquamarine smoke flashed and Quinn was at her side, concern filling his eyes as his arms slid around her waist. "Joseline?"

"Find the keys," she murmured, her body going limp despite her protests. Shea's presence comforted her fading warmth, the others rushing forward in her peripheral, but her vision blurred, the power still surging as she collapsed against Quinn in a dead faint.

epilogue

His father's strength was growing. Alvah could smell his aura intensifying the further he walked into the obsidian tunnels beneath Corae.

Three hundred years since they'd planted the seeds. Three hundred years they lay watching, waiting in the dark for the triumph they deserved—for his father's return.

He was tunnels away from the main alcove before he smelled the tiny mortal's fear. She was pathetic, a cowering, blubbering mess of a child. Her fear disgusted him; her sobs filled the air as he approached. His father's beastie curled nearby, head resting along two massive paws stained with blood, but the Houzo was far from asleep. His onyx tail twitched lazily behind him, the ever-present aura he protected shimmering along his body, watching the young girl in the corner. Waiting with predatory focus.

The child's eyes darted toward him, the terror growing, swirling through pine green irises as her violent shaking intensified. Onyx hair clung to her skin, her gown a dirtied, bloody mess. Tears streaked her cheeks, eyes puffy and red from crying.

"What do you want?" she whispered through cracked lips.

Alvah smiled, cocking his head. "Nothing, little princess."

"Then why did you bring me here?"

A soft chuckle from the Houzo. Her eyes darted toward him as he uncurled from the wall where he lay, stretching and approaching her. She yanked against the chains binding her to the floor, frantic and useless. "You are so precious." He trailed a nail delicately down her neck, his eyes gleaming, delighted by her fear. "So precious. So...useful."

"Where's my sister?"

Her voice was slightly stronger, but her expression still belied her fear.

The Houzo snarled, and he caught the anger before it flared. "I haven't the slightest idea where the fire-haired brat is."

"Good," she whispered. Alvah could have sworn she relaxed.

The Houzo recovered, tail swishing as a deep chuckle rumbled from his chest.

The beast had always been there—his father's most trusted pet, the obvious vessel for his essence. The blackness of it shimmered along silken fur, Aeron's soul flickering down the beast's spine.

Soon, Father. Alvah turned his gaze to the helpless child beside him. *Soon.*

"Good for her, for now." He knelt beside the princess, taking her hand in his. She shook furiously, stumbling as she tried and failed to stand. "But not so good for you, I'm afraid."

Her eyes widened in terror. "No," she sobbed, "no, please..."

Alvah glanced at his father's pet. Then, with a final nod from the Houzo, he plunged his nail into the soft flesh of her wrist, slicing the skin to her elbow.

Julia barely registered the pain as the shriek erupted from her raw throat. The agony shook her to the core as she watched, helpless, her blood spilling from her forearm. She covered her mouth with her other hand, fighting the urge to vomit.

"The Waeshorn bloodline," the shadows along the beast's fur whispered. "Blessed by the wretched Goddess herself to honor Alaric, the first king. How funny, their hopes of protection would be their undoing."

Julia convulsed, the loss of blood too much for her small, weakened body to handle. She nearly fell over, caught when the nightmare gripped her forearm.

"At last," he purred.

The shadowed man laughed, the strange teardrop markings beneath his eyes shimmering gold in the dim light. Another cry sent her writhing in agony as her blood pooled around the beast's mouth, matting dark fur.

When he pulled away, the darkness shimmered around him. "Thank you, little princess."

She braced her uninjured arm against the ground, cradling the wounded one to her chest. The monster's eyes glowed with excitement. For a moment, she could have sworn they were blue mixed with green—a trick of the light.

But the silken, haunting voice that fell from those bloody lips was different. Beautiful.

The monster blinked once, twice. Then, turning to her, it cocked its head, and smiled.

The shadowed man bowed. "So, Father, it has begun at last."

"Indeed, it has." Again, that beautiful voice. "Thank you for your blood, little one. Without it, I would remain trapped forever. But your bloodline has set me free. Soon, it will be my complete release. Then, and only then shall my children and I bring darkness to this world. A darkness that not even the cursed Twelve could stop, not without their mother."

The shadows separated from the beast, straightening until they formed a man. He shimmered, his shadowed body transparent—incomplete, but alive. He reached a hand toward her and Julia yanked away. He laughed. "Thank you."

Julia opened her mouth to question him, but the words vanished. She met his gaze, terror trembling on frozen lips as she whispered the truth—the word, *the name* that even now, Navarre feared most.

"Aeron."

Glossary

Words and Pronunciations

Sielapora- (say-LAH-pour-AH): ancient Dorwynnian term for kindred souls or warrior soul mates, a unique, non-romantic bond between fighting companions.

Sirdispora- (seer-DIS-pour-AH): ancient Dorwynnian term for paired souls, or mates, a romantic bond between destined hearts.

Kitsugon- (kit-SUe-gone): An original mythical creature crossover between a dragon and a fox. Fox-like body and head, and dragon-like tail, wings, legs, and face.

The Shadowplains- the demon realm
Narcio- (Nar-SEE-oh)
Dorwynn- (DOOr-win)
Rekiv- (Rah-KEH-v)
Rathal- (Rah-thAH-l)
Ebondenn- (Ebb-OHN-den)
Chiron- (Ch-ih-ROne)
Raenya- (RAY-een-yah)

Joseline- (JAHss-eh-LYN)
Evalyn- (Eh-VAH-lyn)
Edan- (AY-den)
Aeron- (Ay-RO-n)
Rowen- (ROW-en)
Neirin- (nEE-ir-in)
Naoi- (Nah-OY)
Vien- (VEE-ehn)
Albion- (All-BEE-on)

Nichol- (NEE-kohl)
Zarin- (ZAH-rin)
Alvah- (AL-vah)
Houzo- (how-OO-zoh)
Akuma- (ah-COO-mah)
Nakoiyaa- (nah-COY-ah)

<u>The Twelve (Navarre's Gods, also the names of the months)</u>

Noria- (no-REE-ah): Goddess of Healing
Eona- (ee-OH-nah): Goddess of Love and Desire
Rinoa- (rih-NO-ah): Goddess of Life, the Sun and Precious Minerals
Syvi- (sIH-vee): Goddess of the Sea
Ywone- (yih-WOE-n): Goddess of Beauty, Morality, and Fertility
Ryenas- (riy-NEE-ahs): God of Trade, Agriculture, and Wine
Malous- (MAL-oh-oos): God of Wealth
Kyaos- (kiy-AH-ohs): God of Wisdom
Nova- (NO-vah): Goddess of the Moon
Era- (ERR-ah): Goddess of War and the Hunt
Yvaos- (YAH-voh-s): God of Strength
Sauda- (SA-ou-da): the Goddess of Death

Acknowledgments

First and foremost, I need to thank my Nana. She was my light. My rock in so many things. Even though she's gone, I've never felt like she truly was; her presence is always within my heart and soul, braving the doubts each time I face them.

To my loving Gram, for your support from the very beginning. I am so blessed an honored to have such an amazing woman in my life. From staying up late on vacation to help rework plotlines, to reading my work in the very beginning stages and helping me tweak the story, to never failing to remind me that I can do anything I put my mind to. Thank you, for lending me your strength. <3

To my parents. Mom and Dad, thank you for never doubting me. For showing me every day the beauty that is our imagination, and for never trying to crush mine no matter how old I got.

To my dear sister, Kiara. For the stunning author headshots and for listening to me ramble about plot points when you had no idea what I was talking about. I am forever grateful I got stuck with a flawless human like you for a sister.

To Aunt Dana, for being one of the most amazing people I know and an endless wall of support.

To David, who despite being a non-reader, has never failed to love me unconditionally and support me as I pursue my writing dreams. You are truly the love of my life, and I would be lost to the madness we without you.

To Laura, the first friend who truly believed in me. My alpha reader who isn't a writer. My writing wing woman. Girl, you have been there from the very beginning. You've never failed to support me and be there to read my work with endless praise, even in the beginning when I knew it was awful. I would be completely lost without you, and I cannot thank you enough for your friendship. <3

To Andie, for being the best Instagram friend a girl could ask for. We are half a world away, literally, yet I feel like we were meant to be friends. You've been by my side cheering me on for several years now. Several years of crazy long emails sobbing over the cruel yet satisfying plot twists we have planned, gushing over our precious babies and their relationships, over the endless flow of worldbuilding. Thank you, for being by my side. <3

To Lina, my dearest partner in crime. My soul sister. Where to begin? If we lived closer, we'd be inseparable, that's all there is to that. We started this journey into the fire together, and I couldn't imagine it with anyone else as a staple by my side. You are a beautiful, kind, exquisite soul, and I am so grateful for your friendship.

To my Beta Readers. Thank you all, from the bottom of my heart for your help and motivation and for loving my world even in its more primitive stages.

To my editors. Renee, darling, my love for you knows no bounds. Not only did you edit Whispering Shadows for me with love, but I will be forever grateful for your suggestions in making this story what it it today. Thank you, for helping me when I struggled and for never failing to give flawless advice and wisdom. Your neverending friendship is so precious to me, and I still want to cry from your kindness.

To Jess from Lizard Ink Maps for helping me bring Navarre to life. Literally. I still can't believe how absolutely STUNNING that map is! I will be forever grateful that I got the chance to work with you. <3

To Celin (@celingraphics) my fabulous cover designer, for continuing to bring my imagination to life.

To all the authors who sparked the excited look in my eye every time I picked up a fantasy book and made me want to pursue those dreams myself. Tamora Pierce, J.R.R. Tolkien, C.S. Lewis, Holly Black, Kerri Manslicaco, Sarah J. Maas, Leigh Bardugo, I am forever grateful for the beautiful worlds you created, thus inspiring me to create my own.

To my fabulous street team and ARC team for continuing to help me bring the magic of Navarre into the world by storm! For your beautiful reviews and endless excitement. I can guarantee you I would not be here without them. I cannot thank you lovely humans enough!

And to you, my lovely faeries, my magical readers. Thank you for believing in me and my realm. For cherishing my characters the same way I do. For spreading the word about my books to other future readers. For your love. For your undying support. For making my dreams a reality. Your support is worth more than any precious gem in this world.

About the Author

Sydney has been devouring fantasy for as long as she can remember. She dabbles in theater, crafting, and cosplaying or cooking (badly) when her free time isn't consumed with reading or writing. She's the oldest of three and co-parent to two precious kitties, (Pandora and Panther Lily) and enjoys discussing the struggles of life with them whenever she can. After five years of nursing school failures, Sydney finally has her Associate of Arts and is currently dancing through life with her soulmate and partner-in-crime.

For more information on her journey, her work, or simply to fangirl over fictional characters, feel free to follow her on Instagram—@sydneysbookshelf or Tiktok—@faeriequeensydney, check out #thelilacbookblog for book reviews, and sign up for her newsletter, The Lilac Letter! (**www.worldofsydneyhawthorn.com**)

the story continues!

Anxious to know what happens next?

Follow me on Instagram (@sydneysbookshelf), visit my website and subscribe to my newsletter for updates and behind-the-scenes goodies, or visit my shop for signed copies, merchandise, and more!

Made in the USA
Middletown, DE
16 May 2022